BETWEEN

Megan Whitmer

SPENCER
HILL
PRESS

Spencer Hill Press

Please visit our website at www.spencerhillpress.com

First Edition: July 2014.
Megan Whitmer
Between: a novel / by Megan Whitmer – 1st ed.
p. cm.
Summary: A girl learns that she's in a witness protection
program for magical creatures and the future of their
world depends on her, but saving them means sacrificing
someone she loves.

The author acknowledges the copyrighted or trademarked
status and trademark owners of the following wordmarks
mentioned in this fiction: Chuck Taylor, Coke, Gibson
guitars, iTunes, Jeep, Kleenex, Little League, M&Ms, Men
in Black, Shrek

Cover design by Nathalia Suellen
Interior layout by Jenny Perinovic
Author Photo by Priscilla Baierlein Photography

ISBN 9781939392152 (paperback)
ISBN 9781939392169 (e-book)

Printed in the United States of America

ONE

Buck. Muck. Truck. Duck.

"Duck!" I lift my head and turn to Sam. "What the duck!"

Sam sits cross-legged in the grass beside me, his guitar resting in the bend of his knee. He's been strumming the same chords over and over again, turning the tuning pegs while he tries to match the melody in his head. "Duck," he repeats, and looks at me from the corner of his eye. His mouth turns down on one side. "It doesn't feel right."

I tap my pencil against the sketchbook balanced on my legs. My long red hair pools on the page, covering most of the drawing I'm working on. We've been playing this game for a few months, ever since I made the New Year's resolution to stop swearing. Mom set a jar on the kitchen counter back in December and started making me and Sam put a dollar in every time we use language she doesn't like. It took ten bucks to convince me to come up with words that won't cost me anything.

Sam, on the other hand, throws in a ten every Monday as insurance. He's much fonder of swear words than I am, and he's a much harsher critic of my substitutes.

I think "duck" works pretty well.

Duck. Ducking. Ducker.

The perfect swear stand-ins are so elusive. "Do you have a better suggestion?"

"Chuck." His answer is immediate, like he's been waiting for me to ask. His eyes stay on his guitar strings, and his grin is equal parts deviousness and delight.

I slap the headstock of his guitar. "My name is not a swear word."

"Of course not." He wriggles his eyebrows. "Your name is Charlotte."

Ugh. I wrinkle my nose and look back to my drawing. Charlotte *should* be a swear word. I hate my name. I only hear it from substitute teachers. Everyone else knows to call me Charlie if they expect a response. Except Sam, of course, who calls me Chuck.

Sam snorts. "Why don't you just put money in the swear jar like I do?"

"I need my money for my art supplies."

He shrugs. "Then give up peanut M&Ms."

Give up my M&Ms? I need those like I need air. A sketchbook, some pencils, and a party-sized bag of peanut M&Ms—that's all I require in life. I lower my chin and fix dead eyes on him. "Sometimes, I don't know how you're my brother."

"Older brother," Sam reminds me, drumming his fingers against the body of the guitar. "You could learn a lot from my experience, Chuck."

We share a birthday, but he never misses an opportunity to play the Older Brother card. I smirk at him. "Six minutes older. I'll keep my M&Ms."

"Suit yourself." He rakes his fingers through the mess of light brown curls on top of his head and nods at the swells of farmland across the one-lane road in front of our house. The sun slips below the top of the highest hill, splashing the sky with orange and pink and turning our neighbor's horses into dark silhouettes. Black wooden fences divide the farmland into a patchwork of fields dotted with animals, wells, and a couple barns. "You're gonna run out of light soon."

He's right. I turn back to my drawing and pull my colored pencils from the zippered pouch beside me. I usually prefer to draw with charcoal, but these colors—the variance in greens in the grass, the blue-gray ponds, the brown mares, the fruity blend of colors hanging in the sky—deserve to be recorded. In mere minutes, the entire scene will shift as shadows stretch across the fields and all the colors fade into one. I can fill in the details later, but I'll have to work quickly to capture these colors.

I feel Sam's eyes on me. His hands are still, resting against his guitar. He's watching my face, and I know what's coming. He's been waiting for an opportunity to bring it up since we got in the car after school. I'd filled all our silences with as much random conversation as possible, but he's got me now.

I stare hard at my lines on the page. Maybe if I don't look at him, he won't mention it.

He draws in a quick, short breath, about to speak.

I brace myself.

"You know your drawings are incredible, right?" he asks. "The Collis Society made a mistake."

And there it is. My pencil stops moving, and I close my eyes. It had never occurred to me that I wouldn't get into the prestigious arts program at the Collis Society. Drawing is my thing, and everyone knows it. Sam has his guitar and notebooks of song lyrics and melodies; I have my worn-out sketchbooks and shelves filled with charcoals, paints, and brushes. Doing an independent study at Collis this summer was supposed to be a given. I'm Charlie Page. Of course I'd get in.

Except I didn't. Mrs. Huffman gave me the letter in homeroom this morning. I thought getting it on my birthday was a good sign.

I was wrong.

"Not incredible enough, I guess," I tell him. I hate the way my voice shakes. There are a million worse things that could happen than being rejected from Collis's art program. I know that.

Still, I was counting on it. A summer residency at Collis would automatically set my college applications apart and practically guarantee me a spot in any of the best visual arts programs in the United States.

Without it? I don't know.

Dear Ms. Page, We regret to inform you...

The air seems heavier, pressing down on my shoulders.

I know what an acceptance from Collis would've meant for me. I can't decide what the rejection means. I'm not good enough? I'll never be a real artist? I'm wasting my time?

Maybe I'm supposed to do something else. Sure, I'm one of the best artists in my high school, but what does that even mean? It certainly wasn't enough to impress Collis's admissions board. Every high school in the world has its best somethings. I'm a big fish in a tiny, supportive pond, and Collis can choose from an ocean filled with special, sparkly fish far more gifted than I'll ever be.

Why did I even think I'd get in?

Sam sets his guitar aside and rests his arm over my shoulders. He pulls me close, mixing sympathy and reassurance into his easy, close-lipped smile. "Your drawings are incredible. You're amazing. This changes nothing."

I lay my head against his shoulder and we sit without words, listening to the water dribble across the rocks in the creek across the road.

"Hey, you two." The screen door creaks as Mom comes outside. She's changed into khaki shorts and a pale pink T-shirt that makes her golden skin look even more tan. She trots down the stone porch steps and seats herself next to me, stretching her long legs alongside mine in the grass. "Anything exciting going on out here?"

I give Sam a meaningful look. Mom doesn't know about Collis yet. She'd been so busy since we got home getting everything ready for our birthday dinner that I didn't mention it to her. Besides, her hugs always bring out my tears if I'm on the edge of crying, and I'd like to avoid a breakdown.

"Oh, you know." Sam sighs heavily and withdraws his arm from my shoulders. "I'm trying to concentrate on drawing this sunset, and Chuck won't shut up about the new Amos Lee album. You know her and her hipster music—it's pretty annoying."

I snort. Sam's iTunes library is three times the size of mine and filled with artists I've never heard of. He never leaves the house without his earbuds in. His obsession with music rivals my love for art, and we're equal in our respect for and ignorance of each other's passions.

"Mm-hmm. I imagine it would be." She presses her lips into a wry smile and rubs my back, studying the blend of colors on my page. "That's beautiful, hon."

Sam picks his guitar up again. He's been fiddling with a new tune all afternoon, penciling notes in his composition book, but now he plays one of his old songs. I call it "Ol' Faithful," because it's the one he plays most often. No words, only melody. Sometimes fast, sometimes slow, just enough to feel the strings beneath his fingers.

I lean into Mom while he plays. My wavy red hair stands out alongside her stick-straight brown locks, mingling together down our arms as she rests her head against mine. I gaze at the barn near the bottom of our hill, admiring the contrast of the fireflies igniting in its shadow.

I can't imagine loving anywhere more than I love this place in the spring. The sweet scent of hay mixed with cut grass, the occasional whinny of the neighbor's horses, the way the breeze drifts through the wildflowers and wanders over my skin. While nearly everything in me knows that my only chance for a career in art means I have to get out of this tiny town, there's a piece that knows no other place will ever really feel like home. It's why I've drawn nearly every scene it has, inside and out, in my sketchbooks. Wherever I go, it'll be there, too.

When Sam's hands go still against the guitar, Mom sighs. "I could sit out here all night, but Seth will be here any minute. Who wants to come inside and help me set the table?"

"I would, Mom, but the sunset..." Sam waves his hand toward the sky before settling it over his heart. He presses his lips together in the most dramatic display of feigned emotion I've seen since the time he pretended to be devastated after Mom bought a dishwasher, and we no longer had to wash them by hand. "It moves me."

I flick his forehead with my finger. "Go away."

"How much longer are you going to work on that?" Mom asks, nodding toward my sketch.

Darkness trickles down from the sky over my head, slowly chasing the sun away. "A few more minutes. I'll come inside when Seth gets here."

"Good, then you and Seth can make the salad," she says, and I nod as Sam follows her into the house.

It's quieter without Sam and his guitar, but the crickets start their chorus to keep me company. I lean over my sketchbook, penciling in details as the night settles around me, my nose nearly touching the page. What little light I have suddenly dims, and I look up to watch a cloud press its way across the sky. I look back to my drawing and sigh. I'd hoped to pencil in some of the finer details, but the faster the light fades, the harder it becomes.

Five more minutes, cloud. That's all I need.

I glare at the sky, begging the cloud to move. Something tingles in my fingers, and I drop my pencil, shaking them out.

Five more minutes.

Light gradually begins to peek through the cloud as a breeze pushes it away. The cloud isn't the only thing moving. The prickly feeling climbs from my hands to my elbows, and I draw my arms into my body.

I curl my fingers into fists and squeeze, digging my fingernails into the heels of my hands, and then relax, spreading my fingers wide. I repeat this over and over until the tingling subsides.

It's like my arms fell asleep, which makes no sense. I've been drawing the whole time. I rest my hands palm-up on my sketchbook and stare at them. Even after the weird sensation vanishes, its phantom lingers right below my skin. I lift my shoulders and shake my arms, flinging the feeling away.

I hear a car coming down the road, followed by the sound of gravel crunching beneath tires. I flip the cover shut on my spiral-bound sketchbook and stand to watch Seth's red Jeep climb the winding drive to our house. With the sun almost completely hidden, the breeze has picked up a chill as it drifts over the grass and across my bare skin. I tuck my sketchbook against my chest and wrap my arms around myself. Bright headlights shine directly into my face when

Seth reaches the top of the driveway, and I turn my head away for a second. He steps out of the car, and the front porch light bounces off the chiseled curves of his face as he lifts his head toward me.

"Hey," Seth calls, walking closer, holding two bright yellow envelopes in one hand. He's dressed up more than usual, in dark jeans and a light blue button-down shirt with the sleeves rolled up once or twice, and his hair has that meticulously messy look that shows me he took his time getting ready.

Seth is always good-looking, but even more so in that shirt. Everything about him is dark, from his brown hair to his tanned skin to the sharp look in his chocolate-colored eyes, and the contrast of the light shirt does all the right things. He'd be downright crushworthy if he knew how to have fun at all. He's far too grown-up to be nineteen, and sometimes it takes every bit of patience I have to get through a conversation with him.

Everything Seth says is right, even when it's not, and I've never met a bigger rule-follower in my life. I'm the quintessential "good kid," as Sam often reminds me, but even I know I have to break a few rules now and then if I'm going to live any kind of life at all.

Not Seth, though. His world is black and white. While I prefer to draw that way, I have deep appreciation for the gray areas, too.

He waits until he's beside me to say, "Happy birthday." His perfect lips spread into a brilliant smile. His eyelashes are ridiculously long, making his eyes impossible to ignore. I wish for the millionth time that he wasn't so attractive. Or that he was mute.

"Hi." I tuck my hair behind my ear. "We're on salad duty."

"Sounds dangerous," Seth replies. We go up the front steps and he reaches around me to open the screen door. We're greeted by the aroma of tomato sauce, garlic, and oregano. "Spaghetti?"

I respond with a polite nod. Birthdays always mean spaghetti around here, just like Thanksgiving means turkey and Christmas is desserts only. Spaghetti is Mom's best meal, with her homemade sauce, salad, and the garlic bread she makes from scratch. He's been spending birthdays and holidays with us for the last few years, so I know he knows this.

"Seth!" Mom says as we enter the kitchen. She wipes her hand on a dark-blue dish towel and embraces him like she would me or Sam. She always calls Seth her other child. His parents died when he was younger, and he'd wound up living down the road with his aunt. She worked all the time, and still does, I guess. I've never laid eyes on her.

Sam and I met Seth about five years ago when Mom hired him to mow our yard. He'd wanted to earn money to buy a car, and Mom basically adopted him when she learned he was eating frozen meals every night by himself. Pretty soon, he was having dinner with us two or three nights a week and spending all the major holidays with us.

Sam sets four glasses of ice on the table and greets Seth with a hug of his own. "Hey, man!"

Sam doesn't understand why Seth drives me crazy, but it takes a lot to get under Sam's skin. He's as patient as I am impatient, as loud as I am quiet, as messy as I am meticulous. To be fair, while Seth acts like a protective big brother to both of us, I'm convinced he's harder on me.

"I'll take those," Mom says, pulling the birthday cards from Seth's hand, "and you two work on the salad."

Seth goes straight to the cabinet beneath the sink to grab a cutting board. I collect vegetables from the refrigerator while Seth picks a knife from the block by the stove. I turn on the water in the sink to wash tomatoes.

"How was your day?" he asks.

I shrug. "It was all right."

"Just all right?" Seth's eyebrows come together, forming a crease directly over his nose.

The Collis Society's bright white stationery flashes in my mind, along with that crushing first line: Dear Ms. Page, We regret to inform you...

I nod and turn the water up higher, hoping it's loud enough to keep him from asking more questions. Seth has this weird knack for knowing when I'm upset about something. It's comforting when I want to talk about whatever's on my mind, and annoying when I don't. I feel his eyes on me as I turn the tomato over and over in my hands and set it on the cutting board. We finish the task in silence, even though I know he's not going to let me off that easily.

When everything's ready, we choose our regular spots around the table. Mom's pulled out the ironstone dishes, like she always does for special occasions, and the brightly colored foods pop against the stark white serving plates. I don't know if she does that on purpose, but I always notice. I take a mental snapshot to sketch later. Sam pours sweet tea into our glasses, and the ice pops as it settles.

When we're all seated, Mom picks up the platter of spaghetti and passes it around. "How was everyone's day? Seth, did your finals go well?"

"Yep! My last two were this morning," Seth says, piling noodles onto his plate. He takes classes at the local university about an hour away. Pre-Med.

"Just normal school stuff," I say, taking the bowl of marinara sauce from Sam.

"No stories?" Mom asks.

"Nope," Sam answers.

I raise my eyebrows and shrug like nothing in the world happened today, like I didn't find out I'm less talented than everyone thought, like the thing I've planned on for the last two years suddenly isn't an impossibility. My breath hitches, and I focus on swallowing.

"What's wrong?" Seth asks, his dark eyes on me.

"Nothing." I spoon sauce over my noodles and paste on a smile.

"Something go wrong at school?" he presses, because he just can't let it go. He keeps watching me, waiting.

I speak through my teeth, maintaining my grin, "I said nothing's wrong."

"You don't have much of a poker face, hon," Mom says. "What's up?"

"Ugh." I slump against the back of my chair and let the corners of my mouth drop. There's obviously no escaping this conversation. "Fine. I didn't make it into the Collis Society's summer arts program. The one with the artists in residence? I got my letter today."

Saying the words out loud brings on a fresh wave of the humiliation mixed with the frustration I've been battling all day. The worst part is how sure I'd been of my acceptance. I should've at least thought of a backup plan. Everything was resting on that program. Heat spreads across my chest and up my neck.

Mom's shoulders fall. "I'm so sorry, hon. I know that meant a lot to you."

I shrug. *Everyone* knew it meant a lot to me. That almost makes it worse. Everyone at school, all of my teachers, they all thought I'd be a shoo-in. I let them down, and tomorrow I'll have to tell them.

"Those people at Collis are obviously blind," Sam adds, twirling spaghetti around his fork, "with no taste in art whatsoever. And they're probably senile. I bet everybody on that board is super old. Old people smell funny, Chuck. The whole place probably smells funny. Who wants to spend a summer there? You'd miss us way too much."

I raise my eyes to his and smile. Leave it to Sam to make the arts program I'd wanted to get into for years sound like spending a summer trapped in a nursing home. "You're so full of sheet."

Sam winks at me, his cheeks bulging with spaghetti. Of all my swear words, "sheet" is his favorite.

"Didn't you send the drawings I suggested?" Seth asks. "The ones from the lake trip last fall?"

The way he phrases the question annoys me. Didn't I? As if choosing something different than his suggestion is the whole reason I didn't get in. Like not listening to Seth is automatically asking for trouble. Because he's clearly never been mistaken in his life.

"No." I smooth the hair above my ear. "I sent the series I did of the buildings downtown. The old library, the courthouse, and the mill." The lake drawings were watercolors. They were pretty, but not all that artistically challenging. The admissions board at Collis would be looking for something more impressive. The buildings had more intricate details—more perspective, deeper angles. They were my best shot at getting in.

But what do I know, anyway? I didn't get in.

"But the lake ones were so much better," he says, lowering his brow, genuinely confused by my choice.

Thanks, Seth. That's the most helpful thing to say.

"I think all of your work is incredible," he continues, "but the paintings from the lake show how broad your talent is. Like how well you draw people and landscapes and a little bit of everything."

The worst part is that it's entirely possible he's right. Maybe I'd completely screwed up by picking the wrong samples. If I'd sent the lake series, would we be celebrating my acceptance right now?

Seth leans over his plate and looks at me. "Sam's right, though. You're incredibly gifted. Your buildings were great. Don't take this too hard. Really."

I nod, unwilling to look back at him. I help myself to a piece of garlic bread from the basket on the table. It's pointless now, anyway. Whether I made the right or the wrong choice, it's over. I reach for my glass of water, swiping the cold condensation with my fingers.

"You should see the sunset she was working on tonight," Sam says. "Did you finish it?"

I take a sip of water. "No. My hands started acting funny and I gave up."

"Your hands?" Mom asks, picking up the shaker of Parmesan cheese from the middle of the table. "What do you mean?"

"I don't know. They started tingling, and it wouldn't stop. It was like they both fell asleep at the same time, and then it sort of spread up my arms." I shake my head and tear the crust from my bread. "It was really weird."

Seth clears his throat and asks, "What were you doing at the time?" because obviously, on top of knowing everything about art, he's also an expert on tingly hand disease.

"Nothing. It didn't last long. It's not a big deal."

"Well," Mom says, her eyes landing on my hands, "let me know if it happens again."

I shove a piece of bread in my mouth and nod. Seth watches me a moment longer before glancing at Mom.

"So anyway. Happy birthday to us, right?" Sam lifts his hands and beckons, asking for applause, grinning broadly.

Mom's head bobs up, and she laughs. "Happy birthday. I can't believe my babies are seventeen. It won't be long until you're off to college and getting jobs and starting new lives without me."

She's smiling, but something in her words digs into my chest. It's been the three of us here for as far back as my memory reaches. Dad died in a car accident when Sam and I were only a few months old, and I only know him through old photographs and Mom's memories.

"Aw, don't worry, Mom." Sam leans over and pats her hand. "Chuck's an artist and I'm a musician. You know we're never getting jobs. With any luck, we'll live here forever and you'll be able to keep feeding us and doing our laundry long into adulthood!"

Mom laughs. "Every mother's dream!"

Sam high-fives me, lifting my mood like he always does, and even Seth cracks a smile. Sam's right about one thing—I'd miss this if I spent my summer at the Collis Society. I can't really imagine going weeks without seeing Mom and Sam. At least now, I'll have them to keep me company while I draw as much as I want from my favorite spot on the front porch.

I meet Seth's eyes across the table. His shoulders relax and he lowers his chin, holding my gaze, waiting for me to forgive him. I take a deep breath and look toward the ceiling, breaking eye contact. He shouldn't have pushed it. I clearly didn't want to talk about the Collis Society. It's my birthday dinner, and I don't want to spend it thinking about the rejection.

When I look back, he smiles at me, a warm, genuine look of affection that slices through my frustration.

I guess it would've been strange to go all summer without seeing Seth, too.

I smile back.

As much as I would've loved Collis, at least now I can spend my last summer before I graduate high school here with my family.

Without them, it would really suck.

Two

The moon hangs high in the night sky by the time Seth heads home. I watch from the screened door while he climbs into his Jeep. When his headlights come on, I rest my finger on the light switch by the door and wait.

"You guys are weird," Sam says, leaning against the doorway behind me.

"Shut up." Just when I think Seth's not going to do it, the headlights blink three times. I smile and flip the porch light in return.

Off. On. Off. On. Off. On.

The Jeep backs up and turns, crawling back down the driveway. I wait until it's completely out of view before shutting the light off for good.

The day Seth bought his Jeep, he came to our house to celebrate. We put the top down and drove the fifteen-mile strip from one end of town to the other, before coming back to enjoy Mom's famous double-chocolate-chip brownies. When he left, Sam and I watched from the doorway while Seth fumbled with all the controls inside the Jeep, trying to figure out how to turn on the headlights. When he finally found the switch, he flashed the lights at us. On impulse, I flashed the porch light back at him. We've been doing it ever since.

"You ready to do our gifts?" Sam asks.

I turn around. "Sure. In the kitchen?"

"Nah. Let's go outside."

"Okay," I tell him. "I gotta get yours from my room. Meet you on the porch in five minutes."

When we were younger, Mom gave us matching gifts every year. If I got shoes, Sam got shoes. If she bought him a video game, there'd be one for me, too. She quit doing it when we got to high school, so for the last couple of years we've given each other coordinating gifts as a little private joke. A few weeks before our birthday, one of us decides what type of gift we're going to buy each other. Last year, Sam chose hats. He bought me a green knit hat with a little flower on the side, and I got him a gray flat cap. This year, I decided on bracelets. He's going to love the one I got him—black leather string laced through a metal guitar pick.

I run up to my room to grab Sam's gift from my desk drawer. I hate wrapping presents. I'm terrible at it. I usually get a white box or bag and draw all over it instead, but for this I'd dropped his bracelet in a clear plastic bag and drawn blue and orange swirls all over it from top to bottom.

By the time I make it back downstairs, Sam's waiting in one of the green wicker chairs on the front porch. All trace of the clouds from earlier have disappeared. Tonight's moon is enormous, lighting up the sky and stealing the spotlight from the millions of stars scattered over our heads. I take a seat in the chair beside him and hold Sam's gift up. "You first."

He plucks the bag from my hand and shakes it. "What could it be?" he asks, his eyes too wide and his voice too high-pitched.

I roll my eyes. "Nerd. Open it."

He pulls the bracelet from the bag and grins, pressing his fingertips to the rounded corners of the pick. "This is awesome!"

I watch his eyes light up and can't help but smile too. Giving someone a gift I know they'll love is one of my favorite feelings.

"Thanks, Chuck." Sam slips it over his wrist, adjusting the knots to make it fit, then turns his bright eyes on me. "Your turn!"

He hands me a small square box. I shake it, widen my eyes, and say, "What could it be?" in my best Sam impersonation ever.

He purses his lips, unimpressed. "Dumbest joke you've ever made."

I open the box and find a red string bracelet with five tiny silver beads in the middle. I put it on and admire the way it lies on my wrist. It's perfect—simple but beautiful, unique without being outlandish. Exactly my style.

I beam at Sam. "I love it."

He nods. "I have great taste."

"I know. You're practically a girl."

"Only prettier." He rests his head on the back of his chair.

The wind picks up, and a collection of leaves toward the side of the yard catches my eye. I lower my arm and watch the darkened shapes lift and trail through the air before leaping across the fence. My favorite tree stands amid the overgrown weeds on the other side. It's tall and wide, with thick, sprawling branches perfectly spaced for climbing. Two smaller trees flank its sides, their leaf-filled branches mingling together. The leaves spiral toward the trees and then dash upward. As my eyes follow them, I catch sight of something else. The curve of the branches, the gathering of the leaves, the shadow from the moonlight–

I stand up, knocking the empty gift box from my lap.

"You okay?" Sam asks, sitting up.

I walk to the edge of the porch, keeping my eyes on the tree. "What is that?"

"What?" he asks, rising from his chair.

"That." I look from him to the tree and point.

His response is slow and measured. "It's a tree."

"No. Hang on. Let me find it again."

I jump off the side of the porch to the edge of the yard, and Sam follows. A few wide, ragged chips of black paint flake off the fence as I step on the lowest slat and stare, eyes straining.

There's nothing.

"Chuck."

"Shh!" I wave my hand to shut him up. "Wait."

The fence gives a bit as he climbs onto it, swings his legs over the top, and takes a seat on the post by my elbow. "What'd you see?"

I don't move, don't even blink. "I saw–" And now I'm doubting myself. What did I see? A face? In the tree?

No. Not in the tree, exactly. Around the tree. In front of the tree. When the wind blew through the leaves.

I'm sure of it. The branches of the trees reached toward each other, forming perfectly arched eyebrows. Clumps of leaves on narrow branches made up the eyes, curved into pointed ovals with darkened edges. The lower, nearly bare branches portrayed full, closed lips. Streams of moonlight through the clouds beyond the trees created the shading of the face itself, showing the rounded edges and high cheekbones.

"There was a face."

"A face?"

"A face."

"Like, a person? You saw someone in the tree?" His eyes are fixed on the topmost branches of the tree, where the leaves are thickest, where someone might hide.

I shake my head. "No, not exactly." But that sounds a lot less crazy than *I saw a giant face floating in the air outside of the tree, rippling in the leaves.*

Sam hops down from the fence before I have a chance to say more. He's already walking slowly toward the tree, his head upturned.

I climb up the next two planks and swing my legs over, landing on the other side. I gather my hair and twist it into a bun while I walk, wrapping the ends around until they stay in place. When I catch up to Sam, he's at the tree's edge, barely outside the leaves' reach. He runs his hand through his curls and stares upward.

It's a large tree, one I'd played in and under a million times growing up, and that's all I've really noticed about it—it's big. Branches spread in all directions with broad leaves hanging wildly throughout.

I take a few steps back and look again.

No face.

It's so dark; who knows what I saw?

"I think the wind and the moonlight played tricks on me," I say. "I must have imagined her."

"Her?"

I'm not sure where that came from, actually. *Her.* Yeah, okay. I guess the face was female. Something about it seemed soft. Too soft for a man's face. Full lips, dark-rimmed eyes, smooth, rounded cheeks— definitely not male.

And definitely not here anymore.

"You sure I shouldn't check it out? Maybe there's a hot chick hiding up there!"

I'm positive I said nothing about the face being hot. The Y chromosome is so weird.

It was pretty, though, now that I think about it. The way the moonlight filtered through the leaves and outlined the face in silver, framing its features—

"Charlie! Sam!" The front porch light comes on, casting a yellow glow across the yard. Mom comes down the steps and around the side, calling for us.

"Coming!" Sam responds.

I lift my feet high as we walk back through the weeds toward the house, trying not to think about how many ticks are out here. Every couple of steps I glance back over my shoulder. It's a tree. A big tree. Just like it's always been.

"What were you doing out in the field?" Mom asks as we climb the fence and drop over it.

"I thought I saw something in the tree," I tell her. As soon as I say it, I know how dumb it sounds.

"What'd you see?" she asks, zeroing in on the tree.

"I, uh..." I watch her eyes dance over the tree's branches from top to bottom. The wind picks up again, fluttering the weeds around the fencepost. She lifts her nose into the breeze and her entire body shudders. She pulls something small and green from her pocket, about the size of a cellphone but more rounded. A calculator, maybe?

"Sam, Charlie." Mom's eyes are focused on the thing in her hands, her fingers tapping across its screen. "Get in the house."

Her tone is hushed, but the alarm in her voice is thunderous. My heart speeds up.

"Huh?" Sam asks. "What—"

A loud keening cuts him off, and we all spin around, each looking in a different direction. The sloping fields distort the sound, and while I can't figure out exactly where it's coming from, I know it's close. It rises in pitch, then ceases.

Mom raises her voice as she shoves the thing back in her pocket. "Now! Go!"

Her hand is firm between my shoulder blades, shoving me toward the porch. I take off running, propelled by fear. Mom never gets scared. Ever.

The whining starts again, louder, closer.

I stop at the front steps and turn around. Sam and Mom are several steps behind.

Something enormous and dark drops down in front of me, landing in a crouch, and I topple backward. I press my hands against the steps until I'm standing again, and the thing rises as well, slowly unfolding itself and stretching upward, illuminated in the light from the porch.

Anxiety creeps up my spine. The sight in front of me is straight out of my nightmares. No, it's worse. I don't even think my subconscious could create something like this. I clench my hands into fists, my fingernails digging into my palms. I feel them tremble against my sides.

At its full height, the creature is easily seven feet tall. It looks like some kind of man-bird hybrid, standing on two legs with a human-like head and pair of hands. Stiff gray feathers cover its entire body, from the tips of its pointed ears to the curved, black claws on its feet, and thick black wings rest against its back. Its eyes are the worst—bright red orbs that glow against its gray face.

"Chuck! Run!" Sam yells.

The creature's head swivels around, rotating 180 degrees, like an owl.

My heartbeat pulses through every part of my body. I've heard about people being frozen with terror, but until now I never really understood how anyone could be too scared to run. Short, unfulfilling breaths burst in and out of my lungs, and my chest heaves with each one.

My feet remain glued to the ground while the creature's wings lift and spread, and the thing grows even larger. Its wingspan must be at least ten feet. My eyes wander from the tip of one wing to the other.

"Holy sheet," I breathe, and its head snaps back around to me.

"Hey!" Mom's voice is loud, clear, and certain. "Mothman!"

Mothman?

The creature lets out a loud hiss, pivoting on its talons until it stands with Mom and Sam on one side and me on the other, its back to no one. I press my lips together, clamping my teeth against them to keep from screaming.

What is she doing?

"That's right," Mom says, tucking her hair behind her ears with both hands. She steps away from Sam and walks backward, taking the Mothman's attention with her. "Follow me, you big freak."

As soon as the creature is distracted, Sam darts toward me and we stand together, watching the giant monster approach our mother. The closer the thing gets to her, the shakier I become, and beside me I feel Sam shudder.

Mom reaches the driveway and leans back onto the hood of her dark sedan. "Come on!" she yells. There's no sign of the fear I heard in her voice when she addressed us earlier. "Come at me!"

"Mom!" I scream. Why is she baiting this monster?

Sam gasps and leans forward on his toes. He gives me a sideways glance and rocks back a bit. His eyes fall to the ground, searching, probably for some kind of weapon. "We have to help her."

I wrap my fingers around his wrist, anchoring him to me. "You'll never make it past that thing," I hiss.

We lock eyes for a moment, and he exhales hard through his nose, then nods.

My knees tremble so hard I have trouble standing. Mom's bizarre composure is terrifying in itself. She must be having some kind of break from reality. Maybe she's in shock. Maybe she's on autopilot, responding to the threat against her children without regard to the fact that this threat is a gigantic freak of nature who's clearly going to kill all three of us.

The creature squats, and Mom stays in place as it launches itself straight into the air.

Oh my God, it's going to crush her. Sam lunges forward, but I yank him back. "No!"

She rolls away right before the thing crashes down on the hood of the car, its long talons screeching against the metal. The windshield shatters. She dashes around the mess and places herself in front of the Mothman with her back to us, keeping her eyes on the creature. "You two," Mom orders, turning her head slightly to throw her voice back to us, "get in the house."

"I'm not leaving you out here alone with that," Sam argues, his voice higher-pitched than normal.

"Samuel!"

He pulls me backward around the end of the porch, and we crouch there. "I'm not leaving her out here," he repeats, and I nod in agreement. We stay with her, no matter what. I raise my head to peek through the legs of the porch furniture, unable to take my eyes off my mother. She's like some kind of warrior, standing out there in the middle of the yard with that beast.

"Mom's a badass," Sam whispers.

"What *is* that thing?" I ask.

"The Mothman. Haven't you ever seen that movie?" A voice whispers next to my ear, and a hand clamps over my mouth before I scream. I grab at the hand and a voice whispers, "It's me, Charlie! It's me!"

I freeze. Seth? How−?

"Seth!" Sam whispers. "Where'd you come from?"

Seth meets my gaze and raises his eyebrows, silently asking if he can trust me not to scream, and

I nod. He releases my mouth and I do a quick scan of the yard and fields behind me.

Where *did* he come from?

Seth's eyes are glued to the Mothman, and his lips are pressed in a thin line. There's no uncertainty, no surprise. Our car has been crushed by a giant feathered man and Seth acts like he knew what he'd find before he got here. "Long story. You two stay down."

I reach for him, but he creeps around the porch before I can stop him.

Mom stands solidly in the middle of the yard, watching the Mothman stagger off the hood of the car. Her head turns slightly as Seth moves closer.

"Do you have it?" she asks.

Seth pulls a long knife from his pocket.

"No sudden movements," she says, and he slowly approaches, never taking his eyes off the Mothman. The creature lets out another hiss, and I whimper.

"Make sure you stab him right below the rib cage," Seth tells her.

"I know that, Seth," she replies, like he's giving her any mundane instruction, not telling her how to kill a monster in our front yard.

The Mothman skulks toward her, his red eyes shifting from Mom to Seth and back.

"On the right side," Seth mutters.

"I *know* that, Seth," she repeats, harsher.

She steps away from Seth, moving in a wide circle that takes the Mothman farther from the house. He follows at first, then stops. The creature's head swivels backward, examining the front of the house. I crouch lower, pulling Sam with me. The Mothman's red eyes land on me when we move, and he releases a shrill scream. Mom lunges forward, releasing a loud grunt as she attacks.

Sam and I run out from behind the porch in time to see her plunge the blade into its chest, twisting it with a jerk before pulling it out. I pump my fist in the air and jump, fueled by more adrenaline than I've ever felt running through my body. Sam is on the ground, clutching his face in his hands while he stares wide-eyed at the Mothman. The creature stumbles, his body weaving from one side to the other, but never falls. Mom doesn't wait to see what happens. She turns and runs toward us.

"I don't think you got him!" Seth yells.

"I know that, Seth!" she shouts, breathing heavily. "We have to go! You take Charlie. I've got Sam."

She grabs Sam, lifting him from the ground in one swift movement, and Seth moves closer to me. I can't take my eyes off the Mothman as he struggles to steady himself.

"Ellauria?" Mom asks, and Seth nods.

Ell-who-ia?

"You take the bridge gate. We've got the one by the woods," Seth tells her.

I look at Mom. "Wait, what? What's going on?"

She cups my chin in her hand. "Listen to Seth," she says, her brown eyes fierce. "No matter what happens in the next few hours, trust in him, and remember I love you. Sam and I will meet you there."

"Where?" I ask.

Sam turns toward me, his green eyes wide with a mixture of confusion and terror, and there's no time for words before he and Mom vanish.

Vanish.

I gasp, frozen by the sheer impossibility of what just happened.

Seth's arms circle my waist. "Don't let go," he orders, and in a blink, everything disappears. My stomach jumps, my head spins, and I am weightless.

Seth releases me when I feel something solid beneath my feet again. I spin around. We're standing at the edge of a forest, barely inside the tree line. The dense trees swallow the moonlight. I step closer to Seth. "What just happened? Is the Mothman dead?"

Seth's arm comes around my waist, pulling me forward with him while his eyes dance over our surroundings, never resting on anything for very long. "No, he's not dead, but Adele slowed him down. You have to get his heart, right under his ribs, to kill him."

Adele. It's so weird to hear him call her something besides Mrs. Page. Seth drags me along, and I can hardly see the path beneath my feet. I'm so terrified by what might be sneaking up behind me that I can't focus on what's ahead. The Mothman is still out there. I squint, trying to see more through the darkness, but it's no use. My knees go all rubbery, and I concentrate on planting one foot in front of the other.

"Where are Mom and Sam?"

"They'll meet us in Ellauria," Seth states, pushing branches away with his hands. He's not running, but he's not quite walking either. We're buzzing through the forest on our way to a place I'm reasonably sure isn't on any map I've ever seen.

I don't know what's happened. I don't know where we're going. All I have right now is Seth, and I'm not entirely certain what to think of him. He'd appeared out of nowhere tonight and jumped into action. He hadn't asked us what was going on. He didn't freeze up. He ran *toward* the Mothman, not from it. Who is he?

He glances at me. "You're safe. I've got you."

I swallow. I don't feel safe. That Mothman showed up with hardly any warning, and he moved so fast, jumping straight up into the air like that. I close my eyes briefly, and long, sharp talons appear behind my eyelids.

Listen to Seth.

I open my eyes and study Seth's profile. "How'd you do the disappearing thing?" I ask. "We were at my house one second and now we're here."

"It's called flickering. The first few times are a rush," Seth says. "After a while you get used to it, and you hardly notice that weird off-balance feeling."

Off-balance. That's the best way to describe how I feel right now. It's like I've just gotten off a very short, very fast roller coaster.

He points at two towering pine trees a few feet away. "Let's get through the gate, then we'll be safe and we'll have a little time to talk."

Gate?

Seth turns to scan the trees and dark pathways surrounding us before pulling me through the middle of the two pines. Beneath them stands a large wooden gate, a little taller than Seth and twice as wide. It's gray and weathered, with paint peeling from its edges like it's been here for years.

Seth pushes it open and holds it there, waiting for me to pass through.

I look from him to the gate, confused. It's only a gate, unattached to anything, with nothing on the other side but more trees. A doorway to nowhere. I stare at it like the emperor in his new clothes.

He shakes his head and huffs. "Go, Charlie. We have to get out of here."

He wraps his fingers around my elbow and pulls me forward with him. The gate closes behind us, and the transformation is sudden.

The night disappears. The sky is clearer, the plants thicker, the scent sweeter. There's a definition here that didn't exist on the other side of the gate. Crisper lines, more dramatic variations in color. It's nature on steroids, clean and untouched.

"Where are we?"

"This," Seth spreads his arms, "is the Between."

THREE

"The Between?" I ask. I try to keep my eyes on him, waiting for an answer, but it's impossible. I'm surrounded by the purest display of colors I've ever seen. Blue, green, brown, red, orange. They're the same colors I've seen in wooded areas my whole life, but they're bolder, more pigmented—like every color I've seen before now had been muted, and I've just discovered what color actually is. "Between what?"

"The worlds."

Right. Of course. Between the worlds. I tear my eyes from the scenery long enough to squint at him. "I have no idea what that means."

"Your world," he points his thumb back toward the closed gate, "and mine."

I blink. He's from a different world?

"Come on," he says, nodding toward the path. "I'll explain while we walk."

He takes off with long, purposeful strides, and I follow, struggling to keep a steady pace when all I want to do is stop and stare. The Between is a wilderness like I've never seen. It's not just the beauty, although the splendor of this place is absolutely hypnotic; I'm also mesmerized by the sheer abundance. The entire space, for as far as I can see in any direction, is filled with growth. Yet somehow, beneath it all there runs an underlying sense of order—there are no dead leaves or broken limbs littering the ground, the dirt paths are clear and well-defined, and every bush, flower, and tree is perfectly in bloom.

The sky is crystal blue, clearer than any sky back home. I stare up through the pointed leaves of the enormous maple trees. The branches burst with leaves, and while every single one of them is green, no two are the same shade. Even the brown of the path beneath my feet seems richer, like dark coffee grounds scattered across the ground rather than plain old dirt.

Everything here is bigger, fuller, taller, cleaner. Everywhere I look, there's more of the same. The eternity of it is as overwhelming as its perfection. I doubt it's possible to truly record this place on paper, but I want to try anyway.

I wish Seth would slow down a bit. "What do you mean, 'your world?'"

He brushes past a bright yellow bush with ribbons of star-shaped blooms that spring straight out from the middle and hang to the ground. "Well, we left the mortal realm—your world—and we're on our way to the mystical realm—my world."

Mystical realm. Sure.

He spins around, looking at my face, and shakes his head. "That's the problem with the mortal realm. You live there long enough, you lose all sense of magic." He steps closer, speaking slowly, as if I haven't been paying attention. "You were attacked by a flying, feathered man tonight. We flickered. I brought you through a portal to a natural wonderland crafted by Mother Nature herself. How do you think anything is impossible at this point?"

I open my mouth, but stop myself before anything comes out. My desire to argue with him is as instinctive as my response to the word "mystical." I take a moment to wrap my head around what he's saying. My world is the mortal realm, and his is the mystical? He's *mystical*? "What are you?"

"I'm a jeravon."

"A what?"

"Jeravon."

I wait for him to say more, and the fact that he says nothing makes me crazy. This is not the time for his "I'm Seth, so you should accept every word that comes out of my mouth" thing. I fold my arms over my chest and shift my weight to one hip before saying, "Well, that's excellent. I'm a shmiddlydee." He lowers his head and pinches the bridge of his nose between his fingers, but I keep going. "That's a human who makes up words that mean nothing. Now you tell me what a jeravon is."

He rubs his hand down his face and over his chin before settling his gaze on me. "I look human, but I'm not. Jeravons live longer than humans because we age at a much slower pace. I'm also able to heal just about any wound a creature may suffer, as long as the creature is closer to life than death."

The words play back again in my head. Magical. Creature. Healer. "Are you telling me you have magical powers?"

"Yes, Charlie." His nod is certain, his gaze solid. "That's what I'm telling you."

My laughter seems even louder than usual here, and it dies quickly beneath Seth's steady stare. "And you age slower," I say, resting my chin against my chest.

"We age about one year for every twelve human years."

I look around. This is a joke. A very elaborate joke. It's something Sam would do. He could totally be behind this. But would he have trusted Seth to go through with it? Ultra-serious Seth? He Who Knows No Humor?

I lower my eyes to my wrist, rolling the tiny beads of my bracelet between my thumb and forefinger, and mutter, "I don't believe you."

It seems like what I should say, but I'm not entirely sure I mean it. It can't be real—none of this can—but at the same time, we're here.

Seth nods. "I know. You've been raised to find excuses for these things. When we reach Ellauria, it'll be much easier to believe. Until then, I'm going to need you to trust me. Come on."

He continues walking, apparently certain I'll follow.

I can't ignore the feel of this place. The Between. There's something about it I can't quite put my finger on. It's calming, like I know it and it knows me.

Trusting Seth shouldn't be this hard. He's Seth. Except what does that mean anymore? What do I really know about anything or anybody? Still, there's something calming about him, too. For once, his annoying self-assurance is exactly what I need.

Listen to Seth.

At least I know that whatever this is, wherever I'm going, Mom and Sam will be there too. She said so.

I swipe a few loose hairs from my face and tuck them behind my ears, then take off after Seth. Honeysuckle crowds the edge of the path, its sweet scent curling around me. Somewhere beyond the trees, water flows. Aside from that, there are no sounds at all. No birds exchanging melodies, no hum of insects going about their business, no wind, no animals. Nothing.

It's the nothing I find most concerning. This woodland should be filled with wildlife. Deer, bears, birds, butterflies, snakes. How can there be nothing?

Something cold and heavy settles in the bottom of my stomach as this new reality creeps in, replacing what I thought I knew. All the things I'd learned and loved about nature from the world I'd grown up in—the deer that roamed the overgrown woods at the edge of our fields, the hummingbirds that buzzed around the zinnias on our porch—none of that exists here. I find it harder and harder to ignore what I've seen and heard today.

I see Sam's face in my mind, the flecks of gold bright in his wide green eyes before he and Mom vanished.

Before Mom flickered with him the way Seth had flickered with me.

"How does Mom factor into all of this?"

"Adele and I work for a group called the Fellowship," he answers without looking back.

"The Fellowship? Like—of the Ring?"

The path curves around a wide lilac bush. He casts a look over his shoulder and says, "Clever," in a way that tells me he doesn't think it's clever at all. "The Fellowship is in charge of making sure those living in the mortal realm don't know anything about the mystical realm."

Well, I'd say they've been doing a pretty stellar job. "How do you do that, exactly?"

"There have been times throughout history when a human sees something he's not supposed to see. Some kid stumbles upon the flower ring left behind when one of the fairies travels to the mortal realm, a dead mermaid washes up on a beach, or someone snaps a picture of Vanessa or Nestor. When that happens, the Fellowship takes care of it."

"Vanessa or Nestor?"

"The Loch Ness monsters." He emphasizes the word "monsters" dramatically, wiggling his fingers in the air.

He throws each new piece of information over his shoulder and they hit me square in the chest, stealing my breath for a moment before I remember to inhale again. Fairies. Mermaids. Loch Ness monsters—all things that exist only in folklore and children's stories. From Seth's mouth, they sound a little less impossible. "How does the Fellowship take care of it?"

His shoulders rise and fall. "Whatever it takes. Sometimes, it's as simple as destroying film or cleaning up evidence. In other cases, the operation is more complex, like when we have to ruin a person's credibility or make someone believe he didn't see what he saw." He reaches back, his hand hovering next to me as the trail becomes steeper. Sparkling granite disrupts the path, peeking out from the ground here and there. "The point is to make sure humans go on believing magical creatures don't exist."

So they're like the Men In Black, but for magical creatures. "And the Mothman? The Fellowship is supposed to hide him?"

"Not exactly," Seth replies, keeping his eyes on the ground as we maneuver through the rocks. "Some creatures aren't really intelligent enough to be part of the Fellowship. They're wild animals. We try to manage those the best we can, since they could blow the lid off the entire mystical realm."

That makes sense. The Mothman doesn't seem like the kind of guy who plays well with others. Images from this evening play on a loop in my mind—the face in the tree, the Mothman's black leathery wings, the knife clutched in Mom's fist. The path levels out again, and I come to a stop.

Seth's not human. He's leading me to the mystical realm, where he works for some kind of mythical Mafia. With my mother.

"What about Mom?" I ask. "Is she..."

I can't even find a way to finish the question.

She went after the Mothman. She didn't run. She didn't hide. She didn't even seem surprised. She and

Seth spoke their own language, using words I knew but in a context I'd never heard. She flickered.

The conclusion is obvious, but if Mom's not human—

My knees turn to water. I reach around until I feel rough bark beneath my hands and press my back against the closest tree. I take a breath, and then another, but nothing seems to make it into my lungs.

The Mothman. The flickering. Two worlds. The Between. Jeravon. And now I don't know what my own mother is or what it makes me.

"Charlie?"

"Sorry." My voice shakes. "I need a second. It just," I take a breath, "sort of snuck up on me." I feel the tears there, right behind my eyelids, and the more I focus on making them go away, the less control I have over them. A tear slips down my cheek and I swipe it with the back of my hand.

Seth fixes his very serious brown eyes on me. "This isn't how I'd hoped to tell you all this. It's a lot to take in all at once, but right now I don't really have a choice. I want you to know I'm going to make sure you get through this. That's my job."

My lower lip trembles, and I clamp my lips together to make it stop. When my face is under my control again, I say, "I thought your job was with the Fellowship."

"It is." Seth steps closer and rubs his hand up and down my arm, squeezing. "When we arrive in Ellauria, you and Sam will begin training as Apprentices in the Fellowship. Each Apprentice is assigned an Aegis to serve as a mentor and guardian. I'm your Aegis. That means my primary concern is your safety." His eyebrows lift. "Understand?"

I sniff. "Aegis? What kind of name is that?"

"Ancient Greek. Used to mean a shield." He smiles. "For you, it means me."

He's my shield. The words bring a strange sort of comfort in the middle of this complete break from reality. I straighten and rest my head against the tree for a moment.

"This will be easier with Adele and Sam," Seth says. "He's going through as much of a shock as you are right now. When we get you two together, Adele and I will explain everything."

He's right. Sam will need me as much as I need him. I pull away from the tree, and more strands of hair fall from my bun. I tuck them behind my ears. "If we're all going to the same place, why don't we run into them here?"

Seth tips his head toward the path and steps toward it, slowing his pace to allow me to keep up with him. "The Between is infinite. With so many different gates leading from one realm to the other, the odds we'd run into anyone else here are pretty slim."

I look around anyway, keeping an eye out for Sam's curls. Even if we're not exactly together, knowing we're in the same space makes me feel stronger.

I smell the hydrangea bush before I see it. Each rounded bloom is made up of several tiny flowers with pale blue centers that grow darker at the edges of the petals. I can't get over how the flowers look here. Everything seems so much healthier, like each plant was given perfect conditions to thrive. I'm already planning the sketches in my head. One of the large weathered gate. The blossoming honeysuckle. The balls of hydrangea.

Splitting this world into scenes helps me process it. One thing at a time. I can do this. We'll get to Ellauria and sort this out. Sam will be with me, and Mom's voice will make it all make sense.

I wish I'd hugged her before she disappeared.

I search my brain for questions I think I can handle. "What do Apprentices do in the Fellowship?"

Please say we stay super far away from all things that might kill us, such as abnormally large bird-man hybrids. And spiders.

"Everyone enters the Fellowship as an Apprentice. That's when you learn everything about what we do and how we operate, and that typically takes a few years." Seth glances at me, making sure I'm listening, so I nod. "Afterward," he continues, "you move into your permanent role in the Fellowship. What that is depends on the strengths you show as an Apprentice."

Permanent role in the Fellowship.

The words sound so final, like I'm heading into the home stretch of a journey I didn't even know I was on. The ball of anxiety in my stomach swells. I'm supposed to be an artist. I've worked at it for years, ever since I found out I could make a career of it. I've never wanted to be anything else. It's what I've dreamed of—my work displayed in galleries for everyone to see. I don't—

"Watch your step," Seth says.

Broad, rolling tree roots erupt from the ground and the dirt path disappears. Soaring golden tree trunks mark our trail on each side. The leaves block the sun and cast shadows over us, but the gilded trunks and branches provide a light of their own as we pass.

The adrenaline I've been running on is fading, and the bottoms of my feet feel like giant bruises. "How much longer until we reach Ellauria?"

"Not much farther," he says, his voice bouncing off the trees.

"Why don't we flicker?"

"Mother Nature created this as a buffer between the mystical and mortal realms. The only way to get in and out of Ellauria is to travel through the Between. You can't flicker past it."

It's the second time he's mentioned Mother Nature. I've never given much thought to Mother Nature as a mythical creature. She's always seemed abstract, without shape or voice—more of a way of personifying Earth itself rather than having an identity of her own. Seth talks about her like she's a person instead of a presence, and I have no idea what to make of that.

We reach the end of the tree-lined corridor, and Seth stops in front of a large boulder covered in a jumble of twisted, olive-colored vines. Before I have a chance to enjoy the fact that we're standing still, Seth's fingers circle my elbow, digging into my arm, and he pulls me toward the boulder. I squeeze my eyes shut, reasonably certain the introduction of my face to the stone won't end well for my nose. The air changes—cooler, damper—and I open my eyes.

We're standing in a rounded tunnel carved from firmly packed ground. It's lit by glowing lanterns hanging from the walls on either side of us at evenly spaced intervals. I turn around, pressing my hand against the solid rock behind me.

We walked through the boulder.

Through the boulder.

Holy sheet.

Seth speaks to me in a slow, even tone. "Listen, you're basically being thrown into the deep end here, and you have to understand—I'm your lifejacket. I need you to do what I tell you, even if you don't always understand why. What you've learned today is nothing compared with what you need to know." He leans over, placing his face directly in front of mine. "You're going to be fine."

I press my lips together and nod.

Seth nods toward the dark end of the tunnel, pressing us forward. "When we get to Ellauria," he says, "try not to act too awed by everything. Your tendency to gawk could be a problem."

Is he seriously criticizing me right now? "I'm not gawking, I'm noticing. I'm studying the details. I've always done that. It comes in handy when I put scenes on paper."

The tunnel grows darker as we get closer to the end. The lanterns gradually become farther and farther apart. I don't like the darkness. I don't like the uncertainty of not knowing what might be in the shadows. Seth takes my hand.

"It doesn't matter why you do it. Pretend you've seen these things a million times. It shouldn't be obvious to everyone that you're new. You're not like the other Apprentices. They've known about the Fellowship and Ellauria their whole lives."

"Why wasn't I raised like that?" My heart races as the darkness grows bigger, and Seth squeezes my fingers.

"It's a long story," he replies, "and I swear I will tell you every detail, but for now, trust me when I tell you that, for your safety, you were hidden from the Fellowship and the Fellowship was hidden from you."

It's just like him to decide what I need to know and expect me to accept it. Before I have a chance to lay into him, Seth says, "We'll be in Ellauria in five minutes. We'll meet up with Adele and Sam, and then Adele and I will tell you everything. Can you wait until we're all together?"

I take a deep breath.

Listen to Seth.

"Fine." I exhale.

But I don't have to be happy about it.

We walk in silence until we reach the end of the passageway. Blank walls of earth surround us on three sides. I barely see the outline of a rounded door in the wall before me. A tree root has grown down into the cave, twisted around, and dug its way back into the earth, forming a handle. Seth rests his hand on it and says, "After you?"

"Whatever." My last twists of hair fall loose from my bun and I run my fingers through it.

"Whatever," Seth repeats, and shakes his head. "We're going to have to work on your communication skills."

My communication skills?

"You're the one who has no idea how social interaction works." I take a step back from him and cross my arms over my chest. "You tell me just enough to freak me out without giving me the entire story, and when I ask questions, you brush them off like I'm expecting too much too soon. You keep telling me to trust you, and quite frankly, I'm not even sure what I truly know about you at all anymore."

"Charlie, take a breath. You know me." Seth's shoulders fall and his eyebrows come together over his nose. "I'm the same guy who's been part of your family for the last five years. What happened today doesn't affect our history. None of this changes who we are, deep down. You can trust me. You've always been able to trust me."

I want to believe him. I want to be convinced everything that happened before today was real, and that he's part of my life because he wants to be, not because of a commitment to the Fellowship.

"Hey." He bends his knees to make me look at him, but I refuse. His eyes distract me. I don't want to get swept up in them right now. He places his hands on the sides of my face, and I finally meet his gaze. It's as sincere as always, filled with certainty and confidence, and a soft compassion around the edges. "You are completely capable of handling this. I know you're overwhelmed, but if you need to find one thing to be sure of, one thing you absolutely know, it's me. I'm with you, like I've always been, and I'm not going anywhere. Okay?"

For the first time since he mentioned realms, my breath reaches all the way down into my lungs. He's still Seth, and as much as he drives me crazy, I can be sure of him. "Okay."

Seth grasps the handle again. "Remember, once we go through this door, we're Aegis and Apprentice. No gawking."

The reminder gets under my skin because, as Seth is still Seth, I am still me. I smile sweetly. "Whatever. Should I call you Mr. Hewitt?"

He smirks and places his other hand on the body of the door. With a substantial push, the door moans and shakes free from the wall. Seth steps aside and presses his hand against my lower back, nudging me forward as the door swings open.

Four

As soon as my eyes adjust to the light, I see butterflies. Everywhere. I go still, sucking in a quick breath. Masses and masses of vibrantly colored wings flit about in all directions—lingering in the shadows between squat stone buildings, hovering above emerald-green grass, and loitering near the arches of wildflowers poised above wide, cobbled paths. The sun hangs low in the sky, and I lose all concept of time. Is this a repeat of today's sunset, or have I already leaped into tomorrow? "What time is it? Is it still today?"

"Yes. The mystical realm is a little behind."

I step away from the tunnel, moving slowly down the lush grass toward the broadest of the nearby trails. The trees are enormous, with trunks as wide as the house I grew up in, and heavily leafed limbs stretch high over my head.

Wooden stairs climb all the way up around the trunks of some of the smaller trees, leading to other buildings and balconies balanced high in the branches. A few of the particularly massive trees have steps at their bases that seem to lead directly into the trees themselves. I stare at one such tree nearby on the opposite side of the path, examining its steps, trunk, and the crowds of leaves spouting from its higher limbs.

Suddenly, a well-concealed door swings open from the trunk. "Whoa," I breathe.

I feel Seth's eyes on my face as I turn my attention to the woman who is stepping out of the tree. She's tall, with long platinum hair and twig-like legs. Her green dress flows behind her, and two broad, shimmering wings protrude from her back.

My heart pounds. *That* is a fairy. Right in front of me. A freaking fairy.

"Seth?" I close my fingers around his arm.

"I'm right here," he whispers. "Take a second, but then we need to keep moving."

I close my eyes, allowing myself a few seconds to clear my head. A million thoughts flood my brain. Every single urban legend I've ever heard. Every tabloid news story. Every fuzzy photograph of a supposedly imaginary creature.

These things cannot be real.

I take a slow, steady breath before opening my eyes again.

The fairy I spotted a moment ago is hovering above the steps of the tree she exited, chatting with another fairy who is dressed in blue. I hear the unmistakable sound of hoofs clopping against the ground, a noise I heard many times back home when our neighbors took their horses for rides along our fence line. The familiarity is only in the memory—the half-horse, half-man hybrids I see trotting down the path are unlike the stallions I'm used to. Centaurs. There are actual centaurs here. And fairies. With the wings. And the flying.

It's real. It's all real. As terrifying as it is, at least I'm not losing my mind. Tonight's events truly happened, and Seth is taking me to Mom and Sam, and we're going to understand everything.

"Charlie?" Seth pries my fingers from his arm.

I spot two large animals behind him, grazing in a field behind a wooden-planked fence. "Are those unicorns?" My voice raises an octave. He hadn't mentioned unicorns.

"Yes," he says. "The apothecary keeps a few here."

I long for my paints. There's so much color, so much depth, and I can't help but grin at the magnificence. If only I had my sketchbook, I could sit down right here in this spot and be perfectly content for the next several hours.

A joyful squeal fills the air and a large streak of sparkling violet swooshes by us, knocking Seth to the ground. I stumble backward, nearly falling.

Seth lies on his back in the grass, and a winged girl hovers over him, eye-to-eye. She's petite—even though she's looking him in the eye, her feet barely go past his knees.

"Seth! You're back!" she sings.

"Hi, Lulu." Seth slides his hands behind his head and stares up at her, lengthening each syllable with exaggerated annoyance.

She smirks at him. "Don't pretend you're not happy to see me," she says, a Southern twang pulling on each of her vowels.

Seth smiles at her. "Lulu, meet Charlie," he says, "my Apprentice."

She lifts her eyebrows. "Apprentice, eh?" She purses her lips and shifts her mouth to the side. "I can't decide if that's a promotion or punishment for you."

Punishment? What does that mean? I lower my brow and glance at Seth.

He snorts. "Shut up and say hi to Charlie."

In a flash, she's in front of me, the tips of her toes resting on the ground. I close my mouth and pull myself together. Lush eyelashes border Lulu's bright green eyes. Her black hair is cropped, with streaks of deep purple running wildly throughout. Even stretched up on her toes, she's an inch or so shorter than me.

Clearly enjoying the attention, she straightens her posture and rotates like a ballerina. Two pairs of broad wings emerge from her back, below her shoulder blades. They look like a dragonfly's wings, opalescent in color with intricate membranes and crossveins. Holding my breath, I bow my head closer and stretch my fingers toward one of the wings. Just as my fingertips brush their velvety surface, the wings flutter and I lurch backward.

Lulu lifts herself into the air with a delighted giggle. "Gotcha!" she sings, and I laugh. She sinks to the ground and grins. "So. What are you?"

I blink at her. "Huh?" What am I? My mouth goes dry.

Behind Lulu, Seth jumps up from the ground. "Oh! Lulu!" he says, a little too loud, a little too eager. "Guess what I brought for you?"

She instantly spins around to Seth. As soon as her attention is off me, I exhale. "You got it?" she asks.

His face goes blank. "Maybe."

"Seth!" Lulu pouts. "Give it to me!"

Lulu reaches toward his pockets, and Seth backs away. His mouth lifts again, this time in a full-fledged grin, and it throws me a bit. I don't see his flirty side very often. I'm so used to his serious face or that half-smile thing he does. This one is—well, it's stunning. He's more relaxed than I've ever seen him. It takes longer than it should for me to tear my eyes from his face. I long for my sketchbook again. I don't want that smile to go away.

He reaches into his back pocket and pulls out a tiny black circle. He holds it out to Lulu, then pulls it back quickly when she reaches for it. "Promise me you will never ever play this when I'm at your house."

Her shoulders fall. "Seth."

He raises his eyebrows and holds it up higher. "Promise."

She flies up and snatches it from him. "No way!" Her lips bounce off his cheek and she giggles as she takes to the air, leaving a trail of twinkling violet in her wake.

Seth and I stare after her.

"Lulu," I say.

"Lulu." Seth nods, watching while she shrinks in the distance. "The sweetest, feistiest pixie you'll ever meet."

The fondness in his tone makes me turn to look at him. "I like her," I say, watching him watch her.

"Everyone does."

"Is she your girlfriend?"

Seth's eyebrows bounce, and I'm already wishing I hadn't asked. "No, but she's my best friend."

I feel a weird twinge of jealousy. I've never really thought much about Seth having friends besides Sam and me. Not that it matters. Obviously he can be friends with whomever he wants.

I mean, of course.

Why am I even contemplating who his friends are?

"Was that a record you gave her? It was so little."

"Yeah, it's for a phonograph some of the elves invented. That record was Patsy Cline," he says. "Lulu will only listen to vinyl, and she's a country music fanatic. The classics. Patsy, Willie, Hank, George. You know."

I nod like I have some idea what he's talking about. I know those names, thanks to Sam's obsession with music, but I don't know any of their songs off the top of my head.

"When she asked me what I was—" I ask, and he coughs, nodding.

"Right. We shouldn't talk about that out here." Seth's eyes wander, drawing my attention to other creatures nearby who might overhear us. Three fairies and a couple of centaurs linger off the side of the path. "Let's get to your room. Your things will already be there. We'll track down Sam, and Adele and I will explain."

"Awesome," I say, reminding myself to be patient. For as long as I've known him, Seth's had an answer for every question asked since the beginning of time. Standing around in his rightness is his happy place. Today, the one day I would appreciate his need to enlighten the world with all his knowledge, he finds a filter.

Seth points to a gigantic tree not far ahead. It's larger than any of the other trees, as tall and wide as one of the nicer hotels in the neighboring cities back home. There are multiple stairways leading from the base to various areas of the tree, some of them extending far above my view and disappearing into the leaves. Lights twinkle throughout its canopy like a scattering of fireflies. I see a few creatures lingering near the steps leading to the large double doors at its base. "That's Artedion, where the Apprentices live."

"Awesome," I say again, completely unexcited.

"Remind me to find you a thesaurus. Between 'awesome' and 'whatever,' your vocabulary leaves a bit to be desired."

"Your face leaves a bit to be desired." *Self high-five.* I haven't had a good "your face" remark in days, and that one was pure instinct.

Seth wrinkles his nose. "What does that even mean?"

"What does your face even mean?" *Boom.* I grin at him, grateful for a little normalcy. I'm glad he's here. I don't know how I would've handled this with a stranger.

One of his eyebrows dips below the other. "Two 'your faces' in a row? Really?"

"Oh, I can do this all day," I tell him, lifting my hands palms-up by my sides, daring him to try me. Sam and I once conversed only in "your face" jokes for an entire evening. It drove Mom absolutely insane.

He leans closer and says, "Your face can do this all day."

Wait, what?

Seth made a joke?

I burst out laughing, more from surprise than the joke itself because, come on, that was terrible.

The happy smile he used with Lulu is back, and I don't want it to go away. We lock eyes long enough for it to feel a little awkward. I fight the urge to smooth my hair. He glances over his shoulder toward Artedion. "Come on," he says, and I fall into step beside him.

In contrast to the pure, still beauty of the Between, here in Ellauria the magic feels almost tangible, like I could scoop it in my hands and drink it right out of the air. The colors are so clear and vivid they almost don't look real, like I've stepped into a painting, and the palette stretches far beyond the browns, blues, and greens of the Between. There's a glow here I've never seen anywhere, as if the sunlight beams down from all directions and pulses through everything it strikes.

A lion with the head of an eagle trods past us, its wings folded across its back. I can't help but turn my head to watch it walk away, momentarily forgetting to act unfazed. A long tail swishes back and forth with every step it takes.

How can I keep from gawking when things like this continue to pop up and blow my mind?

As we walk, the enormous trees to my right are replaced by a forest of willows. Wide, sprawling branches are adorned with curtains of long purple blooms. Beyond them, I spot taller, narrower trees stretching high into the sky.

"That's the library," Seth says, jolting my attention forward again. He points to a building on the left. Brilliant bursts of light break through the canopy overhead, shimmering down on the white brick building.

That's a library? I scrunch up my nose. It's not much—two stories that basically look like one room stacked on top of another, large windows framed with black shutters, dark green vines climbing the walls. I prefer a library like the one back home—three stories high and lined with books from floor to ceiling. "But it's so small."

The idea that this tiny building is Ellauria's idea of a library actually makes me sad. All this magic and wonder, and this dinky building is the best they can do?

"It's big enough to house a thesaurus, which should be your number-one priority," he says with a smirk, and I stick my tongue out at him. He smiles and nods at the library again. "Principal Command meets on the second floor there. That's the Fellowship's governing body. Every single race in the mystical realm has a representative in PC, and they make all the decisions."

I guess every world needs a government. "Like Congress?"

"Sort of," he says, leading me on past the library.

Seems like they could've found a more impressive place for something as important as Congress. As we get closer to Artedion, I see doors and balconies everywhere, all over the outside of the trunk. The wooden staircases form a crisscross pattern from one balcony to the next. I catch glimpses of creatures climbing stairs and standing on landings throughout the tree.

The front of my flip-flop catches on an uneven spot in the dirt, and I direct my gaze to the ground as I do a little step-hop to keep my balance. A tiny animal pokes its head out from behind the leg of one of the flowering arches. It looks like a tiny cat, aside from enormous ears that stick straight out from its head like giant satellite dishes. A thin tail drags across the ground as it walks. "What is that?"

Seth squats and lays his palm at ground level. The creature hesitates before cautiously placing one paw on his outstretched hand. Seth remains still, speaking in a soft, soothing voice. "This is a fejib. Those enormous ears pick up every single sound in existence. That made it very hard for them to live in the mortal realm, so we pulled them all out. Anything they hear can be played back, like a living recorder."

I crouch next to Seth. The fejib blinks its wide black eyes, then stretches its neck to run its cool nose against mine. The movement tickles, and my giggle causes it to jump from Seth's hand and scamper off into the grass. I stand up. "Why haven't I ever heard of fejibs?"

Seth gives me a funny look. "That's the whole point. The Fellowship protects creatures like the fejib. Humans aren't supposed to know about them."

"Right, but I've heard of unicorns, fairies, and lots of other things I see around here."

"For every one of these creatures you've heard of, there are probably ten you haven't. We've worked very hard to keep their existences secret. Sometimes, like with the fairies, humans have enough encounters with a certain creature and a legend is born."

He's moving toward Artedion again, and I follow. We pass more and more creatures, and I do my best to keep my gaze steady and my posture as relaxed as possible. I deserve an award for all the gawking I'm stifling right now, acting as if men with goat hooves and women with heads full of wriggling snakes are completely normal parts of my life. Several of them wave and greet Seth as we walk by, and he responds with a quiet, "Hello," or a head nod but never much of a smile.

I have no idea where to look. I try to remember the things I know from legends. The snake-haired ladies, the gorgons, they'll turn me to stone if I make eye contact, and I seem to recall that satyrs are basically drunk musicians who love women. I don't know if any of that is accurate, but I keep my eyes on Seth when they pass by just to be safe.

When the coast is clear, I look around again, watching a group of leprechauns topple over each other as they run across the path in front of us. Seconds later, a couple young centaurs chase after them.

While they're all mind-blowing to see in person, not many of these creatures are new to me. After all, entire industries have been built around things like fairies and the Loch Ness monster. "So, if humans have heard of the creature, it's because you guys failed?"

"Oh, I wouldn't say that," Seth says, slowing a bit so I walk next to him rather than behind him. "You may have heard of fairies before today, but did you actually believe they existed? Besides, the majority of those legends began a long time ago, before the Fellowship was formed. There are much fewer sightings today than there were fifty years ago."

"What about Bigfoot? There's a Bigfoot sighting every few months."

Seth shakes his head and waves his hand in dismissal. "Oh, we gave up on Bigfoot a long time ago. She's a lost cause."

"She?"

"Yeah," he says, missing my point. "Total attention whore. No matter what we said or did, she refused to follow the rules. After getting caught on tape one too many times, we had to kick her out."

I break this information into tiny snapshots in my brain. The infamous image of Bigfoot walking through trees is real. The large, hairy so-called urban legend—the topic of T-shirts and comic books and several bad TV shows—is a creature that exists.

And apparently, she's a bit of a diva.

"What happens if she's discovered? Wouldn't she expose everything you've worked so hard to hide?"

"Nah." Seth points to a dip in the path and I step over it. "She's been banished from the mystical realm."

"Banished?"

"She's no longer welcome here," he explains. "She can't return. So she can't lead anyone to us. Besides, she's the only Bigfoot left. So whenever she dies, which we expect to be in the next thirty years or so, the sightings should stop. We do have someone who keeps an eye on the situation, though."

"Bigfoot has her own watchman?"

"There are several creatures with specific units assigned to them, sometimes for their safety, sometimes for ours."

Ooh. I connect the dots. Mom and Seth work together. Tonight they handled the Mothman like experts, completely without fear or confusion. They knew exactly how to handle him, with no hesitation whatsoever. "So you and Mom are assigned to the Mothman?"

"Hmm?"

"You two are part of his unit? You keep an eye on him?" They must be in charge of keeping him from being a threat to the mortal realm.

"Uh, sort of."

"Sort of?" I stop walking and look at him. "What do you mean?"

He looks past me, drawing my attention to the darkening horizon. "Let's get you settled into your room before dark."

I fold my arms and shift my weight to one hip. I know this trick. I use it all the time when I'm babysitting toddlers. They ask for something I don't want to give them, I distract them with something shiny.

I am not a toddler.

I move my hand in a circular motion in front of his face. "This whole mysterious thing isn't nearly as intriguing as you think it is."

"Believe it or not, intriguing you isn't my primary concern at the moment," Seth replies, pursing his lips. "I'm more interested in getting you settled into your room and reconnecting with Adele and Sam. The sooner we get there, the sooner you'll get your answers."

Right. Mom and Sam are waiting. The mention of my family is enough to make me push aside my questions for the moment. I'm sure Seth did that on purpose, but I allow it. I have a feeling I'm going to want Mom and Sam with me for whatever comes next.

FIVE

Seth presses against the heavy wooden doors of Artedion's entrance, pushing them open. "Welcome to Artedion. You and Sam will live here like the rest of the Apprentices."

Artedion's lobby is wide and brightly lit. Overflowing bookshelves line the wall on my left, and plush chairs and sofas are arranged for conversation in front of the shelves. Small tables and lamps are strategically placed, providing light. In the far back corner there's a large, wide fireplace with a hearth made of stacked gray stone.

There's no one around aside from an older woman standing behind a bronze pedestal to my right. She's completely still, her head bowed and her hands folded on top of the leather-bound book lying on the pedestal. The book is as large as the pedestal itself, with worn, rounded covers and golden-edged pages.

"This," Seth points to her, "is Vera. She keeps a record of everyone living in Artedion."

Vera is painfully thin. The long dress she's wearing would find more shape on a clothes hanger than it does draped over her wiry frame. Her slender face is pointed at the top and bottom, with a wild mess of silver curls piled above her forehead. Her bulging eyes are closed, and her narrow lips are slack. I can't decide if she's praying or asleep, but either way I want to shush Seth when he loudly says, "Hello, Vera."

As soon as he completes the phrase, her head snaps up and a smile spreads across her face as she looks down at us. "Hello, Seth."

There's something off about her, but I can't put my finger on it. She looks human, but then, so does Seth. Maybe she's some sort of robot?

"Vera, I'd like you to meet Charlie, er, Charlotte Page," Seth says. "She's new here. I'm showing her to her suite."

Vera's large eyes travel to me as she slips a pair of square-framed reading glasses over her nose. A second pair of glasses is nestled in the curls on top of her head, and a third dangles from the scooped neck of her dress. The book before her lifts, and the yellowed pages make a crinkling noise as they fan open. Her head moves up and down as she traces the lines on the page with her bony finger.

Her fluid movements and natural voice seem too real for a robot. Then there's her book, which seems like it might have a mind of its own. When her eyes reach the bottom of each golden-edged page, the page lifts and turns without her assistance.

"Ah! There you are!" she announces. The book hops up and turns on the pedestal for me to see. My own blue eyes stare back at me, like I'm looking in a mirror.

"Very good!" Vera says, and the book slams shut, pivots on its spine, and lays flat. "You may take her up."

I lean over the strange book. "Is Sam, I mean, Samuel Page here yet?"

Vera says nothing, and I watch while her hands fold back into place on the book's cover and her head slowly turns downward.

"You have to greet her first," Seth says.

"Huh?" Didn't we already do that?

"Vera is a slape. Their brains operate at extremely high speeds, devoting all of their energy to collecting and processing information, so they go into a hibernation state when they're not interacting with anyone."

Seth steps toward her, bringing his face right next to her cheek while he talks. She doesn't react to him at all. I inch closer, staring up at her. I can see the slightest ripple beneath her eyelids as her eyes move quickly from side to side.

"It allows more focus for their cognitive processes. You have to use certain phrases to get their attention," he says.

A human computer. She reminds me of some of the brainiacs back at school—super brilliant, terrible social skills.

"Hello, Vera," Seth whispers, prompting me.

Huh? Oh, right. I step closer to her. "Hello, Vera," I say, loud and slow.

I watch her come alive again—her head popping up, her eyes landing on me. I repeat my question, and the book's heavy cover swings open. Vera scans the pages. After a few seconds, she shakes her head.

A cold sensation pours over my shoulders and down my arms. They're not here yet? My eyes dart to Seth's face.

"Hello, Vera." Seth steps closer. "He hasn't checked in yet?"

"No. When was he expected to be here?" Vera's tone is too pleasant to be delivering such troubling news. They should be here, right? Seth's been telling me all along that they would be here.

Seth hesitates for the slightest moment, his eyes falling across the pages of the book. "Never mind. He'll probably be here any minute. Send him to Charlie's room when he arrives. Adele will be with him."

The book slams shut again, and I shiver. Where are Mom and Sam? They left before we did. What's taking them so long? Seth's hand finds my elbow and pulls me along, thanking Vera over his shoulder. I watch her recede into herself again before I ask, "Where are they?"

"They'll be here any minute," Seth says, but he won't look at me.

I stop, pulling my arm from him. "You're not the least bit concerned?"

Seth's eyes finally meet mine, and he swallows. "Adele is the best. There's nothing to worry about."

I raise my eyebrow, studying his face. His expression is blank, and his stare is steady. I want to believe him, but I saw his reaction when Vera said Sam wasn't here yet. He'd expected them to be here. What if something's happened? Sam and I hadn't even said goodbye. Would Seth lie to spare me the worry?

Seth lowers his chin, staring me in the eye like my thoughts are displayed there. "They will be here."

I take a deep breath and study the grain of the wood floor beneath my feet. I blow out a breath and shake off my worry. They're going to meet us here. Mom said so.

Listen to Seth.

If he says they'll be here, they'll be here. A sprawling burst of color on the wall behind him catches my eye.

"What's that?" I ask. I take a step to the side and take it all in. The painting on the wall stretches from the corner by the fireplace to about halfway across the room, covering the wall from ceiling to floor.

"That," Seth turns around, "is a map. What you see there is the entire mystical realm."

It becomes clearer as I approach. "Ellauria" is written in large script, slightly off-center. I recognize a miniature Artedion drawn there and run my fingers along the broad, painted brush strokes, tracing the path back to the unicorn's field, noting the library along the way. A giant lake sits at one end of Ellauria, and an apothecary center beyond a vast wooded area marks its western boundary. Ellauria is the largest, most detailed section of the map, but there are several other clusters of drawings outside of it, each labeled in the same curved script with names like Ether, Hollow, Gelata, and the Territory of Giants.

Giants! Giant people? Giant plants? I chew on the inside of my lip, reading the names of these places again. What do they mean? Who lives there? I wonder how many of the Grimm's fairy tales are based on actual events. I walk from one end of the wall to the other, scanning the locations. "Will I get to see all these places?"

"Eventually. But for now," Seth plants a finger on Ellauria, "you stay here. Apprentices aren't allowed outside Ellauria's borders without an Aegis."

On a scale of one to ten, rating how tired I am of being told what I can and cannot do or feel or know, I'm about a thirty. I file this little Ellauria rule under "To Be Ignored."

Seth leads me around a corner and down a narrow hallway that ends at another door. Beyond the door, we climb one of the staircases that encircle the outside of Artedion. Halfway up, he stops and nods toward the ground. "See that field?"

I lean over the railing. There's a flat, vacant area behind Artedion, about the size of two football fields, with a wooden platform on the end closest to me. I spot a line of fairies cutting across it. From this high up, they almost look like dragonflies.

"We call that the Clearing," he says.

Of course they do. The Between is between the realms and the Clearing is a clearing in the woods, but I'm the one that needs the thesaurus.

"The Fellowship holds a meeting there every week," Seth continues. "Creatures come from all over the mystical realm for updates on Fellowship activities and missions. You'll attend those meetings every single week to learn more about how we do things. The next one is tomorrow morning."

I gaze at the Clearing, now empty as the last fairy drops down the slope on its far side. Creatures from all over the mystical realm? From Ether and the Territory of the Giants and everything? Tomorrow morning, I'll see for myself while I listen to the updates.

Will I be part of the update? Because of the Mothman?

We continue up the stairs, and I gaze above at the network of stairs that lead to different landings in the tree. There must be nearly a hundred Apprentices living here.

Seth stops in front of the door at the top of the first landing and turns to me. The sun slips lower in the sky, casting his face in a golden-pink that makes his brown eyes look even darker.

"This is your suite," Seth says. "First things first—all of the Apprentice rooms are charmed. Only you, as the occupant, and I, as your Aegis, are able to unlock the door. There are no keys, and there's no way anyone can get inside without our permission, okay?" He waves his hand over a barely discernible knot in the wood, and the door slides open. "Go ahead."

I step inside and stop. My "suite," as Seth calls it, is more of a studio apartment. It's one deep room, with a bed in the back, a living-room setup in the middle, and a kitchen here at the front. Everything has a vintage feel to it, with painted white furniture accessorized in bright colors. It's exactly how I would've chosen to decorate my own place, if I'd been asked.

To my left is the tiny kitchen, complete with a sink, refrigerator, and narrow island. I step toward it, running my hand along the smooth countertop. Seth leans against a small square table surrounded by four mismatched chairs. A teal bowl filled with fruit sits on top of it, and the sight of food momentarily deafens every thought in my head except for how hungry I am. I reach around him to grab a banana.

"I knew you'd be hungry," Seth says, like he's some kind of genius for realizing a girl would want something to eat several hours after dinner.

I strip the peel away and gulp it down in three bites. "Starving," I say. I drop the peel in a small wastebasket tucked between the countertop and a dark brown leather couch.

All the little details—from the brightly painted lamps on the end tables to the turquoise and melon throw pillows perched in the corners of the sofa—they're just like the random splashes of color in my room back home.

On the far wall, there are two arched doorways to the right of my bed. One is my closet, large enough to step inside but not exactly a walk-in, and the second is a—

"Bathroom," Seth calls as I peek inside.

No *sheet*, *Seth*. I poke my head back into the main room. "Is that what that is? The toilet and claw-footed tub threw me off."

"Your sarcasm is completely wasted on me," Seth says, flopping onto the couch and resting his feet on the white coffee table in front of it.

I wander back to the closet. "Where did all the clothes come from?"

"They're yours."

"Really?" I step inside and drag my fingers along the clothes. He's right. I recognize everything, from the light blue sundress I bought last week to my beloved gray Chuck Taylors right down to the faded, ripped jeans Mom hates so much. "How?"

"We have a pretty extensive process in place for bringing Apprentices to Ellauria. I set yours in motion when I brought you into the Between. Basically, there's a spell for everything. All of your clothes, jewelry, makeup, shoes, some photographs—whatever we can do to make it feel like home."

A silk-covered jewelry box sits on the dresser between the bathroom and closet. I flip the lid open. Yep. It's all there. I don't wear a lot of jewelry—just a few random pieces that put me in a good mood—but it's nice to have them. I glance over my shoulder toward the bookshelf on the other side of the bed. The shelves are mostly empty, aside from a couple of notebooks and a jar of pencils. "Art supplies?"

"They're not here?" Seth sits up and turns toward the shelves, then stands to inspect them. He stares at the meager amount of supplies for a moment and frowns. "They should be here," he murmurs. His brow lowers and he shakes his head. "I'll look into it."

"But we can still get them, right?" I worked a long time on my collection of colors and charcoals. More than that, I want my sketchbooks.

He runs his fingers along the notebooks and looks at the empty space that should be filled with my things. "I think so, but—"

"Everything that's ever meant anything to me is in them," I say. The idea of being here without my drawings brings on an unexpected quiver in my belly. I need them. They're more "home" to me than anything else I own.

The sooner Mom and Sam get here, the better.

Seth nods once, meeting my gaze. "Don't worry. I'll take care of it."

I nod back.

He'll take care of it. It's going to be okay.

Listen to Seth.

I step backward until the edge of the bed presses into the backs of my knees. I sit down and stretch out across the bright-green duvet cover, melting into its softness. A weird mix of exhaustion and alertness settles over me, like my mind and body are at war. I glance at the clock on the nightstand. "Seven o'clock? How big of a time difference is there?"

He turns toward me, leaning his shoulder against the bookshelf. "It's seven here, but almost one o'clock in the morning to you."

Impossible. Four hours ago, Sam and I were sitting on the front porch, trading bracelets. I run my fingers over the silver beads, remembering the way Sam's face lit up when he saw the guitar pick.

There's a knock at the door, and Seth pushes off the shelf with a grin. He's halfway across the room before I make it off my bed. "That must be Adele and Sam," he says.

They're here!

I hop off the bed and run to the door, ready to throw my arms around them in a hug that would bring every other hug in the history of hugs to shame.

Seth places a hand on the door, and it slides open. A towering man in my doorway stops me in my tracks.

He's at least a foot taller than Seth and almost twice as wide, with the dark, hardened skin of someone who's spent some time in the elements. Thick blond hair streaked with silver flows freely past his shoulders and down his back, like the pictures of Vikings I've seen in history books. He's dressed like one too, wearing brown pants tucked into tall leather boots and a long gray tunic with a drawstring tied around his middle.

His shoulders are broad, his arms enormous. His eyes are his most striking feature, a vibrant mix of green and yellow. The peculiar color practically glows against his tanned skin. It's all at once beautiful and unsettling.

Nothing about him looks huggable.

Seth's posture straightens. "Alexander! Come in! I didn't expect to see you tonight!"

The surprised expression on Seth's face makes me feel somewhat better about the fact that I'm staring. I have never seen such a large person in my life.

I clamp my mouth shut and pull my shoulders back. No. More. Gawking.

Alexander ducks his head as he steps inside, shrinking the room. He nods at Seth, then turns his attention to me. Something like a smile happens on my lips, but I'm not entirely sure it's believable. This man is the very definition of intimidating. He holds my gaze, and I have no idea where to look.

Sam and I found a stray dog in the barn once. When we tried to get close, it bared its teeth and chased us all the way up the hill to the house. We'd practically leapfrogged over each other to get inside the door. Mom told us to never look a strange animal in the eye because they might consider it a threat. I've never forgotten that.

On the other hand, she also told us it's respectful to maintain eye contact when you're dealing with people so they know you're paying attention.

I can't decide if Alexander is more human or animal.

"Hello, Charlotte," the giant man says, his yellow-green eyes bearing down on me.

"Hello," I say, but it comes out like a whisper. I take a deep breath and raise my voice a bit. "It's nice to meet you." I force myself to blink, breaking away from his eyes. I don't even correct him on his use of "Charlotte." I lift my hand in a tiny wave and immediately regret it. I should've shaken his hand or nodded at him or something. A wave is far too frivolous.

Seth clears his throat. "Charlie, I'd like you to meet Alexander, one of the Fellowship's founders. If Principal Command is Congress, then Alexander is the President."

Alexander nods at me, his eyes barely softening, before he looks back to Seth. "We have a situation."

"What's wrong?" Seth asks.

"Adele hasn't crossed into Ellauria yet."

The weight that had lifted before comes crashing down again, stealing my breath. Heat rises from my knees to my arms to my cheeks. I pushed my fear away before, but now it's clear—there's a reason to worry. They should be here by now.

"What does that mean?" I ask, stepping closer. "Where is she? Where's Sam?"

My voice is a little too high-pitched, too loud. I suck in a breath and hold it, waiting for an answer. Seth and Alexander stare at each other, conversing in silence. My heart pounds against the front of my chest.

Alexander didn't mention Sam. Why wouldn't he mention Sam?

"Where are they?" I ask again, louder.

Seth can't quite make eye contact. "We don't know."

They don't know.

They don't *know*?

Tears form behind my eyes, and pressure builds there, waiting for me to break down and release them. I swallow hard and look at Alexander. "Are they still in the Between?"

He shakes his head. "They haven't left the mortal realm."

Are they together?

They haven't made it out of the mortal realm. So either Mom's hurt and Sam doesn't know enough to know where to go, or Sam's hurt and Mom doesn't want to leave him. Or they're both hurt. Hurt. Not dead. Oh God, are they dead? Would the Fellowship know?

I'd know. Right? I'd have to know. If my twin brother was dead, I'd feel it.

I stare at the red string knotted around my wrist.

The air is too heavy. I have to get out of here.

"Charlie." Seth steps toward me, lifting his hand like he might hug me. A hug is the absolute last thing I want right now.

I need air.

I push past Seth and step around Alexander toward the door. Two giant hands lift me by my arms and place me by the table, and I gasp.

"You need to stay calm," Alexander orders.

"Stay calm? What if the Mothman found them?" The room closes in on me. I imagine the Mothman tracking them, howling, toying with them before he finally swoops down and—

"We've already sent a team to the mortal realm," Alexander says. "Whatever the outcome, we'll know what's happened to them."

Whatever the outcome. No three words have ever sounded so terrifying.

Neither of them says it, but I know. It's possible Mom and Sam are dead. Seth's fingers brush across my shoulder and I jerk away, glaring at him. This shouldn't have happened. The Mothman should never have been so close to us. We shouldn't have left them. "You should've been there. You're supposed to be watching the Mothman. That's your job."

Alexander's forehead creases. "Watching the Mothman?"

Seth blinks and squints at me before he shakes his head. "*You* are my job. I'm supposed to be watching you."

"Oh, I know I'm your Apprentice," I say, waving my hand in the air and rushing my words, "but you're on the Mothman's unit. You're supposed to make sure he doesn't hurt anyone."

"No, Charlie. I never said that." Seth rubs his hand up the back of his head. "The Mothman doesn't have a unit, and even if he did, Adele and I wouldn't be on it." He takes a deep breath. "We're on yours."

Alexander leans against the kitchen island.

Mine? I can't even comprehend what this means. "What do you mean, mine? I thought the units were assigned to creatures that need extra—"

I grab the edge of the table when my head starts to spin.

Oh my God.

I stare down at my white-knuckled grip on the table.

I was right. Back in the Between. Mom isn't human. And I am my mother's daughter.

My lungs fill with air and stop, like the world will wait for me to exhale.

I look to Seth.

I am an assignment.

"Charlotte," Alexander says. He keeps his voice low and even. "Have a seat on the sofa. There are things you need to know."

Alexander's hand presses against my upper back, and Seth stays beside me as the three of us move toward the sofa. The cool leather chills my thighs as I sink into it, and I slip my hands under my legs for warmth. Seth sits next to me. A stained glass window hangs on the wall across from me like a painting, and I focus on it. There's a wide, white chest beneath it topped with a lime-green cushion. I stare at all of it, through it, until the colors blur.

The founder stands in the middle of the room, larger than ever. He's waiting for me to look at him, I know, but I can't yet. My mind races. I'd pushed away these thoughts back in the Between. It's so obvious. Seth flickered. Mom flickered. If Mom's not human, I must not be. What am I? I comb through memories, searching for anything that seems out of place, any clue to a different sort of existence, until I become lost in the complete impossibility of it all.

I need Sam.

Seth leans back and grabs the chenille throw from the corner of the couch and drapes it over my shoulders. His hands linger there, warming me. The blanket's softness glides over my arms like a hug. I turn my head slightly to look at Seth, and his eyebrows pull down. I focus on the feel of his fingers sliding down my back. He nods, silently assuring me, and I take a deep breath.

Okay.

I exhale and slowly raise my eyes to Alexander.

"What happened today was no coincidence, Charlotte," Alexander says, clasping his hands together. He looks down at me, pursing his lips, and continues. "You are an extremely unique being with a specific mix of powers that makes you a valuable asset to the mystical realm. For this reason, there is a unit assigned to protect you from those who would harm you."

"I have powers?" I look from Alexander to Seth. How have I lived seventeen years without noticing this? Seth's already watching me.

"You are a muralet, a direct descendant of Mother Nature herself."

Mother Nature. The faceless, shapeless entity I'd considered back in the Between enters my mind again—a wide vision of nothing, pulling in from all directions to create a more human shape. She was a person. She lived.

I press my fingertips to my forehead, dragging them down my face and over my eyes. Beside me, Seth shifts, pulling his leg onto the couch and turning his entire body toward me. He rests one warm hand on my back, and I look at him with my fingers pressed to my lips.

Mother Nature lived, and I come from her.

I release a quick burst of air and lower my hands. "I come from Mother Nature."

"Well, in a way, we all do." Seth leans forward, resting his elbow on his knee. His eyes are on the blanket as he speaks. "Mother Nature is the reason magic exists. After she created the Between, she built the mystical realm. Each and every one of us comes from her design, because of her abilities."

She was real and she's sort of a god? I picture the beauty of the Between and the enchantment of Ellauria. The architect of all of this is at the top of my family tree?

"A lot of creatures have the ability to call upon magic for various purposes. I can. Alexander can. But you..." Seth's voice trails off as he lifts his head to look at me.

And does he ever. Seth's gaze travels from my eyes to my hair to my hands, and he shakes his head like he can't quite believe what he sees. "Essentially, Charlie, you *are* magic. It's woven into every fiber of your being."

I don't know if it's what he said or the way he said it or a combination of the two, but I'm suddenly unable to look at him. Warmth creeps across my cheeks before flooding down the rest of my body. It's a little ridiculous, really. Having a gorgeous guy say you're magical is super-dreamy until it means "terrifying creatures show up to attack you at your house after dark."

Muralet. I whisper the word to myself. Descended from magic and requiring the protection of a secret organization dedicated to guarding the secrets I've learned today.

"Why would anyone want to harm me?"

Seth looks to Alexander, and the floor groans as the founder paces from one side of the room to the other. "The story goes that, a long time ago, an ogre killed a muralet. After feeding on her, he noticed a drastic increase in his strength. From that point on, muralets were hunted for their blood. Whatever powers a creature possesses, drinking muralet blood makes them better—stronger, smarter, faster, and in some cases, nearly invincible."

My middle feels like one giant knot. Hunted for their blood. My blood. They want to drink the blood from my body. I curl my hands over my knees, squeezing them to keep from trembling. The Mothman could've grabbed me and drained me in no time. Did he already do that to Mom and Sam? I flinch at the thought, and goosebumps explode across my arms. Seth pulls the blanket more tightly over me.

"It was slow at first," Alexander continues. "Muralets didn't live together in large groups, so when one or two of them vanished it wasn't immediately noticeable. By the time we realized what was happening, there were less than thirty left in the entire world. Then they started disappearing, too."

Alexander's expression changes, as though he's grown tired of holding his mask in place. His eyes turn downward; the corners of his mouth droop. "Many of them were completely empty when we found them."

Pale, lifeless bodies scattered throughout Ellauria's brightly colored landscape flash in my mind—dead eyes, bodies lying in impossible positions, pale skin glowing against lush green grass and sparkling flowers. I close my eyes, but the visions only become larger, squeezing out all thoughts until I see my own face on one of those bodies, dead and staring. Then Mom, then Sam. All of us in danger, simply for being born. My whole body clenches. I open my eyes again, but everything is blurry. A tear slides down my face.

"I think that's enough for now," Seth says, his fingers curling into my back again, rubbing up and down. He sounds too far away to be sitting next to me.

"No," I tell him, and blink rapidly to clear my eyes. I look at Alexander. "I want to know everything."

Seth sits up straighter and turns away, placing both feet on the floor. He rests his forearms on his knees and leans forward, balancing his forehead on his fingers.

Silence stretches across the room for several seconds before Alexander rubs his chin and continues. "In the mortal realm, the amount of money a person has often determines his station in life. There's no rhyme or reason to it—a child doesn't choose the family he's born into. In our world, powers are our currency. For a creature with little or no magical ability, the lure of muralet blood is very enticing."

Seth places his hand over mine on my knee, and a tingle spreads from his fingers all the way up my thigh. "That's why we have to be sure nobody finds out what you are. Alexander, Adele, and I are the only ones who know. Sam will know, of course, but it is absolutely crucial that nobody else finds out. If anyone asks, you're a siren."

I take my eyes off his hand on my knee. I've read about sirens—beautiful women who lured sailors to their deaths by singing to them.

I don't sing.

Wait. Did he just call me beautiful? "You think I can pass as a siren?"

Seth's eyebrows wrinkle and the corners of his mouth turn up, as if he finds my question completely absurd. "Of course you can. And it's perfect because a siren's power is wrapped up in singing, and no one will ask you to demonstrate it since the siren's song is so deadly."

Seth thinks I'm beautiful.

It's not that he's never complimented me before. He's always been quick to admire my artwork, praise my intelligence, and even laugh at some of my jokes, but he's never said a word about my appearance. Of all the mind-blowing information being dropped on me right now, the idea that Seth finds me attractive shouldn't even register on the scale, but it does.

His hand is still on mine, covering it completely. I want to scoot closer to him. His fingers curl around my hand, squeezing, and I look up to find his eyes on my face. I bite my lip, wondering how long he's been watching me.

Alexander clears his throat, crashing right down on my moment. Seth pulls his hand from mine and shifts away. What was that about? I look from Seth to Alexander, but they give nothing away.

As soon as Seth's hand is gone, I want it back again. Something in his hunched shoulders tells me not to reach for him. I get up from the couch and take the photo from the nightstand, studying Mom's face and searching for signs of the enormous secret she'd been keeping for years. No wonder she's always so overprotective. If anyone found out our secret, we'd all be dead and drained.

My fingers itch for my charcoals. Drawing is my favorite mode of transportation, my quickest escape route. I can work through what's happening in my head while I break my feelings into visible pieces. Right now, I'd draw what I need to see—something to replace the images in my head. Sam's twinkling green eyes instead of his terrified stare. Mom's soft, gentle hands instead of her white-knuckled grip on that knife.

"I need to return to Central Hall to keep an eye on things," Alexander says, interrupting my thoughts. I turn to face him. He nods to me and then looks at Seth. "If there's any sign of Sam and Adele, I'll let you know."

Seth rises from the couch as Alexander disappears in a ripple of air.

I clutch the framed photograph, remembering the way Mom stared down the Mothman earlier. He could've killed her so easily, but she jumped right out there in front of him. For us.

My eyes burn with tears. I need her here. I need her soothing voice to explain all this to me in a way that makes sense. I need her to tell me this will work out, that our blood isn't a death sentence, and then I need to hear Sam make some stupid joke about it.

Mostly I just need to see them to know they're safe.

My throat goes dry. They have to be safe.

I lower myself onto the foot of my bed and set the photo beside me.

"How did he find us?" I shake my head. "If no one is supposed to know muralets still exist, how did the Mothman show up at our house tonight?"

Seth paces between the coffee table and the stained glass window. "You remember that thing with your hands earlier?"

"The tingling?" I look down at my hands, remembering the itch of pins and needles crawling across my skin, spreading outward from my palms. What's that have to do with anything?

"When did it start? What were you doing?"

I tell him about the cloud, and Seth nods. "Muralets have power over everything Mother Nature created. You can manipulate natural elements—earth, air, fire, and water. When you were born, Alexander repressed your powers. Tonight, it appears, his spell slipped."

Slipped? That's a thing that happens? What good is a spell if it's not reliable enough to keep scary birdmen off my lawn? "How did it slip?"

"We're not entirely sure." He pauses by the window and rubs his hand over his chin. "It's never really happened before. We already have someone looking into it. But with what you've described, it's the only thing that makes sense."

His earlier words replay in my head. Power over everything Mother Nature created.

My powers.

Powers. In me. Mine. Like a motherfluffing superhero. I flop back on my bed and stare at the ceiling. I am Mother Nature's granddaughter, and I have power over her creations. My mind is flooded with possibilities—things I've only seen in comic books and movies. Parting water. Raising wind. Trembling ground. I'm capable of this? I control these things?

"You're saying I was controlling the cloud?"

"It's more like the wind was trying to obey your wishes, but yes."

I bring my hands over my eyes, pointing my elbows upward. Tonight, I wanted to draw the sunset. I wanted to make something pretty on the day when I thought the Collis rejection was the worst thing that would happen to me.

That seems like ages ago, not hours.

I had to draw that sunset. If I hadn't done that—if I hadn't started talking to clouds—would I be here right now?

I hear Seth's footsteps move across the room again.

"How many of us are left?" I ask. "Muralets? Just the three of us?"

My question is met with silence. I let my arms fall to the bed and push myself up again. Seth is frozen by the sofa, staring at me like it's physically painful for him to do so. "No," he says, his voice barely above a whisper. "It's only you."

Only me? But how is that possible? If I'm descended from Mother Nature, the bloodline has to run through my mom and brother, too. That's three of us. Three muralets. Not only me. That makes no sense.

"Adele is the Aegis assigned to your unit," he says, slowly stepping toward me. "She's responsible for taking care of you."

"Well, of course," I say, "because she's my mom." Who better to serve as your ultimate protector than your mother?

Seth stands over me, his gaze falling somewhere between my mattress and the floor. I can't figure out his problem. He's wrong. Clearly, there are three muralets. This is a mistake. I can't be the only one. I'm not alone.

He meets my eyes again, and the pieces fall into place. I realize what he's not saying. The question swells in my throat, aching, but I can't find a way to release it.

It can't be.

"She's Sam's mom," Seth says. He exhales, and everything about him deflates a little. His shoulders slump, his eyes darken, and his voice seems smaller. "Adele and Sam are jourlings, basically the human form of bloodhounds. Very strong, keen senses, excellent trackers and hunters," he pauses before adding, "and they have no relation to muralets."

No.

"I'm not—" I lean forward, trying to find air. "We're not related?"

Seth crouches in front of me and says something, but I can't hear him over the roar of blood between my ears. I wrap my arms around myself, curling inward, closing him out. The weird twitching thing that always happens when I cry starts, where my lips and cheeks seem to have minds of their own. I stare at the floor, focusing very hard on not losing it completely. It's all I can do to hold back the sob filling my chest. My fingers dig into my arms so deeply it hurts, but I can't stop hugging myself.

Seth peers up at me. He's so close I feel his breath on my legs. "Charlie."

How is this even possible? She's not my mom? He's not my brother? My *twin*?

"Don't." I don't want to hear explanations. It doesn't matter. I'm alone. One muralet surrounded by creatures who she thought she knew, but doesn't. How did this happen? How did I not know? I stare down at the photo.

Mom and Sam are tall. I'm not. Their skin tone is the same—the kind that turns golden in the sun, whereas my fair skin only explodes with pink splotches when I try to tan. There's little sign of me in the woman I call Mom.

Even so, it's not like Sam looks a lot like her either. Her dark brown eyes match her hair; Sam's blessed with clear green eyes, and his light brown curls have that naturally lightened look people pay a good amount of money to achieve.

Seth grabs a Kleenex for me from the table by my bed. I feel his eyes on my face, but I keep mine on the picture.

Boy-girl twins can only be fraternal, never identical. I never expected to look exactly like Sam. The idea that our differences mean anything at all never crossed my mind.

I feel so cold. My mother is my mother and my brother is my brother. How could they not be?

"What about the rest?" I ask, fighting to keep my voice steady. "Aunt Becky? Granny? Our cousins?" I cradle the picture against my chest and look at Seth directly. "Was any of it real?"

Seth's face is a struggle—drawn eyebrows, clenched jaw, tortured eyes. When he shakes his head, I can't hold in the sobs any longer. The mattress sinks a bit when he takes a seat and slides his arms around me. I curl into him, letting my tears fall onto his shirt.

My family is so much of who I am. The things I believe, the things I care about, even the foods I like best—they all started with them. I've been shaped by a life that should never have been mine, by people who were doing their jobs.

How much of what Mom did tonight was about saving me, her so-called daughter, and how much of it was about saving the last muralet? Is that why she sent me with Seth? Did she choose to guard Sam over me?

I stiffen.

Is Seth here right now, rubbing my back and holding me tight, because he cares about me? Or because it's his job? The laughter earlier? The comforting touch? What's real?

"Please leave," I tell him, pushing him away.

"I'm so sorry," he says, brushing my hair from my face with his fingers. "I always hoped you'd never have to find out."

Even with all the emotion in his voice, everything he says feels empty. Where does the Aegis stop and Seth begin? Is there any difference between the two? Has there ever been? I scoot farther up onto my bed, resting my head on my pillow with my back to him. "Please. I don't want you here."

The words are out before I can take them back, and I don't even know if I mean them. I don't want to be alone, but I don't want him to be here out of obligation either.

I feel him rise from the bed, and I squeeze my eyes shut.

"All right," he says. "Alexander or I will come for you in the morning. Wait here."

Tears roll across my cheeks and nose, creating sideways paths to my pillow. I wipe my nose with the wadded Kleenex in my hand and hold my fist to my lips to capture my sobs. When I finally turn to look, he's gone.

SIX

I wake up the next morning in the same clothes I wore yesterday. There's an intense throbbing behind my eyes that only comes after hours of crying, and for one peaceful, not-quite-awake moment, I can't remember why.

It all comes rushing back. The Mothman. Sam. Mom. The photograph is still cradled against my chest, and its corners leave stinging imprints on my arm when I pull it away to look at it again.

Mom and Sam.

They're my family in nearly every sense of the word, except they aren't.

Nothing has changed, and everything has changed.

I set the picture on my nightstand and force myself out of bed and to the bathroom, where I shower yesterday away. Afterward, I lean over the sink, searching the mirror for answers.

I'm a stranger in my own life now. I can't return to what I used to know—I don't belong there. I study my face in the mirror, swiping condensation away until my blue eyes stare back at me.

So many of the choices I've made in my life have been under the Fellowship's influence, and I didn't even know it. I am Mom's mission. Her job. An assignment. I could have easily been assigned to a different Aegis. I would've grown up without Sam. Maybe in a huge city. Who knows how my life would've been different?

Who am I, really? Who would I have been without the Fellowship?

I slip into a gray-striped T-shirt and blue-jean shorts, then finger-comb my wet hair before winding it into a braid that lies across my shoulder. I find my eyes in the mirror again, searching them for the things I surely know to be true.

My name is Charlie—of that, I'm reasonably certain.

I don't like spiders or heights.

Peanut M&Ms make me happy.

Memories are precious to me. My wish to preserve the things I care for spawned my love of drawing and painting. I memorialize people, places, and moments that have meant something in my life.

In the life the Fellowship created for me.

I step away from the mirror and swallow hard. My memories don't even belong to me anymore. They belong to the other Charlie, the girl with a life that made sense. Yesterday's Charlie.

I want that life back.

I close my eyes and lean against my dresser, pushing the emotion away. That life is gone. That Charlie doesn't exist. I don't know if that Charlie ever really existed at all. She was a work of fiction crafted by the Fellowship and developed by the creatures that work for it, including Mom and Seth.

I shake my head involuntarily as soon as I think of Mom.

Mom loves me. She must. Regardless of her job here and no matter what my blood means, she's more than my Aegis. She's happy when I'm happy, angry when I'm hurt, and strong when I've needed someone to take care of me. She handles the line between mother and friend like an expert—as quick to throw a *That's What She Said* at me as she is to remind me to use my manners and follow her rules.

And no one will ever convince me that Sam and I aren't connected at our very cores. He knows me better than anyone, and I can tell what he's thinking without even looking at him. I am incomplete without him.

I need them. What if the last time I heard Mom say my name is the last time I'll *ever* hear it? What if that last glimpse of Sam is all I have?

I didn't even hug him.

My stomach drops.

Where *are* they?

I can't do this. I can't wait around and wonder if someone will show up any second to tell me they're dead.

I place my hand over my chest, willing my heart to settle down. It slams against my fingers in return, over and over, entirely too fast. I glance at the clock by the bed and take note of the time—way-too-early o'clock. I doubt the sun is even up yet, but I have to get out of here.

I head down the stairs and through the door into Artedion's lobby, pausing by the map on the wall. My eyes sweep over the elaborate drawing from top to bottom. I need quiet and solitude and something familiar. I want to go home, more than anything, but I know I can't. Even if I could find my way back, I have no idea what awaits me there.

I close my eyes and rest my forehead against the map.

I can't be here. I can't be there.

I open my eyes.

The Between. Its beauty and stillness call to me, offering an escape from both of my worlds.

Already, I'm breathing a little easier.

I put my finger on Artedion and trace the path back to the unicorn field again, just like yesterday. I lean closer, my nose nearly brushing the wall. There, across from the field, is a tiny golden dot marking the gate to the Between. If I hadn't known where to look, I'd never have noticed it.

I study the location of the gate we came through yesterday. It's awfully close to the library, right there off the main path. Someone would probably see me if I tried to use the gate there.

I run my hand over the map, searching for other gates. They're there, barely discernible circles of gold scattered throughout the painting. There's a forest of purple willow trees across the path from Artedion, and gates cluster at the far end of it. It doesn't look like there are any buildings nearby.

That'll do.

The lobby's empty again, aside from Vera. I tiptoe past her, even though I'm pretty sure there's no need. She's frozen in place, head down, hands folded and resting on her book, exactly like she was last night.

I pull on one of the heavy double doors, opening it just enough to look outside. The sun peeks over the horizon, splashing the sky with lavender and peach. Cool air sprinkles my legs with goosebumps as I creep out the door and ease it shut behind me.

There's hardly anyone on the path this morning. Ellaurians must not be early risers. I see a few creatures here and there, nothing I recognize, but for the most part, I'm alone.

I move toward the trees, trying to look like I know exactly where I'm going.

A man with a beard longer than he is sits on a swing near a tiny house beneath one of the larger trees. His two hoofed feet dangle back and forth as the swing moves. He waves when he sees me, and I wave back.

Houses of every size and shape are tucked in and among the willows. There are larger stone cottages with flowering vines stretching across their outer walls, as well as tiny huts made of long, thick sticks. As I hike farther, the willows' low-hanging curtains of purple leaves are replaced by towering elm trees. They're supersized versions of the trees that line the entrance to one of the nicer neighborhoods back home.

Home. I stop and stare up at the trees. The old farmhouse I grew up in feels like a very distant memory, even though twenty-four hours ago I was in my bedroom there. I walk closer and run my hand along the rough bark. It has a gleam to it, like the trunks have been dusted with gold that's settled in their cracks and crevices.

Nowhere feels like home right now.

I won't be at home until Mom and Sam are with me.

I catch a glimpse of shimmering wings above me and look up. The elms' branches are long and wide, growing in and around the branches of the trees next to them, creating natural walkways and bridges. It's like going from the middle-class area of town to the ritzy section. The homes at ground level are nothing compared to the magnificent treehouses suspended in the maze of branches over my head. More wings flutter about in and above the leaves, and I keep my eyes peeled for Lulu's purple sparkle.

I'm so caught up in studying the treehouses that I almost walk into a row of flowering rose bushes surrounding a large, oblong rock. A strikingly gorgeous winged girl with long, platinum hair sits on top of the rock painting her fingernails. She moves the tiny brush over her nails and then holds her hand up in the light, admiring the color.

So even magical girls do stuff to make themselves prettier. How beautifully ordinary.

No *gawking*. I close my mouth and try not to be too obvious, but it's so hard to look away. She looks different from Lulu—more goddess than punk rocker.

"Why don't you take a picture? It'll last longer," she says. She couldn't sound more bored if she tried.

I cringe. "I'm sorry. I was noticing the roses, and then I saw you here." Though most of the roses on the bushes are spread open in blooms the size of my palm, those nearest to the girl are closed. I watch as she dips her nail brush into one of the closed roses and pulls it out. The bristles drip with fluid that matches the brilliant pink of the flower, and she patiently swipes it across her fingernail.

Oh. I guess it's not quite as ordinary as I'd thought.

"I'm Charlie," I tell her. My tone is bright, my smile brighter.

She plunges her tiny brush into the folded petals and slowly withdraws it again. "That's a boy's name," she says, her eyes on her fingers.

I hold my smile a moment longer. Is she really not going to introduce herself? Or smile? Or even look at me? Seriously?

The muscles in my cheeks twitch.

No. No, she is not.

She extends her fingers upward, lightly blowing on her nails, then finally glances at me out of the corner of her eye. "Do you need something?"

It's official. I hate her.

"No, I, uh, just wanted to introduce myself." Ugh. I sound so lame.

"Well, you did." She focuses on her nails again.

It's my turn to be annoyed. "Do you have a name?"

She fixes her lavender eyes on me. "I'm Clara, Empress of the Fairies."

I raise my eyebrows. Empress? Well, la-dee-dah. Am I supposed to curtsy?

"Well, Clara," I say, "it has certainly been a pleasure talking with you." I've perfected the ability of mixing sweetness with sarcasm, to the point that the other person has no idea if I'm being rude or not. It's an art, really.

Clara, of course, doesn't respond. She wiggles her fingers toward the closed blooms. The roses shake slightly, then open and stretch toward the sun. The nail brush disappears. She rises to her feet, smooths her bright pink dress, and shoots me one last disdainful look before straightening her wings and taking flight.

I watch her disappear above me. Unlike Lulu, there's no trail of sparkles following Clara, and I make a mental note to ask Seth why later as I continue through the trees.

Eventually, the houses become sparse, growing farther and farther apart until there's no sign of anyone but me out here. By the time I reach the edge of the giant elms, I'm out of breath and my legs are killing me. I stop there and lean against the nearest trunk, looking for gates.

The ground stretches into the distance in waves of knee-high, deep-green grass tipped in blue. Random spurts of jewel-toned flowers appear throughout, twinkling like stars on the ocean's surface.

It's breathtaking.

I hike through the grass and stop near the middle, turning in a circle. The map showed at least four gates out here, but I don't see a single one. Crap. I should've known I wouldn't be able to find them that easily.

I flop down right there next to a growth of wildflowers. The velvety flowers are scented with a mixture of vanilla, honey, and cinnamon—sweet enough that I'm seriously pondering their taste. A breeze ripples through the grass, and a faint tinkling noise floats in the air. I dip my head closer and realize the sound is coming from the field itself.

I stretch out on the ground, enveloped by the tall grass, and close my eyes while I listen. The wind continues to blow over me, creating a symphony of notes that crescendo and decrescendo as the breeze comes and goes.

The fields are literally alive with the sound of music.

Sam would ducking love this.

Something thumps in the distance, interrupting the serenade, and I open my eyes. What is that? Drums? I sit up, leaning on my hands, and stare across the field. The thumping sound grows louder, completely unaffected by the wind.

Whatever it is, it's coming closer.

I keep my eyes open and try to pinpoint the source of the noise. Soon, I spot the outline of a large bird in the sky above the trees. Each flap of its impressive wings results in a whooshing thud.

I remain still, mesmerized. As the bird draws nearer, I make out the head of a woman with dark, matted hair attached to the body of a hawk. Her gnarled red lips are twisted with rage, and her piercing black eyes are fixed on me with a menacing glare.

Oh, sheet.

My lungs fill with air and stop. I shove myself up from the ground, landing in a sprint toward the edge of the field. I throw one foot in front of the other and look back over my shoulder.

She's still there, growing closer and closer, flying right at me. Pain pierces my chest with each breath. The grass whips against my shins as I lift my legs higher and higher to get back toward the woods or the path or anywhere at all besides this ridiculous vacant field.

Seth told me to wait in my room for him or Alexander to come get me. I should've listened. What happens if this thing catches up to me? Nobody knows where I am.

I can't think about that now.

Run.

My legs are shaking so violently I hardly feel the ground beneath my feet. I make the mistake of looking back again, and her eyes lock with mine.

I think my heart may actually stop.

My toe rams against something, and I'm falling. My knees hit the ground, then my hands, and I'm facedown in the grass, trembling to the point that I can't make my body do what I want.

She's getting closer. Air whooshes against my skin each time her enormous wings flap up and down. The biting odor of mildew and decay encloses me, choking out the sugary scent of the field. I try not to inhale, but my lungs are burning. I breathe in and the foul air tastes bitter on my tongue. Every breath tastes stronger.

She's practically on top of me.

Move!

I press my hands to the ground and push myself upward as she swoops down with her long black talons extended. I roll out of the way, and an enraged screech sounds next to my head.

The world goes mute, silenced by the ringing in my ears. I'm up and running again, propelled through the air by sheer terror. I dart into the trees, zigzagging around the large, wide trunks of the elms.

Something digs beneath my arms and lifts me into the air. She's got me.

"No!" The ringing in my ears is replaced by my own screams. I twist my body and fling my legs back and forth, fighting to free myself.

"Stop it, you idiot, you're slowing me down!"

The voice beside my ear sounds strangely familiar. I freeze and turn my head enough to see Clara's flawlessly sculpted profile.

"Duck!" she says, zooming toward the largest of the willow trees.

I'll say. Duck this whole day.

Oh, she meant–

Long strands of purple blooms whip against my eyes and cheeks. Clara dives toward the middle and shoves me to the ground next to the trunk. "Stay down," she orders, crouching beside me and keeping her gaze upward.

I squeeze my eyes shut and hold my head between my knees, praying my red hair isn't visible through the tree.

I see Clara's hands on the ground, her fingers pressed against the dirt as though she might push off at any second. An angry shriek echoes through the air, and I shrink into myself.

Please go away.

I sit until my breathing is made of quiet, shaky breaths rather than scream-tinged gasps. Beside me, I hear Clara's breathing slow to a more manageable rate, too.

Please.

Clara's hands relax and she rocks back on her feet. The tightly corded muscles across my neck and shoulders unwind enough for me to lift my head. The thumping sound dies away, and then there's nothing.

What in the name of all that is good and sparkly was that thing?

Clara slowly rises. I follow her out from under the willow, and we stop to examine the sky.

All clear.

I shift my original opinion of the fairy from Horrid Witch to Heroic Savior. "Clara, I'm so–"

She cuts me off with a jerk of her head. "You have got to be the stupidest creature I've ever met. Summoning a harpy? Are you out of your mind?"

Nope. I was right the first time. Horrid Witch. "Huh?"

Clara places her hands on her hips. The willow trees around us make her eyes look even more lavender, and they flash when she speaks. "You Apprentices are all the same. You think this is one big game, that your powers are playthings," she fumes.

I step farther away from the trees onto the open space that runs between them. "I didn't summon anything!"

"Sure you didn't." Clara rolls her eyes. "Harpies were banished from Ellauria. How did it get in?" It's more accusation than question. Her tone makes it clear she doesn't believe me.

"It wasn't me! I can't even use powers. I'm a—" I inhale sharply, catching myself, "siren."

She blinks as though I've slapped her. The anger on Clara's face is momentarily replaced by surprise, but she recovers quickly by curling her upper lip. Her eyes travel up and down my body, sizing me up. "A siren? Really? You're not *that* pretty."

What a beach. I've been meangirled once or twice, but never by a charm-impaired fairy who just saved my life. I swallow all the things I want to say and level my gaze at her. "Thank you for saving me."

Clara's fingers glide over her skin, dusting her shoulders and arms and smoothing her hair. "If you'd been killed by a harpy so close to my territory, I never would've heard the end of it. Not to mention the mess she would've left in the Meadow of Music. Harpies are notoriously untidy eaters."

I bite my tongue and look at the clouds. Between the harpy and this fairy, my wonderstruck impression of Ellauria is fading fast. This place may be magical, but it's not without ugliness.

"You really didn't summon the harpy?" Clara asks, studying my face.

I level my gaze on her and enunciate my words as clearly as possible. "No. I didn't."

She releases a loud, annoyed breath. "I guess I need to let PC know about this. Who's your Aegis?"

PC has to know? Oh, God. Seth is going to kill me. "Seth Hewitt," I mumble, shaking my head. I shouldn't have left my room.

I bet he's looking for me right now. From the not staying in my room, to the trying to find a way to get into the Between, to the being chased by a scary ladybird—nothing about this story is going to go over well.

"Seth, eh?" She raises her perfectly shaped brow. "You must be one important siren."

I don't know what to say to that. Am I supposed to be an important siren? I try to maintain a blank expression while I comb through last night's conversation.

No. I'm sure he didn't say anything about being important. I'm supposed to blend in. Clara purses her lips, waiting for me to respond. Why hadn't I stayed in my room like Seth said? "I, uh—"

"Clara! Hey!" a male voice calls.

She lifts a few inches off the ground, looking over my shoulder, and smiles. Like, a real, actual, full-faced smile. "Keiran!"

I turn. There's a group of creatures passing through the trees, some winged, a few hoofed, and one who looks as human as I do. His eyes are on us, and he says something to the others as he changes direction and heads our way.

I could use this time to exit. Maybe she wouldn't notice if I slipped away. I glance around, not sure which direction to go in.

Clara lights up when the guy reaches us, floating around me to be closer to him. "Hi there," she coos, shattering my assumption that she's a hateful hater who hates everyone.

"Hey, you," he replies with a grin, then looks at me. "I don't think we've met. I'm Keiran."

He's taller than me, with broad shoulders and the kind of bronzed tan I'll never have. His eyes are the most unusual shade of gray, with a shadow of pale blue flames around his pupils.

The thing is, he's gorgeous. Ridiculously gorgeous. From his dimples to his flawless skin to the hint of muscle definition beneath his shirt, he's the kind of pretty that doesn't actually exist in real life. Airbrushed pretty.

"I'm..." I have a name. I can't think of it at this exact moment, but I'm certain I have one.

Keiran laughs. "No pressure. I'll just call you Freckles."

My hand immediately flies to my nose, the only place on my body with a scattering of freckles on it.

Clara rolls her eyes. "It's George, or something."

Her voice makes my teeth clench. I close my eyes and give myself a shake. "My name is Charlie Page. I got here yesterday."

"Nice to meet you, Charlie Page." Keiran's messy hair matches his outfit—carefully wrinkled khaki shorts and a red T-shirt that looks like he picked it up off the floor. There's a blue ribbon pinned in a loop to the front of his shirt. He grins, and a few strands of blond hair fall across his forehead.

Of course his teeth are perfect. Of course they are.

"She's a first-year," Clara says, like she's announcing my leprosy. She places a dainty hand on Keiran's shoulder. "We're about to head over to the library to let PC know there's a harpy in the area."

We are? I didn't realize I actually had to go with her. Fantastic. My first morning in Ellauria and I'm about to go in front of PC without Seth. He is going to kill me.

Keiran's brow lowers. "A harpy? Those were banished ages ago. How'd it get in?"

It's the same question Clara asked earlier, and without the sharp tone, I realize the significance of what he's saying. Seth had said Bigfoot couldn't return after she was banished. I'd assumed that this was basically a suggestion or a rule put in place, but now I'm guessing banishment is supposed to be much more permanent.

Is another spell slipping?

"Well, she says she didn't summon it, but you know how stupid first-years can be." Clara looks down her nose at me. "If I find out you're lying, PC will strip your powers for a month."

I huff and speak slowly so she can understand. "I didn't summon anything. I don't even know how."

"We'll see. Regardless, it flew off toward the mountains, so at least it was heading out of Ellauria. PC will need to alert the rest of the territories in the mystical realm." She flips her hair and runs her finger down Keiran's arm. "Want to come with us? You and I could go to the lake after."

"Sure." Keiran shrugs. "I'll walk with you."

Clara plants herself beside him, linking her arm through his. I take a spot on his other side, doing my best to ignore her and focus on how I'm going to explain any of this to Seth. I guess there's no choice other than to tell him I was trying to get back to the Between. Besides, maybe I can distract him by bringing up the banishment thing. Surely spell failure is more important than my aversion to rules that make no sense to me.

Then again, maybe not. Seth loves his rules, almost as much as he loves reminding me of them.

"So, a harpy," Keiran says to me. "Are you okay?"

"Yeah, I—"

"Oh, she's fine," Clara cuts me off. "I grabbed her, and we hid until it flew away. There's no telling what might have happened if I hadn't heard the harpy scream."

I grind my teeth and keep my eyes forward. I can't exactly argue with anything she said, but I'd still like to punch her in her perfect, tiny nose.

"Wow. That's intense. I've never seen a harpy up close," he replies.

We cut through the trees, walking around all the homes I'd passed earlier. More and more creatures are out and about now, some familiar, some not. Aside from a few nods, they pay little attention to us.

"So, Charlie Page," Keiran says. "It's barely eight o'clock, and you've already been to the Meadow, played with a harpy, and found a reason to visit PC. Do you always get up so early, or were you on a mission to get into trouble today?"

"What? Oh. No, but I wanted to..." I rack my brain for something besides the truth. "I was looking for someone. Something. I was looking for, um, donuts? I like donuts."

Do donuts exist in Ellauria? Lying is hard.

Keiran's eyes twinkle, which doesn't help my momentary lapse of intelligence. "It's okay. I did a lot of sneaking around when I first got here, too. The Fellowship keeps a pretty tight leash on first-years." He lowers his voice. "FYI, food is probably the worst excuse you could come up with. You'll find literally any food you want at Mesmer, the patio at the very top of Artedion."

Oh. Well, at least they have donuts. I'm going to have to work on my game if I'm going to pull off this whole "living a lie" thing. Which is hilarious, considering I've been living a lie for seventeen years. Maybe Seth can give me some tips.

Clara leans forward, shooting me a wrathful look. Her eyes are narrowed, her nostrils flared. I don't think she wants Keiran to pay any attention to me at all. I ignore her and smile at him.

We reach the edge of the trees and make our way onto the crowded path. I spot Artedion's canopy in the distance, but we turn left toward the library. I can't help but steal a glance at the sky now and then, and I notice Keiran doing the same.

"Do you think it'll come back?" I ask. Just the thought of it makes my knees quiver.

His eyes roam the sky. "I doubt it."

"I'm sure it won't," Clara declares. "There are too many Ellaurians around now. Harpies don't attack crowds."

Her voice is making it really hard to pretend she's not here.

I keep an eye out for Seth. Maybe he doesn't know I'm not in my room. I'm torn between wanting him here to help me face PC, and wanting him to stay ignorant to this whole ordeal. There's got to be a way out of this.

As though she's reading my mind, Clara asks, "Does Seth know where you are?" Her face is the picture of innocence, but her tone says she already knows the answer.

"Seth?" Keiran asks, looking from Clara to me.

I nod. "My Aegis, and no, Clara, I don't think he does." Now there's no way I'm getting out of this. She's obviously looking forward to watching me squirm.

A group of dark-skinned elves runs directly toward us, and the three of us split apart to allow them to pass through. Keiran watches me as I step aside and then back to him.

"*Seth* is your Aegis?" He raises his eyebrows. "What *are* you?"

Clara's words echo through my mind before I answer. *You're not that pretty.* I brush a few loose strands of hair from my face. Why do I have to be a creature mostly known for being drop-dead gorgeous? Something like a banshee would be so much easier to live up to.

"I'm a siren."

"Oooh," he says, nodding. "I don't think there's been a siren in the Fellowship for years. That must be why you got Seth."

Why are they making such a big deal about Seth being my Aegis? "What do you mean?"

"Seth's never had an Apprentice," Clara says, lifting up to look at me over Keiran's head while she speaks. "He's too busy being Alexander's right hand in the mortal realm."

"Oh," I say, "right." A smile tugs at my lips and I put my head down. She doesn't know he's been my Aegis for years. The fact that I know something Empress Evil doesn't makes me happy.

"Speaking of Alexander," Keiran mutters, tipping his head forward.

I look up and the founder is standing in the middle of the path, his yellow-green eyes locked on me.

Oh, sheet.

Keiran slides his hands into his pockets. My first instinct is to stop walking, followed quickly by a will to hide, both of which would be completely pointless.

"Alexander!" Clara calls. "I'm so glad you're here. I'm on my way to Central Hall right now to call a meeting."

Alexander's stare is heavy enough to bury me in the ground. He keeps his eyes on me a moment longer before acknowledging Clara. "Hello, Clara. What reason do you have to call a meeting?"

"There was a harpy in the meadow," Clara says.

Alexander folds his arms across his chest while she tells him the entire story, from hearing the harpy's scream to rescuing me from the field to hiding with me in the willow. I bite the inside of my lip, remembering the details as she speaks. I'm going to see the harpy's face every time I close my eyes, right after my personal replay of the Mothman attack.

Keiran shifts, moving behind me while Clara speaks.

The fairy's broad gestures and loud retelling of the attack attract the attention of other creatures on the path, and before long a circle of onlookers surrounds her. Seth is going to be really happy about how good I am at staying under the radar.

Alexander's fingers tighten around his bicep, and he shoots me a sideways look. The fury etched on his face is enough to make me wish muralets could control time. I'd take a do-over on this morning in a heartbeat.

Keiran nudges me. "Might've been better to have let the harpy have you this morning," he whispers, nodding slightly toward Alexander.

So I'm not imagining it. I'm in serious sheet here.

Alexander waits for Clara to finish before saying, "There's no need to go before Principal Command. I will handle this."

"But—" She rises off the ground, bringing herself eye-to-eye with him.

He cuts her off with a wave of his hand. "You've told me everything I need to know. I'll issue a warning about the harpy."

"What about her?" she asks, pointing a carefully manicured finger at me. "She never should've been out there, and how do we know she didn't—"

"I said," he says sharply, leveling his eyes on her, "I will handle it."

Clara clamps her mouth shut and slams her feet to the ground, glaring at him.

"Now, if everyone will excuse us," Alexander says, nodding to Clara, Keiran, and everyone else who stopped to listen, "I'd like a word alone with Charlotte."

Keiran straightens. "Yes, sir. Clara and I are going to go for a walk."

Ugh. Every part of me that didn't want to see Seth a few minutes ago is screaming for him now. The rest of the crowd slowly backs away, drifting off to wherever they were headed before Clara's dramatic tale drew them in, until there's no sign that anything newsworthy had happened at all.

Keiran pulls Clara's arm, and she shakes her head as she sulks off. Keiran winks at me and whispers, "Don't mention donuts." His dimples are in full effect now, and I literally have no words. He's like a work of fine art you can't stop studying, appreciating the sheer genius behind its creator.

And then they're gone, and I'm standing alone with Alexander the Intimidating. I wipe my hands down my sides and square my shoulders, giving my head a quick shake. I brace myself, waiting for him to say something. My stomach begins a complicated series of acrobatics.

"Did you believe it was wise to leave your room without telling anyone where you were going?" Alexander growls. "After you'd been specifically ordered by your Aegis to stay there?"

Ordered? It hadn't felt like an order from my Aegis, so much as a suggestion from the guy whose suggestions I've had the choice to ignore for years. I fight to keep from shrinking beneath his stare. "I couldn't sit there and wait. I had to—"

His nostrils flare. "Do you have any idea what could've happened if Clara hadn't been there to save you?"

I recall the harpy's black talons and razor-like teeth. The mere memory is enough to catapult my heart against the front of my chest. "I'd be dead."

"Undoubtedly," he states, his eyes hard. "What were you doing out there?"

I take a deep breath, reminding my heart that I am with Alexander and the harpy is long gone. I rack my brain for an answer he'll like but come up empty, so I give up and admit the truth. "I was looking for a gate. I wanted to go to the Between. I couldn't sit in my room and wait for someone to come tell me Mom and Sam are dead."

My voice cracks on the last few words. I can't believe I even said that out loud. They can't be dead. I rest my hands on the backs of my hips and look at the ground. They simply can't be.

"You really aren't grasping the situation," Alexander says quietly. "You cannot ignore direct orders."

I haven't even been here a full day and I'm already tired of this "orders" talk. As soon as I learn the world is three times larger than I ever knew, my personal existence becomes more and more confined. Three realms to explore, and I'm restricted to Seth's reach.

Alexander's shoulders heave, and he releases a frustrated sigh. He stares over my head for a moment before saying, "Follow me."

I spin around as he marches past me toward Artedion. "Where?"

"Where you wanted to go this morning." He doesn't stop to look back. "The Between."

SEVEN

We're leaving Ellauria?

I guess that whole, "only with an Aegis" rule is trumped if there's a founder around.

When we reach Artedion, he steps off the path and strides past the giant steps. I stumble along, desperate to keep up with Alexander, anxious for more answers. The ground slopes downward beyond the Clearing, and he guides me down the clover-covered terrain until it levels out again. I didn't study this part of the map at all. I hadn't paid any attention to what lay beyond the Clearing.

We're surrounded by a mess of thin, stark-white trees with copper-colored vines hanging from their sprawling branches. I pause once to look back at Artedion, but the crowded trees block my view. Completely disoriented, I scramble to catch up with Alexander.

When I reach him, he's standing between two trees, taller than the others, and I stop beside him. He reaches into his pocket and pulls out a small plastic device like the one Mom had used before the Mothman attacked.

"What are you doing?" I ask, watching his fingers move across it. It's definitely not a calculator.

"Letting Seth know you're with me," he replies, focusing on his fingers while he talks. "We didn't find any trace of Adele and Sam last night, so I sent him to the mortal realm before dawn to do a search of his own. He knows all of you better than anyone. I thought he might have more luck."

Alexander looks to me and drops the device back in his pocket. "I'm sure he'll be looking for you when he returns."

I can't decide if it's good or bad that they didn't find any trace of Mom and Sam. It could mean anything. They're alive and running. They're dead and—my stomach flips. They're not dead.

They're not.

Alexander nods toward the ground. "Watch your feet."

Huh? I look at the leaves scattered across the darkened grass. It's a flat space between the trees. Watch my feet for what?

He grabs hold of a branch over our heads and bends it toward us. The ground beside my feet shifts and collapses, transforming into a set of stairs leading downward.

I tilt forward, peering down into the shadowy passageway. He steps around me and descends the steps. I stare, open-mouthed. There is no way I am walking down a dark stairwell made out of dirt.

When his head is at ground level, Alexander looks up at me. "Come," he orders.

Nope. I shake my head and add Fear of Being Buried Alive to the list of things I'm absolutely sure of about myself.

"Charlotte, if you want your answers, you will come with me now," he says.

I fumble with the hem of my shirt, twisting it beneath my fingers. I *do* want answers. More than anything. Where are Mom and Sam? Who am I? Aside from being a muralet, where did I come from? If Mom isn't my mom, who is? Is the man I called Dad my actual dad?

Yes. I definitely want answers.

I lift one trembling foot and set it on the first step. It's surprisingly firm, and my knee nearly buckles beneath me.

OK. One step at a time.

I bring my other foot to the next step, and repeat, following Alexander into the cool darkness. The smell of earth surrounds me as we go down and down, darker and darker, until I'm relying on the sound of his muted steps to guide me. I grope for the wall and dirt crumbles beneath my fingers. I draw my arms in again and clasp my hands in front of my chest.

Completely blind, there's no choice but to keep moving forward.

Suddenly the world flips and gravity tugs at my back rather than my front. Rather than walking down, we're climbing up—the air warms, the passageway brightens, and we emerge into the sunlight.

The Between spreads before me, calm and welcoming, and the unease in my chest diminishes.

"Where are we going?" I ask. Like before, I can't focus on anything except how green the greens are and how the blues are so clear they glow. Everything is bigger, fuller, taller, cleaner. Everywhere I look, there's more of the same. The eternity of it is as overwhelming as its perfection.

"You'll see." He strides toward a clean, clipped path nearby.

The grass under my feet is so thick it doesn't seem real. "Is it far?"

Alexander doesn't turn around. "You'll see."

I give up trying to talk. I'm out of breath in no time, struggling to keep up as we march through the trees. Every leaf is as big as my hand, edged in olive green that gradually becomes yellow in the center. I want to pick one and take it back with me, press it into my sketchbook and draw pages and pages of them, but it feels wrong to take anything from the Between. It's soothing in its stability. I know what to expect here. I don't want anything to change.

Hills rise and fall under my feet, carpeted in green and dotted with daffodils of the brightest yellow. Seth can't get my sketchbooks soon enough.

The farther we walk, the louder the sound of rushing water becomes, and I spot an enormous waterfall in the distance. We turn on a new path and I lose sight of it, but the growing roar of the water tells me we must be getting closer.

I feel the cool spray of water moments before the roar becomes the only thing I hear, and I shield my eyes, searching for the top of the waterfall. I tip my head back, taking in the wall of water flowing from the soaring peak above. The water is the clearest shade of turquoise, almost impossibly blue. Its gleam is so bright I can't look directly at it, like rays of sunlight pouring from the very top of the sky. Alexander stops and stands with his hands behind his back, observing the water, so I do the same.

"As Seth told you," Alexander says, "Mother Nature is the reason magic exists. When she left the mortal realm, she created this place from nothing. The Between is the foundation of the mystical realm and everything in it. All magic starts here, and this," he nods toward the waterfall, "is its source."

The water flows down, cresting into clouds of white before leveling into the river below. My eyes travel from top to bottom, side to side, memorizing every detail. I want to come back with my sketchbook.

This is a painting. There's a soothing familiarity in the gurgling splashes of the water and the collections of leaves and pebbles alongside the embankment.

The Between itself is a work of art. Mother Nature took her time here. But this, the Source of magic, is an experience. I don't merely see it. I feel it—an immediate sense of welcoming, a homecoming with this place I've never seen before.

Alexander walks along its edge and I follow, farther and farther until the current calms and the roar fades. The river opens up into a wide pool of water. If the falls are sunlight, the pool is composed of stars glittering beneath its surface. The sounds of the waterfall are muted here, replaced by the hushed swish of air sending ripples in my reflection.

Alexander's face appears beside mine. "Do you feel it?"

I meet his eyes in the water. Does he know? Is it this way for everyone? Do we all feel this connection to magic?

"Clear your head." He clasps his hands in front of himself and lowers his gaze on me. "For a moment, forget Adele. Forget Sam. Forget everything that's happened and be here. Right here, right now."

Forget Mom and Sam.

Forget what's happened.

I look away from him and back to the water.

Be here.

I close my eyes and breathe in, filling my lungs completely before exhaling.

Calmness wraps around me, settling in my chest until I feel as still as the Between itself. When I open my eyes, the air is thick with light. It glows, in and around me, in the space above the water and between the trees.

What *is* this?

I blink, and the moment is gone. Everything is as it was.

I whip around to face Alexander. "You felt it?" he asks, and something ignites in his eyes. He squints at me, awaiting my answer.

What did I feel? What was that glow? I press my fingers to my eyelids and rub them before I look again. Nothing.

"I'm not sure. I mean, I felt like everything inside me stopped. My heart, my lungs, everything. And then I saw–" I shake my head. A trick of the light? Something about the blinding waterfall mixed with the pool's reflection?

"What was it?" Alexander steps closer. "What was it like?"

"Everything was," I glance over my shoulder, peering at my surroundings, "different. It glowed. Almost like everything was made up of a billion little points of light."

He raises his shoulders and releases them, like the tension that had held them in place has diminished. His chin falls to his chest, and he nods at the grass, obviously pleased. "Perfect."

"What's perfect?" I don't even know what just happened.

"As we told you, muralets descended from Mother Nature. Because of your blood connection to her, you have the unique ability to draw upon the magic in her designs." Alexander tilts his head and looks at me. There's something different in his stare. A new respect? Pride? "Do you recall how Seth said you are the personification of magic?"

I run my fingers over my braid, ignoring the flutter in my stomach when he mentions Seth's name. Oh, yes. I'm going to recall that for quite some time.

"The magic here is the same magic that flows through your veins. You are the same. Muralets have always been completely in tune with the Between. You felt that connection. The Between is an extension of you."

An extension of me. This magnificent place and I—we share a life source. It's as much a descendant of Mother Nature as I am. Without Her, neither of us would exist.

I study the Between, and it studies me back.

We are the same. No wonder it feels so alive to me.

"Al!" A booming voice calls out behind me, disturbing the silence. I spin around to look across the water but find no one.

"Joe." Alexander smiles in the direction of the voice. He beckons for me to follow and leads me around the water. I slow to a stop as we get closer to a line of trees on the other side.

They're the oddest-looking trees I've ever seen. Their bases are thick, and their rich brown trunks twist and turn at unnatural angles, like we've caught them in the middle of a dance. Several branches extend from the trunks, covered in broad leaves of many colors—not only greens and yellows, but various shades of purple, red, and orange as well. The surface of each trunk is covered in knots and grooves of varying depths, but the branches are perfectly smooth.

"Joe," Alexander says again when we reach the trees, "I'd like you to meet Charlotte."

"Charlie," I blurt out, and Alexander raises an eyebrow at me.

I glance around. Who's he talking to? I peer beyond the branches of the strange trees, searching for movement. Alexander nods toward the one in the middle, the largest.

The knots and grooves in the trunk begin to squirm and revolve. The branches on each side quiver. The tree writhes and bends, and then it stops as suddenly as it started. A face emerges with two large, empty eyes, a prominent nose, and a wide, expressive mouth.

"Hello, Charlie," the face speaks. "I'm Joe."

At some point, I need to accept that nothing here is what it seems, even the trees. A super-scholarly expression takes over my face, with bulging eyes and gaping mouth. I'm full of those lately. I almost remind myself not to act like a newbie until I remember Alexander knows all my secrets.

"You'll have to excuse her, Joe," Alexander says. "She's never been around treefolk."

"What a shame!" Joe says, and the tree's mouth spreads into a grin. If Santa Claus were a tree, this would be him. His leaves rustle as he spreads his branches wider. "Go ahead, then. Check me out."

Alexander steps aside, and I walk right up to the tree. My fingers drift across the bark and examine the length of the tree, as high as I can reach all the way down to its roots. I timidly touch my finger to Joe's nose. He scrunches up his wooden face, and we both laugh.

"The treefolk are one of the oldest magical races in existence," Alexander tells me, holding his hands behind his back. "Their centuries of experience observing people make them excellent judges of character. With only a look, Joe can tell more about you than people who have known you for years."

I look from Alexander to Joe. How much can he know about me, when so much of me is a secret and the rest is a lie?

"You need to know your story," Joe states.

"That depends on your version of my story," I mutter, and Joe releases a deep, rumbling laugh.

"Treefolk are natural historians," Alexander says, circling behind me, "and secret keepers. They existed long before the Fellowship, even before the mystical realm. Joe knows your story better than anyone."

I look to the ground, gathering my thoughts. "Alexander and Seth have told me *what* I am. I'm having trouble figuring out *who* I am. I need to know what's real. How much of me is *me* and how much of me is the Fellowship?"

I raise my eyes as I finish the last sentence. Alexander steps in line beside me, watching my interaction with Joe.

"Who you are is very much tied to the Fellowship itself. To understand that, you will need to know a bit about the Fellowship's history." Joe's eyes soften, and he lowers his branches to my knees. "Have a seat, loved one."

I slide onto his outstretched limbs and settle into him. He stares at me, through me, and it takes some getting used to. Alexander takes a seat directly across from me, his enormous body taking up most of Joe's branches.

"Years ago," Joe begins, "before the formation of the Fellowship, creatures were sighted all the time in the mortal realm. Fairies, mermaids, leprechauns—they were spotted so often that humans became obsessed with finding them. There are stories of fishermen capturing mermaids and ripping them to pieces, certain they were demons."

I recall what Seth had said yesterday about how legends are born from too many encounters between the mystical and the mortal.

Joe's branches move while he talks, and it reminds me of the way Mom can't tell a story without using her hands. "Four Ellaurians—Alexander, Marian, Max, and Whalen—realized mystical creatures would have more luck staying under the radar if they worked together under one system. That way they could communicate with each other and coordinate the best times to slip in and out of the mortal realm unnoticed."

I look at Alexander when Joe says his name, but his eyes stay down, focused on his lap. I know he's a founder, but until now I haven't considered the implications of his title, aside from the fact that it makes him Seth's boss. But this whole thing—the organization of the Fellowship, the weekly meetings Seth had mentioned, the different roles to be filled—he helped create that. I wonder about the other three founders, but Joe continues before I can ask.

"It took a while to bring the entire mystical realm together under the Fellowship. Some creatures refused to take part—they didn't want to be told when they could travel to the mortal realm and when they couldn't. Those creatures were eventually banished from the mystical realm."

"Banished?" I ask.

"They can't return," Alexander explains. "They're no longer welcome here."

Wow. They didn't want to go along with the Fellowship so they were kicked out of the realm completely? Away from their home? That seems a little harsh. "Where do they live, then?"

Alexander shifts on the branch, smoothing the front of his dark-green tunic. "It depends. The obvious creatures find remote areas of the mortal realm to reside, but some of the more human-looking ones live out in the open. We keep an eye on them for our own safety, but for the most part, they're on their own."

He must see the disapproval on my face, because he sits up straighter and quirks his eyebrows. "Not going along with the Fellowship puts the entire mystical population at risk. Everyone that lives in the mystical realm must agree to be part of the Fellowship."

Alexander may have a point, but all I hear is "Follow our rules, or we'll throw you out," and I can't decide how to feel about that. What if the banished creatures aren't able to stay in hiding on their own?

What if they have different ideas about their safety? Would it matter? It seems extreme to throw them out of their homes when they aren't really given a choice about how to live their own lives. I know how it feels to be thrown out of your world unexpectedly. Even if the mortal realm was never supposed to be the one I belonged to, it's the only home I've known.

I'd give almost anything to be sitting on the green wicker loveseat on my front porch, sketching the panoramic views of the neighbors' farms.

I never did finish that sunset.

I close my eyes as the deep ache returns to my chest. I want to go home, and I can't. I want to go back to everything I knew, before I realized I knew nothing.

"Where did I come from?" I ask, looking at Alexander. "Don't say from magic. Who are my parents?"

"You are the daughter of two of the founders—Marian, a muralet like you, and Max, a mureling," Joe replies.

The daughter of founders. I sit up a little straighter.

Alexander's expression turns wistful, and the longing in my chest is reflected on his face. What is he longing for?

Marian and Max. Max and Marian. My parents. The names seem too foreign to belong to the two people who created me. "What's a mureling?"

"All muralets are female," Alexander says, his voice quieter than usual. "Males born to the bloodline were called murelings. They were much less powerful, without the elemental control or blood characteristics of muralets. Murelings had the ability to converse with every creature in existence. No language was foreign to them—human, animal, or otherwise."

I catch the past tense. The murelings are gone too? "Were?"

"The murelings died out after the muralets," Joe explains. "Muralets are rare to begin with—only born once every few generations. As their numbers dwindled, the bloodline eventually came to an end."

I stare across the rippling water of the Source, its surface silver under the sun's light, and process his words. I feel empty. It's not grief, really. I never knew Max and Marian, but there's a sense of loss for the parents I will never have a chance to meet. I'll only know them through the memories of others. Just like the man I knew as my father.

"What about William?" I ask. The man Mom had always recalled so fondly. The one supposedly responsible for Sam's curls and my double-jointed thumbs. His picture sat framed on my bookshelf for as long as I can remember. The story of his death, in a three-car pileup in the middle of a highway only weeks after Sam and I were born, plays in my mind any time I see a car accident. "Who was he?"

Alexander shakes his head. "There was never a William. He was an invention of the Fellowship."

"But the pictures? The stories?"

"It was all part of the mission, Charlotte. There had to be a reason Adele was a single mother."

All part of the mission—of the elaborate backstory created by the Fellowship. It's like losing the father I never knew all over again, except this time the sadness is tinged with anger. I'd mourned a completely fabricated loss my entire life. Every Father's Day. Every anniversary of his so-called death. All for nothing. I grip Joe's branch as if it's the only thing grounding me. "So who's Sam's father?"

"Another jourling," Joe states. "Thomas. He died before Sam was born."

The ache in my chest becomes a churning in my stomach. When we were little, Sam had mentioned his want for a father more than once. He was constantly picking out Little League coaches or school teachers for Mom to date until we got old enough to realize

Mom wasn't interested in dating. I *wanted* a dad, but Sam needed one.

I fiddle with the red bracelet on my wrist.

"So there's you," I raise my eyes to Alexander, "Max, and Marian. Who was the last founder, again?"

"Whalen," he says. "A shapeshifter."

"And where is he?"

"Gone," Alexander declares firmly. I watch his eyes harden, but he doesn't say any more.

"Whalen was in love with Marian," Joe tells me, and the shape of his eyes becomes pointed with sadness. "It was useless, of course. She and Max were completely devoted to one another, but she was beautiful and charismatic, and Whalen believed she had feelings for him too."

Alexander's eyes follow a scattering of leaves blowing through the open space between the Source and the forest. "It became an obsession for him. He would look for hidden messages in her words and actions, anything to support his delusion that they would be together." A shadow passes over his features and he goes quiet, staring at nothing. The emptiness in my chest grows bigger.

Joe speaks up when it becomes clear Alexander can't continue. "She rejected him over and over, politely at first and then with more force. His obsession turned to hatred. He threatened to kill her, repeatedly, and told others about all the things he would be able to do after he drank her blood."

I chew on the inside of my lip. Hearing about what my mother went through makes it even more horrifying. It must have been terrible to be a muralet— to constantly look over your shoulder, wondering if you could trust the creatures you met.

"Shapeshifters don't have an active power—they can change their shape to mimic another creature, but Whalen wanted to become more threatening,"

Joe continues. "The first rule Principal Command put into place when the Fellowship was formed was that drinking muralet blood results in automatic banishment from the mystical realm. As soon as PC realized a founder was hunting one of the creatures he was sworn to protect, they took the extra step of ordering Whalen to be stripped of his powers. It's the only time in the Fellowship's history that a creature's powers have been forcefully removed."

My shoulders become too heavy to stay upright and I fold into myself, leaning against Joe. What would it be like to live in a world where everyone is a threat? Is that my world now? Marian's downfall was being born a muralet. Like me.

I clutch my stomach. "What's going to happen to me?" I whisper. The tears surprise me, crowding in my eyes, and I look down, letting them fall on my lap.

"This is why we've hidden you," Alexander says quietly. "When Marian found out she was pregnant, she and Max went into hiding. Until then, she had refused to give in to the fear of living as the last muralet. But they didn't want that life for you. If no one knew Marian had a child, no one would come looking for you."

I sniff, shaking my head. "What happened to them?"

I don't ask what I really want to know—why did my parents leave me?

"They fled Ellauria to areas of our worlds so remote we hardly remember they exist at all, but Whalen never stopped looking," Alexander says. He reaches into the pocket of his tunic and retrieves a folded cloth handkerchief. He presses it against my arm until I take it.

"They were constantly looking over their shoulders, waiting for the next attack," Alexander continues. "Your father died defending Marian from a couple of minotaurs. His sacrifice gave her time to get away, but she realized you would never be safe with her."

The tears fall more quickly now. I unfold the handkerchief and press it to my eyes. Max died to save Marian, to save me. It's a huge responsibility to know I'm alive because of someone else's sacrifice. He did what a father would do for his child and the woman he loved.

Again, all for me. They were in hiding because of me. She was attacked because of me. He had to protect her.

Because of me.

Alexander tilts his head. "I suspect Whalen is behind the Mothman's appearance on your lawn. He must have had tracers in place to detect muralet magic. When the binding spell slipped and exposed your powers, Whalen must have thought he'd finally found Marian."

I twist the handkerchief in my hands. "Tracers? You said he was stripped of his powers. How can he do anything?"

"Whalen joined forces with other banished creatures still in possession of their powers," he grumbles, "like the Mothman. They do his dirty work. When the prize is muralet blood, nearly any creature can be convinced to play the game."

Joe's branches curl around me, the leaves brushing against my arms and neck. Tiny twigs rub against my back. The gesture of kindness makes me more emotional, just like Mom's hugs always do.

"Where is Marian now?" I ask, my voice teetering between talking and crying.

Alexander leans forward. "After she gave birth to you, she brought you to me. No one has seen or heard from her since."

I finally raise my eyes from my lap to look at him. He's not saying she's dead. Is she still alive? Could she still be out there?

Alexander's gaze becomes alert and he straightens, looking past me. I turn to investigate.

Seth's walking toward us in a black T-shirt that looks completely out of place here. He waves when I look at him. My mind switches gears from my official family to my adopted one. I ease myself off Joe's branch and meet Seth just outside the tree's reach. Alexander stands, too.

"Did you find anything?" I ask. I bite my lip, searching his face for clues. Please say yes. Anything would be better than nothing at this point.

A crease forms between Seth's eyebrows, and he shakes his head. "No. But there are more of us out looking right now."

I look away, swallowing my anxiety. They're out there, somewhere. We have to find them.

"What have you two been doing?" Seth asks.

"Charlie wanted to know more about her family history," Alexander says.

Seth's eyes drop to the ground, and when he raises them to mine, he presses his lips together in an almost-smile that isn't happy at all. He exhales heavily, and I can tell he's glad he wasn't the one who had to tell me about my parents. I nod at him. I'm glad, too.

"You'll be interested to know what our young muralet did this morning," Alexander adds, stepping away from the tree.

Great. I slump back into Joe's shadow and sit down again, disappearing into his leaves, while Alexander recounts the morning's events for Seth. I watch Seth's face go from annoyed to concerned to downright angry.

"Really?" Seth asks me when Alexander's finished. "You couldn't just stay in your room like I asked? Your first morning in Ellauria and you had a run-in with a harpy *and* attracted Clara's attention?"

Seth's eyebrows pull together and his mouth sets in a straight line. The fact that he considers attracting Clara's attention to be on par with attracting a harpy is endlessly amusing to me. "Why does Clara matter?"

"Clara is a member of Principal Command," Alexander says. "We have no interest in any PC members taking notice of you. Speaking of which, I should head to Central Hall to manage any rumors Clara may have already started. The weekly status meeting starts soon. The two of you will be there, correct?"

Seth stares me down and replies, "Yes. We'll be there."

The founder nods and takes off walking in the direction from which we'd come. I watch him leave. Like last night, the world seems bigger the smaller he gets. "What is Alexander?"

"Alexander," Seth says, turning his head to watch Alexander disappear, "is a dragon."

I snort. Of course he's a dragon. Obviously.

Seth's expression doesn't lighten. He shifts his mouth to the side and watches me, waiting for me to get it.

No way. "Wait, you're serious? He's actually a dragon?"

He nods. "He's actually a dragon."

"Like, a fire-breathing animal. That kind of dragon?" I fold my arms across my chest and nod along with my words. I can certainly see the personality traits of a dragon. But the rest?

"Well, no. The fire-breathing thing is sort of an embellishment that humans came up with," he says, stepping into Joe's shade and finding his own branch to sit on. I watch the branches move as he sits down, shifting together and providing support wherever he needs it. "Dragons work with energy, not fire. Alexander, like most dragons living among other creatures, uses a glamour spell to mask his appearance. No matter how pleasant they are, dragons are pretty terrifying to look at in their true form."

"That's an impressive spell," I mutter, looking back to where I'd last seen Alexander. No wonder I can't quite get a handle on whether Alexander is more human than animal.

"Dragons are highly skilled in the use of magic. Every famous wizard in history has been a dragon," Joe says, speaking up for the first time since Seth arrived.

Seth smiles at the tree's friendly face. "Hey, Joe. Long time no see."

"Good to see you, Seth," the tree replies. "I hear you've been given the task of guarding Miss Charlotte."

"Charlie." Seth and I correct Joe at the same time, and then we smile at each other.

"Charlie," Joe repeats, and the corners of his mouth lift, too.

So today, I've been chased by a harpy, saved by a fairy, and brought to the source of magic by a dragon wizard where I met a talking tree. I close my eyes and press my fingers against them, rubbing.

"It's okay if you're overwhelmed," Seth says. "It's a lot to take in."

I want to roll my eyes and thank him for giving me permission to be freaked out. Instead, I open my eyes and study him. "You've always had a weird way of knowing what I'm feeling."

Seth hesitates, and Joe says, "Oh? She doesn't know?"

His eyes roam over the leaves above our heads while he talks. "Well, I told you I'm a jeravon, and I have healing abilities. In addition to that," his eyes flicker to mine for an instant, "I'm an empath. I sense emotions. So, for example, if you're angry, I know it."

Is that supposed to be impressive? I'm pretty good at telling when someone's angry, too.

"But not just anger," he adds quickly. "Any emotion. Like right now, you think I'm full of crap. Or sheet, as you say."

I smirk. "I always think you're full of sheet, Seth. It's my default opinion of you."

He shakes his head, and the slightest smile runs across his lips.

What would it be like to feel another person's emotions? Does he feel mine all the time? "How does it work? You just feel the emotions of everyone around you?"

"No." Seth scratches the back of his head. "I choose who I'm tuning in to. I have to be pretty close by. I can't just read what you're feeling from any part of the realm."

"So you can tune in and out of anyone you choose?"

Seth shrugs. "Pretty much, although the closer I am to a person emotionally—like you or Sam or Lulu—the more easily I can read that person."

"You two should get going," Joe interrupts, ruffling his leaves and bouncing us from his branches. "The meeting will have started by the time you make it back to Ellauria."

"Right," Seth says, raising his eyebrows and looking across the Source in the direction Alexander and I had come from. "Thanks, Joe."

I dust off my shorts and smile. I awkwardly pat one of Joe's branches. "It was nice to meet you."

Joe laughs. "I've known you for years, love. We've just been waiting for you to come home."

The treefolk around him rustle, and I step back as they twist and release a burst of laughter. Seth catches my eye and winks.

I look back as we make our way around the Source, but the treefolk have stopped their dance. Joe's face has receded, and while they don't look like normal trees, they don't look like talking trees, either.

Whatever a talking tree is supposed to look like.

I watch the Source's surface as we pass. I wonder what it feels like. What it tastes like. Is it like water?

"Listen," Seth interrupts my thoughts. "I meant what I said earlier. You can't go off on your own like you did this morning. I have to know where you are. We can keep you safe, but you have to let us. I have to be able to trust you to follow the Fellowship's rules."

The same rules that had kept me so well hidden from the Mothman. Right. I smile a tiny close-lipped smile that means nothing other than that I heard what he said. "Sure."

He stops walking and releases a huff of air. "I mean it, Charlie. I'm responsible for your safety. If you can't do as I ask, I won't hesitate to use extreme measures."

Oh, good grief. He'll have an ankle monitor on me by the end of the day.

Seth smirks.

"What?" I ask.

"Really?" Seth tilts his head. "I just told you I'm an empath. You think I don't know what you think of me?"

I smile, thinking of all the times he's annoyed me and been fully aware of it. And then I cringe.

What about all the times he hasn't annoyed me? Sure, they're few and far between, but all the times I've noticed his smile? Or the way he wears a T-shirt better than any guy I know? Every single time I've felt nervous around him or wondered what he thought of me?

Oh, my God. He could feel that? Can he feel my horror right this very second?

He clears his throat, unable to look at me. "Come on. The meeting's about to start."

Ugh. I'll take that as a yes.

EIGHT

Seth and I make our way back through the tall, white trees. My legs ache as we climb the steep hill to the field behind Artedion. I hear the crowd in the Clearing before I see it. The entire area is filled with creatures I know only from fairytales and movies—leprechauns, griffins, fairies, centaurs, and even a cyclops, plus several species I've never seen before.

No gawking. Eyes forward.

"This is the weekly meeting I told you about," Seth says, his words tickling my ear. He keeps a hand on my arm and leads me toward the front of the crowd. It's a mess of wings, hooves, long hair, and brightly colored creatures. Tall, thin, short, round, with two, four, or six legs—I do my best to keep my gaze steady and my mouth closed.

As we move toward the head of the Clearing, closest to the wooden platform where Alexander is talking, the crowd takes on a different shape. The closer we get to the front, the more they look like me.

Yesterday I would've called them human; today I know better.

I mention this to Seth, and he nods. "Right. There's a reason for that, actually. The creatures who actively work for the Fellowship are the intelligent ones—critical thinkers, complex languages, et cetera."

Seth tips his head toward a line of creatures crouching on the ground to my left. They look part-human, part-monkey, each with a five-fingered hand at the end of their tails. "The ahuizotls there, they're nice and they mean well, but they're never going to be able to run missions. They're pretty erratic, and we can't trust them not to try to eat a mortal if the opportunity arises."

I instinctively take a step to the right, stepping on Seth's foot in the process. He stumbles a bit and snorts. "They're nothing to be afraid of. They just enjoy the taste. Besides," he ducks his head closer to my face to give me a pointed look, "you're not a mortal."

Right. Still getting used to that.

I keep an eye on the ahuizotls as we move forward. Seth places his hand on a gargoyle's shoulder; the creature smiles, revealing a mouth full of pointed teeth, and steps aside to let us pass.

"Anyway," he continues, "all kinds of creatures work for the Fellowship, but to be an Aegis, you have to be able to pass as a human. The ones near the front are Aegises. We stay up front in case we get called up to report on our missions."

I spot Lulu standing right next to the stage. There's no way she can pass as a human with those wings. "What about Lulu?" I ask.

"She's the pixie delegate on Principal Command. She stands wherever she wants," Seth says and changes direction slightly to head toward her. Good. I could use a little Lulu time.

I try to listen to Alexander, but a group of younger creatures catches my attention. They're all different species and all wearing royal blue ribbons, like the one pinned to Keiran's shirt this morning.

"What's with the ribbons?" I whisper, nodding at them.

Seth follows my eyes. "Those are Apprentices. That's not a ribbon, it's an aernovus. It signifies to everyone that the creature wearing it is an Apprentice."

So Keiran's an Apprentice. Good to know. I swish my mouth from side to side and look pointedly at the obviously blank spot on my own shirt. "Where's my aernovus?"

"I'd planned to give it to you in your room this morning." He emphasizes *planned* enough to remind me that I hadn't followed orders. I look sideways, pretending not to notice. "We'll find time later today," he adds.

"Should I stand with them?"

"No." His answer is so quick it almost makes me laugh. Of course he wants me right under his thumb.

"Hey, guys!" Lulu scream-whispers and flashes a gleeful smile when we reach her. "You missed it. Alexander told off one of the fairies because she forgot to close a fairy ring yesterday. I thought she was gonna cry!"

Seth stands beside her, and I place myself slightly behind him so I can look around without Alexander realizing he doesn't have my undivided attention. It's not that I don't want to know all the updates, but it's hard to ignore this many creatures all in one place.

I glance back at the Apprentices, performing a quick headcount. Thirty, maybe? Several of them look mostly human, but there are other populations represented as well. Pixies, fauns, gorgons, and a couple very short, ugly creatures covered in green hair. Trolls? Ogres? They definitely belong to the family of Shrek.

I spot a tall blond head of perfectly mussed hair in the middle of the Apprentices. Keiran turns just as I realize it's him. He lifts his chin in a quick nod of recognition, and my cheeks burn on instinct.

"He's cute," Lulu comments. I immediately snap my attention frontward. Seth turns to see who she's talking about, and now I'm sure my face is a shade or two brighter than my hair.

"Don't stare!" I put my hand over the side of my face, hoping Keiran isn't watching this all unfold. Seth studies me for a moment, his expression unreadable, before turning back to Alexander.

Oh, crap. What did he just get from me?

OK. Emotion check. I lower my chin to my chest, staring downward like I can see the emotions radiating from me. Embarrassment. A little nervousness. Thinking someone's cute isn't an emotion, right?

I've never been the kind of girl who broadcasts her feelings. The idea that Seth sees right through all of my fronts is terrifying. This is completely unfair.

Seth glances over his shoulder again, and I tilt my head upward, staring straight into his eyes.

Feel that, Seth? Annoyance mixed with irritation and a dash of I-hate-this.

"Why can't I stare at him?" Lulu whispers. "You think he doesn't know he's hot? Here's what I've learned about boys, Charlie—the good-looking ones expect us to stare at them. They'd be all freaked out if we didn't."

I widen my eyes at her, giving her the universal shut up face. I don't want to talk about Keiran. I especially don't want to talk about Keiran with Seth standing right in front of me.

"What?" she asks. "You don't think he's cute?"

I shake my head, shrug my shoulders, and do a million other little gestures to demonstrate how much

I couldn't possibly have any idea what she's talking about.

"You okay?" Her green eyes dance. "Having some kind of seizure?"

A couple Aegises give us disapproving looks for talking. I clamp my lips together to keep from laughing, and she winks at me. Seth nudges me and tips his head toward the stage.

"Next up," Alexander's voice booms. "We were able to take care of the fairy sightings in Wales last week. We all need to be particularly vigilant in Europe. The number of sightings there has increased nearly twenty-five percent since this time last year. At this point, we're not sure if it's negligence on our part or a sign of heightened awareness in the mortal realm—but we're keeping an eye on the situation. If this continues, we may have to declare all of Europe off-limits from nonessential creatures for a few years."

A murmur of objection rises from the crowd. "Who decides who's nonessential?" an Irish brogue sounds from the back.

Lulu lifts into the air and looks back at a group of squat, green-clad men with fiery orange hair. "Those leprechauns are so ridiculous," she mutters. "They know they're a big part of our sighting issues over there."

Alexander raises his hands to quiet everyone. "Moving along, I'm sure many of you have heard about the Mothman incident yesterday afternoon."

The mention of the Mothman sends my heart into overdrive, and Seth moves backward to stand beside me. He crosses his arms over his chest and brushes my arm with his fingers. It's a small gesture, but it's nice.

"One of our Aegises was attacked," Alexander announces, "and at this point, she has not returned to the mystical realm. There are no further updates on her location at this time. All of our Aegises in the mortal realm are on alert, and more have been dispatched to join the search."

Alexander recounts the attack, careful to leave me out of it. He doesn't mention Sam's name at all. I nudge Seth and stretch up on my toes to whisper, "What about Sam? He's making it sound like they're only looking for one person."

"Of course they're looking for Sam, too," Seth murmurs, lowering his head a bit. "But you have to understand Adele is the priority for the Fellowship."

The hair on the back of my neck bristles. Priority? No one ever mentioned anything about priority playing a role in finding them. Mom and Sam went missing together. Why would they be treated as two separate cases? I concentrate on keeping my voice low. "And you have to understand I couldn't care less about the Fellowship's priorities. Mom and Sam are equally important to me."

"Finding Adele means finding Sam, Charlie," Seth replies.

I let my emotions speak for me while I stare at the stage, keeping my focus on Alexander. Seth watches my face a moment longer before looking to the stage as well. "We have reason to believe Whalen may be involved," the founder says.

Whalen's name rumbles through the crowd. Eyes widen and lips curl. Every single face reacts to it. At least we're all on the same page about that one. If Whalen is behind this, I want the entire Fellowship to bring him down. I steal a peek at Keiran, but his eyes are on the ground.

By the time the meeting ends, I've heard details of a captured changeling in Canada, three troll sightings in South America, and a missing sandman in Africa. Various Aegises come forward to update the Fellowship on less dramatic operations, like monitoring the migration of the merfolk.

When it's over, Aegises pair up with Apprentices and everyone heads in different directions. Lulu flutters beside Seth and asks, "What are you guys doing now?"

"Gotta get Charlie started on some Apprentice training," he says. "I'm going to show her around Central Hall, maybe do a little mirror work."

She places her hands on her hips. "Groovy. You two want to meet up for lunch later?"

Yes, please. I rock up on my toes, nearly jumping at the suggestion, and nab a chuckle from Seth. Lulu waits for his nod before kissing both of our cheeks and flying off. I watch her sparkling purple trail drift into the grass and disappear behind her.

Seth and I leave the Clearing and walk around the front of Artedion. I watch more Aegises, unattached to Apprentices, split into groups and head off to take care of whatever missions they're involved in at the moment. The Fellowship is so much bigger than I realized last night. "How many missions is the Fellowship operating right now?"

"Hard to say." Seth looks toward the sky. "We have several ongoing situations that are constantly being monitored, like yours. Aside from those, we have things that pop up and need to be dealt with, like sightings and rescues and all the things you heard Alexander talk about back there."

I focus on my footsteps, remembering the leprechaun's question earlier. "Who decides what's most important?"

"What do you mean?"

"I mean, you already pointed out that Mom is higher priority than Sam. What's higher priority than Mom? The missing sandman? The changeling?"

"Shh," Seth mouths, reminding me that I can't talk openly about this, and I huff.

A large horse-like creature crosses the path in front of us, bringing foot traffic to a stop as it lumbers across. It has one large horn protruding from its forehead, and another lying across its back. I look everywhere but at the creature, trying to play it cool.

Seth bends his head close to mine. "Alexander isn't going to let Adele and Sam fall through the cracks."

The creature steps off the path on the other side, and we're moving toward the library again.

I'm sure Alexander will do what he can for Mom and Sam, but in the meantime, I'm waiting. Useless. Hoping that, out of however many missions the Fellowship is running at this very moment, everyone's going to somehow come together to find my family. I pull on the ends of my braid, absentmindedly separating it between my fingers. "How do I know? How do you know they're doing everything they absolutely can?"

Seth's pace slows as he studies my face. "Where's all this doubt coming from?"

I shrug. I saw the Mothman. I saw how quickly he moved. Even if the Fellowship is doing everything it can, who says it'll be enough? How do I know it isn't too late already?

"Charlie." Seth stops in the middle of the path. "Trust me. I told you I would bring them back, and I will."

I want to believe him. I know he loves them like I do. How do I trust anything anyone tells me anymore? The last two days have been one big blow after another, and I'm still not convinced I know the entire truth about the Fellowship or even myself. Everyone I meet—Alexander, Seth, Joe, and who knows how many others—seems to hold a new piece of the puzzle.

Everything is so much bigger than I am. I bite the inside of my lip. "There's a lot happening at once. The mortal realm is huge. I get the impression the mystical realm might be even bigger. How are they going to find Mom and Sam in the middle of everything else that's going on across the two realms and the Between?"

He puts his hands on my shoulders and lowers his head until our foreheads nearly touch. "You need to meet PRU."

Great. Another person who knows more about me than I do? "Who's Prue?"

Seth gives my upper back one swift pat and nods toward the library. "You'll see."

We stop outside the doors of the tiny little building that supposedly houses a library, as well as the entire operation in charge of finding Mom and Sam. Two fairies sit on a stone bench outside the doors, heads bowed together over a book.

"It looks like such a dump," I say, studying the tiny cracks in the white stone walls. You'd think a magical organization like the Fellowship would do a little more upkeep on one of its most important buildings. Surely someone could snap her fingers and turn this into a more respectable library.

"Just wait," Seth says, stepping up to the double doors. He glances back at me before pushing one of them open, then steps aside and guides me ahead of him.

The ceiling soars over my head, so high I can hardly make out the faded mural painted on it. I barely see the shapes at all, just splashes of muted colors—pale red, buttery yellow, and a strip of periwinkle. Rows of books are arranged on shelves five times taller than I am. I watch pixies fly to the topmost shelves and arrange the books there.

A winding staircase tucked in the corner leads to a few closed doors on the second floor before the landing opens up to more bookshelves. The shelves are topped with arched windows that stream sunlight throughout the building and cast spotlights on the library's most striking feature—the broad tree growing in the middle. Its branches extend up and out from every side, perfectly symmetrical. It's wide but short, tucked beneath the second floor's balcony. A couple of gargoyles pass beneath it to the far side of the room.

I turn, open-mouthed, and look at the door. Seth chuckles as I exit the library and re-enter.

It's like walking into Mary Poppins's bag.

I make my way farther inside and Seth walks with me, pausing beneath the tree. The leaves are sprinkled with flecks of gold that shimmer through the branches in waves of light. It continuously sparkles, though there doesn't seem to be any pattern to it. A leaf right next to my head shines briefly, then goes dark. Through the mass of green, I see several other leaves doing the same.

It's incredible.

I step closer, brushing my hand across a dark leaf. It's hard, almost plastic-like. Seth pulls something thin and green, about as wide as a deck of cards, from his back pocket, just like the ones I'd seen Mom and Alexander use. He holds it up by the leaf. They match.

"This is PRU," he says, gesturing to the tree. Light from the leaves bounces off his dark eyes. "The Principal Recording Unit. It's how we keep track of every single operation the Fellowship is involved in. Any sightings, any issues, they're all logged here. Everything I do for the Fellowship is recorded. I enter it here in my leafkey," he swipes his finger across the leaf-shaped device in his hand, "and it's directed to PRU. That's all the light you're seeing—each time a leaf lights up, someone's entering information into the system."

I tilt my head back and peer straight up through the leaves, watching them glow. It is without a doubt the coolest thing I have ever seen.

And that's saying something, considering everything I've witnessed in the last twenty-four hours.

Seth slides his leafkey back into his pocket and steps closer. "Events that seem random take on a completely different shape once they're logged into the system. This is how we're going to find Adele and Sam in the middle of everything else the Fellowship is doing. Trust me. We *will* find them."

Each little light is a glimmer of hope that Mom and Sam are that much closer to being found. I look at Seth. There's not a shred of uncertainty on his face. "Okay," I tell him. "I believe you."

He smiles, and with a quick nod of his head he pulls me away from the tree. We follow another Aegis-Apprentice pair up the winding staircase, and I run my hand along the iron railing, peering down at the shelves of books below. We stop outside a closed door with a frosted glass window. It reminds me of the principal's office back home.

"Over there." Seth points to a door on the far side of the second floor. "That's where Principal Command meets. And this," he opens the door with the frosted window, "is Central Hall, where the real work happens."

As the door swings open, two hooved women dart past us, staring at their leafkeys as they trot down the stairs. Seth places his arm around me to keep them from knocking me down.

The room is the very definition of clutter. Scattered rows of wooden chairs line one side, and an assortment of tables take up the other. Mostly, the room is filled with Aegises. Male and female, Seth's age and older, some more human than others, I think. Talking to each other, drawing pictures on white boards, passing out papers. I get the feeling no one stands still long enough to straighten up this place.

A muscular guy with blond hair and pointed ears looks up when we enter. "Hey, Seth. Didn't expect to see you around here today."

"Hi, Justin," Seth says. "This is Charlie, my Apprentice. I'm just showing her around Central Hall. Charlie, this is Justin. He keeps everything in order around here."

I take in the hardly organized chaos and wonder about his idea of order.

Justin sizes me up. "Right, right. I heard about you. Charlie with the harpy."

Thanks, Justin. I was really hoping someone would bring that up. I don't have to be an empath to interpret the sideways glance Seth lays on me.

"Anything interesting going on today?" Seth asks. A tall gorgon passes behind us, pushing me and Seth into Justin.

Justin steps backward and fans a stack of papers in his hand. He spreads them out for us to see, but they're completely blank. I blink, and then a bulleted list in scripted type crawls across the page.

"PRU generates that info," Seth tells me. "It's constantly updating."

Justin scans the list. "Let's see. Two more units were added to the search for Adele. We've had a chupacabra sighting, a couple of leprechaun issues, somebody found a unicorn fossil—oh, and a couple fairy rings malfunctioned this morning. It was brief, but Clara wants to set up an inquiry."

Well, look at that. The mention of Clara's name is already producing a reflexive snarl on my face.

Seth rolls his eyes. "Of course she does. The fairies need to be more responsible with their rings."

Justin laughs a good, hearty laugh. I decide I like him. I love genuine laughs. "You know Clara. Nothing's ever the fairies' fault. We should give Alexander a heads-up before she launches into one of her tirades."

"I'll mention it to him," Seth says. "Charlie and I are going to do a little mirror work, but I'll see him this afternoon."

"Perfect. One less thing on my list." Justin slides the pages back into one stack and tosses it on the desk behind him. "You need anything?"

"Not at the moment," Seth replies.

Justin nods to us and directs his attention to an Aegis who entered the room behind us. I follow Seth to the far side of the room. I remember what Lulu said about a fairy forgetting to close a fairy ring earlier. "What's a fairy ring?"

"Circles of flowers or mushrooms in the mortal realm. Fairies use them instead of gates to travel from the mortal realm to the Between. If they leave them open, it causes big problems."

He leads me to a wall covered in mirrors in various shapes and sizes—ovals, rectangles, hand mirrors—all outlined in metallic frames. A couple Apprentices are standing with their Aegises there, too. One Aegis is standing with her nose so close to the mirror it almost touches, and her Apprentice watches over her shoulder. He nods at me, and I smile.

Seth points to the wall. "These mirrors serve as windows throughout the realms. When there is a problem to be addressed, it's revealed in the reflection. So," he says, stepping up to a long, skinny mirror trimmed in bronze, "I pick any mirror I want and wait."

"It doesn't matter which mirror?" I ask.

"No. The mission is specific to the viewer. The mirror makes no difference. You get the mission you're supposed to get."

I stand to the side, watching.

Seth's rugged features appear in the glass, his mouth closed, his eyes alert. For a few seconds, nothing happens. Then the edges of the mirror begin to quiver, and ripples dance across his reflection. The collar of his black shirt swells upward. His brown hair melts into his skin; dark eyes morph and blend together. The entire image swirls until a new one appears—the enormous head of a black-haired beast crowned with horns. Black curls of smoke drift from its nose, and I barely make out the tips of fangs slipping over its bottom lip.

I shudder. I've never seen anything like it.

I look from Seth to the reflection and back. "Is that you?"

Seth snorts. "Of course. Doesn't it look like me?"

I have no idea if he's joking. At this point, if he told me he was the Tooth Fairy, I'd believe it.

"No, Charlie," he keeps his eyes on the mirror, "it's not me. That's a hodag, one of our more problematic creatures. They're pretty large and not all that intelligent, so it's hard to get them to stay on the down-low."

I gaze at the hodag's hideous face. "I've never heard of them."

"They live in the mortal realm, but there are so few of them they're not spotted very often," he says. "We did a pretty good job of discrediting the only photograph that's ever been taken of one. Made it look like the guy had constructed the thing himself out of cow and ox parts and some wire. No one believed it after that."

I hold up my hand, palm facing him. "High five! Way to go, Fellowship!"

He chuckles and half-heartedly slaps my hand. "Anyway, looks like somebody spotted a hodag last night."

Seth runs his forefinger across the surface of the glass and the image distorts, pulling toward the edges of the mirror and splashing back again. A young girl, six or seven years old, tiptoes across the top of a log, her arms straight out from her sides for balance. The hodag appears at the edge of the frame, moving slowly across the grass. As soon as it appears, I press my hand to the base of my neck. My eyes dart from the hodag to the girl and I hold my breath, waiting for her to see it.

Seth groans and mutters, "Right in front of her."

She freezes and draws her arms inward, keeping her wide eyes on the monstrous creature. The hodag seems completely oblivious and lumbers on, disappearing beneath a growth of bushes on the other side. The girl quietly slides to the ground, putting the log between herself and the hodag. Even though I know it's coming, I still jump when she screams. The glass heaves, and Seth's chocolate eyes peer out from the mirror once more.

It's only then that I realize how close I am to the mirror now. I bob backward and blink. "That's it?" I ask. "But what happened? Is she okay?"

He steps away from the mirror. "If there were any more to it, we'd see it. So no one else saw the hodag, and the girl must be fine."

A couple Aegises pass behind us toward another mirror, and I move out of their way. "As long as by 'fine,' you mean 'terrified and scarred for life,'" I say, and Seth smirks. "We're not going to go talk to her?"

"No. We stay out of it as much as possible. Sightings by children are the easiest to deal with. Her story will be dismissed as just that—a story made up by a scared kid. But we'll keep an eye on it." Seth walks to a small table in the corner scattered with cloth-covered books, spiral-bound notebooks, and an assortment of pencils. He pulls his leafkey from his pocket and taps it with his forefinger, logging the info into PRU. I imagine the tree lighting up with each keystroke, twinkling with information. He slips it back into his pocket and looks at me.

I lean against the table's edge. "Shouldn't we make sure she's okay? Let her know there's nothing to be afraid of?"

Even as I say them, I question the words. There's plenty to be afraid of. I'm learning that more and more by the minute. Chances are, this girl isn't the target of a homicidal shapeshifter with an inferiority complex, though, so she might actually have a better shot at the whole "Happily Ever After" thing.

He turns and leans against the table, too, his shoulder touching mine. He crosses his arms and addresses the wooden floor when he speaks. "I know it's hard for you to see it this way, but what happens to her only concerns us in regard to how it affects the safety of the mystical realm."

I let that simmer for a moment. It's probably the coldest sentence I've ever heard him say. She's not mystical, so she's not worth the Fellowship's time? "So humans don't matter at all?"

"Our job is to protect the mystical realm. The more involvement we have with humans, the riskier it is for us. Validating what she saw might make her feel better, but it would also put our world in danger." He pulls a worn pencil from beneath a stack of papers and writes something in one of his notebooks.

I think of all the stories I used to trade on the playground about monsters under beds and boogeymen in closets.

I wonder how many were real.

When we were little, Sam and I caught the very end of a werewolf movie on TV. For weeks afterward, Mom had to perform monster hunts in our rooms every night—inspecting our closets, peering under our beds, whatever it took to get us to go to sleep.

Looking back, Sam and I would've felt a lot better if we'd known Mom was basically the monster hunter to rule all monster hunters. I see her facing down the Mothman and my chest swells with pride before longing deflates it. She's a great mom, whether she's really mine or not.

I hope that little girl's parents humor her, and then I hope she forgets. I hope she lets it go. I hate to think of the hodag's face finding a permanent spot in her consciousness. There's a certain kind of peace in ignorance—I miss it more and more.

Maybe it's easier for Seth since this is what he's always been. Everything the Fellowship does is as natural to him as it is unnatural to me. I don't know why one realm has to be more important than another. The mortal realm is still home to me. So far, the mystical realm hasn't provided the kind of comfort I used to feel there. Without Mom and Sam, I'm not sure it ever will.

I gaze at the blank reflections covering the wall. "What about Mom and Sam? Wouldn't they show up in the mirrors?"

Seth nods. "I hope so. There's no way to know. The mirror shows you whatever mission you're supposed to get—we can't ask for certain ones, and we can't turn away from anything that's shown to us."

A few Apprentices wander in, and Seth stuffs a couple notebooks into the drawer of the table before pressing me toward the door.

"PRU can put pieces of several missions together and a bigger picture emerges. So whether they show up in a mirror or not, any little clue we find here will be accounted for in our search," Seth says.

PRU will do its job. I twist my fingers under the hem of my shirt. I have to trust that as much as Seth does.

Central Hall's frosted door closes behind us with a heavy *click*, and we head down the curved staircase. When we reach the bottom, he turns a corner and we're surrounded by shelves. I pinch the back of his shirt, its softness sliding between my thumb and forefinger, and tug on it to make him slow down. He reaches back for my hand and pulls me deeper and deeper through the books, turning in one direction, then the other, until we reach the end of the passage.

Seth sinks to the floor, resting his back against the gray wall, and I join him there. Shelves filled with books rise on either side of us, and I can't see the rest of the library from here. It's completely private. "This is my favorite place in Ellauria," he says. "I come here sometimes to sit and be around the books. My mom was a librarian. I feel close to her here."

I lay my head back. I don't know why I'm surprised by the realization that Seth's history was made-up too. His parents didn't die when he was young. They were mystical creatures. I chuckle and sigh at the same time. I need to forget everything I thought I knew. "Your mom worked here?"

"No." He pulls his knees to his chest and rests his folded arms on top of them. "My parents never came to Ellauria. They weren't really into the whole magic thing."

I bend my knees and rest my arms across them too, pressing my elbow against his. "What do you mean? How could they not be into it? Were they banished?"

"No, they just had no interest in the mystical realm. My parents lived as mortals and did everything they could to shield me from this place. When Alexander approached me about the Fellowship, they didn't want any part of it. They thought it was too dangerous." His

Adam's apple bobs up and down, and he studies his fingers. "When I decided to join, my father never got over it. They chose the mortal realm over me, and I turned my back on them."

I don't know what to say to that. All I want is my family, and Seth willingly left his. But I get a sense that he feels betrayed by them, too. It must've been hard to be forced to choose between his family and his birthright. No one should ever have to pretend to be something they're not. "How long have you been here?"

Seth takes a deep breath and blows it out, counting. "I've been in the Fellowship for about fifty years."

I remember what he'd said before about how jeravons age. I try to do the math in my head and give up. "So that makes you, like, a hundred?"

He smiles. "I've been alive for over two hundred years."

"Two hundred years?" I push off the wall and shoot forward, staring at him. That means he was alive for a good portion of the things I learned in US History class. My mouth hangs open for a second before I clamp it shut and lean back. "You are the seniorest of citizens."

Everything on Seth's face lifts—his eyebrows, his cheeks, the corners of his mouth—and he releases a loud laugh, the wholehearted kind I love. "I guess so."

I giggle, and then it hits me. "You knew Marian and Max."

His smile dims. "Yes. They founded the Fellowship about ten years before I came here."

I sit up straighter. "What were they like?"

He lifts his head and scans the books lining the shelves around us, looking at them without really looking at them. "They were you, split in two. Marian was brave and extremely intelligent, and as stubborn as anyone I've known, aside from you." He closes his eyes for a moment before continuing. "Max was quiet and creative—constantly coming up with ideas for the Fellowship to run more smoothly. His whole life was devoted to your mother and the Fellowship."

I close my eyes while he talks, caught up in a weird mix of sadness and self-pity. My parents are strangers, but when he describes them, I see myself in his memories. The creativity, the strong will—Max and Marian are a part of me.

"They were good," he says. "They were the best kind of creatures."

"I wish I could've known them," I reply.

"I wish you could have, too."

I study his face, mentally tracing the lines of his nose, his lips, his chin.

Seth doesn't look the way I'd expect a two-hundred-year-old to look. I would've thought he'd be more skeletal, with stringy hair, drooping eyes, and a creaking, withered voice.

He's just Seth. The guy I've known for years. The pseudo-member of my family. My shield.

He lifts a finger on the hand closest to me and rests it on my elbow. It sits there, like he simply needed to touch me. A chill travels all the way up my arm to the back of my neck.

I freeze, hoping he won't move away. What does he feel from me right now?

Don't shiver. Do not shiver.

Seth sighs heavily. "I just want you to know I have some idea of what it's like to move forward without a family."

I breathe again, letting my shoulders fall. I can't imagine willingly walking away from my family. Not for anything. "You must really believe in what you're doing, to choose the Fellowship over them."

I'm rewarded with his half-smile as he turns to look at me. "I questioned my decision for years until the day Alexander entrusted me with your secret and made me your Aegis. When I first laid eyes on you five years ago, I knew I was in the right place."

And there's the shiver. He looks at my arm and rubs his hand across the goosebumps covering it.

"I didn't mean to embarrass you. It's just—" His hand stops moving and his gaze lands on the floor again, like he can't decide what to say. Finally, he squeezes me and says, "I hope someday I make you feel like you're in the right place, too."

I stretch out my fingers until they brush against the thin material of the sleeve around his arm, trailing down until they overlap Seth's hand. He lifts his hand and our fingers tangle together for the slightest moment before he shifts away from me. He scoots away until no part of his body touches mine. "We should probably grab some lunch."

I nod. What just happened? We were talking, and all of a sudden he's touching me and I'm touching him, and now I don't know what to say.

I want him to touch me again. Did I do something wrong?

He grabs a shelf and pulls himself up, then offers his hand to help me. I consider taking it for a moment, but decide to stand on my own. I get to my feet and brush off the backs of my legs. Whatever moment we had is definitely over.

NINE

Seth leads me up a narrow set of wooden stairs to a covered deck balanced in the branches of the upmost level of Artedion. The entire area glitters with bright shoots of sunlight that bounce and sway as the wind nudges the leaves over our heads. Picnic tables filled with creatures are scattered across the patio. Gorgons dressed in golden dresses sit alongside green-clad leprechauns, winged men and women line a table at the very back, and black-and-green ogres sit to my left drinking from dainty porcelain mugs, pinkies raised. I hear Lulu's delighted giggle before I spot her purple hair. "There." I point, and we push through a line of satyrs carrying frosted mugs.

"Hey! Y'all made it!" Lulu beams at us from a long, wooden table of pixies, each with vividly colored hair. Lulu's saved us some space at the end, and Seth takes the seat beside her while I slide in across from him next to a pixie with blue-tipped blonde hair. She grins, her smile every bit as cute and adorable as Lulu's, and I smile back because I can't help it.

"We're all here!" Lulu says, patting the table. "Let's eat!"

The empty dishes tremble slightly then appear laden with food. The plate in front of me nearly overflows with white-cheddar macaroni and cheese, my all-time favorite comfort food. The heavenly scent of warm, melted cheese envelops me and transports me to Mom's kitchen, sitting next to Sam and arguing over the last helping of macaroni.

I inhale the tiny slice of normalcy.

Seth lifts his eyebrows a bit, and I smile at him. "I wasn't expecting mac and cheese."

"It's an enchantment," Seth explains, cutting into the juicy ribeye in front of him. "Whatever food you want, you get."

I didn't even realize I wanted mac and cheese. Even the dishes know me better than I do.

"Be careful, though," Lulu warns. "You can't eat macaroni and cheese every day."

I tilt my head to the side and gaze at the wide array of chocolate surrounding Lulu, from the pudding in her bowl to the chocolate milk in her glass. There's even a second bowl in front of her that holds two scoops each of vanilla, chocolate, and strawberry ice cream, topped with chocolate and caramel sauces as well as white chocolate chips and two cherries.

I look across the table, noting more of the same on each pixie's plate. Cookies, cake, pie, and lots and lots of ice cream. Unless my nose is deceiving me, the pixie to my right is digging her spoon into a bowl filled with pure buttercream icing. My teeth ache just looking at it. She giggles at me as she lifts it to her lips.

I raise an eyebrow at Lulu.

"Don't give me that look," Lulu says, lifting her nose into the air and pursing her lips. "Pixies thrive on sugar. It's as important to our diets as green, leafy vegetables are to yours."

Seth shakes his head and smiles at me. "Don't come between a pixie and her sugar."

"Noted." I take a bite of the creamy, cheesy goodness on my plate and close my eyes. Holy. Cheese. Lulu doesn't know what she's talking about. I could *absolutely* eat macaroni and cheese every day. I don't want to eat anything but this for the rest of my life.

"Freckles! You found Mesmer!"

I look up to see Keiran standing to my left, as rumpled and adorable as ever. He flashes his dimples and asks, "Mind if I sit here?"

"Uh, sure," I tell him, scooting closer to the blonde pixie beside me to make room for him. My mind goes completely blank while I watch him swing one leg over the bench, then the other.

"Hi." He directs his greeting to me, and then nods at the rest of the table.

"Well, hi!" Lulu grins broadly. She sits up a little straighter and leans forward. "You're a second-year, right? Keagan?"

"Keiran," he corrects her, picking up his peanut butter and jelly sandwich with both hands.

"I'm Lulu," she replies, then tosses out the names of the other pixies sitting around us. Jojo, Lala, Mimi, Deedee, and the one next to me, Kiki. "And this is Seth. I guess you already know Charlie."

"Yeah," Seth says, like he's accusing Keiran of something, "how do you know Charlie?"

I tear my gaze away from Keiran. "We met this morning."

"This morning?" Seth sits up straighter and rests his forearm on the table. "Where?"

"In the woods with Clara," Keiran answers, his eyes shifting from Seth to me and back. I realize he doesn't know what I've told Seth about the harpy.

"It's okay," I tell him. "I came clean about exploring the meadow this morning."

Keiran grins. "Good. I thought about it all morning and couldn't come up with any excuse that would've made sense anyway." His eyes are like a thunderstorm, intense and gray. My charcoal would capture the color perfectly.

"Helping her come up with an excuse, huh?" Seth comments, chewing slowly. "That's cute."

I don't have to be an empath to know he's annoyed, but I wouldn't mind being able to understand why. Typical overbearing Seth? Or something else?

Lulu sets down her spoon and throws a napkin at Seth. "Don't be rude." She fixes her sparkling eyes on Keiran and winks. "Don't mind him, doll. He's overprotective."

Keiran laughs and Seth shoots Lulu a look.

"You guys seem to be having fun," a familiar, snooty voice comments. I stifle a groan. Lulu doesn't bother hiding hers. The rest of the pixies make various sounds of disgust before getting up to leave.

Wow. Clara's presence is enough to clear a table? She doesn't seem to notice, but she must. She's probably too proud to admit it. Maybe she truly doesn't care? If all fairies are like Clara, I imagine that pixies and fairies don't mix well.

Of course, I can't imagine Clara mixing well with anyone.

"Hello, Empress," Seth says.

Clara acknowledges Seth with a lift of her chin, and her eyes settle on Keiran. "Hi, Keiran." Her lips spread across her face in a barely upturned line. I guess it's technically supposed to be a smile, but the rest of her face doesn't move. It's a little disturbing.

"Hey." Keiran's greeting combines with his dimples, creating a lethal mixture that renders me speechless. Clara blinks, and I see a more normal face–lips parted, dazed eyes–completely hypnotized by Keiran's grin. Seth rolls his eyes so hard I can almost hear it.

For a split second, Clara seems normal–like any of the girls back home who become a little silly when they're crushing on a guy. If Keiran weren't so universally gorgeous, I'd be a little concerned that Clara and I share the same taste in anything at all.

The moment passes so quickly I'm not certain I didn't imagine it. Clara lowers her eyelashes and says, "I'm about to fly over to the rock garden. Care to join me?"

She has the kind of confidence I'd admire if she were the least bit likable. I've always wanted to be the girl who makes a move when I'm interested in a guy.

"That sounds great," Keiran responds. He wipes a dollop of peanut butter onto his napkin. "What are you doing this afternoon?"

I'm so busy thinking about what a stunning couple Keiran and Clara would be that it takes me a second to realize he's looking at me. "Huh?"

"Are you busy? Do you want to go to the rock garden with me and Clara?"

Across from him, Lulu releases a short, surprised giggle and quickly presses her napkin to her lips.

"I, um..." I glance at Clara, pretty sure that this was not what she had in mind when she invited him. The creepy dead smile from earlier is nothing compared to the positively murderous glare she wears now.

Her lavender eyes darken to plum. "I'm sure she has other things to do. Don't you, Charlie?"

I have no idea what Seth has planned. Even if I'm free, do I want to go? Is time with this beautiful boy worth time with that horrid fairy? What exactly is a rock garden, anyway?

I give her one of those smiles where I purse my lips and squint my eyes a bit, every girl's "I hate you" smile. She returns it, and I know we're speaking the same language.

"Charlie's had a really busy morning," Seth interrupts, his tone more challenging than informational. "She needs to rest this afternoon."

Rest? I wrinkle my nose. I'm not a child. I don't need nap time.

"Come on. She just got here yesterday, right? I could show her around a bit. Introduce her to Ellauria. Maybe take her to the lake," Keiran says, flashing his smile at Seth. Who says no to that face?

"Nah, that's really not necessary," Seth replies, including an equally impressive smile. "I'll introduce her to Ellauria."

So, Seth. Seth says no to that face.

Lulu lowers her napkin and rests her chin on her hand, switching her gaze from Seth to Keiran and back. Clara puts her hands on her hips, still glaring at me. Seth and Keiran stare at one another, each waiting for the other to give in.

Hold up. Is Seth jealous?

"Hi." I raise my hand. "I'm seventeen years old. I can totally handle a full day's worth of activity without a nap. Been doing it for years."

Seth lays a heavy stare on me. He obviously knows I want to go. I'd love to see more of Ellauria, and I wouldn't mind making a few friends. I need distraction and a little bit of freedom. I channel my emotions and wait for him to process them. His expression doesn't change.

"Keiran, I don't really think you should get involved," Clara says, her rosy lips drawn in a perfect heart-shaped pout.

He winks at her. "Don't worry, beautiful. I'll catch up with you at the rock garden."

The pout vanishes, and her face contorts into one of rage. Thin, flattened lips, flared nostrils, and one very sharply arched eyebrow.

And for duck's sake, even that looks good on her. I want to bang my head against the table.

Lulu ruffles Seth's hair, studying his face. "Come on, Seth. Keiran can give her a tour and you can take a break."

"I don't need a break," Seth grumbles, tipping his head away from her fingers.

"Well, I know when I'm not wanted." Lulu makes a face at him and rises from the table. "I'm going to head to the Hollow for a bit, but we should talk this afternoon." She winks at me before flying off.

"You're not going," Seth says to me. "We have work to do." He picks up my plate along with his and stands to make his way to the dumbwaiter in the corner.

I glare at his back, hoping he feels the full effect of my frustration. Aegis or not, there's no need for his tone. Resting is the very last thing I want to do right now. The idea of being alone with my thoughts is terrifying. I exhale through my nose. This is ridiculous.

Clara puts her hand on Keiran's shoulder and smiles sweetly. "So that's settled. Shall we?"

Keiran shakes his head while he watches Seth move through the crowded deck with our plates. He throws his napkin on his plate. "I don't really feel like it right now. Can I catch up with you later this afternoon?"

"Ugh. Fine." She scowls at me and stalks off in the opposite direction.

"You'll pay for that later," I mutter to Keiran as we rise from the table. A gorgon passes by carrying a stack of dirty dishes, and Keiran adds his plate to the top of it, thanking her with a smile. I head toward Mesmer's entrance to wait for Seth, and Keiran comes, too.

"Pretty sure you've got a debt to pay yourself," he says, tipping his head toward Seth, who's making his way back to us. Keiran smiles at me. "You have fun with that. I'm sure I'll see you later today."

"Sounds good." I smile at him. He's sure he'll see me? How can he be sure? I wait until his head disappears down the stairs before I drop my shoulders. I hate how quickly Seth goes from treating me like his friend to bossing me around like his Apprentice. Keiran's right. This argument is only going to continue when we're behind closed doors. I can hear it now:

I'm your Aegis, Charlie. I know everything. Blah blah blah, safety, blah blah blah, Fellowship.

Seth meets me by the staircase and hooks his thumbs in his back pockets. "You ready? I'll walk you to your room."

I take his arm and pull him toward the corner where we have a little more privacy. I don't even care that I'm pouting. "If Keiran was a girl, would you have let him show me around?"

His face twists into one big smirk, and he squeaks, "What? That has nothing to do with it. I'm your Aegis, I'm—"

"I know, I know." I wave my hand and recite the Seth Speech. "You're my Aegis. You keep me safe. Fun is for other people."

He snorts. "I never said fun is for other people."

"Whatever." I shake my head. I could almost appreciate Seth's jealousy if it didn't add another bar to my cage.

Seth folds his arms across his chest and sighs. I can't help but notice the way his sleeves stretch across his biceps when he does that. "The whole time I've been your Aegis, you've been hidden from nearly everyone else," he says, so quietly I can hardly hear him. "You're not so safe anymore. Somehow, someone's figured out what you are. Two times in the last twenty-four hours, you've been within arm's reach of a creature hell-bent on killing you. I want to lock you in your room until every threat to you is destroyed."

It's just like him to completely ignore all the wonder I've experienced in the last twenty-four hours. I touched a pixie's wings. I watched a fairy paint her nails with a rose. I wrapped myself up in the tree equivalent of a hug. I ate from an enchanted plate. I step closer, stare up into his dark eyes, and speak with as much force as I can at a low volume. "You're so focused on keeping me alive that you're forgetting I need to live."

Seth studies me for a moment, then slowly nods. "Point taken."

That's all I wanted—acknowledgement that he gets it. "Fine. Walk me to my room." If I'm being completely honest with myself, I really am exhausted. Today's been a whirlwind since the moment I stepped out of my room. I wouldn't mind a bit of a break, although I'd never admit that to Seth now.

One side of his mouth lifts in his patented half-smile. "Bossy."

"I learned from the best," I reply, and take off down the stairs.

We stop at the landing outside my door, and I wave my hand to open it. Sunlight pours through the doorway, and all the table lamps illuminate as we enter. I pull the elastic from the end of my braid and unwind my hair as I walk inside, shaking out the thick waves as I drag myself further into the suite. The door clicks shut behind us. On my bed sits a box with a red towel draped across the top. I raise my eyebrows at Seth, and I swear I see a flush creep across his cheeks.

"I brought you something," Seth says.

Birthdays and Christmases have always meant cards from Seth. An actual gift for no occasion whatsoever? Suddenly my head is in the library again, drawing lines down his arms with my fingers and wondering what it all means.

Wait.

"Seth, if it's a thesaurus, I will throw it at you."

He laughs and stands beside me at the foot of my bed. He smells nice—like an early spring morning with fresh-cut grass, wet earth, and sunshine—and I almost tell him so before I realize that might be a little weird. "Just open it, Charlie."

I pull the towel away and my breath catches. All my loves are there—my worn charcoals, soft pastels, half-empty watercolors, pencils, paintbrushes—everything I need. He must've grabbed them from the mortal realm this morning. I bite my lip and dig through them until I find my sketchbooks at the bottom of the box. He's remembered every single one of them, even the leather-bound one from the shelf over my bed.

I turn and throw my arms around his neck without thinking. It takes the longest second, but his arms finally come around me as well. One hand slides around my waist while the other moves up my back, pressing me closer.

Warmth spreads through me, as much a result of having my sketches here as having Seth's arms around me. For the first time, I feel a little less restless, like this is a place I could get used to.

Ellauria as well as Seth's arms.

Several seconds pass, and neither of us pulls away.

Seth and I have always favored the quick one-armed hug in the past, our bodies barely touching. Hugs of habit, not warm embraces. Like everything else here, this is different.

I close my eyes, inhaling him, and I feel his face turn into my hair, breathing me in as well. There's a hint of lavender mixed into his fresh morning scent. It must be his shampoo. His breath on my neck makes me arch toward him. His heart beats against mine, and I relax, allowing myself to be wrapped in his strength, security, and all the things that are so very Seth.

It's not that kissing Seth has never crossed my mind, but before it's always been more about curiosity than need. I wait, all too aware of how close his lips are to my skin.

Kiss me.

Seth releases me so quickly I almost fall. I take a step forward to catch myself and then force myself to step backward, coming down on my feet and tucking my hair behind my ears. Seth's hands fall to his sides. I stare at his chest, embarrassed. Did he do that because I wanted him to kiss me? Am I completely misreading everything here?

When I finally lift my head, his eyes are already on mine. He clears his throat and says, "I brought something else, too."

So we're pretending that didn't happen. Right.

Seth goes to my closet and reaches inside. When he turns, his hand is wrapped around the neck of a wooden acoustic guitar with a sunburst finish. A Gibson.

My hand lands on my mouth.

Sam's guitar.

I release a shaky breath and run my fingers along the strings Sam had been touching only yesterday, and it's almost like I'm touching him.

"So he'll have it when he gets here," Seth explains. He sets it on the floor at an angle, leaning against the wall and my dresser.

"Thank you," I tell him. My bottom lip trembles, and I swallow the urge to burst into tears. "He'll love it. I love it."

Seth presses his lips together and nods. His smile is filled with compassion so touching that I almost lose it. He seems to realize this and brightens his grin before turning his attention to the box on my bed. "I'm sorry you had to wait. I hope I got everything."

I press my hands to my cheeks. Don't cry, Charlie. You can do this.

I turn to the box and take out each item, laying everything on my bed. I pull out the leather-bound book, the ones with sketches of my home, and ease onto my mattress. Seth sits next to me while I flip through them.

The worn white picket fence around Mom's flower garden. She added something new to it every year, usually an herb of some sort, if she could dig out enough mint to find room. Wild strawberries grew in the corner of the garden, and when I was little I pretended they were there for the fairies living among the blooms.

Mom's front porch, scattered with furniture and flowers. Wind chimes hang on the side above the bright yellow forsythia bush at the end of the house. I'd drawn Mom sitting in the wicker loveseat with her feet propped up on one of the tables. She loved that porch. I could almost always find her there in the mornings, sitting in the chair and drinking coffee, watching hummingbirds fight over the feeders in the yard.

I trace her with my fingers, and a teardrop hits the page below the front porch steps.

Seth's arm curls around me, pulling me toward him. "You'll see her again."

I lay my head against his shoulder and turn the page.

Sam's hands on his guitar, plucking its strings with one hand and gripping its neck with the other. I remember the day I drew this. He'd been working on a new song, but it wasn't coming out right, and he'd spent hours playing the same tune over and over in various keys and rhythms.

I close the book.

What if this is all I have left? These drawings? These memories?

Will we have the chance to make new ones?

"How can I keep going, not knowing where they are or if they're okay?" My voice is cloaked in tears, creating a raspy whisper. I don't really expect an answer. I don't know how Seth could say anything to make this better, anyway.

He rests his chin on my head. "Because that's what you do. You keep going. You get up every day and you believe you're going to see them. You live like they'll be here tomorrow. Prepare for it. Get ready." He pulls away and looks at my face. "You can do this."

I swallow hard. He has more faith in my strength right now than I do. I rub the soft leather cover of the book and then hug it to my chest.

"Oh, while I'm thinking about it, here." Seth reaches into his pocket and pulls out a royal blue ribbon—an aernovus. He loops it around his finger and presses it to his chest. The ribbon glows for a second, then vanishes. I feel a tiny pulse below my collarbone, and when I look down, the aernovus is glimmering against my white-and-gray shirt.

"Now you're officially mine," he says, then quickly adds, "my Apprentice, I mean."

The aernovus curls itself against me before relaxing into a loop. I don't feel any different. Seth says I'm official, but I still feel like a poser. To be honest, I still feel like a mortal.

I need some time to think, process, and unwind.

"I need to talk to Alexander about this fairy ring business," Seth says. "You think you'll be okay here by yourself for a few hours?"

I smile. We both know I want to be alone. I stand to place the sketchbook on my nightstand and pull one I haven't used yet from the box. I could fill an entire book on today's events alone. "Sure. I think I'll draw for a bit."

I'll draw things for Sam. Mom, too. Even though none of this is new to her, she hasn't been here for a while. It'll be their welcoming gift.

Because they're going to come home.

I realize I just thought of Ellauria as home and nod to myself. This is good.

"That's perfect. If you take a break, there are some books on the coffee table for you. One is about sirens, and the other is a bestiary of mystical creatures."

I turn to see two books on the table. One has a shiny red cover and the other seems older, bound in faded green cloth.

"Oh, and one more thing." He reaches around me and pulls open my nightstand drawer.

I burst out laughing. Inside are bags and bags of peanut M&Ms.

Seth smiles. "I'll be back later."

"I'll be here."

His shoulders relax and he nods before flickering away.

I spend the next couple of hours marking up pages with my pencil. I love new sketchbooks. Pages and pages of possibilities, waiting to be filled with whatever I want. The hate-filled eyes and crooked snarl of the harpy. Clara painting her nails on the rock. Lulu's sparkling wings. Seth's arms.

I spend quite a bit of time on Seth's arms, actually. Along with his eyes, trying to balance the seriousness of his stare with the sweetness of his smile. I round out his bottom lip and then rub my thumb across it, smudging the line for softness.

There's a knock at the door and I yell, "Come in!" before I remember I should probably find out who's knocking first. Stranger Danger 101. Seth would not be pleased.

The door slides open, revealing Keiran on the landing outside. He leans against the edge of the doorway, and sunlight shines around his silhouette.

Seth would most definitely not be pleased.

I slide my pencil into the spiral binding of my sketchbook and throw it on the bed as I jump up. "Keiran! Hi!"

"Hey," he says, and steps inside. "Is Seth around?"

"No. He went to see Alexander about some fairy thing." I comb my fingers through my hair. Why is Keiran standing in my kitchen? Do I have pencil smudges on my face?

Keiran's eyes wander around the room before he looks directly into mine with a shy smile. "Well, I'm heading to the lake and thought you might want to see it. If you've had enough rest, of course."

"Oh!" I'm about to say yes before I realize it's not that easy. I bite my lip. "I don't know."

Seth will kill me. He will absolutely murder me.

I really want to go.

Keiran laughs. "No pressure. I totally understand if you don't feel up to it."

Seth didn't technically tell me to stay in my room. And all I'd really said was I would be here when he got back. There was no direct order, and no promise of anything on my end. "Is it far?"

"Nope." He pushes his lower lip out. "Maybe a fifteen-minute walk?"

Fifteen minutes there and back. Even if we stayed for thirty minutes, I'd be back in an hour. It's not like I'm wandering around alone again. This time Keiran will be with me.

Keiran's blue-gray eyes lock with mine, and a smile spreads across his lips as he watches my face.

That's it. I'm going. "Sure. Let me grab my sketchbook."

TEN

Keiran and I navigate through the darkest trees I've ever seen on our way to the lake. The trunks are black, and the leaves alternate between dark purple and navy. He stays beside me, his pace slow and steady, catching me every time I lose my footing. The ground here is covered in tree roots and vines. I try to watch where I'm walking, but I don't want to miss a single sight. The dark canopy chokes out most of the sun, transforming Keiran's golden skin to a blueish-gray slightly lighter than his eyes. I barely see sunlight bouncing off water through the branches ahead.

"What's with all the butterflies?" I ask, tucking my sketchbook under my arm and batting at one of the bright yellow insects flitting near my hair.

"Butterflies? Oh, you mean the petits?"

I pull my sketchbook out and swat the butterfly again. "Petits?"

"They're not butterflies." He dips his head toward me, speaking quietly. "They're petits, the smallest fairies of all."

"Oh!" I drop my arm and lean closer to the petit fluttering around my face. The petit's delicate features are twisted with anger. Her mouth is moving, but I hear only the tiniest hum. "I'm so sorry!" I tell her. "I didn't know!"

He half-smirks, half-smiles. A smirkle. "Don't sweat it. They're fairies, so you pretty much annoy them just by existing."

I raise my eyebrows and smirkle back at him. "So it's not just Clara, then? All the fairies are like that?"

He nods. "Yeah. They can be a little unfriendly."

I laugh lightly. A little.

The petit flies right up to my nose and glares. I still can't understand what she's saying, but I suspect that's a good thing. "They really do look like butterflies," I say, holding my sketchbook to my chest and looking over my shoulder as we walk away.

Keiran places his hand on my elbow, helping me step over a particularly thick growth of vines stretched across the ground between the trees. "Watch out for the gate."

I stop, looking back to examine the vines. "*That's* a gate?"

He bends down to wrap his fingers around the thickest of the vines and pulls upward. A shimmering portal lifts with it, like he's pulling a window from the ground. I lean closer, dipping my hand into the opening. It vanishes, and my mind sees a detached hand floating on the other side in the Between. I pull my hand back and stretch my fingers, examining them.

"I never would've guessed," I say as he lowers the vine to the ground.

"Yeah. Seth will go over all this with you soon, I'm sure. They make the gates hard to spot because of the less-intelligent creatures. We can't have a troll getting loose in the Between and breaking into the mortal realm. Eventually, you'll be able to see the things that don't quite belong here. Like, look," he points across the ground, "none of the other vines are that big or dense. The ones making up the gate aren't even attached to anything."

Keiran's right. They simply stretch across the ground, ending at nothing.

Look for what doesn't belong. I need to keep this in mind next time I want to go exploring in the Between.

I think back to this morning in the meadow. I don't recall anything out of the ordinary, aside from every single thing about the field being out of the ordinary. I'll have to go back and look again.

We keep walking, and Keiran's hand brushes against my arm every now and then. Round pebbles gradually replace the thick vines beneath our feet as we step out of the shadows and the enormous lake stretches before us.

The glittering body of clear blue water is much larger than a pond, but it's not nearly as big as I'd expected. Every lake I've been to covers acres and acres of land, enough to support hundreds of speedboats, sailboats, and pontoons. Here, only a few rowboats scatter across the surface, and it couldn't handle much more. Amid the boats, heads bob up from the water now and then before diving back underneath. To my right, a giant catfish jumps out of the water and glides through the air before crashing back through the waves, and some young centaurs squeal in delight as water splashes on them.

I'm so glad I have my sketchbook with me.

There's a trio of gorgons having a picnic on the far right, their toes barely touching the water. Almost directly in front of me, two pixies sunbathe across the flat top of a large silver rock that juts out over the water like a diving board.

A four-armed girl with long green hair calls to Keiran as we approach, and he lifts his hand, flashing the million-dollar grin. She waves for him to come over, and he shakes his head politely.

Most of the girls I see are eyeing Keiran, and I snort. "Please tell me your powers have something to do with attracting women."

He grins, his cheeks reddening. "Are you saying I need supernatural help?"

"No really," I say, walking with him along the edge of the water. "What are you?"

Keiran stops and takes a deep, heavy breath. "I knew I'd have to tell you eventually." His grin vanishes, and his gray eyes turn serious. "I'm a vampire."

I can't decide if the split-second I spend believing him is a good sign or a bad one. I'm either finally adapting to the mystical realm or I'm the biggest sucker there is. I stare at him until I see a twinkle behind his serious expression, and then I laugh.

"What?" he asks. "Don't I look like a vampire?"

"Well, it certainly explains your sparkle."

He smiles crookedly. "I'm an elf."

An elf? Without thinking, my mind places a red, pointed hat on his head to match his shirt. My mouth falls open. "Shut up."

"It's true."

"Shouldn't you be shorter?" I ask. "With pointy ears?"

"Right," Keiran says, lowering his eyebrows, "and I live inside a tree where I make delicious chocolate-striped shortbread cookies all day."

"Fair enough." I start walking again, and he moves with me. A few older centaurs are resting under a group of trees watching the younger ones play. One of the women smiles at me, and I smile back. I'm getting really good at playing it cool. Some of this already seems normal to me. "So what do elves do?"

Keiran shrugs. "Build things, mostly. I can look at something and immediately tell how it was made so I can re-create it. For the Fellowship, we design and create tools and weapons."

I step right up to the edge of the water. Along this side, the water drops off from the shore immediately. There's no gradual decline into the depths. "How deep is it?"

"Bottomless. All lakes and ponds in Ellauria serve as portals for the water-dwellers," Keiran says. "They take them to any body of water you can imagine on the other side—from the oceans to a puddle in a parking lot, and vice versa."

Pretty deep.

Bouncing lights shimmer within its depths as though the lake is lit from below the surface. I bend over the water and my reflection grows larger, expanding more and more even after I stop moving. Just when I realize the face staring back at me isn't my reflection at all, it bobs up from the water's surface. I jump backward, dropping my sketchbook to the ground. Keiran shoots out a hand to keep me from falling.

I can't take my eyes off the girl rising from the water. Her golden hair is streaked with pale blue lines that run the entire length of its waves. Her eyes are the color of the sea, a dark mixture of green and blue with flecks of silver, like sunlight glittering on water. She smiles at me before turning and diving back into the water. As she does, a gleaming silver tail splashes behind her.

I completely forget not to gawk. My inner five-year-old screams, "Mermaid!" and it takes everything in me to behave normally. I clamp my hand over my mouth and watch, wide-eyed, until I can't see her anymore.

"You all right?" Keiran asks, holding me steady.

Oh, crap. Act normal. I bite my lip and smile. "First time I've seen a mermaid."

"Really?" He drops his hands from my arms. "I'd have thought you would've seen a few, being a siren and all."

Sheet. Right. I press my lips together and shrug. A breeze blows off the top of the water and swirls through my hair. I grab a few strands and twist them together.

"Well," he sits down, "you handled it like a pro."

My hands are still trembling with excitement, and I drop my twist of hair to show him. "It wasn't easy."

"You'll get used to it." He takes off his flip-flops and slips his legs into the water.

I sit down beside him and slide my legs in alongside his. It's warm, almost too warm, but it's refreshing. Four rowboats float near the middle of the lake filled with creatures I've never seen. A few of them look nearly human, aside from animal-like ears or hair made of flowering vines sprouting from their heads. The young centaurs are in a boat, tossing a ball back and forth with a group of mermen. Merfolk appear all over the water, springing up from the surface and splashing back down again. They gather in groups, talking and laughing in high-pitched squeaks and grunts.

Keiran rests his hands on the ground and leans back, tilting his face toward the sun with his eyes closed.

I don't want to get used to this.

I want to feel this alive, this enchanted, every day. Getting used to things means losing sight of what makes them special. I don't want to miss a single bit of the magic here.

I pull my pencil from the sketchbook's binding and flip to the first blank page. Before long, the lake takes shape beneath my fingers, stretching from one end of the page to the other. The centaurs are a challenge— I've always had trouble drawing horses. Something about the way their legs move makes it difficult for me.

I'm so lost in tracing details that when I feel someone watching over my shoulder, I forget for a moment that it's not Sam. I glance up, and Keiran's gray eyes snap me out of it.

My gaze lands back on the page, and I shake my head. Of course it's not Sam.

"I'm sorry." Keiran shifts his weight, leaning away from me. "Would you rather I not watch?"

"It's not that." I let my pencil fall and rest against my thumb. I wrestle with what to say; I don't want to give away too much, but I'd like to be honest. I choose my words carefully. "There are things I miss about home. Drawing makes me remember them."

Keiran rubs his hands through his hair, nodding. "Oh man, I know what you mean. Ellauria's incredible, but there are things I miss, too. Snow. I miss snow like crazy."

"It doesn't snow here?"

He shakes his head. "Never. And sometimes, you need to watch it snow, you know?"

I study Ellauria's clear sky. I guess there's no reason for snow here. I've never wanted to live in parts of the world that only had one or two seasons. I love all four. The different sights and colors each season brings, the change and growth, the way the same place looks so completely transformed at certain points in the year. Bloom, grow, die, rebloom. I appreciate the cycle.

"Where'd you grow up?" I ask.

"I lived in the mortal realm up until I came here two years ago," he says. "Different places. My dad moved around a lot."

"So," I roll my pencil against the page, "no specific place you think of as home?"

He gazes upward. "Not really. We never stayed in one place very long."

I study his profile. What would that be like? I lived in the same hundred-year-old farmhouse in the same lonely little town my entire life. I feel so unsettled without a place to truly call home. Keiran doesn't seem to care.

He sits up. "What do you miss most?" he asks.

"My family," I murmur. I snap my head up when I realize that might not have been a safe thing to say. "I mean, they're not here yet."

He leans over his knees, looking into the lake. "Yeah. I really miss my dad. I haven't seen him in a couple years."

A couple years. I hope I don't have to wait that long for Mom and Sam.

Keiran's eyes stay on the water, but his hardened gaze and tense jaw tell me his attention is elsewhere. It's so different from the smiling, flirty side of him, and I'm so curious about what's behind the contrast. Is he wearing a mask as restrictive as mine?

There's so much I'd like to ask. Where is his dad? Why hasn't he seen him? Is it by choice, like when Seth left his family? Or something else? Is he dead? I open my mouth, then shut it. If I ask more questions, he might ask about my family, as well.

His head stays down, and I can't decide if he wants to talk about his dad or if he's embarrassed for mentioning him. Why *did* he bring it up, anyway? I wonder how similar our situations are, and if the Fellowship is forcing a secret on him, too.

There's so much awkward filling the space between us right now that I'm struggling to find my way out of it. I rack my brain for something, anything, to say, but nothing seems right. "I should probably head back before Seth realizes I'm gone."

It doesn't exactly help with the awkward, but it's the truth. I have no idea how long I've been gone.

Keiran's head jerks like he'd forgotten I was there. His eyes land on the ground, my sketch, my face, and then he nods. He stands up and reaches down to help me to my feet. Trails of water stream down my legs, and the breeze feels cool against them. My skin will be dry in no time under this heat.

"Do you want to go back the way we came, or see a little more?" Keiran asks. "It'll take the same amount of time either way."

I can't resist the option to see even more of Ellauria, so he leads me to the far end of the lake. We pass the centaurs again, but this time the younger ones are arguing with their parents about leaving. The path gradually slopes upward, carrying us high above the trees. He points out Artedion. I see the giant oak and the Clearing behind it in the distance. Below me and to the left I see the navy waves of the Meadow of Music. Another excellent viewpoint for a sketch. This would be gorgeous on canvas, with the rich, deep colors provided by oil paints.

The trees become scarce as the trail gets steeper and steeper. When it levels out, we're at the top of a plateau. Piles of large and small rocks are arranged in various shapes. Flowering plants bloom amid the rocks, scattering the gray landscape with bursts of crimson and amethyst. Fairies flit about through the plants, tending to the flowers and positioning more rocks throughout the area.

Whoa.

I stop walking and stare at the fairies.

How had I not noticed this?

They're all the same. Every single fairy is exactly the same height. They all have the same long, twig-like limbs. The only differences among them are from the neck up, like a variety of heads have been stuck on the same body. Even then, while their hair colors vary, all the styles are the exact same length. Their wings are sparkling pastel shades of pink, blue, purple, and yellow, matching their dresses which, of course, are all identical in style.

"Keiran! You made it!" Clara's voice rises behind us, and I spin around.

She gets more and more breathtaking every time I see her. Her lips are fuller, her dark eyelashes thicker, even her eyes look more lavender than they did back at Mesmer. Her long, platinum hair flows across her shoulders in flawless, shiny waves. It's like a team of hair and makeup artists jumps out to freshen her up when no one's looking.

This does not endear her to me.

"Hey, Beautiful," he greets her. She glides toward him, wrapping her arms around his neck and hugging him, pressing her body against his. He hugs her back, glancing at me over her shoulder.

I roll my eyes and smile. There are an awful lot of Beautifuls around here. I wonder how many girls' names he actually knows.

"Charlie and I are on our way back to Artedion," he says, pulling away from her. "Just passing through."

"Your garden is gorgeous," I tell her, leaning over some of the rock piles and brushing my hands along the tops of the flowers. It really is nice, especially set up here amid all the gray. If I had more time, I'd sketch it.

"Can't you stay for a bit?" Clara frowns at Keiran, completely ignoring me and my compliment.

I look to the sky. I've never been good at telling time by the sun, but the fact that it's noticeably lower than the last time I checked makes me nervous. Seth's totally going to bust me. "I really need to get back."

She purses her lips and exhales through her nose. "Then go," she says, moving her neck back and forth.

I match her expression. "I don't know how to get to Artedion from here."

Clara wrinkles her eyebrows. "Haven't you ever been to Ellauria before?"

The look in her eye shifts from curiosity to confusion. Being new to the Fellowship is my secret, but being new to Ellauria isn't, right?

This is probably why Seth prefers me to be with him all the time.

Before I can respond, a boom shatters the air, loud and sharp like a gunshot. Keiran's arms come around me and Clara, guarding us on instinct as he turns his head toward the sound. There's a split second of silence before the screams follow, coming from everywhere at once, bouncing off the rocks.

"Oh no," Clara breathes. "The lake." She pulls away from Keiran and zooms down the mountain, the rest of the fairies swarming behind her.

Keiran grabs my hand and we're running and sliding down the rocky dirt path we just climbed. The screams stop and a strange, sickly sweet scent invades the air—familiar, but wrong. It grows stronger the closer we get to the lake, assaulting my nostrils and stinging my eyes. I open my mouth to inhale and the odor sticks to my tongue, making me gag.

Keiran freezes at the bottom of the path. He gasps, and his fingers clench around mine.

Mom took me and Sam fishing exactly one time, back when we were seven. It'd been a long day and we hadn't caught a thing, so when Sam and I spotted a little island in the middle of a cove we passed, we begged Mom to take us there to swim. We'd hopped out of the boat as soon as we were close enough and splashed through the water to the rocky shore. The torture of an afternoon spent still and quiet with a fishing pole in hand was quickly remedied by a game of pirates staking claim to the island. We'd wandered to the far side and stumbled upon a shallow pool of lake water filled with dead fish, baking under the sun's heat.

Dead fish. That's the smell. Familiar, but completely wrong here.

My sketchbook falls to the ground, and my brain processes the scene in pieces.

The inky surface of the lake.

Pale, motionless bodies.

A mess of human arms crossed and piled on top of each other at the water's edge, fingers digging into the shore, unmoving.

Silver glints on top of the water. Mermaid tails. Hundreds, unattached to anything.

The adult centaurs I'd noticed earlier lie on the ground near the shore, unmoving.

In my peripheral vision, I see creatures gradually moving in, drawn by the screams. Like us, they freeze as they struggle to make sense of what's happened. The fairies are the only ones who don't keep their distance. They've positioned themselves at various points around the lake, and several of them drift in a grid inches above its surface, back and forth, their faces broken but focused on the water. Every now and then one of them bends closer, studying the remains but never touching anything. Clara hovers above them all, hands on her head, staring in disbelief.

I take shallow breaths to keep the rancid air from filling my lungs. It hasn't been more than fifteen minutes since Keiran and I sat on the shore with our legs in the water. How is the smell of death so strong already?

"Stay here," Keiran says, and he's gone before I can reply. He drops my hand and runs closer, darting around the dead centaurs and the other creatures gathered at various spots on the lake's perimeter. Ellaurians from all directions creep closer, and I know the hopeless horror on their faces reflects my own.

I stare at the ground, trying to escape what's in front of me. A tiny hoof catches my eye, tucked beneath a rock formation on the shore. I run toward it and drop to my hands and knees. A young centaur with blond curls stares back at me, his blue eyes wide. I reach for him, dipping my hand into the shadows.

Hands circle my rib cage and yank me backward. A slender man with arms that drag the ground peers down at me. "Are you out of your mind? That's necrolate!"

I blink at him. Necrolate?

He nods toward the lake. It's black and lifeless, and this close I can see the tinge of yellow floating on its surface. The yellow on the water lends its nearly neon glow to everything it touches, from the merfolk to the centaur near my feet.

The man crouches beside me and peers beneath the rock. He turns his head immediately, his face twisted with pain. "He's gone, honey. Necrolate doesn't leave survivors. They were all dead as soon as it hit the water."

My gaze wanders to the severed arms of the mermaids. They were trying to get out. I close my eyes, wishing I could unsee the hands reaching for help that could never have made it in time. My stomach turns. I'd heard the screams. The sound of their collective terror is one that will stick with me, replaying in my mind when I wake up at night.

I wrap my arms around myself, suddenly aware of how alone I am. I back away from the lake and its horrors, filled with an anticipation I can't quite put my finger on. Darkness creeps along the edges of my vision, vanishing when I turn my head to look closer. I can't shake the feeling that I'm being watched, like arms I can't see are waiting for the perfect moment to steal me away. I'm stuck at the height of my fight-or-flight response, completely tense, my shoulders growing heavier and heavier. Ice flows down my back. My eyes are wide, staring in all directions.

Keiran walks back to me, picking up my sketchbook along the way. I relax a bit when he reaches me, and we stand and stare in silence. There are no words for this. What kind of creature could've done this and disappeared so quickly? Where is it now?

I'd been here, right here, minutes before this happened.

Those arms, those screams, they could've been mine.

"Charlotte!" Alexander's voice thunders through my daze, and I jump. The founder stands a few feet away. His yellow-green eyes shift from a wide surprise to a narrow angry. Seth stands beyond him, watching me with a stricken look on his face.

My eyes land on his face, and though the mixture of fury and relief is plain in his thinly set lips and creased brow, seeing him makes everything a little more bearable.

Seth's here. I'm safe.

I finally allow myself to crumble. Seth's in front of me in a blink, pulling me close as a sob escapes my chest.

"You," Seth growls over my head. I don't have to look to know who he's talking to.

"No, Seth." I want to tell him it's not Keiran's fault. I knew what Seth wanted me to do, and I did the opposite. That's on me, not Keiran, but I'm too drained for words. I rest my forehead against his chest and breathe in his shirt.

"Calm down. She's okay," Keiran responds. His voice is low and lifeless.

"You better thank every god you pray to that she's okay." Seth rips my sketchbook from Keiran's hands.

Alexander strides over and barks at the two of them. "Enough."

Keiran's nostrils flare, and he lifts his head toward Alexander. "One of the gorgons said they saw a shadow hanging over the lake and he dissipated when they spotted him."

"A bogman," Alexander says, gazing across the water. His eyes settle on the dead merfolk for a moment before he looks at Seth. "Get her out of here. These creatures are beyond your healing."

Seth cradles my head against his shoulder, and we're gone.

In my room, Seth drops my sketchbook on the table and holds me until the sobs slow to sniffles. For a moment, I think he might tell me everything is okay. It's not like he needs to point out how lucky I am. I don't need the lecture or the "I told you so."

Then he turns his back to me and puts some space between us, and I know he's going to make his point. I lean against the table and brace myself for what's coming.

"I was standing in the middle of Central Hall when we heard the explosion. I dropped everything, literally dropped it right there in the middle of the floor, and came here." He turns around. His eyes are wide and staring, his face pale. He looks so young right now, so unabashedly afraid. "Do you have any idea what it was like to show up and find this room empty? Then I heard the screams." His voice cracks on the last word.

Seth closes his eyes, and I wonder if he's hearing them now, like I am. High-pitched cries of anguish. I release a shaky breath.

"What the hell were you doing out there?" he asks, anger punctuating every word. "Why can't you just be where I tell you to be?"

I shake my head. My nostrils burn as my eyes fill with tears again. None of the reasons I come up with will mean anything in the face of what happened at the lake. I never should've left. "I thought you didn't want me to go because of Keiran. I thought—"

"Oh for Pete's sake, Charlie!" He cuts me off and slams his hand down on the island in the kitchen. "I'm not your jealous boyfriend! It's my job to know all the different things that could harm you and anticipate threats before they happen. This isn't about keeping you away from some guy, it's about keeping you alive!"

I rub my forehead. He's said it a million times—his job is to keep me safe—but until now I've only thought about what those words meant for me, not him. His life is built around mine. The way he zeroes in on the things that could hurt me is as natural to him as the way I look at a scene and see all of its lines. It's who he is.

Shaped by the Fellowship, just like me.

"I'm sorry," I whisper. For so many things. For today. For last night. For the years he's dedicated to me without question.

Seth's shoulders fall. "I know. I just need you to understand." He walks to me and takes my face in his hands, spreading his fingers through my hair. "Nothing can happen to you. Not because of what you are or what it means or any of that, but because nothing can happen to *you*."

I hear what he doesn't say. His protection is more about *who* I am than what I am, more about his feelings than his job.

I'm more than my bloodline.

My heart flutters. He swipes his thumbs beneath my eyes and across my cheeks, wiping tears away. I close my eyes and allow myself to enjoy the feel of his fingers on my skin. I'm acutely aware of every spot he touches.

When I open my eyes, he's looking at my lips. His eyes are a shade darker than normal, and his cheeks are flushed. His gaze flickers upward, meeting mine, and he blinks a few times. His grip on me loosens, and he says, "Do you understand?"

I nod, unable to speak. Again, I'm overcome with the desire for him to kiss me, but I try not to focus on it. I don't want him to move away again.

He releases a breath and his hands fall from me completely. I bite my lip, stifling my disappointment.

"Okay." He pulls two chairs out from the table. "Tell me what happened. I want to know every single thing you saw."

I slump into the seat, rest my forehead on my fingers, and stare at the tabletop while I tell him everything, starting with Keiran showing up at my door and ending with Seth's arms around me by the lake. I have to stop a couple times, picturing the arms of the dead merfolk and the blond curls of the young centaur. Through it all, Seth says nothing. When I raise my head, he's lost in thought.

"Why did it smell like that?" I ask. The stench is still clinging to my clothes, and I tug at the neck of my shirt.

"The necrolate. It's basically death in liquid form. Everything submerged in the water decomposed almost immediately. Most creatures die on impact. Historically, jeravons have had some immunity to it, although I hope to never find out if that's still true."

The back of my throat aches. There was no immunity among today's victims. Death was quick, that's for sure, but it didn't seem instantaneous. "It looked like the merfolk had a few seconds to react," I tell him.

He nods, tracing invisible lines on the tabletop with his finger. "I saw that, too. They knew what was happening."

It's too horrible to think about, but I can't seem to think about anything else. Their last few seconds must have been filled with mindless terror, climbing over each other to get out of the water, screaming in fear and agony.

"Where did the necrolate come from?" I ask. "How did this happen?"

"If the gorgons are right, and I imagine they are, it was a bogman." He raises his eyes from the table. "You know him as the Boogeyman. Where you and I have blood in our veins, bogmen have necrolate. They expel the liquid from their bodies, and it kills nearly everything it touches."

His mention of the Boogeyman takes me right back to the young girl and the hodag. "The Boogeyman is real?"

Seth leans forward, rubbing his neck with his hands. "Tall, slender death spirits without faces. They live in shadows, and as such, they can enter and exit places very quickly. Like the harpies, the bogmen were banished when the Fellowship was created. They shouldn't be able to pass into the mystical realm."

"Why would they do this? Are they connected to Whalen?" I have to know. Is this about me? Is there any chance it isn't?

Seth shifts in his seat. "Possibly. Whalen has worked with bogmen in the past."

His name slithers over my skin, and my heart sinks. The deaths pile on top of me, pressing me lower and lower. As much as I'd hoped there was no connection, I knew it couldn't be a coincidence. I add the incident at the lake to the list of trauma caused by my mere existence. "But why? What does attacking the lake and killing the merfolk have to do with me?"

"I honestly don't know." Seth presses his fingertips to the table, one after the other, thinking. "He may be sending a message."

It worked. The things I saw and heard today will stick with me for as many lifetimes as I get. "I was so scared," I whisper.

The last of Seth's stony expression fades away, and he rests his hand in front of me. "Trust me, I know. I felt every bit of your fear, standing by the shore today."

Dealing with my emotions on top of his must be exhausting. I couldn't have handled any more grief or horror than I felt on my own today. I place my hand over his, and he rubs his thumb across my fingers. I can't decide if it's more intrusive that he knows my emotions, or that I put them on him.

"Can you tune me out?" I ask. "Do you have to take on my emotions as well as your own?"

"I suppose I could, yes, but I never have. I'm used to handling both of us." His eyes move from my hand to my face. "Would you prefer me to tune out?"

I press my lips together. I don't want to be any more of a burden than I already am. So much of the pain I cause is beyond my control, but this is something I can do. Besides, I liked it better when my feelings were my own. "Yes."

He nods. "I'll keep that in mind. It'll be an adjustment, but I can stop reading you all the time."

"Thank you."

After a moment, he pulls his hand from mine. "You should get some rest, and I should go see if there's anything I can do at the lake."

I don't want him to leave, but I know I have to let him go. Whatever's happening at the lake is more important than me right now. I hope he's already tuning me out.

He rises from the table, and I join him. My whole body feels heavier, weighed down by exhaustion and memories. I yawn. "You're right. I'm going to go to bed."

"Alexander wants to work on your powers tomorrow. I'll be here first thing in the morning." He reaches a hand toward me then lets it fall, like he's changed his mind. I want to step closer, to get inside his arms and stay there until I go to sleep, but I know he has a job to do.

"Seth?"

He lifts his eyebrows. "Yes?"

The bogmen live in shadows, and I spot several around my room. All these creatures I should be safe from are finding ways to get close to me anyway. I almost ask him to stay, but instead I say, "Nothing can come in here unless I let it, right?"

"Right." He turns toward the door and stops, turning back to me. "Charlie?"

Stay. Please say you're going to stay. "Yes?"

"You're safe."

ELEVEN

I miss sleeping with my window open. I love waking up and listening to the random noises of the night. Crickets. Cows. A lone car on the road. Even the coyotes. I miss the sounds.

And the breeze. I miss lying in my bed, absolutely burning up, and letting the air flutter through the curtains and chill the sweat on my skin. My room here at Artedion is fine, with a perfectly controlled temperature that leaves me neither hot nor cold at night.

But I long for the breeze.

I miss everything about my life before Ellauria. Back when everything made sense and no one wanted to kill me, as far as I knew.

I've been lying here staring at darkness for hours. My body is completely drained, but my brain is working overtime. I roll to my side and pull my blanket over my shoulder. My eyes land on Sam's guitar, and I wonder where he's sleeping and if he's comfortable. Is Mom with him? Does he close his eyes? Is he scared? Does he know where I am? I don't let myself question whether or not he's alive.

I flop onto my back and lay my arms on top of the blanket, fiddling with the beads on the red string tied around my wrist. "I swear," I whisper to the ceiling, "I won't give up until you're with me."

At least Mom chose to be in the Fellowship. At least she knew what she was getting into when she became my Aegis. Sam? He was born into this life, same as me. There was no choice, no exit clause. Nobody told us the lives we'd planned for ourselves would have to come second to what the Fellowship had already mapped out.

I sit up and lean forward, resting my elbows on my legs and pressing the heels of my hands to my eyes. There's the dead centaur, right behind my eyelids, just like every other time I've closed my eyes tonight.

If I weren't in Ellauria—would he be alive right now?

I push the covers away and turn on the lamp on my nightstand, tired of forcing sleep when it so obviously isn't going to happen.

I grab a glass of water from the sink and carry it back to the sofa. I'm carrying too much of this on my shoulders. I'm not delusional enough to think I'm to blame for the deaths of the creatures at the lake or the trials my family has gone through. I'm not Whalen. I'm not evil. His actions are beyond my control.

Still, they happened because of me. I feel a weird sense of responsibility for what's been sacrificed in my name.

Mom gave up Ellauria. Sam gave up normalcy. Seth gave up living a life solely for himself. Max gave his life. Marian gave her freedom. Now everyone in Ellauria is in danger, simply for sharing space with the last muralet.

I have to make it right.

I reach past the book about sirens for the tattered green bestiary Seth left earlier, and curl up beneath the chenille throw with the old book propped on my knees. The title has long since worn away, leaving empty indentations and gold flecks of thread where it once adorned the cover. I trace it with my fingers. The first letter is a large capital "B," but the rest of the word is too shallow to trace. I flip it open to find pages filled with elegant handwriting, too curly and extravagant to be modern.

I thumb through the pages. There's a page or two per creature, and each entry includes basic facts like who they are and what they look like, along with strengths and weaknesses. There's no order to the list, just one creature after another. I stop when I notice a page titled *Harpy.*

Winged death spirit. Giant hawk with the head of a woman. Extremely violent. Fond of torturing victims before consuming them alive.

Ick. There's a sketch of a harpy in the bottom right corner, complete with empty black eyes and sharp, curved talons.

The next page has a drawing of a spider with ten legs covered in long hair, two of them held above its head like antennae. A pair of extremely large jaws protrudes from its mouth. At the top of the page are the words *Solif Spider.*

The size of a dinner plate. Runs at speeds of up to thirty mph. Can jump up to five feet. Victims report hearing a shrill scream before attack. Highly aggressive. Will typically aim for the neck. Venom is not poisonous, though bite can leave large wound.

A giant, screaming, jumping spider. That's about the most terrifying thing I can possibly imagine. Awesome.

I flip back to the front of the book and notice a signature at the bottom left of the inside cover.

Maxwell, founder

Everything goes blurry except for those two words. Max created this book? Max, my father?

I fan the pages, studying the drawings with new eyes. They're elaborate and detailed, more than just quick sketches—these are realistic, careful representations. I turn to his signature again and run my finger across it.

My father was an artist. A truly gifted artist.

I hug the book to my chest and smile, savoring a moment of connection with a man I will never know. My father was an artist, and so am I. One more thing I can be sure of.

I read the pages in the order they were created, stumbling across terrifying creatures like banshees and chimeras tucked between more pleasant entries such as pixies, unicorns, and hobbits. I study the facts and drawings until my eyelids grow heavy, and scoot further down the couch until my head rests on the pillow. When I close my eyes again, the centaur is gone, replaced by a slideshow of hand-drawn creatures and scripted handwriting.

Seth knocks on my door the next morning as I pull my black T-shirt over my head. When I step out of the bathroom, he's standing by the couch, eyeing the wrinkled throw and sunken pillow. His hair is more chaotic than usual, but it works on him. Everything works on him. The messy hair, the light stubble on his jaw, and definitely that yellow button-up shirt with the rolled-up sleeves. I run my fingers through the still-damp waves of my hair and say, "I had a hard time sleeping last night."

"Me, too." He grabs Max's book from the table where I'd left it, upside down, opened to the page where I'd stopped reading. "After everything you saw yesterday, you chose this as your nighttime read? No wonder you couldn't sleep."

I pluck the book from his hands. "You didn't tell me Max was an artist."

Seth grins, and I'm so grateful for his smile. "Who do you think painted the map in the lobby?"

"He painted, too?" My father was an artist. He loved the things I loved. Warmth spreads through my chest and down my body.

"Different mediums." He drops his chin and looks me in the eye. "Just. Like. You."

I smile, unable to say or do anything else. All these things make my father more real, like he was someone I would've loved, if I'd had the chance. Maybe even as much as Mom and Sam.

I set the book on the table and look at Seth. "After what happened at the lake yesterday, I never heard if there was anything new on Mom and Sam," I say.

The corners of his mouth drop. "Yeah. Let's sit." Seth steps around the coffee table to sit down, throwing the blanket across the end of the sofa. The expression on his face tells me I'm going to hear something unpleasant, and I bite the inside of my lip. I sit beside him, crossing my legs beneath me and pulling the pillow into my lap.

"We found evidence of harpies near the gate where they were supposed to enter the Between," he tells me. "Alexander and I are now certain the harpy yesterday morning was here for you."

"What kind of evidence?" I hug the pillow to my chest and brace myself. The bestiary said harpies ate their victims alive, and Clara had called them messy eaters. I try not to imagine what might be left behind, but it's useless.

"Nothing to make us think Adele and Sam are dead, Charlie," he says quickly. "At this point we think they're being kept somewhere."

I close my eyes and exhale into the pillow, overcome with relief. They're alive. Probably.

Definitely.

They're definitely alive.

But why? I saw the harpy yesterday. She could've ripped me to shreds in seconds. Why show restraint with Mom and Sam? "Why would someone keep them? Who? Where?"

Seth turns toward me and lays his arm across the back of the sofa. "Whalen is obsessed with power. Neither Adele nor Sam is particularly useful on their own, but they become pretty valuable if they're important to, say, a muralet." He lifts his eyebrows. "We think he's going to offer you a trade."

My stomach churns. A trade. My family for my blood, like goods in a market. That's all they are to him—a means to an end. They're only worth what they can do for him. They're completely unimportant on their own.

I clench my jaw. He doesn't value them as living creatures. They're bargaining chips.

Not that I'm questioning his ruthlessness after what I saw yesterday. "What about the lake attack? Did you guys find anything else?"

Seth bends his arm and rests his head in his hand, spreading his fingers through his hair. "No. There wasn't much we could do. It'll be a few days before we can remove the bodies. The necrolate has to be gone before we can touch anything. The fairies took care of a lot, though. Alexander helped Clara create a spell to mask the decomposition until we can get everything cleaned up."

I remember the way the fairies flew back and forth across the lake, studying the massacre. "What were the fairies doing yesterday?"

"They sense death," he explains, sitting up straighter and removing his arm from the back of the sofa. "The humans got a lot right in their fairy legends—fairies create life throughout the world with plants of all kinds. But they also play a very important part in death. They're in tune with every step of life's cycle. It comes in handy for the Fellowship when we're searching for survivors or dealing with death of any sort."

"Would they be able to sense Mom and Sam?" I ask. "If they're dead, would the fairies know?"

As soon as the question is out, I can't decide what I want the answer to be. On one hand, I'd know for sure, one way or the other. On the other hand, I'd know for sure, one way or the other.

Do I want to know?

The tremor in my pulse says no.

Seth scoots closer and puts his hand on my knee. "Don't think like that. We'll find them. We have a starting point now. We know they made it to the gate, and we'll track them from there."

He's right. Snap out of it, Charlie. They're alive, and they're going to stay that way. If the harpies have them, there must be a way to track them. I lean against him, resting my head on his shoulder. "Do we know how the harpy got inside Ellauria?"

Seth lies back on the couch again, taking me with him. He rests his feet on the coffee table, and I rest my feet on his legs. "Something's messing with magic, affecting some of the older sorcery. There've been too many breakdowns in spells lately. The fairy rings, the gates, even the transport of your art supplies from the mortal realm to Artedion," he says. "It's probably a first- or second-year Apprentice, one smart enough to read magic, but not skilled enough to actually control it."

I go back to what Seth said about having a starting point. My brain starts putting thoughts together and coming up with plans, and I give myself a moment to let it work. "If we figure out where the harpy entered Ellauria," I say slowly, "we could trace it back to where it came from. The Aegises in the mortal realm can trace from their side, and we trace from here."

The plan of action reenergizes me, lifting me off the sofa. This will work. I jump to my feet and start pacing. I talk with my hands, firing off words. "We'll be coming at them from both directions. We'll find them twice as fast."

"Charlie." Seth shakes his head. "You can't be involved."

I spin around. Aegis or not, if he thinks I'm going to stay in my room and draw while my mom and brother are out there being held hostage by a madman and his harem of harpies, he is out of his mind. I have to make this right. This begins and ends with me and my connection to the people I love. They've given up enough for me already. I can sacrifice some things for them, too.

"This isn't about protecting me," I tell Seth. "It's about saving my family. If I figure out a way to find them, I'm doing it."

Seth flies off the couch. "You. Can't." The harshness of his tone silences us both for a second. When he speaks again, his voice is fierce. "Apprentices don't do that kind of work. You can't stand out any more than you already do. It's not just monsters like harpies and the Mothman, Charlie. You don't understand the lure of your blood and what some creatures would do to have it."

His nostrils flare and he stops talking, staring at the floor. When he calms down, he looks back at me. "You're having some kind of overactive guilt complex right now, but none of this—*none* of it—is your fault. I can keep you safe from anything in the mortal realm. But here? If the wrong creature realizes what you are, you're dead." He snaps his fingers. "Like that."

A chill tiptoes up my spine. It's not that I don't understand the threat. I know what happened to the muralets. I know what Marian went through to keep me from all of this and what Seth is trying to accomplish by tying me up with fear.

I also know, no matter what he says, Mom and Sam wouldn't be in this situation at all if it weren't for me. Their only mistake is being loved by a muralet. If they didn't know me, they'd be safe. I swallow and take a deep breath.

"I'm as responsible for them as you are for me. Can't you see? They're out there because of me, and I'm doing nothing."

Seth shakes his head and clutches my upper arms. "You're not alone in this," he whispers. His eyes shine, and I realize his concern is about more than me. He's determined to find them, too. "I swear the Fellowship will find them. I'll bring them back to you."

My chin trembles, but I know he'll do everything he can. He loves them. I have to remember that. "I know I'm not alone. They are family to you, too."

He drops his hands from my arms. "Come on. Let's get out of here."

I drag my fingers under my eyes. Why did I even bother to put on mascara today? Have the last two days taught me nothing? "Where are we going?"

"We've got a little time before Alexander will be looking for you." He laces his fingers through mine. "You need to see something good. Close your eyes."

"Charlie?"

"Hmm?" My nails dig into his arms.

"You can look now," Seth says against my forehead.

I squint open one eye and then the other before slowly releasing my grip and easing away from him. I stretch my fingers as I lower my hands. This flicker was longer than the others, and I sway a bit on my feet. I grab Seth's forearm to steady myself. "Where are we?" I ask.

He raises his eyes and makes a sweeping gesture with his hand. "The edge of Ellauria. This is the Wisteria Tunnel."

Wisteria. Twisted vines arch over our heads, each one dripping with cascades of flowers and creating stripes of pastel colors that stretch the entire length of the tunnel. White. Blue. Purple. Violet. Pink. An intoxicating sweetness hangs in the air. It's straight out of a fairytale.

And I don't have my sketchbook.

"What is it?" Seth asks.

I frown at him. "You're supposed to tune me out, remember?"

He smiles with his lips closed. "Sorry. I forgot. I told you it'd be an adjustment."

I nudge him and smile. "I'm just sad that I don't have my sketchbook. This place is gorgeous."

He tips his head down to mine and whispers, "I'll bring you back."

All my thoughts scatter when his breath mingles with mine. I open my mouth to say something, but I have no words–at least, none I feel brave enough to say just yet. I could go on and on about his lips and his eyes and the way his smell makes me want to bury my nose in his chest, but I won't.

"Shall we?" He holds out his arm, and I close my mouth.

Pull yourself together, Charlie.

I curl my hand around his elbow as we tread beneath the flowering vines.

I try to watch Seth without watching him, admiring the way he moves. Every now and then I sneak a direct glance at his face, and I catch his eyes before they dart in a different direction.

It's quiet and peaceful here, like Seth and I are the only two people in the world. It's easy to forget that there's anything else at all–nothing to cry over, nothing to fear. Just sweetness and splendor, created by the very hands that created me. I run my hands along the blooms and bring my fingers to my nose, inhaling their scent. Seth watches me and smiles when I catch him.

"I knew you'd like it," he says.

Of course I do. I could fill an entire sketchbook with drawings of this place alone. Colored pencils would work. They'd capture the variance in the pastels completely.

When we've walked so far that I can't see either end of the tunnel, I pull on Seth's arm to make him stop, and he turns to face me. "I needed this," I tell him.

Seth nods, looking upward. "So did I."

He pulls a long strand of violet wisteria from the vine over his head and loops it around my wrist. It's so silly and perfect it makes me giggle, and he smiles. My laughter fades, and neither of us find words to fill the silence. I look from his eyes to his lips.

His very soft-looking lips.

Something shifts in his gaze, and there's a gleam, a tiny spark of life that tells me he's still tuning in. The fact that he knows is both exhilarating and terrifying. I want him to kiss me, but I want it to be his idea. Now, I feel like my emotions are making the first move.

Stop looking at his lips.

Don't look at his eyes, either.

Just stop looking at him altogether.

My eyes dart to the wall of flowers beyond his shoulder, and Seth laughs softly. He trails the backs of his fingers from my shoulder to my wrist, and then pinches my shirt at my waist, pulling me closer. My heart beats faster, so much that I'm sure he can feel it. I watch my hands slide up his arms like they have a mind of their own. They move across his shoulders and drift to his chest.

His other hand cups my chin and tilts my face upward as he dips his head closer. When his lips are a breath from mine, he stops. He looks at me, silently asking permission, and I nod. His eyes are mostly closed. His lips part, and he freezes. He blinks, and his forehead creases before he drops his head and backs away.

No. Not again.

I know he was going to kiss me; I may not be an empath, but I know he wants to. What's stopping him?

"Seth?"

When he raises his head again, he looks so lost I can't decide if I want to hug him or wring his neck for bringing his lips so close to mine without sealing the deal.

I step toward him, then change my mind and take another step back.

"Forget it," I say. It's the second time he's pulled away from me in two days. I can take a hint.

"Charlie."

"It's fine." I feel my blood pressure rise as heat branches out from my chest throughout my body. Oh no. I'm about to start saying stupid things. "I don't know why I keep getting so flustered around you. And I get that it's weird for you or something." The words come faster and faster. *Oh my God, Charlie, shut up.* "It's just sometimes it seems like you want me close and sometimes you don't." *Stop talking. Just. Stop. Talking.* "But I get it. You're not interested."

Seth flinches. "Is that really what you think? No, Charlie. That's not it at all." He moves toward me again until something behind me catches his eye. His face pales and he croaks, "Alexander!"

I spin around. The enormous founder stands a few feet away with his arms clasped in front of his belt.

"Seth." That's all he says. One word so full of judgment I nearly crumble beneath its weight myself. I glance at Seth, but his eyes are locked with Alexander's.

What's happening here? Seth wants to kiss me, but he doesn't, but I'm wrong, and then Alexander's here, and now I'm pretty sure I'm missing a giant piece of the equation.

"I'd like to take Charlotte to work on her powers now," Alexander says, raising his eyebrows and staring down his nose. Somehow, he appears even larger than normal. "I assume you two are all finished here?"

"Yes, sir." Seth's gaze falls to the ground. "We're finished."

The founder's lips set into a thin line, and he lifts his hand to me, beckoning.

I twist my bracelet around my wrist. Whatever's happening, Seth must be in trouble. I can't tell if I am, as well. Maybe we weren't supposed to be out here. I try one last time, but Seth won't look at me.

I walk to Alexander, my legs quivering with each step. When I reach him, he takes my arm and we disappear.

TWELVE

We land in front of a charming stone cottage that spreads across an open space amid towering pine trees, and the smell of pine is nearly overpowering. The closer we get to the house, the more the scent is replaced by the perfume of flowers. There are magnificent, well-maintained flowerbeds tucked around the sides of the house and surrounding the wooden porch built across the front.

"Welcome to my corner of Ellauria," Alexander says, his tone decidedly more pleasant than it was moments ago.

I follow him up the steps onto the porch. I pause and look back, wondering if he ever sits on his porch and listens to Ellauria the way I used to sit on mine. He pushes open the door and motions for me to enter before him. I hesitate inside the entryway, taking it in. A dimly lit hallway extends in front of me. To my left, there's a small kitchen with a bricked floor. Yellow wooden cabinets stretch across the wall, ending at a large sink. It's weirdly cheerful. I'd sort of imagined him living in a stone building with cement furniture.

Oh my God.

Is there a Mrs. Alexander?

"You live here?"

"Indeed," he replies.

"Alone?"

He stops midstride to give me a look. "Yes, Charlotte. Alone."

"I'd really prefer you to call me Charlie," I tell him.

He lowers his brow. "I will call you by the name your mother called you." He lays his stare on me a moment longer and then disappears through a doorway to my right.

I guess that's that.

I follow after him. Towering bookshelves line three of the four walls, extending from the weathered wooden floor to the top of the lofted ceiling. Each shelf is filled, sometimes two or three rows deep, and even more books sit on top of the exposed beams running across the length of the ceiling. In addition to those, numerous stacks of books rise from the floor throughout the room, serving as makeshift tables and footstools. A couple of oversized reclining chairs sit in the middle of the room. Alexander sits in one. I take the other.

He waves his hand, and a crackling fire materializes in the large stone fireplace. The orange glow lights the left side of his face, and the warmth shines against my right.

I crane my neck to read the titles perched on the shelf across from me. I twist around, eyeing the stacks and weighing the risk of picking up one of the books for a closer look. I glance at Alexander. His eyes are on me, waiting for my full attention. I sit up a little straighter. The bigger the silence gets, the more I'm pushed to fill it.

"Your house is nice," I say. He glances around the room then back to me, and I scrape my mind for anything at all to say. "I like the ceilings. They're very vaulted."

I cringe as the words come out of my mouth. It would be really outstanding if I could stop making a fool of myself in front of this man.

He stares down his nose at me. "Are you aware of the restrictions on romance between Aegises and Apprentices?"

I glance around the room. Did I miss the segue to this particular topic? "Huh?"

He looks pointedly at the wisteria bracelet on my wrist. "You and Seth, back at the tunnel."

My eyes immediately begin a frantic search for anything else in the room to focus on besides his face. The almost-kiss with Seth ranks right up there next to fashion choices on the list of Things I Do Not Want to Discuss with Alexander.

"Romantic relationships are not allowed between Aegises and their Apprentices," he says.

But—

So Seth and I—

We can't—

Oh.

Suddenly all the times Seth's come so close only to pull away make perfect sense. He would never break a rule. Especially one as serious as that.

I'm a weird mix of confused and disappointed. I'm conpointed.

"Do you have any questions about that?"

My cheeks grow hot. Only about a million, but I want answers from Seth, not Alexander. "No."

He leans forward. "And you understand that what I saw at the tunnel—it can never happen again?"

I need this conversation to stop. "Nothing happened. Seth and I have always been close, but he's never crossed any lines." No matter how much I've wanted him to.

"I hope not. It's important that the two of you maintain a professional distance. Understood?"

Professional distance. "Got it," I reply, resisting the urge to salute.

Alexander nods and sits back in his chair. "The appearance of the harpy in Ellauria is concerning. The spells preventing banished creatures from entering our gates should be fail-proof, but over the last week it appears that the strength of the magic has been compromised." He rests his giant elbows on the arms of the chair and clasps his hands together. "There have been a few slips—your interaction with the wind and cloud being one of them—and until we figure out what's behind the disruption, you need to be particularly cautious."

I nod again, remembering the list of magical issues Seth had mentioned earlier. A mix-up with my art supplies seems much less threatening than a malfunction in the mystical realm's borders, and yet they're all connected.

Max had marked several of the banished creatures in his book. I wonder if others besides the harpies and the bogmen are involved. I don't know what Whalen has to offer, but if it's enough to gain a few creatures' cooperation, it could be enough to attract others, as well.

Alexander stands and stretches, then approaches the window. "Now more than ever, it's important that you learn to defend yourself. Muralet blood can be the Fellowship's strongest asset," he continues, "or our worst enemy, depending on who's in control of it."

I clench my teeth. Everyone talks about my blood like it's separate from me, like it's this abstract thing to possess rather than the actual substance that keeps me alive. "Aren't I in control of it?"

Alexander turns, frowning. "Hmm?"

"It's my blood." I pause to let that sink in. "In me."

"Yes, of course. And we need to make sure it stays with the Fellowship."

He's clearly not understanding my point. I get up from my seat. "Me. We need to make sure it stays with *me*. The two are inseparable." I point while I speak, because come on. Understand what I'm saying.

Alexander studies me for a moment before nodding. "We are in agreement."

"Are we?" I raise my voice. "Because it feels like you see me as a source of muralet blood, and I see myself as Charlie Page, who did not ask to be put in this position."

"You are of no use to anyone dead," he scoffs, as if I'm the one who doesn't seem to get it. "Now let's get started."

I rock back on my heels, confused by his abrupt dismissal of the conversation. That's it? I don't like the way he refers to my use, like I'm a resource rather than a living, breathing person. Is it me they wish to keep safe? Or my blood? At what point does my blood become more important to them than I am?

Alexander marches toward the door and I follow, picking apart his words. He's several feet ahead of me when he stops in the grass in front of his house and turns, surveying the area. He looks at me intently and points to a spot on the ground beside him. I hurry to his side.

"Do not move," he orders. He closes his eyes and lifts an arm toward the sky. His voice is low as he recites words I don't understand.

With a sweep of his arm, a translucent veil appears and descends upon us, covering his home and gardens as well as the open space around them. I am, to say the least, amazed. I take a few steps, turning around.

"Complete privacy," Alexander says. "No one can see or hear anything that happens under the shroud."

Everything outside the covering is a bit murky, like I'm looking through water. "Now what?"

He tilts his head to the side. "Look around you. You need to get in the habit of being acutely aware of your surroundings. Your powers are useless if you don't know which elements are at your disposal."

I turn in a complete circle, examining everything. High, low, one way, and then another.

"We'll start with earth," he says, "which includes anything that grows out of it. See the tree growing by the edge of my porch? Study it."

I look to the bright yellow ginkgo tree to the left of Alexander's home. "Okay."

"Now close your eyes and picture it."

The short, ash-colored branches and yellow fan-shaped leaves of the tree appear vividly behind my eyelids. "Got it," I tell him, keeping my eyes closed.

"I want you to pour yourself into that image. Fixate on it. Maintain your focus."

Pour myself into that image? Who talks like that?

My hands curl into fists at my sides, and I rise up on my tiptoes. My muscles are so tense they begin to ache.

"You look like you're in pain," Alexander says.

"I am." I teeter to the side as I open my eyes. "How long am I supposed to do this?"

"As long as it takes."

I certainly hope I'm going to learn the Fellowship's skill of answering questions without answering questions. "I don't understand. With the cloud, I literally had no idea I was doing it. I wasn't focusing. There was no pouring myself into anything."

"Wind is different. You focus on what you want the wind to affect. Your attention was on the cloud blocking your light, and the wind solved the problem." He raises an eyebrow at me. "Try again."

I take a deep breath and close my eyes. The rounded ginkgo appears once more, and I concentrate with all I have.

"Good, good," Alexander murmurs, his voice steady. "Continue."

The rich yellow foliage rustles in my head. I picture the tree at different angles. Above, below, left, right. Mentally, I gaze at the leaves until I almost feel their texture beneath my fingers. Suddenly, a tingling sensation drips onto my fingertips and climbs to my elbows. I open my eyes with a jerk, turning my hands over and staring at them.

"You felt it?" he asks. Alexander's head lifts with the question.

"Yes," I tell him, rubbing my hands together.

Up until this very moment, a tiny part of me clung to the idea that this was all a big mistake. The cloud thing was a coincidence and what I saw at the Source was a trick of the light. They had the wrong person. Marian's daughter was someone else, and my life still had a shot at returning to blissful normalcy.

But now? It worked. I purposely harnessed this power everyone keeps telling me I have—Marian's power, straight from Mother Nature herself.

I spread my fingers over my chest, just below my neck.

I'm the last muralet.

"Again," Alexander says.

I take a breath and clear my head. It doesn't take as long to feel the tingle the second time. I retain the mental image as long as I can stand it, until the tingle turns to a burn, like several tiny bee stings prickling across my hands and wrists.

"Ow!" I jump backward, shaking my hands and scraping them down my sides until the feeling goes away.

"You're trying too hard."

"Your face is trying too hard," I mutter to myself.

Alexander folds his arms across his chest. "As a muralet, you're soaking up magic from your surroundings all the time. There's no need to strain yourself to make use of it."

"Fine," I huff, readying myself again. I close my eyes and pour myself all over that blasted tree. The muscles in my neck begin to ache. I inhale slowly, keeping the tree in my mind's eye, trying to relax.

Nothing.

"Now you're not trying hard enough," Alexander states.

I groan. "I *am* trying."

"Try harder."

"But not too hard."

"Exactly."

I hate him.

He circles around, standing between me and the tree. "There must be balance, Charlotte. Push too hard and the power becomes toxic."

I shake everything out, rolling my neck from one side to the other and straightening my shoulders. I focus, but not too hard. The tingle sweeps through my fingers, and I try to ignore it, concentrating on not concentrating.

The tingle turns to burning, and I clench my fists. Ugh.

We go through several more rounds, and by the time he decides to break for lunch, I'm hitting the painful stinging tingle only about once every four or five tries.

I still haven't done a single thing with it, but at least I'm figuring out how to control the magic. I feel an enormous amount of pressure to live up to the reputation of the muralets before me. I'm certain they had no idea their legacy would be carried on by a newbie with no magical experience whatsoever.

I'm equally certain the mystical realm wouldn't choose such a person as its defense against a supernatural maniac and his lunatic army.

"I have something for you," Alexander says, and then reaches into the folds of his tunic and retrieves a knife. Its handle is covered in smooth leather, long enough to fit in my fist, and the pointed blade isn't much longer. He lays it across his palm and lifts it toward me.

"It will take practice to gain enough control over your power for it to be useful to you. Given what happened at the lake this morning, I'd like you to keep this with you at all times."

I take it from him, turning it one way and then the other. From end to end, the knife can't be more than ten inches long. "Kinda small, isn't it?"

"It's charmed," he says. "It is exactly as powerful as it needs to be."

I examine the blade more closely. "You think I'll need this?"

"I don't want to take any risks when it comes to you, Charlotte," he says. Alexander positions himself beside me and moves his arm in an upward diagonal motion across his body. The transparent shield above our heads shrivels away.

I tuck the knife in my back pocket. "Now what?"

"Seth should be here any minute," he says. "You'll be working with him for the remainder of the day."

The grass twitches, and Alexander swiftly turns his head. A tiny animal with unmistakable ears rests outside the area where the veil had been. Alexander darts toward the fejib, triggering the animal to dash off into the dense forest.

Seth appears near the yellow ginkgo. I watch his posture go from casual to alert as he processes Alexander's rigid stance and my confusion. He jogs toward us. "What's wrong?" he asks.

"I think someone is trying to listen in." Alexander's tone is dark as he tells Seth about the fejib. "It's the second one I've seen this week."

"But why?"

"Perhaps I can be of assistance," a melodic voice answers behind me, and I spin around to see a slender figure floating several inches above the ground.

Long auburn hair drapes loosely over her shoulders and cascades downward in gorgeous waves. The deep blue of her eyes is so brilliant they practically glow. Her long, shimmering gray gown stops at her ankles.

"Marian," Alexander breathes.

THIRTEEN

Marian.

My voice leaves me at the sight of my mother. I can't take my eyes off her face.

"You." The words spill from my mouth before I know what they mean, and Seth's head swivels toward me.

The eyes, the full lips, the soft lines of her cheeks. It's the face I saw in the tree the night of my birthday. The one I'd convinced myself was never there.

"Charlotte," she says warmly.

I close my eyes and breathe it in, savoring the sound of my name on her lips.

This is my mother. My chest lightens. I don't have to do this alone. She's here. She's come back for me. This all started with her. All the questions I've had about who I am and where I came from, what's real and what isn't—she's the only one with all the answers.

And here she is. Alive.

"Marian?" Alexander repeats, louder, more questioning than before. The expression of awe that had filled his face earlier is gone, and his lips are set in a hard line.

Something seems off. The trees behind her are visible through her body. There's no indication that she hears him at all. She smiles at me. "I knew it was you," she says. Her eyes are kind, but her voice takes on a somewhat threatening edge.

I glance sideways, confused. She knew it was me? Seth is instantly at my side. He grasps my elbow and moves in front of me. Marian laughs merrily, and then her face goes dead. The loving gleam in her eye vanishes. When she speaks, dozens of voices ooze from her mouth. "You won't be able to protect her forever."

"Seth?" I press my nose into his shoulder and stare at Marian from behind him. This can't be right. This can't be the woman who sacrificed everything to keep me hidden. My stomach flutters.

"It's not her," Seth murmurs, keeping his eyes on the floating figure before us. "It's a parallel. See how she's translucent? It's not her."

Worry by worry, question after question, everything piles back on my shoulders and the heaviness returns. I want it to be her. Torn between disappointment and anger, my hands become fists at my sides. I hadn't gotten to parallels in Max's book yet.

"Leave, parallel," Alexander warns. "You are not welcome here."

"I'm not leaving without the muralet." Not-Marian leans forward, and her voice becomes as thick as gravel. "You can't hide her anymore, Alexander. Whalen has promised her to us."

Seth's hand is wrapped around my waist, holding me against his back. Inch by inch, we move farther and farther from the floating creature with my mother's face.

Alexander raises his arms. "You will never have her." He pumps his fists and a blast of energy booms forward, a round ball of pulsing blue light.

It slams into the parallel and dissipates. She erupts in maniacal laughter. "That's all you've got?"

"Keep your mind blank," Seth orders, his words rushed and urgent.

"Huh?"

"They feed off fear. Don't give her any."

Clear. Clear. Clear. Clear.

It would've been a million times easier if he hadn't said a word. Being told to keep my mind blank is the equivalent of telling me not to breathe air.

Clear. Clear. Clear.

Alexander continues to launch his attack. Swirling gusts of energy wrap around her, sending her hair in all directions. She shrieks over the roar of Alexander's bursts of power. "You are nothing!"

Clear. Clear.

I wish I hadn't read Max's bestiary. I know of far more things to be afraid of than I did before.

Something long and black curls around the trunk of one of the large oak trees behind Marian's shape. I stare at it, watching as another one creeps around beside it, and then another, until a head appears. A head with two large, hook-like jaws moving back and forth.

My heart pounds, drowning out all other sound.

No.

I dig my fingers into Seth's shoulders and whimper.

The solif spider howls and launches itself from the trunk, passing through the parallel and landing in the grass. Its legs barely touch the ground as it runs toward me.

"No!" I try to run, but Seth's arm tightens around me, holding me in place.

"Charlie!"

The parallel's laugh echoes through the trees.

I fight against him with everything I have, throwing all my weight into escaping Seth's grip. "Let me go! It's coming!"

"Charlie!" he grunts, struggling to hold on to me. "There's nothing there!"

I keep my eyes on the spider. It's going to be on me any second now. How far did the book say it could jump? Five feet?

There's not enough air. I can't breathe.

"Seth, please!" I scream.

He spins around and grasps me by my shoulders, shaking me. "Whatever you're seeing, it's not there. This is what parallels do. They bring your nightmares to life."

"No, no," I repeat. Seth's wrong. It's there. I'm looking at it right now. It releases a high-pitched scream and springs into the air.

Without warning, a ball of blue fire flies over my head toward the parallel. Seth throws me to the ground and shields me with his body. I wriggle beneath him, looking for the spider. It was just here. It must've jumped past us. It'll be back any second. I try to get up, but Seth's hand presses against me.

"Stay down!" he shouts. A second flame passes over our heads.

"Where's the spider?" I shriek. "Where is it?"

My entire body shakes, and I grab handfuls of my hair, yanking it. Where's the spider?

"Charlie!" He bends his head next to mine and puts his eyes directly in front of my own. "Look at me. Don't let her do this to you. There! Is! No! Spider!"

He's wrong. There's no way the spider wasn't real. I turn my head to the side, peeking through Seth's arms. Alexander's eyes are on something behind me, and he shouts, "Beneath her feet! You must aim for the empty space!"

Another sphere blazes through the air, lower than the others. I feel a wave of heat rush over me, and I raise my head enough to watch the fire connect with its target, perfectly centered in the vacant area beneath Marian's figure. The flame explodes upon impact and spreads upward. Before shattering into pieces, the parallel shoots a look of pure evil at the source of the fire. There's a series of loud pops, then nothing.

The wind dies down. Alexander bends over, resting his hands on his knees. Seth breathes heavily as he moves away from me and stands. I flip onto my back and sit up, gasping for air.

The spider's gone.

I nearly collapse with relief.

It really wasn't there?

Seth stares past me and says, "You've got to be kidding."

I jump to my feet, adrenaline pumping, fully expecting to see a solif spider. Instead, I see Keiran, his dark gray shirt drenched in sweat. His shoulders heave as he tries to catch his breath. When he realizes I've spotted him, he nods and lifts his hand in an exhausted wave. His palm is black with soot.

What's he doing here? I stare at him, then look to where the parallel had been. The balls of flames had flown over my head from behind. Elves create weapons. Keiran seems like a weapon all on his own. "It was you?" I ask. "You threw the fire?"

"Thank you, Keiran." Alexander smiles with his eyes. "You performed beautifully."

Keiran looks from me to Alexander and nods. "You're welcome, sir."

Seth points at Keiran. "You. You're not really an elf."

Keiran points back, like Seth's won a prize. "You are correct."

He's not an elf?! Unduckingbelievable. I slam my hands against my thighs. "Is anyone here who they say they are?"

"Well, technically, you're not even who you say you are," Keiran replies, walking closer.

Alexander raises a hand and steps forward, silencing us. "Keiran was acting under my advisement."

"We're letting flamethrowers in Ellauria now?" Seth helps me to my feet. "Since when?"

"It was as important to hide Keiran's identity as it was to hide Charlotte's," Alexander replies, then adds, "You don't know everything, Seth."

I've been telling Seth that for years, but hearing it from Alexander seems like a blow. Seth's eyes immediately fall to the ground before landing back on Keiran. "Who are you?"

Keiran glances at Alexander, who nods his consent. He hesitates, locking eyes with me for a moment, and says, "I'm Whalen's son."

Every muscle in my body tightens, and I instinctively step backward. Seth grabs my wrist, pulling me backward and placing himself between Keiran and me.

"You're afraid of me?" Keiran peers at me over Seth's shoulder, his expression incredulous. "If I wanted you dead, I would've hit you with a fireball just now and played it off as an accident. Or I would've killed you on the tour yesterday as soon as we were alone."

I narrow my eyes. Is this supposed to make me feel better? To know how easily he could have killed me any number of times?

Seth stares Keiran down, keeping his shoulders and chest high as though he expects Keiran to attack at any second. "Whalen has a son?" he asks.

"Yes." Alexander wipes his hands down his sleeves, dusting grass and debris from them. "After he was banished, Whalen took up with a group of flamethrowers. There is no need to be aggressive, Seth. Keiran is not a threat to us."

Seth's stance doesn't change. His reluctance to believe Alexander only fuels my confusion. Since when does Seth question anything about the Fellowship?

Alexander steps forward. "Keiran has been working for the Fellowship for two years. The intelligence he's provided us has been invaluable. You remember when we learned Whalen had developed the ability to spout necrolate from his hands?"

Seth nods, and Alexander tips his head toward Keiran.

I remember the yellow glow of the lake water. "He spouts it from his hands?" I ask. "I thought he'd been stripped of his powers."

"He was, but we have no control over creatures who may bestow magical gifts on him. The bogmen passed along some of their powers to him."

I twist my fingers together. "Powers can be gifted?"

"It's rare. Principal Command forbids the practice," Seth replies, "but creatures with high levels of magical skill can share powers."

I cover my mouth with my hand as my stomach rolls. The man obsessed with finding me can literally throw death from his fingers. Instant death.

I can throw a little air around and sort of make a tree branch shake.

I'm going to throw up.

"Keiran is an asset," Alexander says, placing a hand on Keiran's shoulder. "We are lucky to have him."

An asset. Like me.

Because we are nothing if we're not useful.

"I can't believe Whalen had a son and I'm just now finding out about it," Seth says, shaking his head slowly.

"You were busy with your own assignment, Seth," Alexander states.

"My assignment," Seth says quietly, staring into the trees. Me. I'm his assignment. His gaze drops to the ground before he lifts his head and asks, "What about Keiran? Is he someone's assignment?"

"I will take care of Keiran, as I have for the last two years," Alexander responds, and then directs his attention to me. "Seth is fully capable of keeping you safe, and with his powers, Keiran will serve as your protector as well. Having said that, if there is ever a time when you feel like you are in danger, I expect you to use your best judgment."

My legs tremble, itching to run. I don't know who to trust at all. Every time I think I've figured it out, something new throws my world off-kilter.

Keiran is still watching me. "You don't need to be afraid of me," he says, more hurt than offended. "Whatever you think you know about Whalen, it doesn't mean anything about me."

I don't know how to feel. Whalen's name paralyzes my thoughts and replaces them with images of death. The idea that Keiran—charming Keiran with the sweet smile and beautiful everything—could be any part of Whalen leaves me numb.

When we heard the necrolate explode on the lake, Keiran shielded me immediately. For a split second, I wonder about our proximity to the attack. Could Keiran have had anything to do with it?

No. The anguish on his face at the sight of yesterday's massacre was unquestionable. He was horrified. As soon as he saw the water, he must have recognized the necrolate. And he ran toward it, looking for survivors.

I tug on the ends of my shirt, watching Keiran shift from one foot to the other. I know I'm more than my bloodline, but is he?

I swallow hard and look at Alexander. "Does Keiran know everything?"

Alexander nods. "He knows about Sam and Adele, yes."

I turn to Seth. "Are you picking up any emotions from him that lead you to think he's a threat?"

Seth's jaw shifts, and he stares hard at Keiran. Keiran stays perfectly still, staring right back. After several seconds, Seth exhales and his shoulders slump. "No," he says reluctantly. "Nothing like that."

"And he can't hide his emotions from you, right?" I study Keiran's face while I talk to Seth. "He can't cover his emotions?"

Seth's chest rises and falls. "No. I see through all of that."

I feel my entire body relax a bit. "Okay then."

Seth's hand hasn't left my wrist, still gripping me tightly. I twist my arm a bit, and he glances at it like he's forgotten he's holding me at all. He releases me immediately.

"Very well," Alexander says. "Given the events of the last three days, we need to move things along with Charlotte as quickly as possible. She can't follow the same schedule as other Apprentices. Her powers need a lot of work, and she needs to know everything we know about Whalen."

"I can do that," Seth says with a nod, but Alexander shakes his head.

"No. I want you in front of the mirrors as much as possible, searching for Adele. If she shows up in a reflection, you can't miss it."

Seth releases a quick breath. "But–"

"And Sam," I butt in.

Alexander's eyebrows lift. "Excuse me?"

I set my jaw in place and hold my arms tight. It's one thing to say Sam's not a priority in front of the entire Fellowship. It's another to say it when every person here knows who he is to me. "Searching for Adele *and Sam*," I repeat, enunciating every word.

"Yes, of course, and Sam," Alexander says harshly, as if I'm insulting him by insinuating otherwise.

He's not an afterthought. He's my brother. He may not be a high-ranking member of the Fellowship, but that's because he's never been given the chance.

Seth steps toward Alexander and points at me. "I'm her Aegis. How do I protect Charlie if I'm in Central Hall all day?"

Alexander lifts his hands. "Finding Adele means finding Whalen. Finding Whalen is the key to Charlotte's safety. In the meantime, she will split her time between you and Keiran." Keiran's head snaps up, and Alexander continues, "Keiran will take the lead on her powers, because of his experience with his own active elemental power. He and I have been studying the other elements, and I will guide his instruction. He will teach her everything he knows about Whalen. You will train her on mission work."

Seth opens his mouth, but Alexander cuts him off. "This is not open for discussion."

Keiran stands a little straighter. "We'll need a safe area to train in."

"You're welcome to use this area around my house. I can create a shroud here like we used earlier," Alexander says, gesturing at the vacant area behind him. "Aside from that, we can determine which areas will be best to practice each power, and you must take care to ensure no one sees you."

I close them out, listening to the blood rush in my ears. Every part of me is stretched tight, held together by my thin veil of control. Muscles I didn't even know I had are aching, spent from today's work but fueled with adrenaline. I hover between fight and flight, and all I really want to do is sit on my front porch and listen to Sam pluck his guitar. I close my eyes, listening to his chords in my mind.

"It's settled," Alexander announces. "Keiran and I will go to Central Hall to record the encounter with the parallel and review our security situation. I want to pinpoint the breakdown. We need to identify where these creatures are getting in. Seth, I imagine Charlotte needs to rest after the work she's done here today."

Yes. Charlotte needs to rest. She needs to go to sleep and wake up and find this is all one big ridiculous mix of dream and nightmare.

Keiran steps toward me and Seth shifts, blocking his way. I touch Seth's arm. I want to give Keiran a chance. If I'm going to expect everyone to treat me as a person separate from Marian, I need to treat Keiran as something besides Whalen's son. We all deserve an opportunity to show who we are, regardless of our histories. "You said you're not picking up on anything bad from him," I remind Seth. "Let's just take it a step at a time."

Seth presses his lips together, but he moves. Keiran's eyes meet mine, and the gratitude there convinces me he deserves a chance.

"I'll find you later and we'll figure out where to start with your powers," Keiran says.

"Sounds good," I tell him, and Seth grunts behind me.

Alexander nods. He and Keiran step together and disappear.

I exhale, staring at the vacant space. There's something purple in the grass and I step closer, picking up the strand of wisteria that must've fallen from my wrist when the parallel was here. I wind it over my arm again. When I turn, Seth's eyes are already on me. "You okay?" he asks.

"I have no idea."

He pulls me close, and I rest my forehead against him, enveloped in his warmth. "I'm going to take you to my place, okay?"

I nod against his chest, and we vanish.

Seth's house smells like his shirts—grass and sunshine. The light-brown sofa in front of me is a shade or two lighter than the chocolate hardwood floors. There's a window seat, shelves filled with books, and paintings on the wall.

My paintings.

The huge watercolor I gave him a couple years ago, of the pond beyond the barn at our house. A framed drawing of the stars that form The Big Dipper as I used to see them from my bedroom window at night. A rough sketch of Seth and Sam from behind, sitting side by side in the grass in our front yard.

All mine. All here. I walk around the room, examining them one by one. "I had no idea you kept these."

Seth's eyebrows wrinkle. "Why wouldn't I have kept them?"

My front teeth dig into my bottom lip, biting back a grin as I take in this gesture that, to him, seems completely natural. It's not just that he kept them. He loved them so much that he surrounded himself with them. I don't even think Mom has this much of my work displayed around the house.

Had. Had this much of my work displayed.

I won't think of her in past tense, but I need to let go of the home I used to know. The sound of the screen door slamming against its frame. The scent of lemons hanging in the air when Mom dusted. Sam sitting cross-legged on his bed, strumming his guitar. Mom curled up on the corner of the couch, reading.

My own room, with every little knick-knack that I thought defined me so well. Every sound. Every smell. Every scene. I close my eyes for a moment and see them all.

Seth stands beside me in front of his bookshelf, and I fight the urge to lean on him. I need to let go of that, too. I'm not going home, and I'll never be with Seth. It'll be easier if I accept that now.

"Hey," he says, keeping his eyes on the books scattered across the shelf. "Earlier, when the parallel showed up..." His voice trails off.

"Yeah?" The last hour held a day's worth of drama. I crawl back through everything that happened, from Keiran to the spider to the parallel.

Her face.

Seth gives me a sideways glance, then turns to study my expression. "It was like you recognized her."

As crazy as seeing a face in a tree had seemed the night of my birthday, nothing seems odd about it now. "Well, I did," I tell him. "I've seen her face before."

His face wrinkles with confusion. "What are you talking about?"

I rub my fingers underneath my eyes and tell him what happened after he went home after our birthday dinner, from the bracelets to the face to Mom coming out to look for us. Seth's expression is skeptical, bordering on complete disbelief. "That's why Sam and I weren't on the porch when the Mothman showed up."

He stares at the ground and rubs his hand over his chin. "And Sam didn't see her?"

"No," I tell him. "She was gone before I could point her out. I thought I'd imagined it."

If I'd known about Marian, of course, I would've recognized her that night. I would've known the face was real, and I would've known it meant something. If I had known about Marian, everything would've been different.

"If you hadn't seen the face, the Mothman could've surprised you..." Seth's voice trails off, and he stares toward the watercolor over his mantle.

I blink. He's right. If I hadn't seen her face, Sam and I would've been sitting on the front porch alone when the Mothman showed up. Mom would've been inside. Who knows if she would've heard anything at all? Even if she had, she couldn't have made it to the front yard in time.

Marian saved me before Adele did.

I press my hand to my chest. She saved me.

Marian risked everything to bring me here when I was a baby. She risked it again by showing her face a few days ago. Both times, she did it for me.

I stare at the curved grain in Seth's dark wooden floor. Have there been other times? Has she been there, watching over me, my whole life? How many times has she saved me without my knowledge?

Seth paces to the other side of the room. "This changes everything. If Marian's coming out of hiding, there's so much more at risk." He stops, pivoting on his feet and staring at me. "What's better than one muralet? Two."

"She'd never show herself to Whalen," I say. She's been in hiding this long. She wouldn't risk it.

He walks toward me until his feet are only inches from mine. "She would if she had to. Think about it. Nothing else has brought her out of hiding in seventeen years—just you."

He holds my gaze until the pieces fall together.

I'm Marian's kryptonite. As long as I'm in danger, she's not safe, either.

Seth's hand goes to his pocket. "I can't put this in PRU. I need to go to Alexander." He tilts his head. "You should rest while I go do that. It won't take long, and when I get back we can figure out this new training plan with you, me, and Keiran."

I wrap my arms around myself, and Seth turns like he's going to leave, then changes his mind and turns back again. He tilts my chin up with his finger and says, "It's going to be okay."

His tender touch on my face is enough to remind me of the way he touched me in the wisteria tunnel. A not-at-all unpleasant chill runs down my neck and across my shoulders. "Alexander told me," I blurt out, like my subconscious has been waiting for the most awkward opportunity to address the Aegis-Apprentice rule. Clearly the most pressing issue right now is how I can't kiss him.

Seth drops his hand. "What?"

"He said the Fellowship forbids us from having feelings for each other." My eyes land on his arms, his lips, his eyes. "Is that true?"

Say it isn't, even if it is. Let's pretend it's not.

His chest rises and falls, releasing a breath like he's been holding it for a lifetime. "I was going to tell you. I couldn't figure out how."

It's more crushing than it should be. I spend as much time arguing with him as admiring him. His constant focus on what's wrong instead of what's right is always going to be a problem. He's never going to be able to separate who we are from what we are. I know that.

Still.

When he's close, I feel better. And I want him as close as he can get.

"So that's that, I guess." I can't decide if I'm angry or hurt or sad or relieved.

He laces his fingers between mine. "Charlie, I–"

"You can't do that." I yank my hand from his with a huff. "That's the problem. You're different here. I never wanted you like this before. You've always been this pushy, overbearing, bossy, infuriating–" I stop as his eyes dance over my face. The corners of his eyes crease, and his lips curve upward. "That's exactly what I mean. Stop looking at me like that. You can't do that."

"Do what?" he asks.

Hold my hand. Pull me to your chest. Breathe against my neck.

I bite my lip. "Don't look at me like you want me. Don't touch me like it's going anywhere."

The smile disappears from his lips. "You're right. I'm sorry. I get close to you and I know what you're feeling and I know what I'm feeling and it's hard not to act on it."

There it is. That's what I need to know. I push off the shelf and move in front of him. "What *are* you feeling? Because I have no idea."

Seth keeps his eyes down like he's afraid to look at me. I walk forward until I'm standing between his legs, leaning against him. His hands move to my hips, holding me there. He lifts his gaze, looking at me through his eyelashes, and I decide I'm an idiot for giving him a list of things he can't do. As far as I'm concerned, Seth can do anything he wants.

"I want to kiss you just to know what it's like," he says quietly.

I close my eyes, committing everything about this moment to memory. His dark eyes. The husky edge in his voice. The way the sun shines through his window blinds and leaves wide stripes of light across our bodies. His fingers resting on my hips.

"But I can't," he whispers, "because once I kiss you, I don't know how I'll ever be able to stop."

I squeeze my eyes shut tighter.

His lips press against my forehead before he flickers away, taking his warmth with him. I don't open my eyes until he's gone.

FOURTEEN

The next morning, Artedion's lobby is packed with Apprentices. They're everywhere—sitting on the sofas near the fireplace, clustered by the bookshelves, leaning against the map—all wearing their aernovuses. My hand flies to my own, stuck to the front of my brown tanktop. Keiran had said he'd meet me here at eight, and it's already five minutes past. He'll be here any second. I ease the door shut behind me so it doesn't loudly announce my entrance and stick to the edge of the room, twisting the ends of my hair around my fingers.

I stand by the map, running my fingertips along it again, looking for more gates. Knowing that I should look for what doesn't belong helps—with that in mind, I shouldn't have so much trouble finding them. I press the tips of my fingers into the tiny golden dots scattered throughout the drawing of Ellauria. A couple beyond the Clearing, five surrounding the lake, two near the library, the four in the Meadow of Music. I memorize them. I'll keep an eye out for them today and sneak back when I find time alone.

An Apprentice with wire-rimmed glasses and a head full of blonde braids brushes past me, and I concentrate on keeping my eyes on the wall. Eye contact invites conversation, and that's the last thing I want.

It's not that I'm afraid to meet new people.

Well, in a way it is. For one, I don't want to have to explain why I'm not going through the regular training like the rest of the Apprentices. They're doing weekly rotations with every major creature population in the mystical realm, learning typical behaviors and schedules, before they'll move into the more technical stuff with the mirrors and PRU.

But the bigger reason is, so far, I haven't been all that lucky with friends here. Lulu is adorable, but I don't see her much. Clara is clearly a beach, and, of course, Keiran's the son of the freak who started all this.

He appears right then, illuminated by the sunlight from Artedion's open doors, and I watch his eyes search the crowd. I lift my hand and Keiran smiles, but it's not the million-dollar one. It's close-lipped and dimple-free, and the fact that any part of his light has gone out makes me feel guilty for thinking the freak thing.

I make my way to him, and he does the same toward me. Heads turn as he presses through the crowd, and he doesn't release a single wink or "Hello, Beautiful."

Great. Keiran's broken.

"Hey," he says when he reaches me.

"Hi." I don't know how to act. I feel extremely close to and far from him at the same time. We've both been defined by our secrets, labeled by what rather than who we are, but it's what we are that's the problem. I'm a muralet, and he's the flamethrower son of the man who wants to kill me.

Except he's also Keiran, my friend—the guy who calls me "Freckles" and makes me laugh at every opportunity.

How do I balance the two?

"What's that?" he asks, nodding at the bulge on my hip.

My hand lands on the knife there, encased in a leather case. "Alexander gave me a knife yesterday."

Keiran nods. "That's good. You never know when you might need it."

We step out of Artedion and pause at the top of the steps. "Alexander wants to move you along pretty quickly," he says. "I thought we'd start by the far end of the willows and mess around a little. Nobody lives out there, so it's usually pretty empty."

He won't look at me.

I can't do this. I'm already exhausted from spending yesterday afternoon with Seth, pretending not to care that he and I can't be a "we," then feeling ridiculous since there's no point in pretending anything around Seth. He didn't acknowledge my emotions at all, and I can't decide if that makes it better or worse.

Duck it. I can't spend today pretending Keiran and I are okay when it's so obvious we aren't.

I'm tired of the charade.

"I don't know what to do to make things normal," I tell him.

Keiran shakes his head and stares at the ground. "I shouldn't have tried to be your friend. I knew you were eventually going to learn who I am. It was dumb."

"It wasn't dumb." I pull him down the stairs and away from Artedion. "Look, yesterday was a shock. I don't really have many friends here, and to find out you're..." There's no good way to finish that sentence, so I don't. "I just wasn't prepared. But Alexander obviously trusts you. There's no way he'd leave us alone together if he thought I was in danger."

He exhales sharply, laughing but not really. "I don't want you to trust me because Alexander does. I want you to trust me because you're sure of *me*."

I don't know how to tell him my capacity for trust is shrinking with every second I spend in the mystical realm. Nothing is as certain as I want it to be, and I can't seem to get a handle on how I feel about anything anymore.

"How can you expect that of me?" I ask. "I'm not sure of who you are. I'm hardly sure of who I am."

He shrugs. "It's not an expectation. It's a goal. I'll keep working until you're sure."

I twist my hair around my finger. "I'm not giving up on you. I want to trust you," I tell him. "Being Whalen's son doesn't make you inherently evil any more than being Marian's daughter makes me exceptionally magical."

He wrinkles his nose. "No, that's probably the worst analogy you could make. Being Marian's daughter actually does make you the most powerful thing in the mystical realm. Good effort, though."

A smile tugs at the corners of my mouth as soon as I hear the teasing tone in his voice, and Keiran gives me the swoony grin that makes girls go stupid. There's something about him that reminds me of Sam, and if there's anything I'm sure of right now, it's the comfort I find in my brother, and how much I need him to be here.

"Charlie," he says, "if I wanted to hurt you, I would've by now."

I'd thought about that very thing all night. He knew when we left my room for the lake that no one knew where I was going or who I was with. We were alone in that dark forest, and all he did was show me a gate, introduce me to petits, and keep me from falling.

"I don't know if it means anything, but," he takes a deep breath and settles his blue-gray eyes on me, "I swear I will never, ever hurt you. I'm not him."

I search his eyes for any sign of deception, but all I see is softness. He wants me to believe him.

I want to believe him.

I want to trust him.

Keiran tips his head toward the path, and we head for the end of the willows.

On the far end of the forest, opposite the Meadow of Music, an old, crumbling stone staircase stretches upward into nothing. It stands right off a narrow dirt path that winds through and around the side of the forest, simply rising into mid-air and stopping. Keiran takes a seat on the steps, and I sit beside him.

"Okay." He claps his hands together. "What'd you and Alexander work on yesterday?"

"I made some tree branches shake."

He waits like I'm going to say more, and when I don't, he snorts. "That's it?"

My cheeks flush. Is his tone entirely necessary? "It's harder than it looks. I'm new to this, you know."

"All right." He rubs his hand over his mouth and chin. "Let's start with something basic. Air. We don't have to worry so much about being seen with that one anyway. Nobody will know you're the one making the wind blow. Alexander said you had some experience?"

I shrug. I wouldn't exactly call accidentally moving a cloud "experience." It's not like I have any idea how to do it again. Keiran steps around me, and I circle, keeping my eyes on him while he talks.

"The thing to remember is that all of these elements," he gestures to our surroundings, "they're waiting for your word. You don't need to force them to do anything. They want to."

It's a variation on what Alexander had said yesterday. Try hard, but not too hard. Command, but don't force.

"My word?" I ask. "Do I talk to them?"

Keiran squints and rubs a finger over his eyebrow. "Maybe I should've said your 'will.' The point is, they're yours. Each of them has a different dialect, but they all speak your language. Yesterday, Alexander had you focus on the tree to shake it, right?" I nod, and he continues. "Right. So for earth, you focus on the object you want to command. With air, you can't really see it. So you focus on what the air is supposed to do. Focus on the object that will be affected by the air."

Alexander said the wind pushed the cloud because I wanted the cloud out of the way. "Okay. I think I get it."

"Let's give it a shot." He turns his head, surveying every direction, and shrugs. "Nobody's around. You can pretty much do whatever you want."

I think that's the first time I've heard those words since I set foot in Ellauria.

I study every single thing around me, considering the impact air could make on each of them. Flutter the grass. Blow dust from the path. Rattle the leaves. Whip through my hair.

"What are you doing?" Keiran asks.

"I can't decide."

"Oh, good grief. You're such a girl."

It's always bugged me when someone says that to me like it's a bad thing. "Yes, I am a girl. Thank you for noticing, *flamethrower*."

The word slips out before I have time to wonder if it's something I can tease him about. If he's going to state the obvious about me, I don't see why I can't do the same about him.

"Yes," he says. "I'm the flamethrower who saved your ass yesterday."

I fold my arms and give him my most unimpressed look. "You're also the guy who lied to me for two days before that."

He lowers an eyebrow. "If I lied, so did you."

He has a point. I roll my eyes.

"He wasn't always like he is now, you know," Keiran says quietly, keeping his eyes on the ground. I don't have to ask which "he" Keiran's referring to. "When I was little, I didn't know anything about this. He was just Dad. He was strict, but he wasn't a bad guy. We used to talk. He'd play with me, he'd laugh with me—he was almost like any dad should be."

I chew on the inside of my lip. How can I respond to that? I know Whalen is his father, but it's so strange to think of him as a dad. I picture a young tow-headed boy with gray eyes playing with the man I'd imagined as a monster.

"How'd you end up here?" I ask.

He shrugs. "Everything changed when I got my powers. At first he thought I wouldn't have them at all. You never know how the powers will work out with hybrids. But when I was ten, the flames started." He stares across the path and into the trees. "After that, he hated me more and more. He lost everything when he was stripped of his powers—his home, his family, his status—and he blames the Fellowship for that. To him, magic is the enemy. I became the enemy."

Adele's not my real mother and Marian didn't trust she could keep me safe, but I've never felt unwanted. I can't imagine being hated by someone who brought me into the world.

"So you left?"

Keiran studies his hands. When he speaks, his voice is so quiet that I struggle to hear. "He said he'd kill me. I left before he could."

My mouth falls open. Whalen didn't just want Keiran gone, he wanted Keiran dead. His own son. I place my hand over Keiran's and squeeze. "I'm so sorry."

"I guess I thought he'd come looking." Keiran pauses every few words, like each sentence is a struggle to say out loud. "I miss having someone care about me. I miss having a dad."

I close my eyes. He could've pulled the words straight from my head. I miss having a mom—someone to take on my joys and sorrows and love me unconditionally. I'm not sure if unconditional love is a thing Keiran's ever known. Mom would never stop looking for me. I'm as sure of that as I am that I will never stop looking for her. I steel myself against my tears. They're not going to help Keiran.

"I care about you," I tell him. "You're my friend."

He is as lost as I am, struggling to cope with an unfair birthright. Mine makes me mystical royalty; his designates him as an adversary of the Fellowship. Like Seth said, I feel responsible for things beyond my control. I see that in Keiran, too. Neither of us asked for this, but here we are.

Keiran's nose reddens and his head drops. If he cries right now, I will burst into tears right along with him. When he lifts his eyes to mine, I see my reflection glistening there. "Thank you. It's nice to finally have someone to talk to."

I smile at him. I know exactly how he feels. Seth knows what I've gone through, but Keiran knows how I *feel*—not because he can sense my emotions, but because he's lived them. We're both trapped on paths that were set for us a long time ago.

He takes a deep breath, puffing up his chest, and releases it. "Okay. We need to get to work."

Work. Right. I pull my hand from his.

Air.

My gaze lands on the tall grass lining the edge of the narrow path in front of us. I focus on it and will it to respond.

Sway.

Flutter.

Dance.

I picture the grass leaning with the wind, gradually bending to the ground as the current grows stronger. A tingle tickles my fingertips. In seconds, a slip of air breezes through, weaving around my ankles and sliding through the grass. Each blade succumbs to it, whipping one way and, when I ask it to, falling the other way as well.

I bite my lip, grinning. It's nothing like the tree yesterday. Air is far easier. It seems so eager to please.

I look to Keiran, and the wind dies. "It worked."

He chuckles. "Of course it worked. Want to do it again?"

We spend the next hour making our way through Ellauria, stopping when the coast is clear and calling upon the air.

I keep an eye out for anything that looks out of place—an elaborate stairway made of tree roots tucked in the Clearing's far corner, a trio of red pine trees standing amid tall green ones, an arch of sunflowers growing behind the library—and make a mental note to check them out as possible gates later.

But mostly, I focus on the air. I want it to go in one direction, and it does. I call for it to switch, and it changes. It ebbs and flows at my will. For the first time, I feel like the powerful creature everyone keeps saying I am. This is nature, and I'm controlling it. At one point, I make air whistle through the trees, and Keiran applauds. It's incredible.

Incredible, but not exactly useful.

"I love this," I say, following him across the Clearing, "but is it really going to help? If something comes after me, air seems a little weak."

"Well, first, you master each element," he says, "then we'll work on combining them. You can do a lot more than you think. They're good on their own, but when you bring them together, you're pretty unstoppable. Your power is only limited by your imagination."

Unstoppable. There's a word I like. "How?"

"Patience, Freckles. Like I said—you have to nail each one by itself before we can move on to the heavier stuff."

We walk down the hill at the Clearing's edge and through the copper-draped white trees. Past the trees lies a still rose-hued pond dappled with bright green lilies. Keiran stops and waits, watching and listening to be sure we're alone. When he's satisfied, he gestures toward the pond. "Now, water."

I eye the pond.

"It's more like earth," he says, folding his arms over his chest. "Focus on the water; command it."

I walk around the perimeter like I'm planning my attack. I crouch beside it, studying its surface, memorizing its shape, just like Alexander had me do with the ginkgo. I imagine its movements as I study its details, picturing what it will do when I command it.

I stand up and take a deep breath to clear my head. All right, Water. Let's do this.

I stare and wait for the tingle.

And wait.

And wait some more.

I grit my teeth and stare harder. Come on. Move.

"It's not like air. It's not so easy," Keiran says. "Command, don't demand."

I press my fingers to my eyes. Command, don't demand. That belongs on a T-shirt. I lay my neck to one side and then the other and roll my shoulders back, then try again.

Water has a completely different feel to it altogether—it's heavier, and the tingle has a pulling sensation rather than a filling one. It drags across my skin, weighing me down, and I want it gone immediately.

A wave ripples across the water, and Keiran snorts. "Really?"

I wipe my hands down the front of my tank-top and shake everything out. "I don't like that feeling."

The look on his face is completely without compassion. "You're just not used to it. Try again. Let it build, so you'll have more force."

The pull comes again, and I let it tug at me as long as I can stand it. The surface of the pond rolls, and its outer edges turn in a circle, faster and faster, until I feel like I'm being pulled to the ground, like the grass is metal and I'm a magnet, heavy with the water's power.

I let it go, and my shoulders spring upward. It's such a dramatic difference, I have to look at the ground to be sure I'm not floating.

Keiran puffs out his lips and nods. "Better. Again."

My neck and shoulders are already starting to ache. I rest my hands on my hips and blow out a breath. I can do this. It's not going to crush me. The pull is the power. Let it build.

This time, I stand my ground until the pull drowns every part of my body. I'm completely weighed down, heavy with power, and the pond begins to shift at my command.

The water's current circles again, faster and faster, and Keiran calls, "You got it! Keep it going!" I hear his smile without seeing it.

The rotation builds until the outer edges lift from the ground and rise into the air. I feel power pouring through me, rushing from one end to the other and back, over and over. It refills as I hold focus, and the funnel of water grows higher.

Keiran circles around to the other side and whistles. "That is the sexiest waterspout I have ever seen!"

He even flirts with water.

My legs start to tremble, and the ache in my neck grows sharper. Uh oh. The waterspout twists and turns, faster and harder. My knees are about to buckle beneath the pressure.

"I have to let it go!"

"No!" Keiran demands. "Push through!"

Everything hurts, like I'm being stretched in all directions. I'm acutely aware of every joint in my body. "Keiran! I can't!"

"Lame!" he responds.

It happens before I realize what I've done. The funnel bends and topples, crashing into Keiran and dumping a pond's worth of water on his head.

I cover my mouth with both hands and clamp my lips together.

Oh. Sheet.

This is the best and worst thing ever.

"I'm so sorry!" I exclaim, but the giggle beneath my words takes some of the strength out of my apology. His blond hair lays flat against his head and everything on his face is slanted downward, from his eyes to his mouth. He looks like a drowned puppy.

Keiran wipes his face with his hands and pushes his hair straight back. "You look sorry."

"Your hair," I tell him, "is amazing."

He wrings water from his shirt and smirkles. "My hair is always amazing."

"Well," I say, "I guess that ends the water training for the day." I don't even try to pretend I'm sad about it. Water sucks.

Keiran shakes his head. "Not quite. I'm not dry yet."

Psh. Easy. It hardly takes a thought to bring air, and a burst of wind begins weaving around Keiran's body.

"Stop!" he says, pointing a finger in the air. "Not air. Use the water. Return it to the pond."

Ugh. I drop my head back and glare at the sky. Air is so much easier.

My fingers dig into my palms as I focus on the sheen of water coating Keiran's arms. Streams of droplets cling to each other, swirling and lifting from his skin. His green shirt lightens as puddles separate, pulling together and upward. There's a tingling, tugging sensation all over my body. Tiny droplets of water gather and take flight, then fall with a splash into the pond. Within seconds, Keiran is dry.

My hair is going to be so much easier to blow-dry now.

Keiran smoothes his shirt and scratches his fingers through his hair. "Nice! All right. Next up, fire."

"Ha!" He must be kidding. His blank expression assures me he isn't. "Wait, are you serious?"

"Earth. Air. Water. Fire." He drops his chin. "What's the problem?"

I exhale sharply. "The problem is, if I lose control of air or water, all of Ellauria doesn't burn in the process."

Keiran's eyebrows draw together. "You can do it. It's not that hard."

"Not for you. It's part of you."

He shakes his head. "That's what you're not getting, Charlie. It's part of you, too."

I wrinkle my nose. I don't want to do fire. Controlling water was difficult enough. Fire can only be worse.

Keiran pats me on the back, one hard slap between my shoulders. "How about this? I'll skip fire today, but that means you need to impress me with something earth-related."

I squint at him. "Like what?"

"You make a tree drop a branch, and we'll stop for the day."

"Any tree?"

He nods toward a line of trees to the left. They're tall but slender, and their branches aren't very thick.

I tug on the ends of my hair, studying the trees. "It won't harm them, right?"

He chuckles. "No, Charlie. The tree will be fine."

"Deal," I tell him.

I study the trees for a moment, then close my eyes and focus on one of the branches until I feel the power pulsing through my hands.

It takes three tries before I get the slightest movement out of the branch, and even then it's so little I'm not entirely certain it happens at all.

"I think you're forcing it," Keiran says.

I roll my eyes. Of course I'm forcing it. Trees don't move around and shake on their own. Any movement is from my force.

"You need to think of it as a conversation between you and earth. Push a little, then let it push back. Try to get a feeling for how much power it needs. Give a little, wait, and give a little more."

Converse with the tree. I shrug. It's worth a shot.

I lace my fingers together and press my hands outward, stretching my arms. I close my eyes and find the calm, quiet spot in my brain where I can relax to call on my powers. I see the branch in my mind and feel the tingle slide up my hands and over my elbows. I picture the limb bending and open my eyes. I keep pressing it with my power, and then I back off. The tingle drips from my fingers.

"Ugh. I lost it."

"Try again. When I say give a little and wait, you have to find a way to wait without losing your focus. Keep your power engaged without pressuring the tree."

I close my eyes and focus until I feel power climb my arms, then picture the branch bending again. I open my eyes to watch, and this time, I let my gaze slip down the trunk as I draw my power back a bit. I look to the branch again and push some more before backing off. As my eyes travel up and down the tree, I see movement in the top. The branch begins to quiver. I keep my breathing steady and start to work with it again. I bend the branch one way and another in my mind, then release it, giving the tree time to respond. We go back and forth for several minutes, until finally, there's a loud *crack*.

The branch falls, crashing through and landing on a web of branches below.

Keiran hoots, and I throw my arms up in a V. He grabs me and swings me in a circle. "You did it!"

And in this moment, I'm sure of him. The joy in his voice, the pride in his face—this is Keiran, my friend.

He is more than his bloodline, just like me.

"I did it!" I squeal, and my cheeks ache from smiling so big.

I can't wait to tell Seth.

"All right. Do it twice more, and then we'll be finished," Keiran orders, clapping his hands together two times.

My smile vanishes. "That wasn't the deal at all."

"The world's an unfair place. Get going."

It's after two before Keiran and I drag ourselves up to Mesmer. The patio is mostly empty, and I spot Seth leaning against an empty picnic table. He jumps up when he sees us. "You're late."

"A-ha!" Keiran sticks a finger in the air. "But we're here!"

Seth is not amused. Imagine my surprise.

What was awkward yesterday is downright annoying today. The fun, fluttery feeling that keeps showing up when Seth's around is back, but now it's just a thrilling anticipation for something that's never going to happen. It's beyond frustrating, and I have to find a way to make it stop before I lose my mind.

It'd help if he didn't wear shirts that fit him so perfectly. Or maybe stop with the dark, soulful eyes.

Sunglasses. I don't want to see his eyes anymore. He definitely needs sunglasses.

I make a show of how much attention I'm not paying to Seth and head to Mesmer's counter with Keiran. We rest our arms across it and wait. Just like the tables, it takes a second before the whole thing shimmies and two white baskets appear. Keiran grabs them both and hands one to me.

BLT and chips with a cherry Coke—exactly what I wanted.

"Good work today," Keiran says. "Same time tomorrow?"

"Sure!" I smile, plucking a chip from my plate. It's the plan we'd decided on last night. I spend my mornings with Keiran, and Seth takes up my afternoons. He nods and takes off toward Mesmer's exit.

When Keiran's gone, Seth motions toward the tables and I shake my head. I'd rather be in a crowd of Aegises in Central Hall than alone with him right now. "It's fine. I'll eat on the way."

He's already walking toward one of the tables and stops. He waits for a lone pixie to pass before asking, "Why? Eat here."

"No, really." I nod toward the stairs. "I'd rather get going."

"We've got plenty of time," he argues. "Let's sit and talk for a few minutes before we get to work."

Sitting and talking and flirting and feeling. Exactly the kind of things I have to stop doing with Seth. "I don't want to."

Seth sets his lips in a line and stares over my head. "Fine. Let's go."

Round One: Charlie.

By the time we make it to the ground my chips are gone, and I've picked most of the bacon from my sandwich.

"I guess you worked up a pretty big appetite," Seth comments.

"Guess so." I take a sip from my straw. I need to go back to the days when Seth acted like smiling too much would break his face. Less joking, less teasing, more of the annoying overbearing, entirely too opinionated stuff.

Distance. I need distance.

"Working with your powers can take a lot out of you."

"Yep."

He sighs. "Are you going to be like this all afternoon?"

"Probably."

He stares at me a moment and then shakes his head, returning his attention to our walk. "I don't have much of an update on Adele and Sam. There's no sign of them anywhere in the mortal realm, and Alexander has suggested focusing more on the mystical realm."

"He thinks they're here somewhere?"

"Well, not here in Ellauria. But since we know banished creatures have been making it past the gates, it's not completely beyond the realm of possibility that Whalen's gotten past them, too."

There's something comforting in the idea that Mom, Sam, and I are all in the same realm. Like they're closer, without the infinity of the Between dividing us.

On the other hand, I'd like several Betweens to separate me from Whalen.

I study the leaves and branches of the trees as we pass beneath them, searching for lines of a face. Alexander had warned Seth that no one could know that I saw Marian's face in the tree that night, but I still keep an eye out for her.

We approach the library, and Seth reaches around to open the door. I step out of the way. "Go ahead. You don't need to get the door for me."

He squints at me. "Just go inside."

"We're not on a date. I can get my own door."

Seth shakes his head and releases a harsh burst of air, something between a laugh and a sigh. "Suit yourself."

The door closes behind him. I wait a moment, then pull it open for myself. I drop what's left of my lunch in the trash and admire PRU on my way to meet Seth by the stairs. When we reach Central Hall, he doesn't even try to get the door for me.

Round Two: Charlie.

Central Hall is mostly empty, aside from a group of five or six Aegises clustered around a desk on the far side of the room, and of course Justin, sitting at his overflowing desk in the middle. Seth heads toward his table in the opposite corner and hands me a notebook and pencil. "I figured you'd want to take notes. I mean, if that's all right with you." He raises his eyebrows. "Would you rather, you know, find your own notebook and whittle yourself a pencil out of one of the trees or something?"

I take the notebook and pencil and purse my lips. "Shut up."

"Just trying to understand your rules," Seth says lightly, sitting down in his chair. He pulls a page from one of the stacks scattered across his desk and hands it to me. "So here's what's going on today. More spell problems. The elves are having trouble keeping their designs in order, the fairy rings still aren't operating properly, and apparently there were some random issues at Mesmer this morning. The enchantments were off. Some gnomes ended up with vegetable soup for breakfast."

Soup for breakfast? That's all kinds of wrong. I lean against the desk, reading the list of failed spells and weakened powers. I jot them down in my notebook and read over the list. "Still no idea what's messing with the magic?"

He shakes his head. "We're not ruling anything out."

I draw circles next to each item on the list and fill them in, digging my pencil into the paper a little too hard. "If the spells aren't working, could that be why we're having a hard time finding Mom and Sam? Maybe something Whalen's doing to block us is messing up magic."

"It's possible, but all this started a day or two before the Mothman showed up at your house. Right now, it looks like a coincidence," Seth says.

I study the notes I've made, looking for connections and finding none. I tilt my head back to the ceiling while I fan myself with the notebook. My reflection scatters across the wall of mirrors, and I walk toward them.

Oval. Square. Round. Tall. Short. So many different views to choose from. I step toward a silver-framed square mirror on the end, moving forward until my face takes up the entire thing.

Come on. Mom or Sam.

Show me.

But the mirrors aren't going to show an Apprentice anything. I step back and pace across the wall, watching all the reflections at once. Of course, I guess the magic of the mirrors is as prone to weakness as everything else right now.

"Hi, Charlie." Justin's face appears next to mine in the long, oval mirror in front of me. "Are you and Seth doing mirror work again today?"

I smile at his reflection. "Yeah. I'm just waiting for Seth to finish what he's doing."

He smiles back. "We haven't had much action from them today," he says. "Not much going on out there."

Justin can't possibly know how much that statement frustrates me. There's plenty going on out there. My family is missing. Why aren't we getting more from the mirrors? "Have there been any problems with the mirrors?" I ask. "Weakness? Failure?"

His mouth shifts to the side. "Nope. They're all operating as they should be."

Would we know if they weren't? It's hard to notice the absence of something you're not expecting in the first place. If there's a mission to be dealt with and it doesn't show up in the mirror, how would we even know until it's too late?

I wander back to Seth's desk and toss my paper down. "I feel like I'm spinning my wheels and getting nowhere."

He leans back in his seat and looks up at me. "I heard what you asked Justin. That was smart. I don't think anyone's thought about the mirrors yet. And really, how can we be sure if they're working properly or not?"

I smile at him. "Don't act so surprised. I *am* smart, you know. And I wondered the same thing about the mirrors. How would we know if messages aren't coming through?"

"I'll be sure to mention it to Alexander," he says. He lowers his voice and adds, "And I know how smart you are. Your brain's always been one of my favorite parts about you."

The way he smiles at me reignites the flutter.

Those. Freaking. Eyelashes.

"Thanks." Leaning over and kissing his cheek seems like the most natural thing to do right now, and the fact that I can't frustrates me to no end. Instead, I stay put and remind myself he's off-limits.

"I think I want a snack. You hungry?" He pulls open his desk drawer, eyes on me. I'm about to remind him I just had lunch when I see the king-sized package of peanut M&Ms.

It's the most glorious sight of my life.

"Starving!" I cup my hand next to his, and he winks.

"I mean, we're not on a date," he reminds me, and tosses a handful in his mouth. "You find your own snack."

Round Three: Seth.

FIFTEEN

"**A**re we really going to start every practice session like this?" Keiran lowers his shoulders and hangs his head toward me, clearly fed up with my favorite trick.

It's our fourth day of training, and the third I've started like this. "You're glam right we are," I reply. "Deal with it."

I take off running through the field, dragging my feet through the knee-high grass, and Keiran laughs behind me. I lift my arms, gathering the air in my outstretched fingers. I run until I'm in the middle, surrounded by a sea of navy. I spread my arms open wide and concentrate, waiting for the tingle to pour over them. As soon as it starts, I close my eyes and grin, biting my lip.

I love this part.

A breeze flutters over me, barely lifting my hair and fluttering the very tips of the grass. There's a collection of jingles, like a hundred tiny bells ringing, and it grows louder as the wind picks up. I relax, letting the power flow through me, conversing with the air.

I open my eyes and watch as the wind grows stronger, bending the grass and twisting the random bursts of jeweled wildflowers.

"Don't get too crazy," Keiran calls.

I know, I know. Air's the easiest element to hide, but Alexander's warned me more than once not to get too comfortable. I rein it in a bit—if anyone were to come along, they'd just see me enjoying the effects of the breeze on the field. Who's to say I'm the one controlling it?

Each type of flower produces a different tone, until we're surrounded by a symphony of sound. Sam would groan at the ruckus I cause. I bet he'd be able to stir the field into one of his familiar melodies, rather than my haphazard way of creating tunes out here.

I can't wait to bring him here.

My hair whips around my face, and I turn in a slow circle. My chest swells with pure elation.

"All right," Keiran calls, folding his arms. "Time to move on."

I sigh and let go of the air, gasping as the power drains away. The wind dies down and the field goes still, replacing harmony with silence.

"Killjoy," I say, when I'm close enough for him to hear.

"Showoff," he responds, and I laugh.

We head back through the willows. "What are we doing today, professor?" I ask.

Keiran raises his eyebrows. "Fire."

We were supposed to work on fire yesterday, but we couldn't find a place secluded enough to mess around with it. Fire's a hard one to hide. I'm anxious to get started on it. The sooner I master my powers, the sooner I can go after Mom and Sam on my own.

"You found a practice spot?" I ask.

He grins and rolls his eyes downward, which can only mean he's up to no good. "I thought of the perfect place. Nobody's there. Completely uninhabited. Lots and lots of space." He leans forward and whispers, "The Between."

My body tingles. The Between! It's brilliant, actually. He's right. Totally private and all the space in the world. Infinite areas to practice my powers. Maybe we could even go back to the Source. I'd like to experience that connection again, especially now that I have a better handle on my powers.

"You're a genius," I announce, and he bows.

"I know." He points to the lone blue willow tree growing amid the purple ones.

Look for what doesn't belong.

"That's a gate?"

"Yep."

He sweeps the long, hanging leaves to the side with one hand and reaches for me with the other. Slipping into the Between makes me notice just how noisy Ellauria is. The stillness wraps around me like a hug. I feel at home, as much as I can without my family, and I take a moment to appreciate the peace.

"You like it here, huh?" Keiran asks.

I smile. "It's the most breathtaking place I've ever seen."

He glances around and nods. "It's beautiful. Let's get away from the gate a bit. We need to find an open spot for you to practice. Triple score if you see a pond."

Water is a must. The only reason I'd agreed to mess with fire at all was because I've become comfortable enough with water to know that, if necessary, I could use it to extinguish the flames.

The Last Muralet Sets the Between on Fire—I can imagine how well that story would go over.

Seth would be so proud.

We walk along the path, my eyes scanning one direction while Keiran checks out another. Something shines through the thick tree trunks, and closer inspection reveals a tiny green pond with a decent amount of open space around it, surrounded by tall oaks and dotted with sunflowers.

"This'll work," Keiran says. He takes a few steps away from me. "You ready?"

I flex my fingers and crack my knuckles, running through all my pre-game stretches before we get started. There's already a tingle in my fingers, which is odd. I mention it to Keiran, and he nods. "Now that you've gotten used to accessing your powers, you'll notice that a lot. And here in the Between, your powers will be stronger than anywhere else. You draw magic from Mother Nature's designs. The Between is her untouched handiwork."

"Really?" I can't let that statement go by without testing it. Before I take another breath, a broad gust of wind howls through the branches over our heads, and I cover my mouth with my hands. Wow. That would've been a gentle breeze in Ellauria.

Keiran peers upward. "Satisfied?"

I smile and shrug. It'll take a few tries to adjust to the strength of my power here.

"All right. Let's talk about fire." Keiran flips his hand over and a glowing ball of flames appears in his palm. "Alexander drilled me forever on it last night, because fire's so different from the other elements we've worked with. When you control fire, you're interacting with the energy the sun leaves all around you. It's one of the fastest elements at your call, but he wanted me to warn you that it's likely to be pretty exhausting."

Keiran bounces the fireball in his hand while he talks, drawing his fingers upward to balance it on the tips, then flattening them again so it drops back into his palm. He crosses one hand over the other and the flame transfers, and then does the same trick with his opposite hand. It's mesmerizing.

"Now who's the showoff?" I ask with a smile.

He grins, floating the fireball between hands. "Let me enjoy the few minutes I have left of being able to do something you can't."

"How do *you* do it?"

He tilts his head to one side and then the other. "Well, for me, the flames come from inside. True flamethrowers hold flames at their fingertips all the time, so they flick their wrists to pitch it wherever they want. As a hybrid, it works a little differently for me."

I keep forgetting he's not a full-blooded anything. "About the hybrid thing—how'd that happen?"

Keiran gives me a look over the top of the fire, then tosses it into the pond. It lands with a sizzle. "Well, Charlotte," he says in a deep, serious voice, "when a man and a woman really like each other—"

I burst out laughing, cutting him off. "I know how you were conceived, jackhole. I mean, how did Whalen end up with your mom?"

He shrugs. "I guess he was lonely. Dad lost everything when PC banished him. His friends, his family, whatever life he had, you know? He had to start over. So he did."

I still can't get used to the idea of Whalen being someone's dad. It simply doesn't fit with anything else I know of him. "Don't call him Dad."

"But he *is* my dad, Charlie." Keiran lowers his eyes. "That's who I am."

"Bullsheet. He doesn't define you; *you* define you."

He shakes his head. "I define myself based on what he's done. When your father is the most hated man in the mystical realm, you figure out what to do to make people like you. So I'm charming." He pauses, shaking his head, and quietly adds, "I'm as manipulative as he is."

There's a noticeable change in Keiran's demeanor. His forehead creases, his shoulders slump, and his entire relaxed persona disappears. It's Keiran without his mask—the real, damaged boy who feels the pressure of his father's mistakes. Tears form behind my eyes. I'm more sure of him than he is of himself.

We're opposite sides of the same coin, both blaming ourselves for things we couldn't have stopped.

"You've adapted to the life you were dealt," I tell him. "That doesn't make you manipulative. It makes you a survivor."

It's what we're all doing, I guess. Surviving the circumstances we were born into. I inherited the hatred of a lapsed founder. Keiran was born under the stigma of a traitor. It's not like we have any choice in the matter.

"There's an awful lot of evil in him," he says softly, holding my gaze. "You don't think I've got just a little of that in me?"

I walk forward until the toes of our shoes are touching, forcing him to look at me. I need him to know he's better than his bloodline, that the horrible person we're all fighting is no part of him. He needs to see himself through my eyes. Whoever taught him to hate himself was a fool. "No. Do you know how easy it would've been for you to go in the other direction? To follow in Whalen's footsteps? And look at you. You chose to come here to help the Fellowship stop him."

"I want the Fellowship to *save* him," he blurts out.

Whoa.

I step back. It's probably the last thing I expected him to say. Is saving Whalen even an option? How do you rescue someone from himself?

"I know you must think it's crazy," he says.

"Keiran, I—"

"Don't." He turns to the side, almost putting his back to me, and rests both hands on top of his head. "I don't expect you to understand. I don't expect anyone to. I've never told anyone. I don't know why I just told you."

I reach for him, then let my hand fall. I know why he told me. He told me for the same reason I believe in him—our lives became forever intertwined the day my mother abandoned me to protect me from his father. On the surface it hardly makes sense. We should be enemies. Instead, we're connected by tragic events that defined us and ultimately cost each of us a parent.

He told me because he needed to tell someone, and I'm the only someone he trusts.

Keiran drops his eyes and speaks to the grass. "He was a founder, you know? There was a time when he loved the Fellowship. I know he'd have to be locked up for a while, but if we could get him to Ellauria, I think he'd remember."

I can't fathom the idea of saving someone like Whalen—the man who stalked my mother into hiding, ordered the murder of hundreds of creatures at the lake just to show that he could, and, most importantly, the man who's keeping my family from me. Keiran talks about Whalen like he's the victim, but he lost everything because of the choices he made.

His choices.

I twist the hem of my shirt. Bring Whalen to Ellauria? As far as I can tell, Whalen has brought nothing but pain to Ellauria—to my mother, to the creatures he's killed, and even to Keiran. Why would I want to bring that monster there?

"He'd still be powerless." I form my sentences gently. Keiran's holding on to the idea of a man I'm not sure exists anymore. Whatever Whalen used to be, he's pure evil now. "He even turned on you, his own son, when you developed your powers. You think bringing him to Ellauria would make things better?"

Let's not forget the reason he was banished—he wasn't powerful enough, and he was willing to kill for it.

Keiran's eyes glisten, and I pretend not to notice. "Don't misunderstand," he says, his voice shaky. "I sympathize with the man who was once my father, not with the man who exists now. I just want to find a way to get rid of one and find the other. I'd spend every day telling him how good he is, how good he can be. I'd make him remember. No matter how long it takes."

This must be what heartbreak feels like. Watching his eyes cloud over, seeing his light fade—it's physically painful. He's as desperate to save Whalen as I am to rescue Mom and Sam.

Is it possible to bring all three back?

I wrap my arms around him and pull him tightly against me. Keiran exhales against my neck. Something aches low in my chest, deepening with every breath.

I let him lean on me while I replay every single encounter I've had with Keiran in my mind—every story, every joke, every laugh. He's the closest thing I have to a brother here, and the pain he's in is very much my own.

"I'll help you," I whisper.

At least, I'll try. Is Whalen redeemable? It seems impossible, but how can I make that call right now?

Keiran lifts his head from my shoulder and steps back to look at me. The hope in his eyes brings tears to mine. "I know the Fellowship thinks he has to die," he says quietly. "I just hope I can figure out another way."

I nod. I don't want to crush the hope that he holds so tightly, but this is Whalen we're talking about. I believe in Keiran's intentions. I believe in his inherent morality. But Whalen? After everything he's done, I'm not sure there's a chance for the happy ending Keiran wants. "If there's a way to save all of them, my family and yours, then I'll help you do it."

"Thank you." He smiles at me, and I smile back.

I take a few steps back and give him some space to collect himself. He looks toward the pond for several minutes, so long that I start to feel like I'm intruding on his grief.

"Okay," he says. "Where were we?"

"You were saying how fire was dumb and I probably didn't need to mess with it," I quip.

Keiran rolls his eyes and puts on his teacher voice. "Like I said, fire's different because you're basically calling on the energy that's already been absorbed by everything around you. Including yourself. So there's no waiting for it to show up or pour into you. Fire is there, all the time." He produces a ball of fire in his hands again. "So instead of focusing outward, you bring your attention inside. Give it a try."

I drop my chin and stare down at my body.

Bring my attention inside.

I lift my hands by my side and wait, focusing.

Focus. Focus. Focus.

I wiggle my fingers in the air.

Focus. Focus. Focus.

"Imagine it pulling out of you, coming from within," he says.

Coming from within.

Focus. Focus. Focus.

I feel absolutely nothing. I drop my hands. "This is dumb."

He laughs. "You're not going to get everything on the first try, Freckles. Let's try a different angle. With the other elements, you're basically asking them to do something and they oblige. So let's try talking to the sun." He produces yet another fireball and yawns. "Maybe the 'focusing inward' is too much for a muralet to handle."

I fold my arms and tip my head toward the pond. A stream of water spouts up from the middle of it like a fountain, arching through the air and dousing the flames in Keiran's hand.

I snort-laugh. Powers are so much more fun in the Between!

His face droops, and he wipes his hand on his shirt. "Classy," he says, and I curtsy. "One more time. Call on the sun."

I roll my neck around and take a deep breath. I find the sun overhead and move my focus there, calling on the waves of light streaming down through the trees. It takes several minutes, but finally I see the tree's shadow shift as the rays of light bend toward me. I'm so surprised I lose my focus entirely, and it snaps back into place.

I nearly collapse to the ground, completely fatigued.

"You did it!" Keiran says. "Sort of!"

I hold my hand to my chest and crouch near the ground, using my other hand to balance. "I hardly did a thing, and it took this much out of me?"

"Alexander warned me that fire would be most difficult for you, but you'll get used to it." He helps me to my feet and slides his arm under mine. "Let's head back. You're not going to be able to do much for a little while anyway."

Keiran pulls me along, cutting through the trees to a different path from the one we took here. I can't believe how exhausted I am from barely interacting with the sun. And that's in the Between. I can't imagine how much more difficult it'll be in Ellauria. Maybe I'll just stick with air, water, and earth.

"Watch your step," Keiran says, and I lift my foot over a lone, crooked limb lying across the path.

Wait.

He realizes it at the same time I do. Why is there a dead limb in the Between?

"That's weird," he says.

I nudge it with my toe, and it rolls a bit, revealing completely blackened bark on the opposite side. I gaze upward to see where the limb came from and notice the upmost branches of tree beside me are mostly bare. I step back, pulling Keiran with me. We move far enough away to get a good view of the tree and see several others in the area with the same problem. Bare branches scattered among those filled with leaves. Dead branches hanging at weird angles, caught by the others as they break away from the tree.

This is wrong.

The Between is about life. Death and desolation of any kind don't belong here.

Suddenly the stillness of the Between seems more ominous than comforting, and I find myself waiting for something to jump out at me.

"What does it mean?" I ask.

Keiran's eyes wander over the trees from top to bottom. "I'm not sure," he says, "but I don't like it."

He pulls me back in the direction we'd come from. I can't stop turning my head, glancing over my shoulder every few steps. Beside me, Keiran does the same. When we reach the gate, he says, "We can't tell anyone."

I press my lips together. "But—"

"If we tell, they'll know we were out here. PC takes its rules very seriously. Apprentices aren't supposed to leave Ellauria without an Aegis." He shakes his head the whole time he talks, trying to convince me. "They'll start keeping tabs on us, Charlie. We won't have the freedom and privacy we need to work on your powers."

He's right. We can't afford that kind of attention. Perfecting my powers is my only hope to save my family. Besides, Seth will kill me if he finds out I went to the Between, right after he destroys Keiran for taking me.

A twinge of guilt curls in my stomach. This feels so wrong. Am I letting down the Between?

"Aegises and other creatures pass through here every day," Keiran tells me. "Someone will notice. Someone will tell. It just can't be us."

Someone will notice.

I feel sick.

"Come on, Charlie," Keiran says.

I take one more sweeping glance at the Between before I follow him through the gate.

Sixteen

I rest my elbows alongside Seth's on Mesmer's railing as I stand beside him, watching Ellauria come to life. A whisper of fog creeps under my feet, settling somewhere between Mesmer and the ground, silhouetting the activities of the creatures below as they start their days. In a few minutes, Mesmer's tables will be filled with Ellaurians eating everything from waffles to flowers to rocks (trolls have the strangest diets).

Seth had asked me and Keiran to meet him for breakfast this morning, and I've been a wreck inside ever since. He wants to discuss our training.

It's been a week since Keiran and I slipped into the Between. I don't think Seth knows. How could he? Besides, he's not the type to wait it out. He'd have jumped all over me as soon as he found out.

Still, my stomach flips over and over while I wait.

I cup my hands around my warm mug—breakfast tea was a strange surprise this morning, but as usual, the mug knew what I needed before I did.

Seth takes a sip of his water. "You seem to be getting more and more stressed out every day."

I knew this was coming. Of course Seth noticed. I lower my mug and stare at my reflection in the clear amber liquid.

"I don't want you to be uncomfortable talking to me," he says. "About anything."

I grip my mug tighter. Does he already know? Maybe he just wants to hear it from me? How much does he know?

"Seth, I—"

"I just miss you," he says. "I miss us. I don't like that you're always on edge around me because of PC's rule about us."

Right. The romance thing. I blow out a breath, long and slow. All of my unease can easily be chalked up to that. I drum my fingers against the mug. That was close.

"Mornin'," Lulu sings, fluttering up from the ground. "You still planning on using the Hollow today?"

"Yes, ma'am," Seth replies, as Lulu drops over the edge of the railing and heads for the counter.

"The Hollow?" I ask.

"Yeah." Seth stands up and turns, leaning his back against the rail. "That's why I asked you guys to meet me this morning. Keiran says you've got a pretty good handle on the elements. I'd like to see how you work under pressure. I'm going to run the two of you through some mock battles. Pixies are the only ones who can let us in and out of the Hollow. Lulu thinks I'm giving you a tour."

"Sounds good." I finish my tea. This should be fun. I'm growing more comfortable with my powers every day, but it's still hard to imagine how they'll be all that useful if I'm in trouble.

"So, you and I are okay?" Seth asks. His eyes have lost all of their certainty.

I smile at him. We're as good as we're ever going to be. "Yes. We are."

I'm not familiar with this uncertain side of him, but I think I could get used to it. As much as I've grown to appreciate his self-assurance here, it's nice to see him a little more vulnerable.

I want to touch him, but I know I can't.

One side of his mouth lifts and he nods toward Mesmer's stairs. Keiran's there, his hair crazier than normal and his eyes only half-open. "Good morning, sunshine!" Seth calls.

Keiran snarls in response. He picks up a bag from the counter and meets Seth and me by the railing. The bag crinkles as he unrolls it and holds the open end near my nose. It smells like powdered sugar and calories.

"Donuts," Keiran says with a grin, and I giggle.

"Everybody ready?" Lulu asks.

Keiran, Seth, and I follow her down the stairs and through the Clearing, past the dark forest, and around the lake, still shielded by the cover the fairies put in place after the attack.

We take an empty path lined with flowering dogwood trees, their blooms dipped in the palest pink. The air turns cooler, and a rectangular body of water stretches across the ground ahead. Everything around the water is flat, but there's a reflection of a large rock shimmering in the tiny ripples of the surface. I stare from the water to the place where the rock should be, but there's nothing.

I study the rock in the reflection. It has four arched openings, each with a tree etched above it. On the far left, the tree is bare. The next is covered in bright green leaves, then dark green leaves, and finally, orange leaves.

"Welcome to the Hollow," Lulu says. She flutters above the water, trailing her toe and sending wrinkles across the reflection. She dips her foot even deeper, then kicks the water forward. The droplets shoot into the air and take shape, draping over an invisible frame, creating the image from the water right before our eyes. In seconds, the reflection comes to life.

"Each opening represents a season. Winter, Spring, Summer, Fall," she explains, drifting across the openings. She rests her toes upon the ground. "Which one do you want to go to today?"

Seth looks to me, and I eye the trees over the openings, settling on the one with leaves of burnt orange. "Fall."

It's always been my favorite time of year. The colors, the clothes, and Mom's warm apple cider. I can practically smell the strong mix of apple, cinnamon, and cloves.

We move toward the rounded opening to Fall. The entire cave is in constant motion, shifting and swelling as waves of water rush over it. It's a strange mixture of magic and mirage. Keiran stretches his fingers into it, and graduating circles of ripples dance across the silvery surface.

"You've never been to the Hollow?" Lulu asks, and Keiran shakes his head. Her eyes sparkle. "You're going to love it. I wish I could be there to watch."

Keiran winks at her. "I wish you could too."

Seth rolls his eyes, and I pinch him.

He chuckles, and my eyes flicker to his lips. His full, soft lips. I press my own together, imagining how soft his lips would feel against mine, and my heart jumps a bit.

He turns his head to look directly at me, eyes wide, barely hiding a smile.

Glammit. He picked up on that. I immediately turn my eyes back to the Hollow. "You're not supposed to be tuning in," I remind him.

"I didn't mean to." He sounds sorry, but the smile is still playing around his mouth.

Emotions are the worst.

Seth laughs silently before turning his eyes forward again. "Thanks for letting us in, Lulu."

"Anytime, darlin'! Lock up when you're done!" She blows us each a kiss, and she's off.

Fall is a mixture of warm brown, burnt amber, and golden yellow. The ground crunches beneath my feet, and the smell of crackling leaves hangs in the crisp air. Crimson and plum chrysanthemums grow in random bursts of color scattered beneath the widespread trees. I step over a narrow stream of water flowing across the ground. The sun sinks lower and lower as we move further from the water portal until it paints a brilliant splash of red-orange through the sky, setting the horizon on fire.

It's beautiful. I stop and stare long enough to note the shape of the clouds and the curve of the horizon. I'll draw it from memory when I'm back in my room tonight.

There's not a lot of wide-open space here, but we find a spot big enough for the three of us to spread out. The ground is carpeted in crunchy orange and red leaves, and I nudge them with my feet.

"All right," Seth says, resting his hands on his hips. "I'm going to yell out a scenario, and I want you two to behave exactly as you would if it were real. Keiran, be careful with the fire around here. Charlie, if I call out a creature you don't know, just say so. Ready?"

Keiran and I exchange glances and nod. I've been studying Max's journal every night. There aren't many creatures in those pages I don't know. I shake out my arms and clear my head.

I'm ready.

"Warg! Behind you!" Seth yells.

The page from Max's bestiary appears in my mind. *Warg: large demonic wolves known for their boundless energy and insatiable taste for blood.*

Even though I know it's not real, my whole body quivers like a tuning fork and my movements quicken, fueled by fear. I thrust out my hand and spin, hurling a blast of wind. Keiran moves to the side. Fire has no effect on wargs. I continue to blast the imaginary target with powerful gusts of straight winds and spinning cyclones.

"Okay," Seth calls. "The wind will throw it off course and diminish your smell, but how will you kill it?"

I stop the air assault and rest my hands on my hips. Fire's out of the question. Water, maybe? I'm not sure. "Physical combat?"

Keiran gives me a You Must Be Crazy look. "You want to go head to head with something three times your size and with teeth longer than your fingers?"

I raise my shoulders. "What would you do?"

"Drown him," Keiran says immediately. "Conjure up a wind strong enough to shove him to the nearest body of water, then command the water to swallow him whole."

Seth points at Keiran. "He's right," he says, "and you know it pains me to say that."

The idea of commanding water to swallow anything never crossed my mind. We've practiced my powers for days, but my mindset needs work, too. I need to start thinking darker. When it comes to attacking, I have to be quick and lethal. These creatures won't hesitate to kill me. I can't hesitate, either.

Seth claps his hands twice. "Again!"

Keiran and I step away from each other. He nods at me, and I nod back, which I'm pretty sure is our new high-five.

"Harpy! Four o'clock!" Seth yells.

Oh, I know the harpy. I can almost hear its screech.

A fireball hisses overhead as a jagged branch dislodges from one of the taller trees and swings heavily through the air.

"Stop!" Seth announces and nods toward the branch. "What's your plan there?"

"Beat it to death?" It's a question, and it shouldn't be. I've got to be sure.

He nods. "I'm not saying it couldn't work, but fire would be a lot quicker."

Boo, fire. I curl my lip, and Keiran pats my back. "Don't worry, Freckles. You'll get there. You still have that knife Alexander gave you?"

I raise the hem of my shirt so he can see the leather case. I still put it on every single day even though I've yet to have a reason to pull it out.

"Good," Seth says. "Don't forget—if you get close enough, you can use it." He turns to Keiran. "Have you worked on combining elements yet?"

Keiran shakes his head. "Not yet. Alexander told me to wait until she's mastered all four on their own."

We run through several more creatures—dark gargoyles, minotaurs, hippogriffs, even the Mothman—before Seth finally says, "Enough!"

I fall to the ground, chest heaving, and stretch my legs across the cool grass. It wasn't a complete disaster. Honestly, I feel a little more confident in my ability to actually defend myself. Air, water, and earth may not be as bland as I thought. I need to get creative.

A shadow falls across my face, and I open my eyes to see Seth standing over me. "You okay?"

"I'm exhausted."

He holds his hand out. "You were amazing. I knew you'd catch on quickly, but that was really something."

I slide my hand into his and let him pull me to my feet. I lean into him a little, finding my balance, and he smiles down at me.

"Take a break this afternoon," he says. "How about we go see the unicorns tonight?"

Keiran's head turns, and I don't meet his gaze.

Every single part of me knows it's not a date. It's *not*.

Well, every single part of me except that delicious flutter in my belly.

Us. Alone. At night. No training.

"I'd love that," I tell him.

It is absolutely not a date.

But his smile says he wishes it could be, too.

Tonight seems like a good reason to wear my new sundress. I'd bought it weeks ago, before I came to Ellauria, but I haven't had a chance to wear it. Cute dresses aren't really appropriate for training to kill murderous creatures.

The dress's fitted top is such a pale blue it's almost white, but the color deepens as it flows downward, ending in a turquoise shade identical to the Source's brilliant waterfall in the Between. The hem brushes my knees when I bend over to slip on my silver sandals. When I straighten, I feel the familiar pulse against my collarbone as my aernovus attaches itself to my dress.

I unwind my braid and let my hair fall in soft waves over my shoulders. A little mascara, some lip gloss, and I'm ready.

I study the mirror.

It's probably a little dressy, but I don't care. Aside from our walks to and from Central Hall, Seth and I haven't spent any time alone since the day he told me he wanted to kiss me. I'm taking full advantage of having him to myself without the eyes and ears of Central Hall around.

Screw Operation Stop Crushing on Seth. I may not be able to convince Seth to break their stupid romance rule, but I can definitely make sure he's thinking about it.

I dab a bit more gloss in the center of my bottom lip and stand back.

I think that should do it.

When my door slides open and I step outside, Seth's expression tells me I'm right. I tilt my head to the side. "Hi."

His lips are parted, caught somewhere between surprise and a smile. "You dressed up."

"I got so gross and sweaty at the Hollow earlier," I tell him. "I felt like being pretty."

"Well," he nods, "success. I mean, you did. You are."

I smile with my lips closed, holding his gaze. He is so thinking about it.

Seth glances down at what he's wearing. "I feel underdressed."

He has no idea how that plain white T-shirt makes his eyes and hair darker or the way his dark jeans hug him in all the right places. That outfit is torture.

The Fellowship is absolutely ruining my life.

"You look fine," I tell him, and now he's the one with the close-lipped smile and mischievous eyes. We stand like that, daring each other, until footsteps pound against the wooden deck over our heads.

Seth's head turns immediately and he backs away, staring over the railing as a group of Apprentices come out of the room above mine and make their way down the stairs, hardly looking at us as they pass.

This is how it will always be. Fun and flirty when no one can see us, rigid and solemn when they can. I stare at the wooden planks beneath my silver sandals. That's not the Seth I want.

"What happened?" he asks, lifting my hand to examine a purple-blue bruise across the top of my knuckles.

"I knocked it against the edge of the kitchen counter earlier," I tell him. "No big deal."

I try to pull my hand away, but he pulls back. He holds his other hand, palm-side down, over mine. A white glow washes over the bruise, and it feels like icy gel is sliding over my hand. When he releases me, the bruise is gone.

I turn my hand one way, then the other. "Thanks," I tell him.

He shrugs half-heartedly. "It's what I do. Ready to head over to the field?"

I nod and wait for his arms to slide around me so we can flicker.

"I thought maybe we'd walk this time," he says.

"Sure," I reply, forcing a smile even though I know it's pointless. He knows I'm disappointed. Flickering is another thing that's pretty much stopped since the day of the parallel attack. He's hardly pulled me close since.

"I just think we shouldn't do anything to make this any harder than it already is," he says quietly, responding to my feelings again.

I shake my head and say nothing. I don't trust anything that might come out of my mouth right now, and besides, how can I argue when I know he's right? Still, he's here, and this is as close to a date as we've ever been on. Surely he notices that, too.

Of course Seth wants to make the rules easier to follow while I'm doing my best to pretend they don't exist. It's one more thing that makes us "us," and one more reason I have to get over this need to kiss him.

"Walking's fine," I say, clipping my words and turning for the stairs. I head down and through the lobby, staying a few steps ahead of him the whole time. When we reach the main path, it takes too much effort to out-walk his longer strides, and I give up.

I never should've worn these sandals.

Or this dress.

Seth doesn't make me talk, and I'm glad. He knows what's happening in my heart anyway. I'm frustrated that we've lost what we once were. He's letting the Fellowship map out his life for him, and I've had enough of it. This is who he is, a rule-follower, and I've always known it. But now, right now, it kills me that he can't look past it.

I know he knows all of that. When I steal a look at him, I'm pretty sure I see the same emotions on his face, too.

Let it go, Charlie.

The rounded hill that hides the door I passed through the first time I set foot in Ellauria rises from the ground on my right. I keep my eyes on it as we pass.

Seth's fingers twitch against mine. "What are you thinking about?"

"I'm wondering what I'd be doing right now if I didn't know about all this."

"You'd be on your front porch, balancing your sketchbook on your knees, drawing something," he says. "You'd be so absorbed in scratching your pencil across the pages, you'd hardly notice when I show up until the lawnmower starts and snaps you out of it. It'd probably startle you so much you'd drop your pencil and say one of your ridiculous words."

I smile to myself, remembering the conversation Sam and I had the last time I saw him. "Duck. I'd say duck."

Seth laughs. "Of course. Duck."

He points to the two unicorns grazing in the apothecary's field. The taller one trots toward us as we approach and dips his head over the broad wooden fence.

"Charlie, meet Dimitrius," Seth says, rubbing between the unicorn's ears.

Dimitrius is almost blindingly white from head to tail with a coat that literally gleams. I scratch my fingers across his velvety snout, and he whinnies. It's the happiest sound I've ever heard—a joyful melody of giggles and neighs.

Seth leans back against the fence. "How do you like training with Keiran?" he asks.

As soon as he mentions training, I see the dead trees in the Between. I keep my eyes on Dimitrius, focusing on staying relaxed. "It's fun. He's been really great."

Bare, broken branches stick in my mind.

Great. He's going to notice.

"You okay?" he asks.

Even if he suspects I'm not telling him everything, he can only know as much as I tell him, right? He may be a human lie detector, but he's not a mind-reader.

I run my fingers from the tip of Dimitrius's snout to the top of his head, scratching the soft hair above his eyes. "Yep. Of course. Just tired of talking about training all the time."

He pushes off the fence and stands with his eyes on me and his hands on Dimitrius. "You sure that's it?"

He knows. He knows. He knows.

I start an inner monologue of everything I want to be true and all the things I want him to feel from me: *We didn't go in the Between. We didn't see anything out of the ordinary. I'm totally committed to following the rules around here. Why would we go to the Between when we were specifically told to stay in Ellauria?*

There's a neigh in the distance, and I see the other unicorn trotting toward us.

"Ah, Cortesia's jealous," Seth says, momentarily distracted. I'm so grateful I could kiss the unicorn right on the mouth.

Cortesia steps up to the fence line and stretches her neck alongside Dimitrius. I oblige, petting each of them with one hand. Cortesia's color is more gray than white, and the shine to her coat makes her look nearly metallic. After a minute or so, both unicorns look so relaxed I worry they might fall over.

"Seth!"

Ugh. Clara. Heat crawls across my chest. I don't mind a diversion, but does it have to be her? There she is, five-foot-ten of perfection personified, and I immediately feel smaller. I look at her because I can't help it, in the same way that I was once fascinated by celebrities back home.

"Hello, Empress." He responds like he doesn't hate her, which is annoying.

"Visiting the unicorns?" she asks.

No, *Clara. We're braiding each other's hair.* I roll my eyes and make a face at Dimitrius.

"Yes," he replies. "What are you up to?"

"I'm on my way to meet a group of Apprentices to take them to the Hollow. It's my turn to give them the lowdown on fairies. Speaking of which," she places a hand on her hip, "I don't think I've seen Charlie's name on any of the Apprentice lists."

Why is she even looking for my name?

"Charlie and I are doing more independent training," he tells her. "Separate from the others."

"Oh, because she's a siren?"

I'm right here. She's doing her best to pretend I'm not, but I'm *right here.*

"Yes," Seth says.

"You must've been really worried after the lake attack," she says. I look up, thinking that one was for me, but nope—still ignoring my presence.

Seth nods. "I was worried about everyone. It was a horrible thing."

"I guess it's lucky Charlie wasn't at the lake when it happened. But then, she doesn't really seem to spend much time near the water anyway, for a siren." Clara finally focuses her lavender eyes on me with a scrutiny that makes me wish she'd go back to pretending I'm not here. "I find it so odd that Seth is your Aegis. It seems irresponsible to assign a male Aegis to a siren. Don't you think it's strange?"

Is she all over me just because she enjoys seeing me squirm, or is there something to this? Am I supposed to be doing something more siren-y? "You seem to be awfully aware of where I am and what I'm doing," I tell her.

Clara places her hand to her chest and laughs. "Oh, goodness no! Is that what it sounds like?" She smiles, but it doesn't reach her eyes. "It's quite the opposite. I have no idea what you're doing here, actually. I've never seen an Apprentice get the kind of special treatment you enjoy."

She's definitely paying too much attention to me. What has she seen? Heat spreads across my chest, but I don't acknowledge the rash of anxiety moving up my neck.

I'm never wearing this dress again.

Seth clears his throat and sharpens his tone. "Alexander specifically designed her training plan, Clara. If you have questions, I suggest you talk to him."

The grin remains plastered to her face. "I may do that, just to satisfy my own curiosity, of course. I'm sure it's not like anyone is keeping secrets from PC." She shakes her hair and brightens, like she can shed one personality and don another. "Well, I'm off. You two enjoy your date!"

I could grab her by her stupidly perfect hair and throw her to the ground and still not feel satisfied.

"This isn't a date, Clara," Seth says, dropping his hands from Cortesia's face. The unicorn whinnies in protest.

Her hand flies to her mouth. "Oh, of course it isn't! What a slip! That would certainly be a problem, wouldn't it?" Her words drip with exaggerated concern. She clearly knows what she's doing. "We'd sure hate to split you two up!"

Clara swats Seth's shoulder playfully, but the look she gives me is anything but friendly. I answer it with a sneer of my own. She lifts into the air without another word.

Split us up? I shiver. They can't do that. Can they? Not in my situation. Nobody else knows what I am. Alexander would never let that happen. They can't really split us up.

Right?

I widen my eyes at Seth. "They'd separate us?"

He stares after Clara before turning his face to me. "If it looks like we're romantically involved, yes. I can't be your Aegis if I can't be objective about you. It puts you, me, and the rest of the Fellowship in danger."

And the Fellowship is all that matters. Not what I want. Not what Seth wants. That all comes second. "I can't have another Aegis, Seth."

I don't want another Aegis. I want him. In so many ways.

"Exactly," he says. "You can't. Which is why we can't. Ever."

Ever.

My stomach clenches.

Ever is too long to be a real thing.

SEVENTEEN

"I think we should go back to the Between," I say, following Keiran through the tall white trees beyond the Clearing. We're on our way to the pond below the Clearing, since he absolutely refuses to let me start anywhere near the Meadow of Music today.

"No." Keiran shakes his head and keeps walking.

Just the one word. No explanation whatsoever. It's like he doesn't even know me.

I pout my lips and shrug my shoulders. "Yes."

Keeping this big of a secret from Seth is killing me. My stomach is constantly in knots when he's around, and every time he looks at me, I'm sure he knows. I've almost blurted it out at least ten times in the last two days. I want to tell him because I feel guilty. I want to tell him because I'd rather he find out from me than someone else. But mostly I want to tell him because I need to know if there's been anything else. Why haven't I heard a word about dead trees in the Between?

Keiran stops walking and puts on his serious face. His eyes are more gray than usual this morning. "We're lucky we didn't get caught the first time. If I'd had any idea what we'd find when we went, I never would've suggested it. Why should we risk it again?"

I doubt he'll have much sympathy for my need to be honest with Seth. "It's been over a week and nobody's mentioned a thing about dying plants in the Between," I tell him. "I want to see if the trees are okay."

"Maybe you haven't heard anything about it, because it's not a big deal!"

I raise an eyebrow. "You don't think it's a big deal that at the same time we're having trouble with spells, the Between is also weakening?"

He opens his mouth like he's going to argue, and then his face goes blank. "I guess I hadn't really put that together."

I hadn't either until the words came out of my mouth. But it makes sense. The Between is home to the Source. If something's not right there, it would explain why magic is falling apart here. "This is more important than me and you, Keiran."

He chews on his lip, looking from side to side. "Okay. We get in, we look around, we get out. Quick and easy."

"Of course," I reply, already steering us toward the two tall trees that mark the gate Alexander led me through when he took me to the Source.

Keiran climbs the tree to reach the limb that activates the gate. He wraps his hands around it and hangs on, lowering himself to the ground as the dirt collapses into stairs. "Creepiest gate ever," he says, gazing into the darkness. "I hate this one."

Glad it's not just me. I feel the same tightening in my chest that I felt the first time I saw this passage.

It's not a crypt. It's not a crypt. It's not a crypt.

I take a deep breath and descend the steps as quickly as I can to reach the other side.

I breathe a sigh of relief as soon as I'm in the Between, happy to see that it's still here at all.

Everything near this gate looks as perfect as ever—the leaves are green and strong, the trees thick with life. Keiran looks at me and smiles. He's as relieved as I am.

I spot the Source in the distance and point to it. "Let's just run and take a look real quick."

"Charlie, we said—"

I take off jogging down the path. "Sorry, what? Can't hear you!"

He groans behind me but I hear him running, too, each footstep falling against the dirt path in rhythm with mine. We make it about half a mile before we see the first dead limb, followed by another and another. I dodge them as I slow to a walk, weaving left and right on the path.

It's more than the trees.

Brittle, empty stems rise from the ground where full hydrangea bushes once stood, the area beneath them covered in dry brown petals. The honeysuckle vines have withered away to nothing. All of the colors—the bright greens, clear blues, and every one of the flowers—look washed with gray. The few flowers that remain droop downward, as if they'd rather lie down and die than reach for the sunlight.

Glammit. We've waited too long.

Keiran and I say nothing, only exchanging glances here and there as we wander through the chaos.

The closer we get to the Source, the worse the damage becomes. Dead leaves cover the ground, strewn across yellowed grass and jagged limbs. The trees are bare and mostly broken, lying on their sides as if a tornado stormed through. I stop and take it all in.

The wide, thunderous flow of the waterfall has slowed to a trickle, and the river before me is a muddled gray. The actual pain doesn't strike until I reach the Source's deep pool. It's lost most of its light.

I only catch a slight glimmer in the waves here and there, nothing like its brilliance the first time I saw it.

I close my eyes. We should've told someone.

"Whoa," Keiran breathes. "What could've done this?"

I have a pretty solid idea of what, or at least who, is behind this, and I can't look at Keiran right now. I raise my head and gaze across the water to the treefolk. They're still there, still alive, although their colors are muted.

"Joe!" I call, and take off running around the Source to reach the large, old tree.

His branches spread open when I get close, and his trunk shudders. In seconds, his face appears. When he speaks, there's none of the jovial boom from before. His voice is quiet and pained. "Charlie," he creaks, "we're dying."

"We have to get out of here," Keiran says from behind me.

Tears burn behind my eyes. I wrap my fingers around one of Joe's branches and squeeze. "What's doing this to you?"

"Tell Alexander," Joe wheezes, "Whalen knows. He knows."

Keiran steps closer. "What does he know?" he asks.

Joe's face starts to recede. "Tell him," he says again.

"Joe, wait—" I put my hands on either side of his face, but he's gone, too weak to stay with me. I let my hands fall to my sides.

"We have to get out of here," Keiran repeats.

I want to spin around and snap at him. I know we have to go. I know we have to tell PC about all of this. I know we should've told them the first time we saw it.

I know his father—who Keiran is so convinced can be saved—is behind it.

Whalen knows.

I turn and start walking to the other side of the Source, back in the direction we came from. "We need to go to Alexander," I say loudly.

I need to know what Whalen knows.

Keiran walks beside me, our feet dragging through piles of deep, dead leaves. I watch the Between, silently begging it for answers.

Something glints on the ground a few yards off the path. I trudge through the decay for a closer look. Keiran calls after me, but I ignore him.

A shiny guitar pick knotted on black string lies in the tall mix of dead grass and fragmented leaves.

And now, nothing else matters—not the Between, not Joe, not Whalen. Just this little charm lying on the ground.

Sam.

I bend to pick it up and let my fingers hover over it, afraid that if I touch the pick, it'll disappear. I close my eyes and snatch the bracelet with my fist, then turn my hand over and open it.

Still there. My chest soars, and I slip the bracelet onto my wrist.

"Sam?" I yell, walking forward and stopping, yelling again, turning and walking another direction, yelling some more. I stumble in all directions, waiting for some kind of indication of what I should do next.

"Charlie?" Keiran calls.

"Over here!" I continue throwing my voice around. "Sam! Sam!"

He's here. Somewhere.

"Sam! Sam!"

I turn by a large dead maple tree that's been split directly down the middle, and freeze.

A dark-haired woman lies crumpled on the ground ahead. Her pale pink T-shirt is covered in streaks of mud and leaf bits, and her khaki shorts are nearly black. The muscles in my legs tighten, and it takes a moment to process the sight. "Mom!"

I sprint to her side and drop to my knees next to her. Why is she here? How long has she been here? Her cheeks and forehead are covered with bruises, some purple and others a faded blue. Wide, black-red scabs cover her arms. Her hair lays in matted tangles all over her head. I brush leaves from her body and lean across her. My chin is trembling so hard I can hardly speak. "Mom?"

Heavy footsteps crunch across dried leaves, and Keiran crouches on the other side of her. I can't look at him. He says nothing. There's no need.

Tears blur my vision. I run my hands over her arm, her shoulder, her cheek. Her skin is so cold and clammy. I pull her hand from her side and wrap my fingers around it, holding it to my chest. I lay my forehead against her fingers and let my tears drip down her hand.

Keiran bows his head, giving me space and comfort at the same time.

I need Sam. He's the only person allowed to hug me when I'm about to fall apart. I don't know how to do this without him.

If she's out here, like this, is he—?

No.

I squeeze her hand tighter. "Don't leave me," I whisper against her fingers. "Please." I murmur the last word over and over, rocking on my knees.

Keiran presses his hand against her forehead.

She releases a long, shaky breath, and a sob racks my body.

She's alive.

"Mom," I whisper, swiping my tears with my free hand and leaning closer to her face.

"Charlie." The frailty of her voice breaks me. It's sickness and fear combined, and it's enough to push me into action.

She's alive, but she won't make it out of here if I don't get a grip.

I pull myself together. "Mom. I'm right here. This is Keiran. We're gonna get you out of here."

"No," she wheezes. "Run."

Keiran jumps to his feet, scanning our surroundings.

"I'm not leaving without you," I tell her. I can't possibly let go of her now that I have her in front of me. "Where's Sam? Is he here?"

She closes her eyes, flinching at something I can't see. "He's with Whalen."

I close my eyes and bite down on my lip to keep it from shaking. My brother is alone with the man who's been ripping my world apart since before I was born.

"Where are they?" Keiran asks.

Her eyes flutter open and close again, and a wet rattle accompanies every breath she takes.

"Mom? Stay with me. We're getting you home." Breaths burst in and out of my lungs, but I keep the tears at bay. They're not going to help her.

She says something so quiet I can't hear it. I place my ear next to her lips.

"Wants to eradicate magic," she whispers. "The Between—purest magic—everything is rooted in its design."

She gasps for air and coughs.

Eradicate magic?

"Poisoning the Between," Mom rasps. "Everything and everyone in the mystical realm will die."

Another cough—a hacking fit that sends her body into convulsions.

Keiran meets my eyes across her body. Whalen doesn't want to gain power; he wants to obliterate it.

"Run, Charlie," Mom breathes. "Run."

"No, Mom." It's more of a sob than a sentence. I shake my head. I can't bring myself to release her hand. Now that I have her back, I'm not letting go again. "I told you I'm not leaving you. You're coming with us."

A long hiss invades the air, and I look up to see the Mothman's glowing red eyes through what's left of the trees. His black mouth gapes open, and a thick, wet hiss sounds again. He stands on the very tips of his talons, like he's going to lunge toward us at any moment.

I stop breathing.

"Charlie." Keiran's voice is low, his eyes locked on the creature. "Don't. Move."

The hissing ceases, and the Between is an entirely new type of silent—the kind that creeps up in the middle of the night and takes your mind to the most terrifying possibilities imaginable.

A chill fills my core.

Mom's eyes pop open, and her chest heaves. I jump as she releases a scream more powerful than I ever could've imagined, given the state she's in.

The Mothman leaps into the air and Keiran lunges for me, catching me beneath my arms. We topple backward as the Mothman lands on Mom's body. We flip over and bounce off the grass onto our feet. I pull my knife from my side and point it at the Mothman.

One clawed foot presses down on Mom's neck, its claws touching the ground on either side, and the other stands on her torso. Mom stares up at the giant creature, her eyes wide and her mouth frozen in a silent scream.

"When I say run," Keiran breathes, "you run. Don't stop running. No matter what. Don't stop until you're in Ellauria."

Everyone keeps telling me to run like it's the easiest thing to do. Mom's here. Sam's here. I can't leave them.

My eyes focus on the sharp, dark talons around Mom's neck. One of them stretches, straightening until it points directly at me. A whimper escapes my lips, and the Mothman's head swivels toward me, rotating in a complete circle. His eyes lock with mine. His mouth gapes open, and a thick, wet hiss sounds again.

"Run!" Keiran shouts.

But I can't. I'm stuck here, frozen by the sight of the only mother I've ever known pinned to the ground by the enormous, deadly creature that started this whole nightmare.

She escaped him before.

A gurgling noise erupts from her throat as his talons squeeze her neck.

She is the bravest person I know.

I tear my eyes away and focus on the tall, blackened tree behind them. In seconds, the brittle branch cracks free and crashes downward, landing directly on the Mothman's head.

The Mothman hisses again, but his stance doesn't waver.

Mom's lips grow purple, and the whites of her eyes explode with red.

No. She will not die here.

"Charlie!" Keiran shouts again, circling around to the Mothman's side. "Run!"

I can't.

Keiran raises his hand, sending a ball of flames screaming through the air. It flies over the creature as he lowers his head until it's mere inches from hers.

Get up, Mom. Get up.

Keiran keeps throwing fire, but even the ones that make contact don't seem to have much effect. They merely sizzle against the Mothman's dark feathers.

Mom's fingers twitch in the grass at her sides, and her face grows redder.

My heart goes frantic. I stare at everything and nothing, desperately searching for a weapon. Water would extinguish Keiran's fireballs. The heavy tree branch had little effect. Air?

A gust of wind blows through, and I steel myself against it as it whips around me. Keiran stumbles a bit and plants his feet in the ground, doing the same.

The Mothman stays solid.

I cry out in frustration, slamming my fists against my legs.

I'm not ready for this. My powers aren't ready.

"Combine them!" Keiran yells. He runs closer, throwing more and more fire. A few feathers ignite on the Mothman's shoulder, but they burn out quickly. "Water and air. Fire and earth. They're not enough on their own—put them together!"

My breaths come quickly, each one shakier than the next. I look from Keiran to the monster.

Combine them.

My mind races, swirling through the most random possibilities. The Mothman launches into the air and I want to move, to help, to scream, but I do nothing. I wait for her to roll out of his way.

Get up, Mom. Get up.

The Mothman crashes down, and the sickening crunch of bone is everywhere, announcing her death in surround sound.

No!

My knees hit the ground, and my vision blurs. *She can't be dead. She can't be.* I say it over and over in my head, all the time knowing it's a lie.

The body on the ground is a fractured mess of bone and blood. There's nothing left of her there.

She's dead.

As much as I want to close my eyes and make the image disappear, I can't tear my gaze away. My world is nothing but the sight of Mom's mutilated body and the sound of my breaths. How did I get this close to her again, only to lose her?

The noises I make are senseless sounds of grief wrapped in terror. A tremor takes hold of my body, sending me into convulsions, and I wrap my arms around my stomach.

No *no no no no.*

I rock forward and back. My throat thickens, and the Mothman's weight is upon me before I can scream.

"No!" Keiran yells.

The sharp points of his talons dig into my neck and hip.

Flames crash into the Mothman, one after the other. I hear Keiran grunt with each throw, but my eyes are locked only on the enormous monster on top of me.

My nostrils sting with the smell of singed feathers. Pressure builds behind my eyes as all the air is pushed from my lungs. The Mothman leans over me, and I feel his scorching breath against my skin, the tips of his feathers trailing over my arms. His blood-rimmed eyes lock with mine, his head tilting to the side as his wings lift and fold over me, enclosing me in a cocoon of darkness.

There's no air.

Mom's dead.

I'm supposed to be the most powerful creature alive, and I froze when she needed me.

I couldn't save her.

"Charlie!" Keiran releases a determined scream of rage and runs toward us, his feet crunching across the leaves.

In a blink, the Mothman's massive wing strikes out, connecting with Keiran's chest and catapulting him through the air. There's a loud *thud* when Keiran hits the ground, and then there's nothing but the Mothman's face in mine.

Whalen has Sam.

What's the point?

Pain tears through me as the Mothman bears down on my body.

I squeeze my eyes shut. *This is it.*

The monster leaps upward, and sweet, fresh air flows over me, filling my lungs. My fingers close over the leather handle still gripped in my hand.

My eyes fly open. My knife.

I will not end here.

I whip my arm out as the Mothman comes crashing down, recalling Seth's instruction to Mom the night this all started.

Below the rib cage. Right side.

My knife connects with something solid and I push in with everything I have, twisting the blade. The Mothman screams—a shrill mixture of hiss and screech—and his weight triples as he slumps over on top of me.

I press against his massive body, craning my neck and gasping for air. I push my feet into the ground and maneuver myself until I find a break in the feathers.

Air.

I drink it in, chest heaving.

A hand reaches beneath the Mothman and grabs my wrist. "Charlie," Keiran says, breathing hard. "Charlie. I'm here. I've got you."

His arms slip over me, lifting the Mothman. I push with all the strength I have left. Finally, the weight is gone. I roll to my side, coughing and sputtering.

In the grass just a few feet away lie the broken and bloody remains that were once the woman I called Mom. I stretch my arm out, reaching for her, and Keiran stands over me, his hands on his head, his face twisted with pain.

The Between swallows my sobs, and we're once again surrounded by silence.

"Charlie!"

I lift my head. Seth?

I blink and he's there, surrounded by Aegises and fairies. Clara stands at the front of the crowd, rising into the air and taking in the death around us.

I push myself upward. Is he really here? How did he know?

"You were in the mirror," Seth mutters. His gaze sweeps from me to Keiran to the Mothman. He flinches when he sees what's left of Mom and turns away.

I push myself upward until I'm standing. Pain rips through my chest, and I press my fingers to my ribs. I'm pretty sure a few of them are broken.

Seth keeps his eyes on the ground. I take a step toward him, and he turns his head to me. His sharp look is filled with warning.

I need him. I need his arms around me. I need to be as close to him as possible, to feel his breath on my skin and his heartbeat against my chest. I need him in unfair ways he can't possibly provide.

There's movement all around me. Fairies hover about, studying the Between's decay and collecting Mom. Aegises examine the Mothman, taking note of my knife and the singes left behind by Keiran's flames. I hear questions, but I can't find words to answer.

Keiran steps closer, gently brushing leaves off of my shirt. When I look at him, his eyes are empty. "I'm so sorry," he says.

I shudder, unable to respond.

Through it all, Seth stands as silent and motionless as a statue, his tortured eyes locked on my face.

I channel all my thoughts to him. *I need you. Please.*

His gaze only hardens. He waits until two Aegises take hold of me and Keiran, then turns his back on me to lead the way back to Ellauria.

Eighteen

Every single part of the room where Principal Command convenes, from the walls to the floor to every single table and chair, is made of dark oak, with black lines marking the grain. There are no windows, and the small desk lamps on each of the tables don't do a whole lot for the ambience.

It's designed to be intimidating, and it works.

Forty-eight members of Principal Command, every leader that could make it to Ellauria on a moment's notice, sit in groups of three at sixteen tables arranged in a half-circle on one side of the room.

Keiran and I sit opposite them in two stiff wooden chairs set far enough apart that, when he catches my eye and tries to whisper, I can't understand his words.

"Do you have something to say, elf?" A giant centaur stares down his nose at Keiran.

They keep doing that—calling me "siren" and Keiran "elf," like our names don't matter.

We've spent the last hour recounting everything that happened from the time we decided to go to the Between to finding Sam's bracelet to the appearance of the Mothman, and ending with the moment Seth and the fairies arrived.

Alexander sits in the very center of PC with his elbows resting on the table and his hands folded in front of his chin. Seth leans against the wall by the door, here only because he's my Aegis and therefore personally responsible for carrying out whatever punishment PC gives me for defying the Fellowship's orders and going into the Between.

Never mind that we discovered the cause of the weakening magic everywhere. Never mind that we killed the Mothman.

Never mind that Mom died.

Seth still hasn't talked to me. He'll hardly look at me. He did at least take the time to heal my cracked ribs, but as soon as he was finished, he walked away. If I weren't completely drained of emotion, I'm sure that would hurt. As it is, all I feel is emptiness.

My feelings dulled when I watched Aegises pick up the pieces of my mother. They were further muted when Seth turned his back on me in the Between. But the final straw was being brought to this cold room to relive today's events, all while being treated like some sort of deviant.

Sam is all I have to cling to now, and of him, all I have is his bracelet.

The only way to survive this is to stop feeling.

"Our rules aren't arbitrary guidelines," says the centaur. "These orders are in place, not only for your safety, but for that of the mystical realm as well."

"After everything we've told you," Keiran says, his tone dripping with disbelief, "your main concern right now is that we broke one of your rules?"

Where I feel blank, Keiran seems angry. I've never seen this disrespectful side of him—a side that isn't concerned with being likable or charming. I don't know if he's angry with Whalen, the Fellowship, himself, or all of the above, and we haven't had a moment alone to process anything together.

His father—the man he's intent on saving—is responsible for my mother's death. I don't know how I would deal with that if I were in his place.

I stare ahead, my gaze falling somewhere between the tabletop and the floor.

"Your irresponsibility could've allowed the Mothman to enter Ellauria or any of the mystical realm's other cities," the centaur growls.

"This is so stupid," I mutter.

"Excuse me?" Clara pipes up, leaning over her table. "Did you say this is stupid?"

I look from Sam's bracelet to her face. "I've said everything I have to say about why we went to the Between." I break the story into monotonous steps one more time. "I'd heard of the trouble with magic. I wanted to look at the Source. Keiran only went because I made him. I've told you what Joe said," my eyes flicker to Alexander, "and what Mom said. Why are we still sitting here instead of doing something?"

Clara leans back in the seat, settling her arms over her chest. "You know, I've been a bit curious about your particular situation," she says, then addresses the rest of PC. "This Apprentice has been kept separate from the rest of the first-years since she got here. She seems to enjoy advanced training and freedoms that the others do not."

I release a harsh, loud laugh and comb both hands through the front of my hair. This is completely insane. "Did you hear the part about how Adele died, about what she said about Whalen, about how he wants to destroy magic?"

"You need to learn your role here," Clara snaps.

"She's not wrong," Seth states. Every head in the room turns toward the door. "Adele's dying words were a warning. Whalen wants to eradicate magic," he says, "and you're all sitting here discussing how to punish a couple of adventurous Apprentices."

It's the first time I've heard his voice since he found me in the Between. He meets my gaze and holds it for a couple beats before looking away.

It's the first time he's done that, too.

I know he thinks going against his orders is a slap in the face to him and a sign that I don't take my own safety or the Fellowship's mission seriously. But he should know me well enough to remember that I can't ignore the pull to do what I feel is best. The Between needed me. The first time we snuck in was foolish. The second time was a mission.

"The state of the Between is a problem," Lulu adds. "Whatever Whalen's doing to it is working. It explains the disruptions we've seen in magic. It's only a matter of time before the decay spreads to the Source."

Heads bow together, murmuring about Lulu's words.

"What did he mean, Alexander?" I ask, raising my voice over the discussion. "When Joe said to tell you that Whalen knows. What was he talking about? What does Whalen know?"

Alexander unfolds his hands and presses his fingertips together. For a moment, I think he either didn't hear me or doesn't want to answer, but he finally speaks. "Everything we are comes from the Between. Magic itself is rooted in its design. The Between," he says, "is life."

"What does Whalen know?" This time it's Keiran talking, clearly as tired of this game as I am. *Get to the point, Alexander. Tell us what's happening.*

"When Whalen was stripped of his powers," the founder continues, "it left him in an in-between state. He's not mortal, but he's no longer mystical. He became something of a blank slate. When he crossed paths with the bogmen and began to use his body as a vessel for necrolate, he became an entirely new type of being."

The entire room is silent. I glance at Seth from the corner of my eye, but he's focused on Alexander.

"Whalen's sole purpose is to destroy," Alexander says. "He is death, and his extended presence in the Between is choking out the life there. The longer he stays in the Between, the worse his effect on the Between and the Source will be. I imagine he discovered this by accident. He's probably been making a home there for a long time. But now that he knows what he can do..." He raises his eyes to make contact with mine. "He's not going to stop until the Between, and magic itself, is dead."

I lay back in my chair. The Between is dying because Whalen is inside it. The only way to stop the process is to remove him.

I look at Keiran. His shoulders are slumped, his eyes on the floor. What would Whalen's presence do inside Ellauria?

"Destroying magic makes no sense." Clara's voice is sharp. "Without magic, we all lose our powers. He'd have to have one hell of a bargaining chip to convince other creatures to help him."

A satyr behind Lulu clears his throat. "I agree with Clara. He'd never be able to convince so many creatures to abandon their own magical gifts. If he wants to live as a mortal, he can."

"Besides," an elf adds, "why bother staging attacks within the realm at all? He can poison the Between and end magic without that."

I rotate Sam's bracelet on my wrist. It's true. If destroying magic is his goal, why bother with the attacks? Why take Adele and Sam? Why target me at all?

"I think it's more about bringing down all of magic than living as a mortal," Keiran says. His eyes stay on the floor. "He hates magic. He doesn't want it to exist."

Well, that would explain why he's targeting me. He hates magic, and I am magic.

Wait.

I raise my head to find Alexander's yellow-green eyes bearing down on me. Fear slices through my shield, assuring me that my emotions are not, in fact, dead.

I *am* magic.

On the far side of the room, a stooped leprechaun with threads of gray in his copper beard speaks up, his voice brittle with age. "Perhaps he is offering something to the creatures in return for their assistance in attacking the realm."

The room goes silent. My heartbeat picks up, gradually gaining in speed and pressure. If the Between dies and the Source is demolished, the creatures who wish to survive will need a new source of magic.

"I believe we are missing a piece of the puzzle," the leprechaun continues. "There must be something in the realm he wants, which may be the bargaining chip Clara spoke of earlier."

Something in the realm that he wants.

I swallow. Me. He wants me.

My hands tremble, and I slip them beneath my legs to hide them.

I *am magic*. The words that had once seemed so incredible now sound like a death sentence. Uncertainty drapes itself over me.

Alexander rises from his seat and stares at the table for a moment. He lifts his head, and his eyes flicker to me before sweeping across the faces of Principal Command. From the corner of my eye, I see Seth's posture straighten. He pushes away from the wall by the door and eyes the founder.

I grip the edge of my seat, curling my fingers around it. I know what Alexander is about to say, and at the same time, I'm certain that he can't say it.

Can he?

"The missing piece," Alexander says quietly, "is Charlotte. She is the bargaining chip."

I shudder, stunned.

The room is silent for a breath, and then Clara says, "What does he want with a siren?"

Alexander stares at the table and then lifts his head, making eye contact with Clara first before glancing around the room. "Charlotte isn't a siren. She is a full-blooded muralet, the daughter of Max and Marian. If Whalen destroys the Between, she will be the only source of magic left. Every creature is going to want control of her blood in order to survive."

"Alexander!" Seth flickers to the middle of the room, appearing in front of me.

Keiran's head snaps up, looking from the founder to me. I'm glued to my chair, held in place by the stares of every single member of Principal Command. Their faces are filled with varied expressions of shock, awe, and, in Clara's case, a bit of disgust.

I gape at Alexander, my heart pounding. All I've been told since the moment I got here is how important it is to keep my bloodline under wraps. I cannot believe he just spilled what's supposed to be the Fellowship's biggest secret. I'm completely exposed in front of forty-eight creatures who may or may not want to rip me apart for my blood right now.

Seth steps backward, closing the space between our bodies. It's the closest he's been to me since he found us in the Between. I want to reach for him, but I don't.

Suddenly everyone's talking at once, louder and louder, fighting for control of the room.

"Marian had a child?"

"—doesn't make sense—"

"So what?"

"I knew she wasn't pretty enough to be a siren."

"—thought she vanished—"

Alexander raises his hands, and silence blankets the room. "Do you recall the first time I took you to the Source?" he asks me. "You said you saw a million balls of light making up everything around you."

I nod, and the knots grow tighter.

"The building blocks of our worlds are at your call. Your blood provides the magic, and your power controls the elements." Alexander leans forward. "Your unique bloodline provides the key to creation, Charlotte. Whalen can't destroy magic without destroying you. As long as muralets exist, magic will never be extinct."

The key to creation. I feel like something between the missing link and a god. Neither is anything I desire to be.

I lean forward until I can breathe. I don't want this kind of responsibility. Keeping myself alive has proven hard enough. Carrying the future of magic on my shoulders is unimaginable.

"As a founder, Whalen knows this," Alexander says. "When my binding spell slipped and you were revealed, he must have been horrified to realize the muralet bloodline lives on."

"Why didn't you tell me?" Seth asks.

"Why would he?" the satyr asks. "Why should you know information that PC doesn't?"

Alexander ignores Seth and addresses the satyr. "Seth has been acting as Charlotte's Aegis since before she was brought to the mystical realm. As the last muralet, she was hidden for her own safety in the hopes that there would never be need to bring her here at all."

The last muralet.

So he's still keeping Marian a secret.

"As magic weakened and the attacks on Ellauria became more frequent," he continues, "I deemed it necessary for Charlotte to master her particular set of skills as quickly as possible. For this reason," he gives Clara a pointed look, "I directed Seth and Keiran to work closely with Charlotte in individual training sessions separate from the general Apprentice population."

Clara points a finger at Keiran as if she's just made a vital discovery. "I knew there was a reason you were spending so much time with her!"

Keiran's face wrinkles with disgust. "Clearly, Clara. That's the most important thing right now."

She leans back in her chair, completely ignoring his sarcasm.

"Why is an elf training a muralet?" the centaur asks.

Keiran's expression fades to fear. His posture goes rigid. If Alexander gave me up, there's no reason to think he'll keep Keiran's confidence either.

"Alexander," Seth says, the word wrapped in warning. He can't give up Keiran's identity. He simply can't. Being the daughter of a beloved founder is one thing; being the son of a murderous traitor is another.

Alexander shakes his head at Seth before announcing, "Keiran isn't an elf. He is a flamethrower, and he's Whalen's son. I've been training him in the ways of the Fellowship for the last two years."

No one hears that last part, because as soon as he mentions Whalen's name, the room erupts. Several creatures leave their seats. Some shout at Alexander, some make accusations at Keiran, but everyone stares. Even Clara looks at Keiran differently—her expression more animosity, less adoration.

Keiran closes his eyes and rests his head in his hands.

Alexander absorbs the commotion in silence until someone suggests Keiran is leaving gates open for banished creatures to pass through, and then he explodes. "Enough! Whalen's presence in the Between is weakening magic everywhere, causing the gates to malfunction. Keiran is an asset, not an enemy."

"Founder or not, you cannot keep this kind of information from Principal Command!" Clara exclaims. "Your inability to give up your secrets will be our downfall."

Alexander slams his palm against the table. "The Fellowship is what it is because of my leadership. If you take issue with any part of my performance, I am happy to discuss it with you after we have secured the safety of the realm."

Clara's eyes are murderous. "I look forward to our discussion."

A cold sweat covers my skin. Keiran won't look up. We are two overwhelming secrets. What other secrets does Alexander have?

The centaur pounds the top of the table in front of him. "The safety of the realm is the highest priority. What can be done to restore the Between?"

Holy sheet, he's looking at me like I have any idea how to restore anything. No one's talked to me about creation. Throwing water. Tossing wind. Breaking trees. Shooting fire. I can almost do those. Creation? Restoring? I shake my head slowly. "I have no idea."

"Can the fairies heal it?" Lulu asks.

"I'm reluctant to send fairies into the Between when we're unsure of the source of the decay," Clara responds.

I find myself torn between thinking that Clara's an idiot on a personal level, and that she's something of a force in her role as Empress. Not that I'd ever say so out loud.

"I agree," Alexander says, then slaps his hand against the table twice. "Effective immediately, all passage through the Between is forbidden. The mystical realm will be on complete lockdown while we develop a plan to stop Whalen."

Complete lockdown? I leap from my chair before he finishes his sentence. "No! You can't do that! What about Sam?"

"Sam?" The centaur's eyebrows come together. "Oh, the jourling boy?"

Seth places his hand at the small of my back. "Yes," he tells the centaur. "Adele's son. Adele filled the role of Charlie's mother in the mortal realm. Sam and Charlie lived as brother and sister."

I hold up my wrist, and the guitar pick glints in the light of the nearest table. "This was out there," I sputter, taking deep breaths between each sentence. "This was his. He is out there. He's waiting."

The satyr massages his temples with the tips of his fingers. "I think he's the least of our concerns at the moment."

I feel the tears welling in the outer corners of my eyes, and my breaths come faster and faster. They can't leave him out there alone with that madman. How will we ever find him?

"No," I announce. Sam needs me. He knows I'll never stop looking for him. Without Mom, he is completely alone. He may be unimpressive to the Fellowship, but he's my brother. I'm on the table, leaning across it into Alexander's face so quickly I'm not sure I didn't flicker myself.

"I don't give a flying duck about your priorities," I continue. "He's my brother. I will not leave him. At this moment, I don't care about any of your rules. My only concern right now is bringing my brother home, and if you expect me to help you save your realm, you better get on board." I push away from the table and stare down my nose at the founder. "I will not abandon him."

The room is completely devoid of air. Every single eye is glued on Alexander, waiting for his response to my outburst.

The founder inhales through his nose, never breaking eye contact. He speaks slowly but firmly. "We have to consider the possibility that saving Sam could put the entire realm at risk. We cannot send Aegises into the Between until we know what we're dealing with."

"Then don't!" I tell him. "I'll go myself."

"You cannot put yourself in harm's way." Alexander's words are soft. "If Whalen succeeds in destroying magic, you are the only creature capable of rebuilding it. Your blood is our key to survival. It's the only way the mystical realm gets through this."

"I. Don't. Care," I bellow. "Without Sam, I don't want to be here!"

Seth's hand rests against my shoulder blades. I take deep, shuddering breaths. I can't be here without Sam. I can't live knowing I'll never see him again. We know he's with Whalen. We know Whalen is in the Between. Even though the Between is daunting, it's the closest I've got to a pinpoint on my brother's location.

No one is going to stop me now.

"He's one of ours," Seth argues. "We can't leave him out there."

"Regretfully," Alexander says, "we've reached a point where the future of the Fellowship must come before any individual member."

"You would sacrifice Sam's life?" Seth asks, staring at Alexander like he's never seen him before.

Alexander squares his shoulders. "Yes."

I launch myself at the giant founder, but Seth catches me, wrapping his arms around mine and spinning me backward. I scream for him to let me go, but he keeps his arms tight until he transitions from holding me back to holding me together. I melt against him, exhausted.

NINETEEN

I walk through Seth's door on autopilot, barely registering the setting sun. We must have been at Central Hall for hours. I slump down onto the sofa and curl into him, hiding my face in his chest and crying, finally releasing the full range of emotions I've been pushing down since Mom died.

He wraps an arm around me and lets me cry for as long as it takes. I tell him everything again, from the first time Keiran and I snuck into the Between to watching Mom die. I relive it all, more for myself than for him. I break it into pieces. Seeing her face. Hearing her voice. Even in the end, she was protecting me. She screamed so the Mothman would go after her instead of me.

She never stopped, lying there dying, knowing she couldn't survive his attack.

She never stopped protecting me.

I clutch Seth's shirt and cry harder, remembering everything about the life before Ellauria.

Mom's bedroom full of books. Her spaghetti. The way she joked with me and Sam about everything. The way she treated us like adults and allowed us to make our own mistakes.

If there was something I wanted, she never told me I couldn't achieve it. As big as my dreams are, her dreams for me were always bigger.

She took me on and loved me as much as she loved her own child.

Even though I knew my life in the mortal realm was over, I've been clinging to the idea that Mom, Sam, and I would be a family again. We'd still be us, no matter where we were.

Now it's just me and Sam.

I have to find him.

By the time I'm able to breathe without sobbing, I'm exhausted. My eyes are so swollen I can barely keep them open, and Seth's shirt is drenched with my tears. I wipe my cheeks with my hand and settle my fist against my lips, like I can capture any further emotion before it escapes.

"I can't lose him, Seth."

He rests his chin on my head. I know he feels my heart breaking, and I'm pretty sure I feel his, too. "Don't worry," he whispers. "I'm not letting him go, either."

It's all I need to hear. One person to tell me he's in this with me. I won't have to fight alone. "Thank you," I reply.

Seth pulls me from the sofa and leads me to his bedroom. He pulls back the thick gray comforter on his queen-sized bed before grabbing a white T-shirt from his drawer. "Put this on. Get some sleep."

I take the shirt from his hand and clutch its softness to my chest. Before he leaves the room, he looks back and says, "I mean it. Sleep. We're going to need everything we've got to save him."

He's right. As much as I want to spend the next few days in bed, grieving everything I've lost, I can't. I have to pull myself together and go on—Sam needs me.

I'm going to save him.

I slip on Seth's shirt and crawl beneath the covers, listening to him pace outside the door until I fall asleep.

It's pitch black outside when I wake again. Moonlight pours through the curtains, illuminating Seth's form by the window. "Seth?"

"Hey, sorry. I didn't mean to wake you."

"What time is it? What are you doing?"

"Midnight," he says. "I came in to crack the window. I know how you like to sleep with it open."

I close my eyes, overwhelmed with affection for the beautiful, frustrating boy in front of me. "Can you—" I take a deep breath. "Will you hold me?"

Seth goes still for a moment, then nods. I lift the blankets, and he stretches his body alongside mine. I pull the covers over our shoulders and snuggle into him, molding my body to his.

"Don't tune me out, okay?" I whisper. I close my eyes and let my walls down, allowing myself to feel all the things I shouldn't.

"Charlie." He shakes his head.

"Please," I whisper against his neck. "I don't care what PC says about this." I run my fingers lightly over his cheek, tracing his jawline. When my thumb sweeps across his bottom lip, his hand lands on my waist, sliding over my lower back and pulling me even tighter against him.

"Charlie," he says again, but quieter. "We can't."

I have a lot of confidence in the fact that we absolutely can. Maybe we can't parade around Ellauria holding hands and trading kisses, but right here, right now, I refuse to let him pull away again.

"Just once," I breathe.

I press my lips against the underside of his jaw, and his sigh makes me smile. He winds his fingers through my hair and whispers my name one last time before his mouth finds mine.

We go still, savoring the moment we've been denying ourselves for weeks. When we move again, the kiss is urgent, full of everything we haven't said and everything we may never be able to admit. He pulls my bottom lip between his teeth, and I curl my fingers into fists in his hair. When his tongue slides over mine, I lose myself for a moment.

There are no thoughts. Just this. Just Seth, and his lips, the way his breaths become my own, and the way his hands know exactly where I want to be touched.

I tilt my head back slightly while he kisses the corner of my mouth, my cheek, below my ear. He lingers at the base of my neck, and my whole body tingles. His fingers slip beneath the hem of my shirt, setting my skin on fire.

We carry on for several minutes, exploring each other. His study of my neck is particularly thorough, and I discover that putting my fingers in Seth's hair is the quickest way to make him melt.

I fall asleep with my head on his chest and my leg draped across his hip, while his hand traces lines up and down my back.

I wake the next morning alone in Seth's bed, wrapped in his scent. I lift the neck of his shirt to my nose and gather his sheets around me, inhaling him. Footsteps in the living room pull me out of bed, and I gasp when my bare feet hit the cool wooden floor. I tiptoe to the doorway, tugging Seth's shirt over my thighs.

Seth's sitting on the sofa with his back to me, flipping through my sketchbook of home. The sight of him sends my mind to last night—the scratch of his chin against mine, the burn of his fingers on my skin, and the sweet softness of his lips.

I quickly finger-comb my hair and say, "Morning."

He glances over his shoulder and freezes. I smile when his eyes travel up my legs. I could've put my shorts on, but part of me wanted this moment. When he reaches my eyes, his mouth spreads into the smile I love so much.

I step around the sofa and he stands. His hand slides down my arm from my shoulder to my elbow and he pulls me close, kissing my cheek. I close my eyes and resist the urge to pull him back to the bedroom. We have too much work to do.

"I was just about to wake you," he says. He releases me and pulls something from his pocket.

My knife. "Where'd you get that?"

He winks. "I have friends in high places."

The only way he could've gotten that knife is if someone on Principal Command snagged it for him. I can't imagine either of us has any friends left on PC, except—oh. "Lulu?"

He nods. I take the knife from him, feeling its weight in my hands. Someone took the time to clean it, and the steel blade shines, showing my blue eyes in its reflection.

There's a knock at the door, and the peace of the morning vanishes. I shouldn't be here. Seth nods toward his room, and I duck back in there to hide.

I close his door, easing it shut as quietly as possible, then back away, staring at it. My eyes fall on every single section of his room—the bed set against the middle of the wall, the tall bookshelf to its right and the short nightstand on its left, the wide mirror-topped dresser behind me. The only decent hiding spot would be his small closet, but that's entirely too obvious.

My heart races. The last thing I need after all of yesterday's drama is to be caught at my Aegis's house early in the morning wearing only his T-shirt.

I creep toward the door and press my ear to it. Keiran's voice sounds from the living room. *Thank God.* I pick up my shorts from the floor and slide my legs into them before dropping my knife into the case on my hip. I leave on Seth's T-shirt.

There's a knock on the door, and Keiran peeks his head in before I have a chance to respond. I'm so grateful I'm dressed.

"Oh, hi!" I put on my innocent face. "When'd you get here?"

He raises an eyebrow. "Just now. When did *you* get here?"

Keiran's smirk tells me I don't even need to bother coming up with a lie, so I roll my eyes instead.

"You know I don't care about the rules," he says. "How are you feeling?"

I take a deep breath, giving it some thought. "Determined."

"Good answer." His eyes bounce around the room. "Do you mind if we talk for a minute?"

I wrinkle my eyebrows. "Of course not."

Keiran steps further into the room and calls over his shoulder, "Seth! I'm gonna do some making out with Charlie, so we're gonna shut the door now!"

"Sure thing!" Seth calls back, and I smile. If I'd known kissing Seth would've chilled him out so much, I would've forced myself on him a long time ago.

I straighten the comforter over the bed and sit, and Keiran joins me. Anxiety creeps over his face; he stares at the floor for a few minutes before speaking. "I'm really sorry about Adele."

I knew he would feel the need to apologize, even though his guilt is completely misplaced. I squeeze his hand, remembering everything he did for her yesterday. Everything he did for me. My chest aches, and a tear sneaks down my cheek. It's all so fresh. "Thank you."

He places his hand over mine and shifts to face me. "I just—I want you to know that I still think I can save him."

I go still. Save him? We're still going to save the man responsible for killing my mother? Yesterday only solidified my stance on Whalen's morality. There's no saving him. Keiran's delusional.

I look at the wall because it's easier than looking at him. "Keiran—"

"No, listen," he says, cutting off the argument he knows is coming. "You only know this side of him, and I totally understand that. I know he's only done horrible things to you—"

It's my turn to interrupt him. "He's done horrible things to you, too! And Marian. And the Fellowship. And Sam. My mom is dead because of him." My voice shakes, and I pause to get my emotions in check. "You said yourself you miss the man he used to be. Are you so sure that man is still there at all?"

He swallows hard and looks at me. "We'll never know if we don't give him the chance."

I lace my fingers together on my lap, squeezing my own hands. How many chances does a madman get before we accept the fact that he's evil? How far will Keiran go to save this completely fabricated image of a father who can't possibly exist anymore?

Seth knocks on the door and opens it. "You two finished?"

He eyes me, and I realize he's been creeping on my emotions from the next room. I shoot him a small smile. It's nothing I can't handle.

"Yeah." Keiran gives me one last lingering look. He's not giving up. "All done."

The three of us move to the living room. Seth and I sit on the sofa, and Keiran picks the recliner near the window. "What happens next?" he asks. "Is the Fellowship really not going to send anyone after Sam?"

My stomach twists. "It certainly doesn't seem like it."

Seth sits up, leaning forward. "We can sit here all morning and pretend we're not going to go back for Sam, or we can skip to the part where we figure out how we're going to find him."

I really, really should've kissed him a long time ago.

"Who are you?" I ask, searching his eyes. "Where's Captain Rule Follower?"

Seth shakes his head. "I can't support what Alexander said yesterday. The Fellowship put Sam in the position he's in, and the Fellowship should save him."

"Yeah. We can't leave him out there. He's your family," Keiran says. "You can't give up on him."

I hear the undertone of his last sentence. I can't give up on Sam. He won't give up on Whalen. I know he sees a parallel between his situation and mine, between my love for my brother and his need for a father, but it's not the same.

Keiran stands. "So the question is, when? How?"

"I think we need to go as soon as possible," I say. "I found his bracelet near the Source, so it'd be a good place to start. But that was at least a day ago. The longer we wait, the farther away he could get."

Seth nods. "That bracelet is the freshest lead we have. We can't waste it."

"We could go now," Keiran suggests.

I wait for Seth to argue, to come up with any reason to wait, but he rises to his feet. Keiran takes a step toward us.

We're really going now. My hands sweat and my knees tingle. This is it. "Thank you for doing this, both of you. It means everything to me. And it will mean everything to Sam."

Seth's arm slides over my shoulder. "Let's bring him back."

Twenty

Thick gray fog curls through the trees, dulling the vivid colors I've come to associate with this place. I can almost feel the life draining from the world around me. Everything seems dimmer, as though a haze has settled over the Between. Brittle leaf carcasses litter the thin, dusty paths through the woods. Nearly black trees stretch into the sky like skeletal hands, shooting up from the ground and reaching for light. What had once seemed so full now feels so devastatingly empty.

"Whoa," Keiran breathes.

"I can't believe it," I whisper. It looks even worse than yesterday.

Beside me, Seth releases a long, heavy breath. "Let's find Sam and get him out. When he's safe, we'll deal with the Between."

When Sam's safe.

Seth's certainty is comforting.

I look at our bracelets, side-by-side on my wrist. I can't allow myself to run through all the possible reasons his bracelet was out here on the ground. He was alive when Adele left him, and I'll cling to that with every piece of my being.

He's out here. We *will* find him. I'll bring him home.

There are so many dead limbs scattered across the ground, staying on the path is almost pointless. Seth stops every now and then to toss a few out of the way, but I get the feeling he just needs to expel energy. Straightening up the Between right now is an exercise in futility.

Only days ago, this place was a comforting reminder of the home I used to know. Will I ever feel that security and warmth in this stillness again?

Next to me, Keiran goes rigid. "Move."

His voice is so calm I don't react at first. He snaps out of it and jerks his head. "Move!"

I look up in time to see a dense, black cloud enveloping the trees. A hum fills the air—a low, droning buzz—and I watch as the edges of the cloud fragment into pieces.

"Locnifs," Seth says, pushing me off the path. "Run. Don't look back."

Locnifs. Max had drawn them as beetles the size of locusts with razor-sharp teeth. It's not an image that's easy to forget.

I turn and sprint. Seth's feet land hard and fast behind mine, and Keiran darts ahead. I feel the bugs on me even when they're not, landing on my skin and crawling through my hair. The buzz grows louder and louder, until it feels like it's coming from inside my own body.

"Faster, Charlie!" Keiran yells, reaching back and pulling me along with him.

As if I'm out for a leisurely jog. I'm giving it everything I've got.

A locnif lands on the back of my hand and I shriek, flinging it away. Then another, and another. Sharp, stinging pain stabs my arms and the backs of my legs. I hear Seth swear behind me as the locnifs find his skin, too.

The locnifs weren't here yesterday. As terrifying as they are, their presence brings a strange sort of hope. Whalen must be close, and where he is, Sam is, also.

We slide over the top of a hill, and Keiran releases me as the rocks fade into dirt and my feet find their grip again. I dash toward the barren trees, weaving in and around trunks and branches before ducking behind a broad growth of bare-limbed bushes. Seth yanks me toward him, and we slap the locnifs from each other's skin. They're everywhere.

We must be on the right track. We must be close.

"Keiran!" I scream.

"Over here!" he calls back. He's to my right, rapidly chucking fireballs into the air. Each one sizzles through the horde of insects, breaking the cloud apart and sending the locnifs in different directions.

Swollen, bloody bites cover my arms and legs. The welts on Seth's skin are already starting to fade. He lifts his hands over me, and I push him away. There's no time for healing. Keiran's flames aren't enough to stop those things from eating us alive.

I step out from behind the brush and welcome the tingle that pours through my hands. Strong gusts of wind whip around me, separating the swarm into pieces. The effects are only temporary. Through the wind and fire, the locnifs only scatter and reunite, constantly moving toward us.

There has to be an escape.

I spot the waterfall and see the angle of the river flowing from it. The deep water where the Source pools beside the treefolk should be straight ahead.

"Can we jump in the water by the treefolk?" I shout.

Seth blinks. "What?"

"The Source! Can we jump in it?"

He wrinkles his eyebrows before his expression clears with understanding. "Yes. I think so."

Seth yells to Keiran and we make a run for it, dodging hanging limbs and hurdling dead logs until we come out on the other side.

The pool of water stretches across the ground. Beyond it, I see Joe and the rest of the treefolk, or what's left of them. Their shriveled, bare trunks are as black as the rest of the trees. The gorgeous leaves that had once adorned them are gone. I run straight toward the Source without slowing down and jump when I reach the edge, crashing through a layer of dead leaves on its surface.

Keiran's and Seth's bodies roar into the water beside me, and everything goes silent.

Is it possible to feel yourself sparkle? It's the only word that seems fitting for the sensation of the Source's pure magic against my skin. I'm completely motionless, embraced by the water. I stay under as long as my lungs will allow. My chest feels tighter and tighter, and I see Seth kick to the surface beside me. Keiran takes my hand and pulls me up along with him.

Cool air glides over my scalp when my head breaks the surface. The locnifs are gone. We make our way to the edge of the water and climb out. I brush my hair back from my shoulders and wring water from my shirt where I can. Beside me, Keiran and Seth do the same.

"Everybody okay?" Keiran asks, looking us over.

The bites on my arms and legs sting a little, but I nod. I'll survive.

Seth pulls a leaf from my hair. "I guess we should—"

I look up when his voice trails off. His eyes are wide, his jaw tense.

A line of harpies stretches across the ground in the distance, as wide and deep through the trees as I can see. They watch us with empty eyes, heads bobbing up and down, teeth gnashing.

"Oh no," I breathe. The terror I remember from my first morning in Ellauria returns. The ugly, twisted glare of the harpy is multiplied across the faces I see in front of me.

One of the harpies releases an earsplitting shriek, and they lift into the air.

Focus.

Survive.

Keiran immediately springs into action, throwing fireballs as quickly as he can produce them. I close my eyes and see Sam's face. Power floods over me more intensely than I've ever felt it before. The weight of the Source's pure magic still clings to me. When I open my eyes, flickers of light pulse through my fingers.

Suddenly, everything looks like a weapon. I launch the limbs scattered across the ground into the sky. Between waves of branches, I command squalls of wind that twist violently through the air, disrupting the creatures' flight patterns.

"Charlie!" Seth yells.

My entire body ignites with power. Golden light shimmers beneath my skin, and my hair spreads across my shoulders, whipping in the wind. Magic fills every inch of my body with a satisfying tingle that spreads from the tips of my fingers to my core. I launch wave after wave of attacks while I run toward the sound of his voice.

The harpies keep coming.

Seth appears beside me, his arms filled with jagged rocks. He throws them into the air, and my mind grabs hold of them, pounding the harpies that are closest to us. The rocks slam against their heads, and their screams echo through the empty trees. Several harpies drop to the ground and stop moving.

Keiran continues his one-man fire show, pitching fireballs into the air. Harpies shriek upon impact, catching fire and falling to the ground. I jump around them, pulling more dead branches and wind into motion. A fireball flies by my head, and Seth yells, "Watch it!"

"Not me!" Keiran answers.

Not him?

Seth and I stop to look. Each flame Keiran throws is answered by at least five more. Through the mass of branches and trunks I catch fleeting glimpses of tall, slender creatures with red skin. Their fingers are capped with flames that take to the air with each swing of their long arms.

Mother. Fluffers.

"Watch out!" I yell.

Seconds later, a loud roar fills the air and a wall of water rushes through. It stops in front of us and hangs there, acting as a barrier from the flamethrowers on the other side. The balls are extinguished as they pass through the wet shield. Keiran runs over to Seth and me.

The pull of the water presses down on every joint of my body, and I gather my strength to raise my hands and push the water forward. It lifts and spreads, encircling the flamethrowers. Through the shimmering curtain of water, I watch the creatures pause to stare. The water rolls and flows inward upon itself, crashing down and swallowing the flamethrowers in its flood. I hold it there, fighting against the weight of the power, until every single flamethrower stops struggling. The water lifts to the sky and evaporates, leaving the lifeless, slender bodies behind.

I release my command of the water, and Seth catches me before I fall backward from exhaustion. I hold on to his arm for a few seconds and allow my head to stop spinning.

Keiran lets out a low whistle. "You are one scary muralet, Freckles."

I smile at him. "Thank you."

A shadow passes over his face. The Between darkens as another wave of harpies flies toward us, filling the entire sky. *Where* are they coming from?

Seth swears under his breath. "Got any other tricks?" he asks.

Keiran had said my power is limited only by my imagination, but I'm the first to admit that I'm running out of ideas.

I think back to the Mothman attack, when Keiran had told me to combine the elements.

I didn't have a chance then. But now, it's our only shot.

I close my eyes, searching for an easy and powerful solution. I still feel the power there, waiting for my command.

I need more. Bigger. Louder. Longer.

I need a natural disaster.

A low rumble sounds in the distance, and I open my eyes.

Holy sheet, it worked.

A line of tornadoes dances across the sky, pulling up branches along the way. They roar toward us, louder than anything I've heard in my entire life, growing in size as they approach. My hair whips around my head and my ears pop.

"Get down! Hold on to something!" I yell. The three of us take off in separate directions. I lose sight of Keiran, but Seth darts behind an enormous hollow log on the ground.

I wrap myself around one of the few trees still standing. The storm rages all around me, targeting the harpies and pitching all of them in various directions. When the tornadoes lift from the ground, the fog settles again, and the Between is thick with silence.

I release the tree and step backward in a daze. Fatigue pulls at every part of my body, bringing an ache that starts deep within my bones. I rest my hands on my knees and survey the carnage.

Dead harpies are strewn across the ground, and the remains of flamethrowers are scattered over them, apparently lifted and distributed by the winds. Seth stands like an island in the middle of it all, his hands resting on his head.

I turn in the opposite direction.

Where's Keiran?

Everywhere I look—more death, more destruction—no Keiran.

I forget the ache in my bones and put all of my focus into spotting his charcoal-gray T-shirt amid the debris. I spin in a circle, taking slow, deep breaths to stay calm. This is not the time to lose control.

Where *is* he?

I finally spot him on the far side of the Source, lying motionless on the ground beneath the treefolk, and I take off running.

I don't see the long, narrow branch lodged in his side until I'm practically on top of him.

"Keiran!" I whimper, falling to my knees beside him.

He takes a ragged breath. "I'm all right," he pants, but the sheen on his pale skin says otherwise. I lay one hand on his chest to comfort him and examine the branch with my other. My trembling fingers barely graze the tip of the branch. Keiran's sharp intake of breath paralyzes me.

"Seth!" I cry. "Help!"

He's beside me in seconds and winces at the sight of Keiran's body. "It has to come out," he says, his eyes on the branch.

Keiran's fingers curl into fists in the grass. He squeezes his eyes shut. "Do it," he gasps. "Quick."

That branch is going to leave a fairly large hole in Keiran's side. I've never seen Seth heal anything like that. "How quickly will you be able to heal him?" I ask. "He's going to lose a lot of blood."

Seth's mouth is set in a grim line, and his eyes are as serious as I've ever seen them. "It's his only chance. He can't move, and we can't leave him like this."

Of course we can't. No one's getting left behind. I place my hand over Keiran's and squeeze. "I'm right here."

He presses his lips together, breathing hard through his nose. Seth wraps his steady hands around the branch and hesitates for only a moment before pulling it out in one fluid movement.

A strangled sputter escapes Keiran's lips as his eyes fly open and roll backward. I press my hands to the dark stain spreading across his shirt. Seth drops the branch and replaces my hands with his own. The glow is quick. I just hope it's quick enough.

There's movement in the distance, beyond Seth's shoulder. A darkened form appears in the fog.

"Seth," I whisper.

He follows my gaze, and we watch while the figure comes closer, separating from the shadows.

His face is a bit slimmer. His brown curls are a bit longer.

But it's him.

"Sam!"

"Charlie, wait!" Seth yells, but I ignore him.

I take off running, and my brother catches me in his arms.

TWENTY-ONE

"Charlie!" Seth yells again, his feet landing in sharp crunches among the debris.

I don't look back. I don't need to.

He's here.

I fold my arms around Sam's neck and hold on for dear life, clutching his shoulders, breathing him in. His arms circle my waist, and he squeezes me in a forever kind of hug.

"Chuck." Sam's voice is laced with affection, and it's the most beautiful sound I've heard in weeks. He tries to pull away and I hold tighter, afraid to let go. I don't want to open my eyes in case it all vanishes. Ever since I left the mortal realm, I've had to accept that nothing is what it seems.

Seth comes to a stop, practically standing on top of us. He grabs my arms, pulling me away from Sam. I immediately feel cooler without Sam's warmth.

"Seth! Stop!" I yank my arms from his hands and study his face, confused. He's watching Sam, his entire body tense. Why? It's Sam.

This is what we've been waiting for. This is why we're here.

"You found my bracelet," Sam says.

His voice is perfection. I scan every inch of his body, from the curly mess on top of his head to his broad shoulders to his long legs and enormous feet. It's him. He's here. I'm afraid to look away. I don't even want to blink. A smile pulls on my lips. "I was so afraid I wouldn't find you."

Seth takes another step until he's closer to Sam than I am. "Where's Whalen?" he asks. "You're just out here wandering around alone?"

Seth's words snap me out of it. My eyes dart past Sam into the fog. Seth's right. Whalen could be anywhere. "Right," I say, looking over my shoulder at Keiran, still lying on the ground. "I want to hug you for days, but let's get back to Ellauria first, where it's safer."

"No," Sam declares. His eyes stay firmly planted on my face, staring past Seth as if he isn't there. "I'm not going to Ellauria."

Huh?

"Come with me," Sam says. "We'll go home. Away from all this," he nods at the Between, then finally settles angry eyes on Seth, "and them."

Home? My skin prickles. I blink, and blink again. The home he speaks of no longer exists. There's nothing left. The house may still be there, but everything that made it a home has been taken away.

"What are you talking about? We can't go home."

He smiles, a sad, lopsided smile. "That's what they want you to think. Whalen told me we can go back. It'll be just like it was. We can forget all of this."

Whalen told him? Like that means anything? Besides, I don't want to forget all of this. This is who I am now. I can't go back. I can't pretend this world doesn't exist or that I'm not a part of it. "Sam, it won't be like it was. We know the truth now. You're a jourling.

I'm a muralet. We don't belong in the world we used to know."

Seth starts talking in smooth, even tones. "Sam, Whalen lied. The two of you can't go back. Nothing will ever be like it was. Whalen wants to destroy the Between."

"I know," he says, looking at me like I was the one speaking, "and we'll go home."

I shake my head, open-mouthed. I feel like the weight of the Mothman is on top of me again, taking away my air. This isn't what's supposed to happen. I came here to find Sam, get him away from Whalen, and take him to Ellauria where he'll be safe.

Seth continues in his hostage negotiator voice. "If he destroys the Between, he destroys magic entirely. The realm, the creatures who live in it—they'll die."

I study Seth, awed by his demeanor. He's as solid as a rock while everything inside me quivers.

Sam lowers his head to look directly into my eyes. "That's why we have to get out of here." He says it like the two of us are the most important parts of the equation. What about everyone else? What about these places? The Between? Ellauria? All the incredible creatures, with their beautiful histories and amazing powers? He can't seriously believe that all those things should suffer.

And why does he keep looking at Seth with such animosity?

Alexander's words echo in my mind. *The future of the Fellowship must come before any individual member.*

No. I'm not giving up my brother.

I lick my lips and try to explain this more clearly. "Sam, the mystical realm is built upon the Between's magic."

Sam closes his eyes and nods like he's tired of hearing about it.

"Without it, the realm and everything in it dies. The creatures in the mortal realm will lose their powers. We're not entirely sure what it'll mean for them, but it'll be catastrophic." I take a deep breath. "We're talking about the end of magic everywhere. That includes me and you. We're magical. We'll suffer."

"No. You and I will be all right. Whalen said he'd make sure we survived." Sam's eyes light up, and he smiles like a missionary spreading his truth, like he's about to give me the gift of life itself.

Seth laughs, short and quick, completely dumbfounded. I am too. This isn't my brother. Sam would never sacrifice an entire population like this. He doesn't even know them. He only knows what Whalen has told him.

Sam pushes past Seth. "We can go back, Chuck. No Fellowship. No magic. Normalcy. Me and you, hanging out on the porch, guitars and sketchbooks, while Mom bakes something in the kitchen."

Oh, my God. He doesn't know about Mom.

My stomach rolls, and a chill settles over me. "No, Sam." I pause, wishing I didn't have to say what is coming next. "Mom's dead. The Mothman killed her."

His face pales, and he stumbles backward. His eyes stay on mine, his expression passing through moments of shock, disbelief, and pain.

"No," he says, over and over. Just the one word. "No."

I reach for him, but he turns away and crouches to the ground, holding his head in his hands.

I look at Seth. He shakes his head slowly at me.

This isn't the Sam that left us a few weeks ago. This is a new Sam, tainted with Whalen's words. Whalen is as much a poison to my brother as he is to the Between, choking the life out of the Sam I grew up with.

Several seconds of painful silence pass before Sam takes a deep breath and says, "She shouldn't have run. Whalen told us, if we ran, he couldn't protect us."

"What?" I ask.

"The Mothman killed her because she left." Sam rises from the ground and turns. "All she had to do was stay with us. She went for the Fellowship instead."

I simply cannot wrap my head around his thought process. The Mothman works for Whalen. How can he possibly blame the Fellowship for her death?

"The Fellowship didn't kill her, Sam. The Mothman that Whalen sent after her did," Seth says.

Sam sniffs and wipes his eyes with his fingers. "She chose that life. She chose to live for the Fellowship, and she died for it." He holds out his hand to me. "No one gave us that choice. We were born into this life, but we don't have to stay. We can leave."

I stare at his empty hand, and something between a stunned laugh and sob escapes my chest. "I can't leave, Sam. I can't let Whalen destroy magic. Muralets are composed of the same elements that make up the Between. I *am* magic. Don't you see? Destroying magic means destroying me."

"It won't happen like that," he says. "Come with me."

He knows what I am. He knows what Whalen wants to do. How can he not understand? I clench my teeth, infuriated by his refusal to see what he doesn't want to see. "I. Can't. It's a death sentence."

Sam's hand closes, and his head drops.

"I'm growing tired of this," a brittle voice announces from behind the shadows. "I told you she wouldn't listen."

A broad man with dark, stringy hair and pale eyes slinks out of the fog and straightens. His ashen skin is illuminated by the bands of sunlight that stream through the cracks in the clouds overhead.

Sam steps aside, moving in the man's direction. It's a silent gesture, but its significance is booming. It's a choice, an alignment, and I stare in disbelief as my brother takes a stand next to the man who hasn't introduced himself, but I already know who he must be.

"Whalen." Seth grabs my arm, pushing me backward and positioning himself in front of me.

The confirmation of his identity chills me. The way he places his hand on Sam's shoulder makes my stomach turn. The man responsible for ruining the lives of nearly every person important to me is comforting my brother, and my brother's allowing it. My heart pounds in my throat, and I struggle to find my voice. "Sam."

He won't look at me.

"She's choosing the Fellowship over you, son," Whalen says. His voice is thick with sympathy, but there's no mistaking the pleasure on his face. "Just like your mother. Just like I told you she would."

Seth drops the composed act and raises his voice. "Sam, he's brainwashing you. Whatever Whalen's told you, it's a lie."

Sam lifts his head and glares at Seth, his eyes shining. "As far as I can tell, the only people who've lied to me are you and Mom, all in the name of your precious Fellowship."

He says the word "Fellowship" as if it is a disease.

I know those feelings. They were mine. I remember the betrayal and anger I felt that first night in Ellauria, when every part of my life felt like a lie. I remember wanting nothing more than to turn back the clock and sit on my porch with Sam. I wanted to forget. I wanted to wipe all of this from my consciousness.

I had Seth to pull me out of it.

Sam had Whalen.

"Sam, the Fellowship kept us safe," I tell him. "I know how you feel. Trust me. I was angry, too. But we can't deny who we are."

Whalen coughs, and I catch a whiff of a stench so horrid it makes my eyes burn. I turn my head away, gasping for clean air.

"You're wrong. Magic is fleeting. It should be denied. It isn't meant to be a part of us at all," Whalen growls.

"Funny how you think that now that you're nothing," Seth fires back, lunging forward.

Whalen wheezes and thrusts an arm in Seth's direction. Seth pushes me away just before a jagged yellow orb slices through the air and connects with his chest. An awful, strangled sound erupts from Seth's mouth before he slams to the ground.

Sam's forehead creases as he watches Seth writhe on the ground, and his eyes shift from Seth to Whalen and back.

"Tell me I'm nothing again," Whalen spits.

The veins on Seth's neck bulge, and his face grows red. He rolls from one side to the other, clutching his chest.

"Seth!" I scream, and rush toward him.

My scream slices through Whalen's influence on Sam, and my brother yells, "Chuck, no! It's necrolate!"

I freeze. Seth's eyes close, then open, then close again. This time they stay that way.

His healing abilities give him immunity. He's not dead. He can't die. The necrolate can't kill him. I repeat it over and over in my head, but nothing prepares me for the moment when his body goes still.

I tremble and stagger backward. My heart throws itself against the front of my chest over and over, pounding all the way up in my throat. My head swims with fear. How do I fight someone who can throw death from his hands?

Sam circles around until he is standing in front of me, facing Whalen. He picks a jagged branch up from the ground and holds it like a bat in front of his body, pointing it at the fallen founder. "You said you wouldn't hurt her."

There. That's my brother.

"You have outlived your usefulness, boy," Whalen growls. He grabs the end of the branch and twists it from Sam's hands before swinging it through the air. The thick end of the branch collides with the side of Sam's head, and he falls to the ground.

I clutch my stomach and scream.

Sam's eyes close and his mouth goes slack. Bright red blood spills through Sam's hair and stains the grass below.

So much blood.

Don't be dead. Don't be dead.

I can't lose all of them. Mom. Seth. Sam. I can't. I can't have gone through all this and still lose everything.

I keep my eyes on Sam until I see his chest rise and fall. He is alive.

For now.

I curl my fingers around the knife on my hip and look at Whalen. When our eyes meet, he erupts in vicious laughter. "Everyone. Every single person you care for will be destroyed." He slithers toward me. "You will pay the price for every muralet that's ever existed."

I walk backward, drawing Whalen away from Sam's body. To my right, Seth lies on the ground, motionless. To my far left, Keiran is beneath the treefolk. I have no idea if the healing Seth performed before Sam's arrival is enough. Around me is the Between, the place I identify with most—between two worlds, between two lives—and it's dying by the second.

In front of me is the madman responsible for every bit of pain I've suffered since the day I turned seventeen. I lift my chin as determination takes over.

He will not win this.

"The price for what?" I counter. "Creating magic? Being more powerful than you? Existing in a world where you cannot?"

"Tell me, muralet," he says, placing a finger next to his chin. "Why do you feel the need to fight for something that has taken so much from you?"

Whalen moves toward me at a steady pace, and I continue to walk backward. "The only one taking things from me is you," I tell him. "You ran Marian into hiding. You sent the Mothman for Mom. You took Sam."

"Magic!" he roars, throwing his arms into the air in a wide, sweeping gesture. "Magic took everything from you just like it took everything from me. I had a life. I had a love. I had—"

"Marian?" I force a loud laugh, just to hurt him. "You think she was your love? Is that why you wanted to kill her?"

His nostrils flare. "Marian and I could've made a life together, if only she weren't blinded by magic."

Blinded by magic? Marian is magic! How do you rationalize with someone so completely insane? The tip of my knife points directly at him. "Magic is who she was, and you wanted to kill her because of it."

"Magic tore us apart. It ruins lives, Charlotte. Mine. Yours. Sam's." He lifts his hand in the air, and I see swirls of yellow sparks circling his knuckles. "I'm doing the world a favor by putting a stop to it."

"You can't kill me," I tell him. "Without me, you have nothing to offer your followers."

"Without you," Whalen's eyes flash, "my followers will die. Every single magical thing in existence will perish. The deals I have made will no longer matter."

I dash to the side as he releases a shower of necrolate. One round misses me, crashing behind me with a sizzle, but the second round strikes my shoulder. Necrolate drenches the wounds left by the locnifs, seeping below my skin.

An ear-splitting wail of agony rings in my ears, and it takes a few seconds to realize the cry is my own. I'm suddenly on the ground, staring blankly at the sky.

Whalen's laughter rings through the Between.

"Dad?" Keiran's voice is quiet but strong.

Oh no.

My eyes drift toward the treefolk. Keiran struggles to his feet, holding tightly to branches to stay steady.

"Dad," Keiran says again. "You don't have to do this."

Pain ravages my body. The necrolate burns as it spreads through my limbs, and I am agonizingly aware of every path of every vein beneath my skin. On top of that, my heart splinters as I watch Keiran's face.

"Aha!" Whalen shouts, parading around with his arms outstretched. "Another life, ruined by magic." He spins around and hurls a ball of necrolate through the air. Keiran releases a fireball in return. The two collide over the water, disintegrating in mid-air. Keiran collapses, too weak to stand, and Whalen laughs.

I need to move.

I need to, but I can't.

My shoulders are glued to the ground, weighted by necrolate. The burn is everywhere now, not only in my veins. My head throbs. My teeth ache. My eyes feel like they're covered in sandpaper. I will my legs to bend, but nothing happens. No matter how I try, my body won't respond to the commands my brain is so desperately sending.

A new sensation begins—sharp, piercing pain strikes at random across my torso, like nails being driven into my skin.

Whalen stretches his arms over his head and sighs. He surveys the bodies around me. "What do you think, muralet? Who dies first? Keiran, Seth, or Sam?" He looks at me with his eyebrows raised as if he truly expects an answer. "Decide quickly, please. I want to make sure you're alive to watch."

My eyes land on Sam's face. Is he aware of any of this?

"Sam it is," Whalen says.

No!

Whalen steps over me to retrieve my knife from where it fell when the necrolate hit. He picks it up and crouches beside me, holding the blade in front of my eyes. "He'll die by the weapon you brought." Whalen grins wildly, his eyes manic. "Isn't that the most poetic thing you've ever heard?"

My knife. No. He can't use my knife against my brother. One swipe of that knife is all it will take to kill Sam.

He can't.

It can't be my knife.

Whalen cackles and rises, circling back to Sam.

Get. Up.

A current of air pours over me, tangled with color. I blink.

More and more colors fade in, swirling in the air. Red, blue, pale yellow, white. They dance and pull together, until I clearly see the outline of a face, *the* face, followed by a tall, slender body.

She steps out of the wind, her blue gown flowing behind her. Her long, wavy red hair spills over her shoulders, and her blue eyes ignite with love, magic, and power.

Marian.

I am lost, overcome by the necrolate and overwhelmed by her presence. I want her with me, but I want her to leave.

No, Marian. Stay away. He'll kill you.

"Mmm." I try to speak, but my lips, like the rest of me, no longer work.

"Shh. Don't speak. You will need all of your energy to survive this," Marian whispers, bending over me. "The necrolate is strong, but you are stronger."

I want her to hug me. I need her to reach down and pull me up into her arms, comforting me the way a mother does. I want to hear her say that everything is going to be okay.

But of course, she can't. The necrolate would kill her.

I find the sky again. Marian is wrong. I'm not stronger than this. Already, I feel my heartbeat slowing. The burning pain and piercing stings have been replaced by a numbness that's settled over my body, growing heavier by the second. It's like something is lying on top of me, forcing me to fight for every breath.

"Are you watching?" Whalen looks over his shoulder and freezes.

Marian rises to her feet, completely calm.

"Marian." Whalen's voice is hate and wonder combined. "You came."

"Marian?" The sound of Seth's voice lifts some of the weight from my chest. I shudder, and tears drip down the sides of my face. My gaze travels down my body to where he lies in the grass. He's moving. I watch him crawl to his feet and sway slightly, pressing his hand to his head.

Seth's immunity continues.

"You're too late, Marian," Whalen calls from across the water. "Your daughter is dying."

"Seth," Marian orders, stepping away from me. "Heal her."

Seth stumbles to me and drops to his knees. He looks exactly like a person immersed in death would look. His face is pale and his eyes are too large, with swollen, purplish bags beneath them. He breathes hard, like every breath is a struggle, and leans over me, giving me strength with his eyes.

"Hang on, Charlie," he says, his voice cracking. "Hang on." Seth lifts his hands over me and light pours from his palms.

Whalen flicks his hand and launches a ball of necrolate at Marian. Her figure dissolves, taking flight before my eyes. Piece by piece, the wind picks her up, and she is gone, vanishing as the necrolate passes through.

Whoa.

Whalen stares at the sky with his arms outstretched and releases a scream of fury. He storms toward Sam, hurling necrolate in all directions and shrieking Marian's name. A wall of air bursts forward from behind Seth and me, launching Whalen's necrolate in the opposite direction.

Above me, Seth curses.

Whalen lifts Sam by his hair, pulling him to a sitting position and crouching behind him.

Marian's voice is beside my ear. I barely see the outline of her face. "Look for what you can command."

I struggle to keep my eyes open. I command nothing. I have no power. There's nothing left.

Whalen grips Sam's shoulder with one hand and brings the other around his neck, pressing the tip of the knife against Sam's throat.

No.

The point of the blade pierces the skin and Sam's body flinches. Whalen flashes me a grin.

"Charlie!" Marian's cry is urgent. "Use your power! Use it!"

Sunlight drips through a crack in the clouds, streaming through the trees and puddling on the ground.

Concentrate.

Live.

"Charlie, no!" Keiran shouts, climbing to his feet again, and I wonder how much he's seen, how much he's aware of.

I can't save Whalen now. Not after this.

A shard of sunlight pulls free, breaking from the puddle of light, and shoots through the air. Everything moves in slow motion. The golden ray arches in the air and comes down like a dagger in the side of Whalen's head. He gasps and goes completely still.

"Dad!" Keiran cries, rushing toward him.

"Good girl," Marian says. The outline of her face shimmers in the air over me.

Whalen releases Sam and falls backward. His eyes drift from my face to Keiran's. Something shifts in his expression. The hatred melts away, and he blinks like he's seeing Keiran for the first time.

Whalen's body swells, splitting at the seams. Keiran covers his eyes as sunlight explodes through the cracks in Whalen's body until he shatters into nothingness.

Keiran releases a loud, miserable wail and falls to the ground.

"Stay awake," Seth orders me, ignoring everything happening around him as he works to heal me. "Don't close your eyes." His hands hover over my stomach. He moves them up and down my body, his face twisting with frustration with every pass. "It's not working. The necrolate is too much. Dammit!"

"He needs your blood, sweetheart." Marian's voice is soft, soothing. I want to curl into her and sleep. She whispers so faintly, I'm not sure I heard her correctly.

My blood.

No. Seth can't take my blood. He'll be banished if PC finds out.

"It's the only way," she says, fading more and more. "He needs more strength."

The only way?

I wince.

I put everything I have into lifting my hand off the ground. A deep gash left by one of the locnifs spreads across my wrist. Seth grasps my hand. "You keep your eyes open." His voice trembles, riding on shaky breaths. "You do not close them."

I pull my hand from his, lifting it higher even as the muscles in my arm fight against me. Further. Upward. My wrist by his lips.

Seth's head jerks backward. His eyes show his horror. "No."

My wrist falls against my stomach. Every muscle in my arm burns.

Seth's hand rubs against my forehead. He stares at my wrist.

We both know that drinking my blood will give him the power to heal me.

We both know that drinking my blood could destroy his life.

His face crumples. "Charlie, stay awake!"

But I can't. There's a pain in my chest so sharp that closing my eyes is the only way to escape it. Every time I close them, things seem a little less real. The longer I keep them closed, the further I flee. I can't feel the lower half of my body.

I hear Seth swear, feel him take my hand in his.

"I love you."

His lips brush against my wrist, and everything fades.

TWENTY-TWO

I approach the sprawling stone apothecary center at the edge of Ellauria and smile at the green-and-black-haired pixie by the door as I enter. It's the third time I've been here since we returned from the Between two days ago, so she doesn't bother to ask which room I'm looking for.

There are Aegises posted outside Sam's and Keiran's doors, their bright orange chairs standing out in the completely white hallways. It's ridiculous. Sam and Keiran aren't threats to anyone in the Fellowship. The fact that they're being guarded like criminals is annoying.

Still, Alexander decided Whalen's death was a suitable trade for my and Seth's complete disregard of his order to stay out of the Between, so I'm choosing my battles wisely. If only Principal Command knew the extent of disregard we had for the Fellowship's rules, I imagine our situation would be far worse.

I stand in the middle of the brightly lit hallway between two doors. The Aegis outside Keiran's door nods. "He's awake," she tells me.

Neither Keiran nor Sam has been awake for any of my visits so far, so I smile like I'm excited by the news, but it really only makes my stomach quiver. I killed Keiran's father. I don't know how he will react to me.

I pause outside his door, dreading this conversation.

If it were anyone else, I wouldn't do it. But this is Keiran. Our friendship is one of the reasons I've survived my time in Ellauria so far. I take a deep breath and rap my knuckle against his door as I push it open.

The rooms are much nicer than the sterile hallways would have me believe. They're cozy, more home-like, and best of all, not completely white. The walls are painted a warm shade of brown, the color of creamed coffee, and the carpet is thick and soft beneath my feet. There are cushioned armchairs in each corner and a bookshelf beneath the window. Magic doesn't require medical carts or IV bags or needles, just a nice, relaxing place to recuperate.

"Keiran?"

He lies in bed, his arms resting on top of the navy-blue comforter, staring out the window. There's no indication he hears me—no movement, no glance, and certainly no words. I bite my lip and steel myself against the painful awkwardness of facing a friend who may hate me.

Our friendship is worth this conversation.

I ease the door shut and set a bag of peanut M&Ms on the table next to the bed. I'm running out of them. Just a few bags left before someone will have to pick up more from the mortal realm. I had a joke all prepared about it, but I don't think he wants to laugh with me.

"How are you feeling?" I ask. I give him a moment to respond, and when he doesn't, I fill the silence. "The apothecary said you'd probably end up with a pretty amazing scar. Is it very sore?"

Nothing.

I shift on my feet, staring at his face. I replace what I see now with an image of him from my head—laughing, silly Keiran, flirting with everything that breathes. I blink, and blank Keiran is back.

Our friendship is worth this conversation.

"Listen," I say, trying to remember the way I'd rehearsed this in my head. "I'm so sorry."

Whalen was a horrid, evil person. I am certain that I, and every single person I love, am safer now that he's gone.

Even Keiran.

Still, I took a life, and that always matters. Keiran's father is dead because of me. Of all the misplaced guilt I've felt over the last few weeks, this one is absolutely correct. My actions caused Whalen's death. Keiran's life will never be the same, and that is one hundred percent on my shoulders.

It's a sick feeling, whether Whalen deserved to die or not. I took a life.

Keiran doesn't acknowledge my apology. Not that I expect him to.

"I didn't have a choice," I tell him.

Keiran may not want to talk to me, but I know he hears me. I walk around the bed, placing myself directly in his line of vision.

"It was us or Whalen. I couldn't save everyone. I'm sorry I had to choose, but I want you to understand," I crouch beside his bed until my eyes are in front of his, "I *had* to choose."

His gaze flickers, the first sign that he's aware of me at all, and he looks directly into my eyes. There's no light in them, only pain, and my own eyes burn with tears. I lower my head and let them fall. I've given up trying to hold them in anymore.

"Charlie," he whispers.

I lift my head, so happy to hear him say my name I cry entirely new tears. "Yes?"

Keiran closes his eyes. "Please leave."

His words crush me, and it takes a moment to breathe again. There are so many things to say, but I hold them in. "Okay," I tell him. "I'll come back tomorrow."

I wait, giving him a chance to tell me to stay away. He doesn't.

It's not much, but it's all he's going to give me right now, and that's enough. The hurt in his eyes is there because I put it there, but I know I can get him back. He needs time, and I can give that to him.

But I'm not giving up.

When I stop in the doorway and look back at him, his eyes are on me. We hold each other's gaze for a moment before he turns his head away again.

I allow a few seconds in the hallway to collect myself before I dip my head inside Sam's door. He's still asleep, just like every other time I've been here, but I go in anyway.

I stand over his bed, soothed by the peace on his face. I can only imagine the things he's seen and heard over the last several days. I can't wait to replace those memories with new ones.

His eyelids flutter, and I brace myself.

Please be happy to see me.

Please don't tell me to leave.

When his eyes focus on me, his lips lift in a tiny smile. "Hey."

I want to pounce on the bed and hug the daylights out of him, but that sort of thing might be dangerous for head wounds. It would've been so much easier if Seth had been able to heal Sam and Keiran like he healed me, but in that moment we'd made a quick decision to tell absolutely no one about drinking my blood, and demonstrating his improved powers for either of them was too risky.

"I'm so glad you're awake." I take a seat on the edge of the bed. I'm not sure when I'll be accustomed to having him in front of me again. I want to keep my hands on him, to assure myself that he is really here.

Sam lifts a hand to the wide white bandage wrapped around his head and winces. "I think I'd rather be asleep. Where am I, Chuck?"

"You're in the apothecary center." I hesitate before adding, "In Ellauria."

The mix of disappointment and disgust on his face is fleeting, but I catch it. He has the wrong idea about Ellauria. He's going to love it here. I know it. He just has to see it. He has to let go of the images Whalen put in his head. I shift in my seat, choosing my words carefully. "I know you spent a lot of time with Whalen, so you don't really see things the way they actually are yet, but—"

Sam laughs, a quick, frustrated burst of air rather than anything joyful. "Along those same lines, perhaps your judgment has been skewed by your time with the Fellowship."

I pout at him. "That's not fair. Whalen hurt a lot of people."

"Magic hurt a lot of people," he replies. "Magic ruined my life."

It's like Seth said. Sam's brainwashed, just repeating the things Whalen drilled into him for days. "Those are Whalen's words, not yours."

"Just because he said them doesn't mean I can't agree with them," he argues. "I've lost everything. My mother. My sister. My home. My life."

"You haven't lost me," I say quietly.

He shakes his head. "I don't want any part of this. If this is what your life is now, I've definitely lost you."

"You haven't lost me," I repeat. I can't understand why he's giving up like this. He's not even trying to hear my words. He's so convinced that he's right, he's not giving me a chance to show him otherwise.

"We should've let magic die," he mutters. "I shouldn't have left the bracelet for you to find."

That bracelet is the reason we were reunited. Without it, we wouldn't be together right now. He'd rather have gone on without me?

"You understand that if magic dies, I die? I *am* magic, Sam. It's in my blood. Whalen wanted me dead because of my connection to magic itself."

His head falls to the side, staring at the wall. "But all of this would've come to an end," he says. "There'd be no Fellowship to dictate lives. There'd be no threat to any of us."

He's not making any sense. "There wouldn't be anything to dictate. None of us would exist. We're all magical. We'd all die," I say.

Sam swallows. "And this would all be over."

I close my eyes and exhale. I'm losing him. With every single second, he's receding deeper and deeper into whatever reality Whalen put in his head. Whalen is dead, but he's still ruining my life.

"You don't mean that, Sam. You can't really feel that way."

His gaze flickers to me. "You have no idea what I feel, Chuck."

Seth's sitting on the front steps of Artedion, and he waves when he sees me coming. He waits until I'm close enough to hear and says, "Sorry. That didn't seem to go well."

"Watch it," I tell him, looking around to be sure no one overheard him.

The increase in his range of empath abilities is the biggest change we've noticed since he drank my blood.

He doesn't have to be near me to feel my emotions. It's my least-favorite side effect of his enhanced powers. All I need is to be even more of an open book to him. Still, without my blood, he wouldn't have been able to heal my necrolate poisoning before we came back to Ellauria, so I shouldn't complain. Much.

He smiles at me. "Relax. We're fine."

If Principal Command, or anyone in the mystical realm, finds out he drank muralet blood, he'll be banished. They won't care that it was the only way to save me.

Seth won't talk to me about it. I tried to ask how he feels, but I think he's putting on a strong front for me. We both know the Fellowship is his life. Even if he's starting to see its flaws, he can't be banished.

His secret is as much mine as it is his. It may have been his final decision to drink my blood, but what else could he have done when I was lying there, dying, pressing my wrist to his lips?

I'm worried enough about how I'm going to find ways to kiss him as often as I want without being separated from him and assigned to a new Aegis. The idea of being separated across realms is a little more stress than I can handle right now.

"You ready to go back to the Between?" he asks.

Alexander wants us to meet him there to get an idea of the work we have ahead of us. A large portion of the Between has been demolished, thanks to Whalen's presence and our showdown with him a couple days ago. It will need to be rebuilt, and the strength of the Source returned, in order to ensure magic's stability throughout the realms.

"Sure," I reply. Might as well find a way to stay busy since two of the three people I love most aren't speaking to me.

"Hey," Seth says, tilting his head. "They'll come around. We'll keep talking to them. Keiran will understand why Whalen had to die, and Sam will see the good we do here. It's just going to take some time."

I nod, swallowing a ball of emotions.

"Come on," he says. He opens his arms, and I step inside. They close around me, and we disappear.

The crash of water is like a train roaring through the Between, and the murky green Source looks nothing like the waterfall I remember. The withering of the Between has stopped since Whalen's death, but the damage done up until then still needs to be reversed. Seth and Alexander stand behind me, allowing me to study the Source.

I'm the key to creation. Somewhere inside me, I have what it will take to fix this.

"Be here," Alexander reminds me.

I close my eyes.

Be here. Peace curls around me, until all I hear are the steady beat of my own heart and the gentle whoosh of my breaths, in and out.

When I open my eyes, I see every atom of every cell of every single thing around me. It's different from the first time I saw them. The brilliant lights I saw last time have faded to only a fraction of the glow they once had.

I turn in a circle and see Seth and Alexander, a million tiny dots filling their shapes. There are outlines of tall, majestic trees and abundant growths of flowers—memories of what the Between used to be.

No. More than memories.

It's a blueprint. The edges of the outlines shine. They're filled with empty space, rather than the glowing orbs that make up the tangible objects around me.

This is her design. Right here, laid out in front of me.

I just have to find a way to create it.

I blink and the lights are gone, replaced by the sad, desolation of the new Between.

I still don't know a thing about creation. Seeing the building blocks doesn't mean I know how to control them. I need someone to show me how to find that power within myself. It's not one that Alexander or Keiran or anyone will be able to show me.

I need Marian.

I'd thought she would return to Ellauria now that Whalen is dead, but there's been no sign of her since we left the Between. I look around, hoping for a glimpse of her here and finding none.

"You're sure I can do this?" I ask, turning to look at Alexander.

Alexander gazes upward, studying our surroundings. "Muralets were built for creation. You create magic where it's needed, and you enhance the power and strength of others. There's no question. This is who you are. It's why you exist."

Alexander can never just say "yes."

ACKNOWLEDGEMENTS

When someone asks if this is my first book, I don't even know how to answer. It is, but as many revisions as it took to get this story right, I feel like I've written at least five books under this title. I wouldn't have kept going if it weren't for my incredible support system.

First and foremost, I'd like to create an enormous THANK YOU out of hugs and glitter and tackle my editor, Danielle Ellison, with it. Danielle, without your push and guidance, this book wouldn't have happened. Looking back on the draft you originally read, I'm insanely grateful that you loved it enough to help me turn it into what it is now. And thank you for being as in love with Seth as I am.

Along those same lines, I will forever be grateful to Brianna Dyrness, Christina Ferko, Britta Gigliotti, and Danielle Rock for taking the time to read *Between* through every one of its many, many incarnations. This book would be a mess without you.

Thanks to everyone at Spencer Hill Press who's had a hand in making this book, as well as Cindy Thomas for everything she's done to help me promote it. You've been an amazing group of people to work with and I couldn't have asked for a better experience. I love being a part of the SHP family.

Nathalia Suellen and Tiffini Scherbing created amazing artwork to represent my story. Nathalia, I was in love with my cover as soon as I saw it. Tiffini, the map you created for Ellauria is absolutely perfect. Thank you both for turning my words into something beautiful.

Josh, you read every single draft of this book, and ripped it apart when it needed it. Thanks for taking the time to talk through plot issues with me and for being such an excellent friend. You, sir, are the sheet.

Kelsey, I can't even list all the ways you've saved me in the last year. Writing and editing can be such lonely experiences, and I'm so glad we've been able share all the ups and downs with each other. Thank you for keeping me going, and for acting like I was totally normal when I went into Crazy Writer Mode.

Sarah and Angi, thank you for being there to laugh and cry with me throughout this entire process. You give the best pep talks, and you always know when to push me. I wouldn't have survived without our music videos, group texts, and general awesomeness.

Samantha, you kept me sane from the first edit letter to the last. Thank you for taking the time to read and reread scenes and to brainstorm with me. Your insights and critiques have been invaluable. You are truly the best.

Chris, your unfailing belief in me and this book kept me going when I was completely mentally exhausted. Thank you for reading it at its worst, and for inspiring Charlie's fascination with Alexander's vaulted ceiling.

Hugs to Gina Denny for being my very first critique partner. You read the earliest draft of this book and loved it anyway. I don't even know how to thank you for that.

Dahlia, Erica, Maggie, Jamie, Leigh Ann, Cait, Jenny, Gina, Marieke, Chessie, Lyla, Jen, and Suz—thank you ladies for supporting me and *Between* for so long, and for being some of the smartest and most selfless writers I know.

Nick, I don't think anyone understands the drama that played out in my head throughout this whole process better than you do. Every time I was convinced I was a talentless hack, you pulled me out of it and reminded me why I do this. Thank you.

Melissa, Becky, David, Justin, and Amy—you're the best cheerleaders ever. Thanks for putting up with my Vanishing Friend/Sister Act during edit cycles, and for reminding me that I do, in fact, love this book.

Mom and Dad, thanks for constantly supporting me. I am very blessed to have you as my parents, and that fact never escapes me. I love you.

Lauren and Ella, you are the funniest, smartest, cutest little people in existence. I'm so lucky you're mine, and every time you speak, I love you more.

Lastly, to my husband Brian—you deserve an award for being married to a writer. I know this isn't what you signed up for, and I am deeply appreciative of the sacrifices you've made to help me make this dream come true. Thank you for being the kind, patient man that you are, and for making me laugh every single day. I literally could not have done this without you. I love you.

breathe
for me

rhonda helms

Isabel's been cursed since the Middle Ages.

Desperate to escape an arranged marriage, she made a
hasty bargain with a demon, asking for liberation from an
oppressive husband-to-be and the excitement of travel. But
the demon's gift came at a steep cost, and the price for her
freedom is much, much higher than she could possibly give.

A. R. KAHLER

MARTYR

THE HUNTED : BOOK ONE

THREE YEARS HAVE PASSED SINCE MAGIC DESTROYED THE WORLD

Those who remain struggle to survive the monsters roaming the streets, fighting back with steel and magic—the very weapons that birthed the Howls in the first place.

About the Author

Megan Whitmer loves all things Southern, and has a soft spot for football, kissing scenes, and things that sparkle. She lives in Kentucky with her family. When she's not writing, Megan spends her time drinking absurd amounts of coffee and dancing in her kitchen. Between is her debut novel. Visit her online at meganwhitmerwrites.com.